SAINTS + SINNERS
2019

NEW FICTION
FROM THE FESTIVAL

Visit us at www.boldstrokesbooks.com

Saints + Sinners 2019

NEW FICTION FROM THE FESTIVAL

edited by

Tracy Cunningham and Paul J. Willis

SAINTS + SINNERS

2019

SAINTS + SINNERS 2019
NEW FICTION FROM THE FESTIVAL

ISBN 13: 978-1-63555-447-2

THIS TRADE PAPERBACK ORIGINAL IS PUBLISHED BY
BOLD STROKES BOOKS, INC.
P.O. BOX 249
VALLEY FALLS, NY 12185

FIRST EDITION: APRIL 2019

CREDITS
EDITORS: TRACY CUNNINGHAM AND PAUL J. WILLIS
PRODUCTION DESIGN: STACIA SEAMAN
COVER DESIGN BY TIMOTHY CUMMINGS

Acknowledgments

We'd like to thank:

The John Burton Harter Foundation for their continued support of the fiction contest and their generous support of the Saints and Sinners Literary Festival program.

Radclyffe, Sandy Lowe, and Bold Strokes Books for their talents in the production of our anthology and their sponsorship of the Saints and Sinners event.

Timothy Cummings, cover artist for the 2019 Saints and Sinners Literary Festival anthology and program book.

Amie M. Evans, whose editorial contributions over the years have informed and shaped the quality of these anthologies. Hope you will be back next year, Amie!

Everyone who has entered the contest and/or attended the Saints and Sinners Literary Festival over the last 16 years for their energy, ideas, and dedication in keeping the written LGBTQ word alive.

Our Past Contest Winners

2018
Jeremy Schnotala "Sand Angels"

2017
J. Marshall Freeman "Curo the Filthmonger"

2016
Jerry Rabushka "Trumpet in D"

2015
Maureen Brady "Basketball Fever"

2014
Sally Bellerose "Corset"

2013
Sandra Gail Lambert "In a Chamber of My Heart"

2012
Jerry Rabushka "Wasted Courage"

2011
Sally Bellerose "Fishwives"

2010
Wayne Lee Gay "Ondine"

CONTENTS

INTRODUCTION

Jeff Mann, 2019 Finalist Judge

The Saints and Sinners Literary Festival has had an enormous impact on many writers' lives, including mine. I've been attending the festival from its beginning in 2003, and I've met a plethora of wonderful publishers, editors, and fellow writers. Both my professional and my personal lives have been immeasurably enriched: most of the material I've published in the last fifteen years has been with the help of fellow SAS attendees, and I've made many friends at SAS, folks I feel great fondness and admiration for, even though I only see them, for the most part, once a year at the festival. When a future scholar writes the history of twenty-first-century LGBT writing, both Saints and Sinners and the many authors it's nurtured will be a big part of the story.

I was hugely honored to be inducted into the SAS Hall of Fame in 2013, and being invited to judge the annual fiction contest is an equal honor. That said, having to choose the top four out of sixteen fine finalists makes me exceedingly uncomfortable, especially since I've met some of the finalists and admire them. Up until the writing of this essay, I've deliberately avoided Facebook posts and SAS e-newsletters so as to remain ignorant of who wrote what and to make my ranking impartial. Yes, I've written and published a lot; yes, I've read a great deal; and yes, I've taught creative writing for years; but still, the end results of this competition are, finally, one man's opinion. All of these tales well deserve to be included in this anthology.

I'd like to say a little something about each of the stories, in the order in which the hard copies sent to me were numbered.

I loved the nuanced and loving relationship between the older brother, Anthony, and the younger brother, Joey, in Stephen Greco's "Washington's Retreat," especially when juxtaposed with Anthony's secret and surprising way of paying the bills and making ends meet. Greco uses the Revolutionary War history of Brooklyn to lend the story a graceful unity and creates gentle romantic tension inside the colorful setting of an expensive Japanese teahouse.

In Daniel Jaffe's "The Importance of Being Jurassic," the author does a fine job of using the setting of Dublin to illustrate Ireland's social changes over the last few decades and to examine the vast differences between the lives of older and younger gay men. The reference to Oscar Wilde's statue in Merrion Square was particularly affecting, and reading the story reminded me of how much I enjoyed visiting Dublin back in 1994 and how much I'd like to return someday.

Being an Appalachian myself, I enjoyed the use of an Eastern Kentucky setting in "Brody's Family Secret," by J. R. Greenwell. The food, the dialect, the customs all rang true to me, and the way an apparently realistic piece of fiction flirts with elements of speculative fiction was an unexpected twist. The romance shared by the young narrator, Brody, and his buddy, Johnny Mac, is deeply touching.

Michael H. Ward's "Omaha" is one of the runners-up. I savored all of it: the gay-bar scene, the realistic dialogue, the drag queen (with the great name of Miss Tiny Cherokee), the erotic tension and release, the tenderness, the sense of future possibility, and the beautifully effective images of the story's close. '

Felice Picano's "Flawed" is a sleek and smart tale of speculative fiction involving a certain San Francisco antique store, a mirror with a certain flaw, and a narrator who's growing accustomed to the luxuries of high society and intends to hold onto those new privileges and pleasures no matter what the risk. I freely confess that I was vigorously rooting for him by the last couple of pages.

The use of first-person narrator in "Solid Gold Saturday Night" by W. L. Hodge is very well done, as is the sharp use of humor and the depiction of gay-bar life in a Texas town. The triumphant way that the transgender protagonist rebukes the obnoxious members of a rude and raucous bachelorette party will make readers cheer, and the poignant ending was just right. You'll think of this story every time you hear that Elton John classic, "The Bitch is Back."

"Salvage" by Karelia Stetz-Waters is another runner-up. I'm not normally a fan of post-apocalyptic fiction, but the spare yet poetic language of this piece grabbed me. The tale beautifully portrays the way that long-repressed erotic urges, once unleashed, can transform, strengthen, and lend both hope and defiance. (I will admit to some bias in my appreciation of this story about a lesbian tattoo artist, since I'm heavily tattooed and nearly all my best friends since my high-school days have been lesbians.)

In "The Unit," Aaron Hughes grabbed my attention fast with his narrator's voice—vulgar, blunt, belligerent, just right for the character. I'm a big fan of action/adventure and military-themed movies and television, so a gripping, fast-moving storyline about love between warriors was bound to impress me. Add to that one of my favorite subjects, Greek mythology, which Hughes uses beautifully throughout the story, and I couldn't help but choose "The Unit" as another runner-up.

The New Orleans setting was a welcome component in William Christy Smith's "Shopping for Others." The subject of the story—how AIDS can transform a life—is full of grim verisimilitude, but there's one scene inside the Immaculate Conception Church that's hysterically funny, and the surprise at the story's end was neatly done, tying up small mysteries and loose ends.

"Stones with Wings" by Louis Flint Ceci was one of my favorites. Here too is post-apocalyptic fiction, but without any of the clichés of that genre and with a focus on agricultural practices that I, once a part-time farm boy, found fascinating. Hand-pollinating okra? Without bees, it makes perfect sense. The slow growth of attraction and fondness between the protagonist, Cyprion, and "the wild boy," Paolo, is perfectly paced, and the metaphor embedded in the title works wonderfully. (To adapt a phrase of Robert Frost's, "So was I once myself a skipper of stones…") As with "Solid Gold Saturday Night," there's poignant triumph here, both in the hermitage garden and in the protagonist's cabin.

Michael Graves' "Trick Hearts" is brimful of the edginess and uncertainties of contemporary youth: pot, horror movies, passionate texting and sexting, colorful parties, polymorphous eroticism, sudden sorrow, and, in this case, porn videos. As in any good coming-of-age story, the teenaged protagonist, Dusty, experiences emotional growth, epiphanies, and a loss of innocence.

Stylistically, Jamieson Findlay's "Arundel's Name" is remarkable. Sentence structure, diction, allusion, irony, imagery…all are masterfully used. The contrasts between public reality and private fantasy are bitterly keen here, and the use of a poem by Sappho creates a beautiful interweaving that continues throughout the story, right down to its final sentence.

Matching losses and mutual desires pervade Maureen Brady's "Fixing Uppers," when a home renovator mourning the end of a love relationship gets far too drunk at a lesbian wedding and meets an intriguing photographer. An important part of any mature relationship, the story wisely seems to suggest, is helping one another recover from past disappointments and present damage.

I loved the sharp delineation of setting in Lewis DeSimone's "Figures of Speech," which takes place in Venice, Italy, "the most romantic city in the world." We experience the story from two points of view, that of a single gay man, James, and his single straight friend, Cynthia, which gives the story a broader perspective than it might otherwise have and illuminates the different ways human beings deal with loneliness and the loss of love, both romantic and Platonic.

Contrasting urban attitudes to rural realities, Jonathan Harper's "Foxes" is a fresh take on a narrative structure sometimes seen in horror movies: thanks to a flat tire, Danny and Kyle, two "proud and naïve" gay teenagers from an urban area, end up stranded in a small town, "the kind Danny understood existed but had never actually seen." There, they encounter locals both welcoming and threatening before being swallowed up by the mystery that dominates the story, a mystery that lends the cry of a fox evocative and sinister meaning.

I chose J. Marshall Freeman's "The Grove of Mohini" as the winner. Like "Figures of Speech," this story has a double point of view. One "center of consciousness," to use Henry James' phrase, is Sid, a handsome young man of South Asian descent who's hired to appear in costume at a wealthy man's ostentatious outdoor party. The other point of view belongs to Leo, one of the middle-aged host's middle-aged friends. As in "The Importance of Being Jurassic," this tale examines the considerable differences between the lives of older and younger gay men. It also uses mythology to fine effect and deals in an especially poignant way with a grim and inescapable fact: the AIDS epidemic decimated a generation. Like several of the stories in this collection,

"The Grove of Mohini" moves toward a sense of erotic renewal, or at least the possibility of it, reminding us of how Eros can heal, inspire, renew hope, and invigorate body, heart, and mind.

The same can be said for fine writing: it can help us endure, especially in anxious times like these. I found these stories a true pleasure to read, and I'm confident that you will too. What a priceless gift this festival is.

Brody's Family Secret

J.R. Greenwell

No one ever told me that growing up in the mountains of eastern Kentucky during a depression was supposed to be difficult, so I didn't know any better. Sure, life had its trials and challenges, but it also had its rewards and blessings, its intrigue and excitement. Mountain people have a bond of camaraderie by heritage. A sense of solitude created by the distance of where we live along the ridge. The holler is our kingdom, sheltered by the edge of the forests and lit by the sky, usually connecting our neighbors to one another by a common stream or creek. We usually protect ourselves by being respectfully private about our problems, thus family secrets are mostly suppressed. However, everyone in Raccoon knew my family's secret—that is, everyone except me.

"Smells good, Mama," I said as I walked into the kitchen, the old screen door slamming behind me. I headed to the white porcelain dishpan next to the sink to wash my hands before supper. I cringed at putting my fingers in the gray murky water that had been used all day, but I knew it still had enough lye soap in it to kill the most ambitious bacteria on anyone's hands. At least that's what my mama told me. My mama never lied. I submerged my hands ever so briefly and wiggled my fingers just enough to create a layer of bubbles atop the old water.

"Where's yer daddy?"

"Oh, he's fixin' to come in," I answered as I dried my hands on the damp dishtowel draped over the sink. "I think he's enjoyin' this day with it bein' warm and all."

"Hard to believe it's the end of February and we got the doors open, but it feels good to git the winter stench out the house."

"Yeah, the air does smell fresh. I see Daddy by the outhouse."

"He better git in here before supper gits cold," she said as she lifted the half-filled cast iron skillet off the woodstove and plopped it down so hard on the old oak table you could hear the clamor clean down to the end of the holler, which was her way of ringing the dinner bell that we didn't have. And sure enough, Daddy walked through the door right on cue just like a bloodhound that had been trained to fetch on command.

"Smells mighty good," Daddy said as he kissed mama's neck from behind. My daddy worked in the waning timber industry, mostly because Mama didn't want him down in the mines. Both jobs were dangerous and difficult, and the coal mines paid a lot more money, but Mama said people working the mines didn't live to be old. Said she didn't want to live the rest of her life as a widow woman.

"Wash yer hands and sit down so we can say grace," she said as she placed three mismatched plates on the table. Daddy obliged by dipping his hands in the gray water and splashed them around, and then he wiped them on his dirty overalls. Mama wasn't looking, but she knew he didn't use the dishtowel to dry his hands. Some things she just overlooked.

As usual at suppertime, we all sat down and I said grace, followed by Mama and Daddy completing the ritual with a heartfelt "Amen!" I was convinced our "Evangelical" version of 'amen' was unlike any other 'amen,' and more powerful, too. Ours had the kind of inflection that brought us closer to God, if at least for just a brief moment, before we ate what Mama had prepared.

"Oh my! Fried rabbit with white gravy and boiled taters. My favorite," I said as though I was being treated to one of the finest meals in a New York restaurant, you know, the kind that serves fancy snails and mushrooms. Mama cooked the best fried rabbit in all of Raccoon, Kentucky, at least that's what my daddy always said, and of course, Daddy never lied.

"Give your daddy some credit. He was the one who went huntin'."

"Thanks, Daddy. You did good."

"Never mind the praisin', just be thankful they was plentiful this year."

"Amen," my mama said. "How is it?"

I swallowed a mouthful of potatoes heavily covered in lard-made, white gravy before I answered. "Mighty good, Mama. Mighty good. Daddy, is it okay if I go down to Becky's house later?"

"What fer?"

"They's listenin' to the Academy Awards show on the radio." My daddy sat in silence either enjoying the morsel of fried rabbit in his mouth or pondering a reason why I shouldn't go visit my friend.

Mama looked at me. "They got one of those talkin' boxes in their home?"

"Yes, ma'am. It's like bein' there. You just sit and watch that box and listen. I saw it last time I was there. Ain't nothin' like it around. Daddy, how come we don't have a radio?"

"Cause we don't have 'lectricity."

"And why don't we have 'lectricity?"

"Cause we ain't a member of the co-op, that's why. Only people with money to waste can afford to have 'lectricity."

"Becky's family ain't rich and they got light bulbs that glow in the dark."

"Nothin' wrong with kerosene lanterns and candles when we need to be up at night, and even then, the moon gives us the light we need to git to the outhouse and back."

"I don't think it's right to go over and listen to it," Mama said as she shook her head. "Almost sinful, if you ask me."

"But Mama, it's the Academy Awards. *Gone with the Wind* is nominated and so is *The Wizard of Oz*. Becky's mama and daddy took her to see both them movies at the theater in Pikeville. She said they was good movies. And the Academy Award show is where all the movie stars git together. They git all dressed up and they drink bubbly champagne."

"More reason not to go. Sounds like a gatherin' of a bunch of demons and sinners. Preacher Thompson told us about them flyin' monkeys in that wizard movie. Said they looked like devils."

"And Clark Gable and Vivien Leigh are supposed to be there too."

"Clark Gable?" Suddenly, Mama's voice took a liking to the topic. "I will say, and forgive me, Daddy, but that Clark Gable sure is a handsome man."

Daddy broke his silence. "You wanna be like Clark Gable when you grow up?"

"Heck no. I wanna be like Vivien Leigh."

My daddy took a deep breath and turned his head to the side to exhale. It was never a good sign when Daddy turned his head to the side before he spoke. Then he leaned back and looked at me real serious. "Boy, quit with the nonsense. You're fourteen years old. You oughta know by now you can't be like her. She's a woman. Don't you know if you talk about this kind of thang, people are gonna call you a sissy?"

Mama placed her hand on my arm. "And you could even get beat up and hurt."

"I ain't sceered of anybody or any name callin'. And what if I am a sissy? Johnny Mac's a sissy and he's my friend. Anyway, Miss Allison says I can be anythin' in the world I want to be. Says if we wanna escape the confines of Pike County, we have to think big."

Daddy paused. "You think that school teacher has the answers to all your problems, don'tchee? Well, I hate to tell you this but you're gonna do what every young man does around here, what we've done for generations. You're gonna git a job in the mines or in timber, then you're gonna find a girl and marry her, and then have a mess of kids."

"I ain't gittin' a job where I have to git dirty."

"There ain't much choice," Daddy said firmly.

"I'll figure it out. Becky says that every girl that gits married in the mountains is knocked up before she gits married. She says they even have shotguns at the weddin's. Mama, can I have some more taters?" Mama lifted the bowl and spooned out the remainder of the potatoes onto my plate. "Did you have shotguns at your weddin'?"

Daddy laughed out loud. Not sure why he thought my question was so humorous, but somehow he must have. "Boy, did we ever. I think we hold the record for the number of guns at our weddin'."

Mama smiled as she recollected the event. "Yes, it was special. After we said our vows, all the men folk, includin' your daddy, went off and went squirrel huntin'."

"That's an odd thing to do."

"It's what men do in the mountains," my daddy said as he wiped his hands on his pant legs.

"So, you two were in love?"

"That's right, son. And still are," Mama added. "So, are you sweet on Becky?"

"Well, I guess I am. She's got broad shoulders, which I find appealin', and I really like her cropped-off hair. Yeah, she's real cute. I could like her if I had to."

Mama sat back and a dreaming kind of smile came across her face. "It would be nice to have grandchildren one day, wouldn't it, Daddy?"

"I reckon. Yeah, it would be nice to have some extra help around here."

I wasn't sure where the conversation was heading, but I didn't like having my life planned out in front of me, especially with me not having any input. "Oh, Becky said she never wants to have any young'ns, that's what she called 'em, eatin' off her titties all day long, and then changin' diapers, then havin' to wash 'em and hang 'em out. Miss Allison says people in big cities adopt children after they're potty trained. That way they don't have to deal with shitty diapers."

Daddy took a deep breath. "Thank goodness for Miss Allison and her words of wisdom."

We were just about finished with supper as my daddy held the leg bone of the unfortunate hare between his fingers and chewed it clean down past the gristle. When Mama turned her head to look out the window, I licked my fingers after running them over the plate, collecting the remaining layer of the white gravy as if it were the last meal I would ever have.

"Leave a bit for Hickory," Daddy said. Hickory was his tick-totin' beagle dog, his hunting companion, his alarm clock, and probably his best buddy. They were inseparable when they were outside, but the old screen door kept the two apart when Daddy was in the house. Mama had a few strict rules, and keeping Hickory outside was one of them.

"Yes, sir," I said as I pushed my bones to the side of the plate. Hickory would have a feast with my share of the rabbit bones as I could not get past eating the gristle like my daddy did. Never could. "Mama, I know what day this is."

"And how do you know what day this is, other than a Saturday?"

"I seen the day on your calendar," I bragged. "Daddy marked it."

"Well, I reckon that calendar is about two years old. 1938, I guess.

I only have it hangin' 'cause I like the pictures, and well, we cain't afford another'n."

"Today's the day before your birthday. Happy birthday, Mama!"

"Brody Josiah Whitaker, you know I don't like celebratin' my age," Mama scolded as she began to blush. "And anyways, it ain't until tomorrow."

"I have somethin' for ya, somethin' special, and I cain't wait," I said as I jumped up and ran to my room. I could hear her and Daddy chattering back and forth, but I paid no mind to what they were saying. I returned with a present wrapped in an old shirt I'd outgrown and tied with hay-bale twine. Mama was playfully reluctant to accept my gift, but I could see the pleasure she was getting. "I know your birthday isn't until tomorrow, but I wanted to give this to you today. Come on, Mama. I made it special for you."

Mama was slow to reach for my present, but she did. Getting presents was a rarity in our household, not because we didn't like to exchange gifts, but we were poor. We were proud survivors of the Great Depression and didn't know any other way. At least I didn't.

"Oh, Brody, you shouldn't have," Mama said.

"I made it myself."

"You made it?"

"Yes, ma'am, with my own two hands. I thought you might want to wear it to church in the morning. I would have gotten you a store-bought present, but you know, we don't have…you know."

"I don't want no store-bought present," Mama said proudly.

Daddy was getting as excited as my mama. "Woman, are you gonna open it, or are you savin' it for next year's birthday?"

Mama gently untied the twine and unfolded the shirt. As quick as Hickory could swallow a rabbit bone whole, Mama's face went from sheer pleasure to horror. She let out a scream that was probably heard through all of Pike County.

"What the hell?" Daddy said.

"Don't curse at the table!" Mama yelled.

"You don't like it?" I asked, pointing to the furry object on the table.

"Brody, is that the cat?" Daddy asked.

"Fluffy?" Mama whimpered.

Everyone was doing a lot of asking and not even giving me a chance to explain. I sat down in my chair, my parents staring at me in disbelief. Fluffy lay motionless on the table.

"Yes, it's Fluffy…the cat," I confessed.

"But that cat got run over by the wagon out front," my daddy interjected. "I threw it behind the woodpile last week."

"Waste not, want not. Ain't that what you always say?"

"Yeah, I say that all the time, but why would you give your mother a dead cat?"

"And I thought Fluffy just ran away," Mama mumbled.

"Well, Mama, you know how every Sunday at church you always comment on that ratty old fox that the widow Ballard wears around her neck? You know, and how it has those itty bitty eyes and it bites its tail so that it don't fall off. And you always give her a compliment on it. You say, 'Why, Mrs. Ballard, that is the prettiest fur I have ever seen,' and she gets embarrassed with pride and says, 'Why, thank you so much.'"

"I know, I know. But Fluffy?"

"Well, you really liked Fluffy, and I thought what better way to keep him around and make you a present by fixin' him up so you could wear him on Sunday or any other special day."

"But how'd you do it?" Daddy asked.

"I just did what we do when we skin those squirrels before Mama fries a mess of them up. I took out Fluffy's innards and dried the pelt, stretchin' it as far as I could, and then I sewed him back up and let him dry. He still looks alive, don't you think?"

"Almost like he's breathin'," Mama whispered. "And it's like he's starin' right at me with those pearly buttons. Are those Meemaw Allen's buttons?

"Yes ma'am."

"I was savin' those for a sweater I was gonna knit one day."

"Mama, I only needed two. They's plenty more in the box for your sweater."

"Well, son," my daddy said as he inspected Fluffy without touching him, "it looks like you did a mighty fine job."

"Thanks," I said. "Did you know Miss Allison says squirrels are a member of the rodent family?"

My daddy's tone of voice always changed for the worst when I mentioned Miss Allison. "That school teacher of yours is always fillin' your head with nonsense. What's that supposed to mean?"

"They's cousins to rats. How come we don't eat rats? Heck, they're all over the place. We'd never go hungry."

"Watch your language at the table."

"But Daddy, it's true."

Mama quit staring at Fluffy and broke her silence. "That's disgustin' to think about eating rats. Enough of that nonsense."

"Rabbits is cousins with squirrels too, and we eat them," I said. "And what about 'possem? They's nasty and we eat them."

Mama stood up and started clearing the table. "We ain't eatin' no rats cause I ain't fixin' 'em, and that's that. It's disgustin'."

"I'll tell you what's disgustin'. Eatin' hog nuts," I said defiantly.

Daddy was quick to quiet me down. "Son, now that's enough. They's mountain oysters and they's a delicacy around here."

"Yes, sir," I said. "Mama, you gonna wear Fluffy tomorrow to church?"

Mama turned to me and smiled. "Of course I will."

"And why don't you wear the gloves I made for you, you know, the white ones with the squirrel fur trim and the danglin' squirrel tails that hang off the edges?"

"Maybe, yes, maybe," she said while she wiped the plates with a soapy washrag. "Why, Lord Almighty, we got company," Mama said as she peered out the kitchen window. "Looks like Mr. Harman ridin' his mule."

"Harman?" Daddy echoed. "Wonder what he wants?"

"I suspect you might want to go and find out," Mama said as she dipped the dishes in fresh well water rinsing them clean to dry.

Daddy got up and went outside. I watched from inside through the screen door as Mr. Harman got off his mule and he and my daddy talked. It was an odd thing for Mr. Harman to visit, as I couldn't recollect him ever coming by before. He didn't stay long, and after the two shook hands, Mr. Harman got back on his mule and slowly rode down the old rutted lane. I could see my daddy wasn't happy as he walked back to the house. I quickly sat back down in the chair, hoping he hadn't noticed that I had been trying to listen. He came in and sat down at the table.

"What is it?" Mama asked.

"It's time," Daddy answered.

"It's time? I expected it would be sometime soon. Yes, it's time," she repeated reluctantly and then she sat down. Mama was on the left and Daddy was on the right of me. From the looks on their faces, either somebody died or I was in deep trouble.

"Mr. Harman tells me you tried to hurt his son yesterday. Says you used some kind of magical power to knock him over. Is that true?"

"No, it ain't true. That Jack Harman is a bully, mean as a hornet. He was pickin' on Johnny Mac, callin' him a pervert sissy. I told him to stop or else, and he asked me what I was gonna do, and I put my hands on my hips and I stared at him real long, and then I snapped my fingers in the air, and he tried to run but he tripped over his own two feet and fell and hit his head on the ground. Face first. He got a bloody nose." I paused for a moment to think if I left anything out of the recollection of my encounter with Jack Harman. "Then he ran like the devil was chasin' him. He just tore outta there and didn't look back. I swear on Mama's Bible, I didn't touch him."

Mama's eyes began to tear up, and Daddy bit his bottom lip. I never saw him get emotional, but he was about to and then he cleared his throat. "Son," he said, "there's somethin' you need to know about who you are. What you are."

All kinds of thoughts and images were racing through my head. *Who am I and what am I?* I asked myself. Do they know something about me that I don't, or do they know something about me that I know and I didn't think they did? Could they see that I was attracted to boys? Did they know I had a crush on Johnny Mac? Could they hear me jacking in my room when I thought everyone was asleep? Surely, to God, they could see that I was kidding when I said I wanted to be Vivien Leigh. Well, I was partially kidding.

"What is it, Daddy? Have I done somethin' wrong?"

"No, son, you haven't. We've just been keepin' somethin' from you. It's time you know."

Mama stared down at the table at Fluffy, avoiding eye contact with me. I was starting to tremble with the anticipation of what my daddy was going to say to me. "Just tell me," I demanded.

Mama reached over and took my hand. She looked me directly in the eyes and said, "Brody, you might be an alien."

Well, that just beat all. Mr. Harman comes to visit riding up on his old back-sagging mule to tell my daddy that I beat up his bully son, Jack, with some magical power that I didn't even know I had, and then my parents sit me down to tell me I'm an alien. Keep in mind my mama and daddy never before lied to me. And I didn't think they were now.

"An alien?" I asked.

"Yep, an alien," my daddy answered.

"From outer space?"

"Yep, like from outer space."

My mama went on to tell me that she and my daddy had gone on a picnic at the top of the mountain ridge that overlooks Raccoon. They stayed late to watch the stars and suddenly a light beamed on them, a blinding light from above. They were brought aboard a spaceship but they had no memory of what happened. Two months later, Mama found out she was pregnant, but she and my daddy hadn't had relations, at least that's what she recollected. She said, "It was our secret, 'cept later old George Adams, the town drunk, told us he saw us git pulled into the spaceship. And then he blurted the story out to ever'one around here. We denied it and got married, and then you was born."

"That's all crazy," I said. "I ain't no alien."

Daddy leaned back in his chair. "We ain't sayin' you is or you ain't. But everbody hereabouts think you might be. They's been looking for signs."

"Signs?"

"Yep, signs. Signs like you ain't one of us, signs like magical powers that humans don't have."

"I ain't got no powers!"

"Mr. Harman and his son think you do, and that's all the proof they need to go to the authorities."

"Brody," Mama said, "we've been worried all along that if there's any inklin' that you're an alien, the gov'ment will take you away. We'd never see you again."

"But, Mama, I'm your flesh and blood. You birthed me. Do you think I am an alien?"

"No, no I don't, but I've had my doubts from time to time. You have red hair and there ain't a redhead in the family, for either one of us. And your eyes are as black as coal, and we're from a long line of blue eyes. And you have to admit, you are a bit different from the other boys here in the mountains," she added as she finally touched Fluffy with her fingers.

"When was the last time you was in a fight?" Daddy asked me.

"I ain't never been in one."

"That's cause ever'one is sceered of you, fraid you'll zap 'em, or eat 'em, or somethin' even worst. They've just been waitin' for a sign, and I guess Mr. Harman's boy took it that way."

It isn't every day that your parents confess that you might be from another world. Hell, I did feel different from the other boys my age, but not this kind of strangeness. I never sensed that people might be afraid of me. I always thought they respected me. Looking back, I was intrigued by the fact that no one had called me a fairy when I was even more effeminate than Johnny Mac, the school sissy. But I was suddenly more concerned about my mama and my daddy. They had been carrying around this burden of a secret from me for fourteen years now, trying to protect me from cruel condemnation and even worse, the government.

Before heading to Becky's house, I promised my parents I would never use my powers, the ones I didn't have. Daddy said when he and Mr. Harman shook hands, it was an agreement that Mr. Harman would give me another chance before getting in touch with the authorities. I reassured my parents I would not give into a challenge and I'd lay low. It was the least I could do, and anyway, I didn't want to be told to go to my room and think about it while the Academy Awards show was gonna be on the radio. And even more importantly, Johnny Mac was invited too.

An early chill came over the hills, and I was glad Mama insisted I bundled up. I walked down the lane and took the gravel road into town. I spotted Johnny Mac's massive mop of blond hair as he approached the end of his lane. He waited for me, and the two of us walked to Becky's house together. Suddenly, the thought of being an alien seemed far behind me.

Mrs. Johnson met us at the screened-in porch, one of the few houses in Raccoon that had one. She was pleased to see us, even calling us "polite young men." Becky's daddy worked at the coal company mercantile store and made good money, which explained why Mrs. Johnson was the best-dressed woman this side of Pikeville. She was pretty too.

Becky greeted us and took us into the living room. It was fancy with doilies on the backs of every chair, lamps with real light bulbs on the end tables, and gold-framed pictures hanging on the walls. And in the corner, the radio sat on top of a large box draped with laced fabric. It looked glorious. We chatted and giggled like school girls, and Mrs. Johnson brought us spoonbread in fine china bowls and we ate with real silverware. Soon, Mr. Johnson came into the room and shook our hands and asked if we were ready. We pulled our chairs around and watched Mr. Johnson and the talking box, and like a conductor leading a train out of the depot, he turned on the radio and fiddled with the dials hoping to find the show we came to hear. He never did find the right channel airing the awards show, but we ended up listening to a broadcast of *Superman*, much to the chagrin of Becky and her mother. I quickly gave up the idea of being Vivien Leigh in a lip lock with Clark Gable and soon got caught up in a wish to be flying in the arms of the man of steel. While listening, it dawned on me about our similarities. He was from another planet and he had super powers. Suddenly, I thought that maybe, just maybe, what Mama and Daddy were telling me might be true. Listening to the radio was the most incredible thing I'd ever done, but we had to deal with Becky and her mother's interruptions as they sporadically quoted lines from *Gone With the Wind*, and more than once saying, "You've just got to see the movie." Even Mr. Johnson's occasional demands to his womenfolk to hush went unheeded.

After about an hour of listening, Mr. Johnson, despite Becky's objections, announced that we had to leave since Sunday was a church day, and they needed to get to bed early. Becky accused her daddy of being cheap and not wanting to pay for extra electricity to keep the light bulbs on. I couldn't imagine talking to my daddy like that. Johnny Mac and I obliged our hosts and said goodnight and expressed our thanks and appreciation to Mr. Johnson for sharing his radio.

It was way past dark and even colder on the walk home. The crescent moon lit the roadway just enough so that we didn't stumble in the ruts. Johnny Mac hadn't worn his coat and his voice trembled as he tried to speak. I offered to share my coat with him, taking it off and draping it over the two of us. He was freezing and I told him to put his arms around my waist and I'd warm him up. We stood there for a few minutes, facing each other in a bear hug trying to warm his body. My cheek pressed against his neck, and I could smell the scent of day-old sweat, a smell I'd remember my entire life. I kissed his neck and he kissed mine. I gently pulled back and looked into his beautiful blue eyes and then kissed him on the mouth. It was my first kiss, and with the sweetness of spoon bread on his breath, along with the nervous warmth of his lips, the moment couldn't have been more special. "Come on," I said. "We need to git home before we freeze to death."

We walked toward Johnny Mac's lane, hand in hand under my coat. "See you at church tomorrow?" I asked.

"Yep, see you in church," he whispered back to me in my ear before kissing me one more time on the lips. "Night."

"Night," I echoed as I watched him trot quickly down the lane to the holler ahead. I smelled the hand that held his and sensed a yearning in my gut that I had never felt before. I stayed put until he faded into the darkness and then I ran home, every now and then leaping into the air, hoping that I would discover the power to fly.

❖

Daddy hitched up the plow horse to the wagon and we headed to church. Mama kept her word and wore Fluffy around her neck and she even blushed a bit when I told her she looked pretty. The fur pelt looked expensive atop her brown Sunday church coat, and the squirrel-trimmed gloves were the perfect accessory to the outfit. *The widow Ballard was going to be so envious,* I thought to myself as we walked through the church door just in time to have a seat before the first hymn of the day was to start. I moved my mouth without singing to *Shall We Gather at the River?* and stretched my neck to get a glimpse of Johnny Mac and his family. Mama kept nudging me to pay attention, but I kept looking, wondering where he was. They never missed Sunday church services.

After what seemed like hours of singing hymns, praying, and shouting back at Preacher Thompson "Amen!" at the tops of our lungs, the service was finally over and we filed out of the church while exchanging "God bless yous" with our neighbors along the way. The line of wagons meandered down the road and up to the hills, and those on foot followed, all heading home to their hollers for a Sunday meal.

As we approached the MacDonald lane, I told my daddy that I needed to check on Johnny Mac, and without any objections, he allowed me to go.

"Don't be long," Mama said. "They's ham on the stove waitin' fer us."

"Yes, ma'am," I answered before I hurried down the lane and up the ridge.

I made it to the fencepost about fifty feet in front of the house before I stopped. There was no one on the porch. Rule of the mountains is that you don't go up to a neighbor's house if there's no one on the porch. It had something to do with nosy revenuers and government workers looking into things they had no business looking into.

"Johnny Mac!" I yelled as loud as I could. "Johnny Mac, are you home?" I waited for a few seconds when I saw Johnny Mac open the door and walk onto the porch. He came down the steps toward me.

"Brody, you gotta leave."

"I didn't see you at church and I was wonderin' if you was okay," I said as he approached me. "What happened to your face?" I brushed back his blond hair to see his swollen black eye and abrasions on his cheek and neck. "Who done this?" I demanded.

"My daddy was beatin' my mama last night when I got home. He'd been drinkin'…still is. I tried to stop him and then he turned on me."

I was getting so angry at the thought of anyone hurting Johnny Mac, even if it was his daddy that did it. "I ain't leavin' you here."

"Johnny! Git in the house, and git in there now!" Mr. MacDonald was standing off the side of the porch with an axe in his hand. He staggered a bit and reached for the porch post to catch his balance.

"I gotta go," Johnny Mac said before he headed up the hill. With his head down, he passed by his daddy who slapped him to the ground. I had all kinds of thoughts running through my head at that moment. It was just yesterday afternoon that I promised my daddy that I would never use my alien powers, the ones I didn't really have, and I would lay low. But now I was faced with the biggest challenge of my life. Mr. MacDonald was no Jack Harman, but he was still a bully, a drunkard bully with an axe who just slapped the love of my life. Johnny Mac went into the house and Mr. MacDonald yelled at me to leave his property.

I was shaking in my shoes, but I stood my ground. "I ain't leavin' here without Johnny Mac!"

The big burly sot started walking toward me, his axe raised in the air. I should have turned and run home, but for some reason, and it might have been a Superman inspiration to fight for good and destroy evil, I couldn't turn so I did the only thing I knew how to do, especially at a time like this. I spread my legs wide, and I put my hands on my hips, and I summoned my super alien powers by glaring as hard as I could, and then I snapped my fingers in the air. If it worked on Jack Harman like he said it did, then maybe if would work on this loony drunk man. He stopped about ten feet in front of me and lowered his axe.

"What the hell are you doin', you fuckin' fairy?"

Somehow, I didn't feel offended by him calling me a fairy. At least he didn't call me an alien. "I'm usin' my powers to knock you down!" I yelled.

"You is crazy like your mama!" he roared back at me, and then he raised the axe over his head. "I'm gonna chop you up into li'l pieces and no one is gonna give a shit!"

I snapped my fingers one last time as he approached me when suddenly the sound of a gunshot could be heard bouncing off the mountain walls. Mr. MacDonald fell forward, the axe landing right at my feet. He had a bloody hole in his back. I look up and Johnny Mac's mama was standing there holding a double-barrel shotgun. She'd shot him dead.

"He ain't gonna hurt no one no more," she mumbled. "No more."

❖

At the funeral service, I watched as the MacDonald family mourned the loss of their daddy, and I felt sad too, but not because Mr. MacDonald was dead. Johnny Mac and his family were moving to Pikeville to live with a relative, and I knew I'd never see him again. As soon as Mr. MacDonald was given a final blessing and covered with dirt, I glanced at Johnny Mac and said goodbye with my eyes. Becky grabbed my hand.

"Come on, Brody," she whispered. "Let's walk." I nodded, and she led me away from the cemetery.

We ended up on Coal Ridge Road where we sat down behind a protruding boulder overlooking Raccoon just as the sun was beginning to set behind us.

"You gonna miss Johnny Mac, ain't you?"

"Yeah, real bad. If I hadn't been so foolish, Mr. MacDonald would still be alive and Johnny Mac wouldn't be movin' away."

"Don't be blamin' yourself. My mama said it was bound to happen. I think what you did was really brave. Daddy said that Mrs. MacDonald shootin' her husband dead is the talk of Pike County."

"Yeah," I said. "So maybe it'll put to rest me bein' an alien with super powers."

"Maybe so, but people like Jack Harman won't be so convinced."

"Guess I need to let him beat me up just once and he'll leave me alone." We sat in silence for a few minutes watching lights slowly appear as the darkness fell across the town. "I cain't figure out how this whole thing about bein' an alien got started."

Becky sat up straight. "Well, I overheard my mama say that your mama made it all up."

"Why? Why would she do that?"

"She said your mama was slow."

"Slow?"

"Yeah, not real smart, and maybe she was afraid about bein' knocked up with you, or maybe she was sceered fer you, like she did it to protect you, you know, cause you're a sissy boy."

"I don't know. And what about the bright light Mama talked about?"

"Maybe they ate some magic mushrooms. My mama says you cain't be too careful when it comes to eatin' mushrooms."

"Could be Mr. MacDonald was right when he said my mama was crazy."

"No, bein' slow and bein' crazy ain't the same thing."

"She did wear a dead cat wrapped around her neck," I said. "Even wore it to church."

"And you was the one who made it fer her. That don't make you crazy."

"I'm not so sure. And I ain't so sure any of this matters."

Becky stood up. "We need to go before it gits too dark to see the trail. And anyway, Brody Whitaker, you got a mama and daddy who loves you, and I got a mama and daddy who loves me, 'cept I got me a daddy who's cheap."

"At least you got 'lectricity," I said as we started our journey down to Raccoon.

That evening, I realized my life was forever changed, and I might not ever understand my family's secret. I gave up using super powers that I didn't have, but like Scarlet O'Hara, I learned coping skills to meet the challenges I faced on a daily basis. I was quick to realize that being a sissy in Appalachia is the same thing as being an alien in Appalachia. I've never outgrown my need to stand up for causes I believed in, and I also never outgrew snapping my fingers in defiance of anything that got in my way. At the very least, the gesture gave me a few seconds of start time if I needed to run in another direction.

FIGURES OF SPEECH

Lewis DeSimone

She's dying for a cigarette. The urge still hits her after every meal, even breakfast. It would be the perfect complement to the bittersweet coffee that now warms her tongue. All around her, people are lighting up, blowing out elegant puffs of smoke that mingle above their heads. Smoking is still acceptable in Europe, almost an art. In America, you have to sneak a cigarette; even on the sidewalk, people stare at you, their eyes accusing you at once of rudeness, pollution, and child molestation.

But she's left the habit behind, along with other reminders of the recent past. Italy is a convenient place for forgetting: so constantly aware of its own history, it leaves no room for anyone else's. New York seems years away as well as miles. New York is beyond remembering. Except for the damn cigarettes.

Facing the bright side of the piazza, she's donned her sunglasses. Everything looks slightly green, though the outlines of people and buildings are clearer without the morning glare. They've been in Venice for only a couple of days, but already she's memorized this spot. Like everyone else in town, they keep returning to it. It's the only place in the city that feels open, the only place she can really see the sky.

James sits across from her, looking down at the faux marble tabletop. He's been unusually quiet all morning. By now, he should be begging her to take a stroll through the twisted, dirty backstreets of Venice. The real Italy, he calls it. Why, she wonders, is reality always associated with ugliness?

Behind James, a group of startled tourists stand in the midst of a flock of pigeons, encouraging them to land on their shoulders—the same vermin they would shoo viciously away at home.

A young Italian man, maneuvering his way through the menagerie, catches her eye, a sickeningly flirtatious smile dancing on his lips. She seals her own lips fiercely and squints back at him. She's tempted to tear the glasses off to show him the anger in her eyes, but decides he's not worth it.

"I swear," she says, grabbing James's attention away from the patterns in the table, "the next guy who looks at me like that is going to find himself dunked head first into the Grand Canal." The words taste like nicotine on her tongue. Everything tastes like nicotine these days; it must be like the phantom pains people get when their limbs have been cut off.

"They think it's charming," she goes on, still staring at the man's back as he disappears under the clock tower. "They probably think I should be flattered—like it's all an innocent game of cat and mouse and the mouse actually *enjoys* being chased!"

"Cynthia, we've been in this country for two weeks already. Shouldn't you be used to it by now?" James stirs his cappuccino with a cinnamon stick and takes another sip. The steamed milk leaves a frothy mustache on his lip.

"That's easy for you to say," she replies. "Nobody's treating *you* like a piece of meat."

A sudden burst of laughter shakes the foam on his cup. "Thank you very much for that testimonial to my sex appeal," he cries. "I'll have you know that I have been come on to several times in the past few days alone."

"Well, that's different."

"Why, pray tell?" A child runs through the square, sending pigeons soaring toward the sky in a sudden rush.

"Well—you're used to it. That's how you—oh, you know what I mean."

"No, Cyn, I'm not sure I do." He sits back in his chair, cheek resting on his open hand, waiting. He loves putting her on the spot like this, goading her to make a remark that he can construe as homophobic. He still hasn't forgiven her for saying that some of her best friends are gay men. It was just a figure of speech, she told him. He should have taken it as a compliment; after all, he *is* her best friend.

"I just don't appreciate being ogled, that's all. I came here to *see* the sights, not *become* one." She taps her fingers nervously on the tabletop. "Oh, let's just change the subject," she says, looking wildly around. "What do you want to do today?"

To her right, tourists, burdened with tote bags and camcorders, meander through Piazza San Marco, drawn toward the wide corridor that leads to the lagoon. Torn between the basilica on one side and the campanile on the other, they hover aimlessly for a moment around the souvenir carts whose proprietors practice their sales pitches in cheerful broken English.

James turns languidly back to Cynthia and smiles. "Absolutely nothing," he says.

A light breeze swirls Cynthia's hair across her face. She brushes it back impatiently and allows her hand to linger on the nape of her neck. She isn't used to the crisp feeling of the short hairs back there—so much for Milanese hair stylists.

"Well, we have to do *something*," she replies. "We can't just sit around here all day."

"Why not? The Italians do."

"We're tourists, dear," she sneers. "We don't sit; we tour. What about all those palaces we still haven't seen—and the Guggenheim collection?"

"Don't you think it's ironic?" he asks. "Here we are, in the cradle of romance—you and me."

She smiles, finally. "It's not so much ironic as pathetic." A group of schoolchildren spill out of the basilica now, screeching their appreciation for summer air if not Byzantine architecture.

"Maybe so," he says, "but let's make the most of it." He glances at the check on the table and pulls a twenty euro note from his pocket. The colorful paper curls up around the cup that he places to hold it down.

It's the height of the tourist season. In the marketplace just off the piazza, the narrow alleyways are crammed with a motley group of people—mostly Americans, of course, but she can still catch snatches of German and Italian in the surrounding din. They hurry through the twisted streets, more concerned with finding open space than achieving a destination.

"Where was it you said you wanted to go?" he asks as they emerge into the light at last.

"The Guggenheim."

"Great. Which way?"

"Search me." The perennial answer to a foolish question. In just two days, they've discovered that one never looks for anything in Venice; one simply finds it. The most they can hope for is to start in the right direction.

She looks over his shoulder at the map they were given at the train station. The city looks so manageable on paper—the canals and bridges organized like the pieces of a particularly intricate jigsaw puzzle. Actual navigation through Venice, however, makes her suspect that the cartographer was blind—or at least mildly sadistic.

They must trust their instincts, each turn to the left requiring a later turn to the right in order to maintain an approximation of a straight line. A distance that should take five or ten minutes to travel (on paper) actually takes closer to forty. But that, of course, is supposed to be one of the charms of Venice.

Crossing a bridge, she looks down at the canal as a gondola slides underneath, a couple snuggled together in the back. Everywhere she goes in this city, she sees the same thing: couples holding hands and smiling. Half of them, she suspects, are on their honeymoon. Venice is Italy's answer to Paris; everyone is supposed to be in love.

"This place is ridiculous," Cynthia says as they backtrack down yet another dead end. "I can understand the tourists—they're attracted by the myth of Venice, I suppose—but why would anyone want to *live* here?"

He affects his diplomatic face now. James prides himself on his diplomacy. "I'm sure they get used to it. Venice is probably as boring to them as New York is to us."

"New York is on a grid, James. You can't get lost."

"I guess you haven't been to the Village lately."

He makes her stop on the crest of yet another bridge and pulls his camera out of its case. "Look out at the water," he says, holding the camera up to his eye and twisting the dials around the lens.

She leans back, both hands on the rail behind her, and turns a three-quarter profile to the camera. After two weeks of traveling, she knows exactly the kind of shot he wants. James seems to live behind the lens; if a tree fell in the forest and he weren't there to take a picture of it, it wouldn't exist.

She turns suddenly at the sound of a large splash in the water. On the other side of the canal, an elderly woman, dressed in a dark apron and matching kerchief, stands with her hands on her hips, staring up at her building. The splash is followed by a clatter on the roof, and Cynthia looks up in time to see a shingle fall off and follow its companion into the canal. The woman throws her hands despondently into the air. Shaking her head, she goes back into the house, mumbling under her breath.

"What's going on?" James says, finally drawing the camera away from his eye. He moves toward the rail and stands beside her, adjusting his camera strap.

"*Venezia*," Cynthia says dryly.

They find the Guggenheim eventually, thanks to a few conveniently placed signs. Entering the courtyard, her feet crunch into the graveled walkway, past Henry Moores and Giacomettis that bring them startlingly back into the modern world.

Inside, they're immediately assaulted by cool, crisp air. "Oh, thank God," Cynthia says, relishing the goose bumps that emerge suddenly on her skin. "I was beginning to suspect that air conditioning hadn't been introduced into this town yet."

"Glad to see you're enjoying yourself, Cynthia."

She sighs and lets out a tiny puff of laughter. "I'm sorry. Guess I'm just a little cranky."

"You were fine until we got to Venice."

They start to the right of the entrance and make their way around in an ellipse through the various galleries. Cynthia stops in front of a Jackson Pollock and they stand back to get the full effect.

"What a relief from all that ancient stuff."

"It *is* nice for a change," James replies. "Reminds me of MoMA."

She turns away from the Pollock and leads him into the next gallery, which is dominated by a display of blue glass objects set on shelves in the window. The summer sunlight pours through, bathing them in the reflected blue. Cynthia speaks softly to the exhibit. "I was supposed to come here with Glenn."

"I didn't know you had plans for a vacation together."

"We didn't. It was just *my* plan. We were going to honeymoon in Venice."

"Honeymoon?"

She turns to him with a scowl. "It was a fantasy, James, all right? Allow me."

James takes the hint and drops the subject. They make their way through the rest of the collection separately, wandering in and out of the galleries a minute or so apart. Cynthia prefers to absorb art silently; she talks about it only afterward, fearing that another person's opinion as she's studying it might interfere with her own and destroy the experience.

She has come to Italy to forget Glenn—especially Glenn. She succeeded, too, until Venice. It's too great a test, she tells herself, being unattached in the most romantic city in the world. Like deliberately wandering through a candy store when you're on a diet.

James is sitting on a bench in the courtyard, waiting for her. She steps down onto the gravel and stands before him. His dark hair spills delicately over his forehead, giving him the look of an innocent yet mischievous little boy. James, she thinks, hasn't changed much since college. He was her best friend then, too. She laughed when her women friends teased her about him, accusing her of having a slight but hopeless crush. To them, James was the epitome of the cliché—all the best men are married or gay. But if James were different—if their relationship had become what she'd once wanted it to be—she has no faith that it would have survived half as long.

Spotting her, he gets up and takes her hand. He seems to know that she needs that right now; she needs the feel of his skin against her own. "Now it's my turn."

"Where to, o wise one?" she asks as he leads her out the gate and back onto the narrow quay.

"You'll see."

Of course, James is just pretending to know where he's going, but she doesn't call him on it. He seems just as surprised as she when their destination suddenly appears before them.

"This is the Ca' Rezzonico," he whispers as they enter the palazzo, "where Robert Browning died."

"Why does everyone come to Venice to die?" she asks. It's never occurred to her before—the irony of the city of love becoming the city of death.

"Can you think of a more beautiful place to spend your last days?"

They step into an enormous hall, brilliant in the sunlight pouring through the French doors. The brocaded walls are hung with paintings in various styles. Their footsteps echo through the nearly empty room: this is not one of the more popular tourist spots in town.

"Paul told me about this," he says, pacing slowly through the room. "It was his favorite place in Venice. He loved Browning."

"I wouldn't have guessed that," Cynthia replies. "Paul struck me as more of a Romantic."

"All poetry is romantic, don't you think?"

She laughs. "'My Last Duchess'? I hardly think a poem about a man who collects wives like some people collect stamps is romantic."

"Well, Paul thought so."

They drift toward the open French doors, and step out onto the tiny balcony overlooking the Grand Canal. The white balustrade is severely chipped, revealing black lines here and there like veins in the stone. Bright sunlight glints off the water as two or three gondolas float slowly by.

She knows very little about Paul. They met only a few times, at parties and other, smaller gatherings. She's always felt somewhat uncomfortable around James's gay friends, like an intruder from the enemy camp. Alone, they get along perfectly; James understands her so well, certainly better than other men, even better than her few women friends. But he behaves differently with his own group. When they're around, she feels like the outsider. She's reminded that James belongs to another world, a world she can't possibly understand.

She went to the memorial service, out of respect. But she sat in the back, apart from the rest. She caught sight of James from time to time, up at the front with his friends. They were smiling, laughing at the stories each speaker told about Paul. It seemed wrong to her somehow, laughing at a funeral. But they had all grown accustomed to death by then, she supposed; perhaps they saw it differently.

Now, with the warm Venetian wind blowing through her hair, she watches James. He's staring down at the water, the gentle waves that shimmer back and forth on the canal. Paul was just a friend, she knows, not a lover, but she wonders if that might actually make it harder. Friends are usually thought of as permanent.

She doesn't know much about James's love life, actually. Perhaps he senses her discomfort and graciously chooses not to tell her. But still, she wants to ask him what it's like—whether it's easier for two men to love each other than for a man to love a woman. She wants to know if gay men are really different somehow; she wants to know if she will ever find a straight man with whom she can feel as comfortable as she feels with him. And she wants to know what it's like to watch your friends die. She wants to know if he thinks about death every time he takes a man to bed, if death lies between them, obstructing or heightening their passion.

"You know," she says, looking out across the canal, "I'm beginning to think the legends are true. Venice *is* haunted."

"Maybe." He looks back at her finally. He's wearing the same smile she saw at the memorial service—painful, but honest. "Let's go," he says. "I think I know the perfect solution."

"A stiff drink?"

"Okay. The second-best solution. We'll have the stiff drink later."

She smiles and takes his hand.

Piazza San Marco, fortunately, is the one place in Venice that you can find without getting lost. There are signs everywhere to lead you there. It takes them only a few minutes to find the square again. They arrive just as a swarm of pigeons springs up from the cobblestones. "Tippi Hedren's worst nightmare," James jokes, leading Cynthia toward the campanile.

They have to wait a while; the elevator can hold only a few people at a time. Other tourists mill about, checking their cameras and conversing in a variety of American accents.

A few minutes later, they are atop the bell tower, looking down upon the city. The domes of the basilica remind her of women in hoop skirts, preparing for a ball. On the other side, she sees a less picturesque view of Venice—an endless cluster of red-tiled roofs stretching toward the horizon.

They stand side by side, looking out over the piazza, James's face once again lost behind his camera. A few large clouds hover in the distance, but otherwise the sky is a pristine baby blue, the horizon miles away. From this height, everything is brought into sharp perspective—the pattern of white lines on the pavement of the piazza, even the route back to the train station; it all seems so simple.

She hears the click of the camera and James lowers it from his eye. His arm brushes against hers as tourists scuffle behind them in pursuit of their own idea of the perfect photo op. On the far side of the piazza, a gold awning ruffles delicately above the table where they had sat in the morning. The wind is brisker up here, bracing. Instinctively, she leans in and James rests his arm on her shoulder to lend her warmth.

❖

Cynthia's right: Venice is haunted. No matter where he goes, he can't escape the ghosts. Every part of the city arouses déjà vu: he's seen it all before, through Paul's eyes. Paul lived here for a year, researching his dissertation. Venice is a veritable treasure trove for the art historian.

There are no surprises left; everything is exactly as Paul described it. The long black gondolas, stroked along the water by gorgeous men in tight striped shirts. The narrow, shadowy canals slicing their crooked paths through the city. The sepia and gray buildings, crumbling piecemeal but still refusing to fall, refusing to surrender to time.

Cynthia has toured him most of the way up the peninsula with her nose in a Michelin guide, peeking out only when one of the standard sights comes into view. Rome zipped by, a jumble of fallen arches around the Colosseum, and Florence was little more than one museum or church after another. Only in Milan did she slow down the pace: shopping couldn't be rushed. He's grateful they've saved Venice for last. Compared to ancient Rome, Renaissance Florence, and depressingly modern Milan, Venice belongs to no particular age. It defies history at every turn, as it defies road maps and the laws of urban planning. Venice is timeless.

Heady from the chill and the view from the campanile, they emerge into the square, not quite sure where they're going. Cynthia's arm is locked inside his, their footsteps matched evenly, like those of languid soldiers sleepwalking in formation. To the hundreds of strangers passing through the piazza, they probably look like just another couple on a romantic stroll.

Cynthia hasn't mentioned Glenn in weeks. Even at the time of the breakup, months ago now, she didn't say much, and he hadn't wanted to push. The end was actually the only part of the relationship he *wasn't* in on: she had told him every last detail when she first developed her interest in Glenn, seeking his advice for how to break the ice; later, James received late-night phone calls with intimate descriptions of each date immediately after she got home; and he was her primary confidant for every bump and turn in the relationship. But she seemed to want to keep the end to herself, as if the pain were her own exclusive property, as if pain could not be shared.

"It's over," she announced abruptly one midnight. Whenever the phone rings after eleven, James's first thought is death, so her choice of phrase was particularly upsetting. He asked her to clarify, visions of funerals hobbling through his still half-asleep mind.

"Glenn," she said simply. "We broke up." He asked for details, but none were forthcoming. She changed the subject almost immediately. He had the feeling this was just an informational sound bite, like an on-the-hour TV news report. "Have you ever been to Italy?" she asked.

And now, two months later, they're lost in the labyrinth of Venice.

"How about that drink?" he says, gesturing toward a café beside the Grand Canal. Miraculously, they've made their way this far without ever glancing at the map. Maybe, he thinks suddenly, that's the secret.

She nods silently, attempting a smile, and follows him to a table near the water. Twilight has begun to fall and the café is lit by a series of tiny colored lamps, whose reflection dances on the waves.

"Still hate Venice?" he asks once they've settled down with their drinks.

She smiles, running a hand slowly through her hair. "I never hated Venice. It's just—" she seems to be searching for the word—"a very moody place."

"I'll drink to that." His mouth twists around the bitter Campari; it's definitely an acquired taste, and after two weeks, he still hasn't managed it. Reluctantly, he sets the glass back down on the table. The tabletop is stained with a series of rings, all identical in size. He wonders how many cups and glasses it took to make all these marks. How many people have sat here before them today? He's settled his own glass in at least five different spots already; the pattern resembles a lopsided Olympic flag.

They're silent for a long moment, lulled by the rhythm of the water that slaps gently against the moorings below. Cynthia's voice finally drips out in a whisper, as if she's really speaking to herself. "I thought I was over him."

"Glenn?"

One elbow resting on the tabletop, she toys with her bangs. Clearly, she isn't used to her new haircut. She said at first that it made her feel naked to have so much of her face exposed. "Yeah. What was it, six months? That's not very long to know someone. Why did it seem so important?"

James settles back in his chair. The Campari is out of reach now—just as well. "You never know what's going to be important," he says. "Sometimes you just feel it."

She sighs loudly and turns her eyes toward the canal. "Oh James, why are men such shits? Why do they always do this to me?"

"Why do you let them?"

She continues to stare out at the water; he can see only half of her cynical smile. "Hope, I suppose. I keep holding out for the one guy who's going to be different."

"How close have you come?"

She laughs. "What do *you* think? Just one long string of jerks, from ninth grade to now." She faces him again and takes a long sip of her drink. "I just keep finding them—or they find me. As soon as one walks away the next one shows up. I don't even have to try."

"Poor baby."

"So how do you manage?" she asks.

"I thought you had that all figured out. One-night stands, right? The back rooms of tacky bars?" There's a sudden rumble as a vaporetto starts up behind her and powers its way along the canal. As it passes, he sees people standing on deck, luggage piled defensively around them, their hair thrashing in the wind.

"I never thought that," Cynthia says, peering at him beneath a furrowed brow.

"You never asked before."

"I know. I guess—"

"It makes you uncomfortable." He smiles and crosses his legs, ankle to knee. "It's okay. Most people seem to feel that way. Even these days."

She's clutching her glass by the base, like a protective talisman. "So?"

"What, the history of my love life? Cynthia, believe me, if I were in love, discretion would be the last thing on my mind. You would already know every gory detail. The fact is, I haven't been in love since—" He lets his voice trail off, surprised to find that he doesn't want to be in this conversation after all.

"Craig?"

Of course, she knew Craig. There were no secrets in those days. "Just dates since then," he says after a moment, long enough for the name to fall and drown in the water beside them, "an occasional almost-relationship. But I don't really want more than that now. I'm just trying to enjoy life."

It's his turn to look away, into the water that seems to be turning black in the encroaching darkness. Paul wanted his ashes emptied into the Grand Canal; he had to settle for the Hudson.

"Who knows?" Cynthia says, apparently taking advantage of the smile that now plays upon his face. "Maybe there are two Mr. Rights out there, after all—one for each of us."

"Stranger things have happened. Jesus walked on water." He laughs and reaches for his drink.

"Well, here's to miracles," she says. They lean in to touch glasses.

The café is only a few blocks from their pension. They walk back through the deepening dusk. Tucked into an alley near the train station, the pension must be one of the best-kept secrets in Europe: in a city that preys on tourists, they've found the best bargain of the entire trip. Of course, what they save in euros they've lost in scenery. As far as James can tell, the only view from any room is the alley itself—a rather narrow, shadowy dead end that is best got through as quickly as possible. But, he thinks, views are for people who prefer to stay indoors. And Venice is certainly not a city for the agoraphobic.

Cynthia begs off dinner in favor of an early night. He leaves her in her room, smiling wanly, encouraging him to go out by himself. She must sense that he's secretly happy to have a chance to explore Venice on his own.

The Lista di Spagna is full of restaurants and shops, the latter just closing for the evening when he emerges from the hotel. The light has grown a deep blue, sinking into the stones of the street and the ancient walls of the buildings. With the darkening sky overhead, the city seems to close in upon itself like a grotto, voices echoing from one side to the other. As he walks through the marketplace, the excited shrieks of last-minute shoppers are countered by the hurried remarks of the vendors, who are now more concerned with going home than making a sale. The disparate voices join in a cacophony of unfamiliar sounds. Arguments arise here and there, people yelling and gesturing wildly to one another—but without a sense of enmity, as if controversy were expected and welcome. The Italians, he has discovered, love to complain; ironically, it seems one of their greatest pleasures in life. If things went smoothly, they would probably be bored to tears.

He finds a tiny restaurant at the foot of a bridge that arches acutely over the water. It's still early, so there are only a few other customers. There are so many restaurants in Venice, though, that none of them ever seems to be crowded. Paul's take on it was that Venice was just notorious for having terrible food. But one doesn't go there to dine, he said; one goes there to live.

In the doorway, James is greeted by a smiling waiter who rushes forward and leads him to an empty table at the front. "Please," the waiter says, visibly struggling through his English, "have a seat." James sits dutifully in the corner. Through the potted plants that line the window, he can watch streams of people passing over the bridge.

The waiter hovers over him as he reads the menu, the plastic smile still in place. James looks over the pasta courses—the *primi piatti*; alone, it doesn't seem worth the bother of having a full-course meal.

"We have special tonight," the waiter intones. James looks up obligingly. The waiter is young, in his early twenties, his face framed by high, sharp cheekbones that make his brown eyes seem huge. "Linguine with clams," he says. "Very good for you, the clams."

"Fine," James replies. He doesn't feel up to making decisions tonight; linguine sounds good enough.

"And some wine? A nice *bianco*, perhaps?"

"Half liter," James says. "And *aqua minerale*." He is taken aback by the waiter's insistence on speaking English, which appears to be only slightly better than James's Italian. But given his obvious eagerness to practice, James decides it's more polite to communicate in his own native tongue than to butcher the waiter's.

The waiter nods and vanishes quickly into the back of the narrow room. Outside, the bustle begins to slow down as the light grows dimmer. The dozens of pedestrians on the street when he left the pension have now dwindled to only a few—couples strolling hand in hand; young Italian men sauntering along, telling jokes and ribald stories in excited tones. It's a different atmosphere from daytime Venice: quieter, more sedate—somehow, he thinks, more Italian.

Suddenly, the waiter is at his side again, holding a bottle of wine up for inspection. "No," James says hesitantly, "*un mezzo litro*." As much as he would like to, there's no point in getting drunk tonight.

The waiter laughs and inserts the corkscrew. "But this is a beautiful wine. You will love it, I am sure."

"No, I—"

The cork is extracted before he has time to form a complaint. The waiter dribbles a mouthful into his glass and, reluctantly, James tastes it. He's hardly a connoisseur, but the wine is quite good. He nods his assent and the waiter fills the glass to the brim. "Is good for you," he says cheerfully. "The linguine comes soon."

A middle-aged couple stands in the doorway, peering around curiously. The waiter rushes over. "*Buona sera*," he chimes, "*una tavola per due? Qui.*" He leads them past several empty tables toward an alcove in the back.

Sipping the wine, James continues to watch the passersby. He relishes the silence, the peace of solitude. This is what travel has always been about for him—watching real people in real places live their ordinary lives.

He's drinking too much. His stomach begins to churn, reacting against hunger and the wine. The waiter is flying back and forth from the kitchen to the few other occupied tables. James notices that the couple who came in after him have already been served, the woman poking her fork timidly into a mound of risotto. She whispers something to her husband, who shrugs in response. James signals meekly to the waiter, who meets his eye with a smile and nods. In a moment, he's hovering over the table again.

"Just a moment, *signore*," he says crisply. "The linguine, she is coming." He picks up the wine bottle and refills James's glass. "You will love it, I promise. Clams very good for you, good for here." And he reaches out quickly and pats the napkin on James's lap.

"Waiter." The man near the alcove is waving a hand. Beside him, his wife is still pushing her food across the plate, as if she's searching for buried treasure.

"*Sì, signore.*" Quickly, the waiter turns away.

James looks down at his crumpled napkin, checking that he hasn't imagined the incident. No one can accuse Italian men of playing hard to get, he thinks. He's been cruised on the street on this trip, even touched by an occasional salesman or hotel clerk; he's come to expect that American inhibitions against physical contact do not exist here. But he's never known whether anything sexual was intended: Italian men walk down the street arm in arm all the time; it doesn't necessarily mean anything. But touching his penis—that seemed pretty sexual. He takes another sip of wine and watches the waiter making his rounds. He's definitely attractive. James remembers how offended Cynthia's been by this sort of behavior throughout their trip. He wonders if he should feel the same way. He wonders if all this flirtation is just a way to get him to spend more money. And yet, at another level, he doesn't really care.

Anxiety churning in his belly, he's almost lost his appetite by the time the dish finally arrives. The waiter smiles broadly as he lays the plate before him. "Enjoy," he says, staring into James's eyes. He lingers a moment before returning to the back.

Once he's calmed down enough to take a few bites, he discovers that the dish is quite good, if unexpectedly spicy. He reaches for a drink. The waiter still hasn't brought the mineral water.

Another couple appears in the doorway and the waiter walks briskly over to greet them. On the way, he catches James's eye and winks. James quickly looks down at his plate, concentrating on twirling the linguine around his fork.

"Is good?" the waiter asks, suddenly appearing at his shoulder.

"Yes," James says, his mouth full. "May I have my water?"

"Ah, of course." He lifts a hand, as if to dramatically smack his forehead.

In a moment, he reappears with a small bottle of water. Pouring it into a goblet, he peers down at James. "The water," he says, "is good only cleaning the face in the morning."

James takes the goblet and empties it in two gulps.

"You have beautiful eyes," the waiter says softly, "very beautiful eyes. You are American, no?"

James nods.

"I love to go to America. You must tell me all about it. Perhaps later, tonight, we could have a drink together; you tell me all about America."

James smiles flatly.

"How are you called?" the waiter asks, tilting his head to one side.

James fumbles with the words in his ears, the familiar idiom so strange in literal translation.

"Your...name," the waiter says.

James debates with the truth. For good or ill, it wins. "Giacomo," he says. "*Mi chiamo Giacomo.*"

The waiter's eyes light up, his mouth hanging open in a perfect O. "Giacomo! That is me, also! *Sono Giacomo.*"

James stares, trying to tell whether *he* is also debating the truth. If he had said Leonardo, would that have been the waiter's name, too? Would they have found themselves lying to each other, both putting on false personas, both playing a game that no one would win? James suddenly understands what Cynthia's been complaining about since they got to Italy—the insincere flattery women have to put up with, the constant, unashamed stares, the suggestive remarks from unremarkable strangers. He's already observed that Italian men seem completely fixated on their penises—constantly scratching, repositioning, or simply holding them—as if to reassure themselves that they're there, or to give the world some indication of their dimensions.

The waiter leans in. "Yes," he says, "we get a drink later tonight. I tell you all about Venezia. Yes?"

"I—I have to meet someone later."

The waiter smiles suspiciously. He's probably tried this line before. "A woman?" he asks. His eyelashes are full, making his eyes seem even darker, more inviting.

"Yes. My—friend is waiting for me at the hotel."

"I see. Well, perhaps another time. You are in Venezia for a few days, no?"

James smiles. "Yes. Perhaps another time."

"*Bene.* Enjoy your dinner," he says, softly tapping the tablecloth.

There's a sudden lightness in James's stomach, though he has been stuffing it hurriedly for the past five minutes. He watches the waiter go, his apron strings flapping delicately against his black pants. So easy. It would be so easy.

He takes another sip of wine. There's nothing to lose now; the bottle is already half gone. He pushes the plate away and cradles the glass in his hand, staring out the window.

When the waiter comes to clear the table, James turns expectantly, but the friendly smile has faded somewhat. "Would you care for dessert?" he asks, scraping the tablecloth and dropping the crumbs into his hand.

"No, thank you," James says. "Just the bill."

The waiter gently tears a sheet off his pad and lays it on the other side of the table. "*Buona sera, signore*," he says. Their eyes linger for a moment. James feels the lightness passing from his stomach to his head before the waiter abruptly breaks the connection and turns away.

The evening has turned very mild, perfect for strolling. He needs to walk off the wine, anyway, and in this state he would probably get lost on his way back to the hotel. San Marco is the only logical choice.

It seems that only tourists are left on the streets; their cameras now safely tucked away, they wander slowly past cafés and over bridges, whispering softly to one another, perhaps truly enjoying the city for the first time all day.

Cynthia sees something ugly in Venice; the aged walls speak to her of sin and decay, of dreams unfulfilled, futile desires. The city frightens her—the dead-end streets that lead only to water, the twisted bridges that defy every attempt at memorization. She wants it all laid out clearly for her—no mystery, no adventure. She wants it all to make sense.

The piazza is nearly deserted by the time he finds his way there. Even the pigeons have gone, resting somewhere in wait for the next day's mob of tourists. His footsteps echo on the pavement. Still dizzy from the wine, he peers up at the domes of the basilica. It seems extraordinary to find such a magnificent building here—extraordinary that this very city even exists. How absurd, he thinks, to create a thriving community on a lagoon—tiny islands connected by footbridges, islands that daily sink further into the muck. Some lunatic took this chaotic landscape and tried to impose order on it, tried to create something solid from the disparate elements at hand. And somehow, miraculously, succeeded.

A nearly full moon peers at him from behind the campanile. Its light falls brilliantly onto the square, accenting the outlines of each building, each shape. The sky itself is too blue, like a color from a palette. The entire landscape seems painted; it's too clear, too three-dimensional, to be real.

Paul kept a Monet print in his room, a palace on the Grand Canal—all blues, greens, and purples. It hung on the far wall, facing the bed. He stared at it for hours, toward the end, when it took too much energy to speak. In those days James sometimes regretted bringing up the subject of Venice, but Paul seemed unable to shut up about it. "That's where life is," he said once. "Life began in the water, after all." And he laughed.

As James paces through the empty square, a fine rain begins to fall—more like a mist, drops of water seemingly suspended in the air. Water is everywhere now, proclaiming its power, washing bits of the city away. But still, it's here. Cynthia's right: Venice is ridiculous. Romance always is.

At the end of the square, bright lights signal the vaporetto station. Laughing suddenly, turning his head up to face the rain, he runs across the piazza, toward the light.

FOXES

Jonathan Harper

What Danny remembered most about the ordeal were the foxes. The day had started with the two of them: Danny and his passenger Kyle, both boys no older than nineteen, both proud and naive, both drunk off the thrill that comes with a road trip. They rode in Danny's bright yellow Beetle, a flashy lemon of a car, the type of gift a parent gives to buy back his son's affection. Now, they were alone on the road, far away from any authority. Nobody knew where they were; only the wrong people knew where they were headed.

They were near the West Virginia-Maryland border when it happened, nervously singing along to Tom Petty, admiring the sprawling farmland that stretched out around them. The road had felt unusually bumpy for a few miles before passing vehicles had waved frantically at them. Kyle had waved back at the first few, amused by the overt friendliness of country folk. "Must be the car. They know we're out-of-owners," he mused. Soon, the Beetle became increasingly unsteady, almost slumping to one side. A little warning light was flashing on the dashboard, what first appeared as a harmless little thing, something an inexperienced driver overlooks until he and his friend are stranded on the side of the road, staring at a flat tire spilling out like loose flesh over the pavement.

Around them were hills and forest, the guardrail bordering the edge of a wooded ravine. There were no other signs of life. It had rained throughout the morning and the air was unusually cold for October.

"What do we do now?" Danny asked.

Kyle lit a Parliament, as if to prove he wasn't nervous. "Call somebody," he said flatly.

"Call who?" At first, the only person Danny could think of was his father. It had never occurred to him that such things could happen, to break down on an isolated road, much less the necessary steps to remedy the situation.

At first, Kyle didn't respond. He crawled over the guardrail and began to descend down towards the woods behind them. "I'm going to piss," he said. "You need to call someone." And then, he was gone.

This was Kyle's habit. He always disappeared, especially in times of crisis and every time it happened, Danny told himself it would be the last. Instead, he pulled out his phone and mused over the little search icons for towing companies, but then, he felt a paroxysm of anxiety: what exactly did one say? How would he describe where they were? Then, he cursed Kyle for leaving him behind to deal with it all. He considered starting up the car and driving off, imagining the car stuttering along like a drunken bumblebee, Kyle dashing alongside pleading not to be left behind.

His thoughts were interrupted by a sudden high-pitch yelp from behind him. Down by the edge of the thicket, he could see Kyle peering into the woods mid-stream. He crossed the guardrail and descended. There in the thicket was the orange and white mask of a fox's head, staring at them. Two kits peered out from behind the bush of her tail. Three sets of eyes, all dark as charcoal. As Danny leaned forward, the vixen cringed and flashed her teeth, but did not move until Kyle took a stick, striking out at them until they scattered.

"What did you do that for?" Danny snapped.

"Whatever," Kyle grumbled. "Did you call?"

"No."

The two boys pissed and then crawled back up the hill where they froze. From around the bend, came the long silver bullet of a police trooper, its lights flashing, pulling up slowing behind the Beetle. As Danny remembered it, the police car had moved in slow motion, his stomach churning into panicked nausea with each passing second, only able to think about the two zip-locked baggies of cocaine nestled in his trunk.

The trip had been Kyle's doing, at least that's what Danny told himself. It should be stated that these two friends did not actually like each other. Their friendship was one of those forced college bonds, the type one would spend years trying to distance himself from.

Danny's father had taken great interest in their relationship from the very start, even though Danny assured him regularly that they were not lovers and never would be. For some reason, this hurt his father's feelings. To him, Kyle meant potential for his son's first meaningful relationship, an image inspired by the young gay couples of sitcoms, maturing together in an increasingly hazy world of expectation and judgment. He thought Kyle was charming, multi-faceted, and someone who would mature with the kind of positive influence that his own son could easily provide.

This was far from the truth, as neither boy was interested in maturing. They wanted to be dangerous, as if they languished in the idea of self-destruction. The previous semester was defined by their competing for the affections of Vince, a self-proclaimed entrepreneur who had a series of vague businesses, a mysterious host of hotel parties, a dark figure who slinked in and out of night clubs. He never seemed to work, yet always had money. He was like an ethereal object unraveling in all directions, messy and fabulous and nearly impossible to contain.

It was Kyle who first learned about the vacation cabin in Proctor, a hazy five hour drive through mountains. It was Kyle who agreed to collect some party favors from Vince's condo and then transport them there. And it was Kyle who convinced Danny to take them in exchange for a weekend in Vince's hideaway.

Thankfully, the state trooper had no interest in opening the Beetle's trunk. Instead, he was cordial and concerned, eyeing the flashy little car with a raised eyebrow, before calling a tow truck for them. The tow was a massive rusted thing, similar to its driver, a weathered old fart with a limp and a habit of chewing on dry air. He gave a single nod to the trooper before inspecting the bright yellow car with a grimace.

"Thank you so much for coming," Danny said, extending his hand. The man ignored it, again glancing back at the trooper who merely shrugged.

"That tires not just flat. It's dead."

"Can you fix it?" Kyle asked in an annoyed tone.

"Nope. Don't do that. I'm just here to take you back to town. That's all." The man wandered around the car in slow painful movements reminiscent of a door creaking shut. "Pop open the trunk." His tone was full of authority.

The boys looked at each other as Danny's chest inflated with a wild panic, so much so that he felt on the verge of floating away. But the drugs were concealed in Kyle's bag and no one seemed remotely interested in searching for what they didn't know existed. A click from his key chain and the Beetle's trunk opened, where the tower retrieved a metal prong and inserted it into the front bumper. He connected it to the hook of the truck's crane and within a few minutes the Beetle was pulled upward onto the truck's bed.

"You boys ride up front with me," he said. "And put that out. I ain't breathing in your cancer." Kyle grimaced and snubbed his Parliament under his sneaker. As they entered the truck's cab, Danny was pushed into the middle of the bench as Kyle hugged the side door. Outside, the trooper was still standing there, smiling even, and watched them drive away.

"We're gonna backtrack a bit. You boys sure picked a bad spot to break down." Within moments, they passed the welcome sign into West Virginia only to immediately make a U-turn in a service lane. "Technically, I'm not supposed to cross state lines, but it can't be helped." The tower spoke as if measuring out every syllable. He asked where they were going. Danny told him Proctor and the man huffed. A few moments later, he added, "It's a fancy little car you got back there," a certain sense of skepticism building in his voice.

"It's the purse dog of the automobile industry," Kyle said and Danny nudged him lightly.

The driver ignored him. "Shame to see it misused. You had no business driving on that as long as you did. Luck will have it there's no damage to the wheel."

"Well we didn't know it was flat," Kyle snapped.

"Not sure how you didn't." He flipped on the radio to a gospel station, volume low enough to create an unintelligible chorus over a pipe organ. "A car like that ain't meant for traveling out here. Sits too low to the ground. Drive that over anything and it'll likely scrape up the underbelly and throw your alignment out."

Kyle grumbled under his breath. Beyond them, the trees meshed into a continuous blur of reds and oranges and browns. When he finally asked to change the music, the tower gave a sorry look and Kyle added,

"I'm Jewish." A white lie; both boys binged and purged on them. The radio flicked to a country station as penance and then it was turned off altogether.

They sat in silence the remainder of the drive.

The exit lane cut into the hills and revealed a small depression of open fields and a two-street town, the kind Danny understood existed but had never actually seen. A no-brand gas station, perhaps the largest building, greeted them at the end of the ramp. There the road split into parallel streets, each aligned with a dozen small houses that looked pasted together: low chain linked fences surrounded by overgrown lawns and homey porches. On one of them, a plump woman sat with an elderly man, watching two children chase each other around the yard. She may have instinctively waved.

The tire shop capped the end where both streets rejoined. It was a large structure, perhaps a barn in a previous life, now with faded red siding and a sloped roof of fitted sheet metal. Broken down cars lurched in the back and a duo of broad-faced mechanics lurked out front. The gravel was still soft from rain and caked into several mud pools. The tower signed as one of the mechanics pointed at the Beetle with mild amusement. But both mechanics went stern as they watched the boys exit the truck.

The Beetle was lowered into place, the fourth car waiting entry to the garage. As Danny stood there, a flash of wind turned the air bitterly cold, the ache of it seeping in through his pea coat. Kyle retrieved his bag from the trunk before wandering off. The driver had also disappeared, presumably inside the garage. Danny, however, could not bring himself to move away from the tow truck. There was something about the shop and the town that unnerved him. The whole place didn't make sense to him. How could people actually live here? There was no grocery store, no businesses, not even a local bar. It felt like a sort of Purgatory, a place of waiting for final judgement. And though Danny felt like he was in no immediate danger, there was the inherent need to get back to the road and to the eventual safety of Vince's cottage. Then, his thoughts were interrupted. The tow driver returned with a clipboard, squinting at it with a methodical stare. He didn't accept credit cards and Kyle hadn't returned.

"Yup. When it's time to pay, people make themselves scarce," the old man grunted. "Happens all the time."

Danny fished out several twenties from his wallet and signed on the dotted line. At least he had the foresight to bring cash. He stuffed the carbon copy of the receipt into his pocket. "What happens now?"

"Go talk with the people inside," he said and crawled back into the truck.

"But you can't go yet! You're going to stay until my car's fixed, right?" The words fell out of Danny's mouth and left behind a perturbed hollow feeling. Why had he said that? The tower squinted at him, a cringe really, and Danny humbled himself. "Thank you for everything. If it weren't for you, we'd probably still be stranded out there."

"Sure thing, kid," he replied. "But one bit of advice. Your friend. A guy like that will get you into trouble. But you knew that already. Take care now."

And then he drove off.

Danny found Kyle inside, sitting cross-legged with his backpack propped up on his lap. The room was surprising warm and overpopulated. The receptionist sat behind the counter, head bowed into a paperback. Metal fold-up chairs held other stranded travelers: a middle-aged couple, a humming elderly woman, a nervous twitching man dressed up like a lumberjack. Sitting next to Kyle was a petite teenage girl wearing a bright yellow fleece whose fingers seem to dance over her cell phone. When Danny sat down, she smiled brightly at him, mouth full of braces, and said "Hi," stretching out the word much longer than necessary. Danny nodded, but his attention was focused on the backpack with Vince's party favors inside.

"Have you been outside the entire time?" Kyle asked.

"I feel sad and lost," Danny muttered. "I just spent all my cash paying for the tow."

Kyle pulled him into a shoulder hug. "Poor baby. I promise I'll make it up to you." The girl next to him giggled. "I spoke with the mechanics. We had a nail in the tire. It needs to be replaced and there's a little damage to the wheel."

Danny gasped. He thought of his father shaking his head in disappointment.

"Relax. It's not as bad as it sounds. The damage is minor. They said you might feel a little bump from time to time, that's all."

"Tell me you're sorry," Danny said. He kept his voice low but the entire room noticed.

"For the tire?"

"You bullied me into taking this trip and then you left me to pay for the tow by myself."

Kyle's face turned very pious. He looked ready for an argument, but feeling all eyes on him, he simply stood up and slung his backpack over his shoulder. "I'll be back," he said.

The girl flashed a little grin, as if she'd witnessed something remarkable, but then was quite happy to talk about herself. She was in for an oil change and on to visit her boyfriend in Morgantown. His roommate was gone for the weekend, so they'd finally have some private time together. She said she didn't even know how to check her own oil and when the little warning light started flashing, she had no idea what it meant. She was like a doll with a chord that when pulled made her say something flimsy. "This kind of thing always happens to me," she said. "If I hadn't pulled over when I did, my engine would've fried up and I'd be in so much trouble!" Danny nodded with sickening recognition that they were a lot alike.

The conversation drifted on until she returned to her phone. There was no one else to speak with, the other customers guarded in their own minds. They would all be stuck here for hours. When Danny stepped outside, it was freezing and he pulled the pea coat tighter around him. He found Kyle out on the side of the building, speaking with one of the garage workers, both looking discreet and failing miserably. The man was tall and lanky, hair pulled back into a dirty ponytail and wore an army surplus jacket. As Danny approached, the mechanic moved back behind the garage and out of sight.

"So, I'll be back in about twenty minutes," Kyle said.

"Wait. What's going on? What was that all about?"

"Look, I'll take care of everything. You just wait inside."

Danny openly stared. "What do you mean? What are you going to do?"

"Don't worry about it," Kyle said. It was strange how Kyle often fancied himself an actor in a sitcom, one of the side characters who was often rewarded for outlandish behavior.

Danny looked back at the backpack. "You're not going to try and sell him Vince's stash are you? He'll kill us!"

"Oh, shut up!" Kyle rolled his eyes.

"Then, what are you going to do? Suck him off for a twenty?"

Kyle gave him an indignant glare, while glancing behind him. "Will you please just relax. I'll be back."

"Look, if this is about money, I'm going to walk down to the gas station. They must have an ATM. Let's go together."

"Why don't you trust me?"

"Because you're out here less than ten minutes and you suddenly are going to wander off with that man and I have no idea why." Danny kept his voice low. He was feeling desperate. "Don't go with him. You are not as good at these types of things as you think you are."

They were both silent for several seconds before Kyle turned around and walked towards the back of the building.

"Fine! Just call me when you're done!" Danny yelled after him as Kyle lifted up a middle finger without turning around.

❖

It was not a long walk down to the other side of town. The sky turned to a mix of purple and gray and he felt the pressure building in his sinuses—another storm was approaching. He started to jog past house after house: a withered garden, a rusted truck, an abandoned tricycle. It was a desolate town, not even a fire hydrant in sight. The whole place could burn down without even a siren.

The gas station housed a small diner with a handful of booths and cheap vinyl padding. The short order cook drearily swayed over the flat burner. He must have startled the old woman because she yelped as he took a seat in one of the booths. Her mouth was missing a few teeth and her chin sagged, but otherwise she looked perfectly harmless. "There's no smoking inside!" she bellowed without cause.

The gas station attendant came out from behind the register and dropped off a black plastic ashtray. "It's not like she doesn't have one every hour. Nobody checks on that kind of thing here." The attendant was a matronly woman with long hair that ran down her back. "My name's Vera and you tell me what you want and Betty over there will fix it up for you." He smiled sweetly, a smile used to charm people his parent's age, and asked for coffee. Vera yelled, "You got that, Betty? Coffee!" Betty grumbled "coffee" and slammed a filled tea cup and saucer on the counter. Then, a van pulled off the highway to the pumps and Vera wobbled back towards the register.

The coffee was burnt with floating grounds, but it warmed him. An old jukebox collected dust in the corner, mostly oldies and country music. But deep in he found an old Sheryl Crow album nestled with Led Zeppelin's "Physical Graffiti" and dropped in a dollar's worth of songs. A great relief yawned within him, like the whole maelstrom of bad luck had finally depleted itself. The songs played and ended. Then Vera took his order and repeated it in a booming voice: "Betty, grilled cheese and tomato! Side of green beans!"

"I'm not deaf," Betty snarled back.

Outside, rain started in a light drizzle. Soon, the storm was upon them, pelting the large windows. Danny checked his phone; the day was eating itself up and Kyle still hadn't called. It was a shame actually. Kyle would have been an ideal companion now, happily smoking and talking whatever crude nonsense that usually spewed from his mouth. He called Kyle's phone. It rang impotently until it reached voicemail.

"Do people come here often?" he asked but Betty had drifted off into her own mental space again.

Vera came by and plopped down, drinking from a bottled iced tea she had liberated from the gas station's cooler. "Not often. As you can tell, we're not a major destination." He nodded and they sat quietly for several moments. "Where you from, honey?"

He mentioned the university, his weekend jaunts into D.C. They compared notes about small towns and big cities, emphasizing crime and racial injustice. Vera kept fiddling with her pack of Marlboros, hesitant at first to smoke one. "I should have quit years ago. If I keep up this habit, I'll end up like haggard old Betty there."

"You know I can hear you," Betty grunted.

Vera just smiled at her and turned back to the boy. "So, tell me. What are you doing here all by yourself?"

"I popped a tire earlier. It's down at the shop."

"Well I figured that," she said. "But it shouldn't take this long to change a flat."

"There was a long line," he replied and then, because it felt appropriate to do so, he mentioned Kyle was still down at the garage, that it was his turn to pay. "He's going to call me when the car is ready." When Vera asked where they were going, he mentioned Proctor, that they were going to visit a friend.

"Proctor? That's a very strange place for a vacation home." She snuffed out her cigarette, pale lipstick visible on the filter. Then, she gathered the dishes and walked off.

Now alone, he sat at the table feeling very tense, casually playing on his phone. Betty leaned against the counter and smoked a long slim cigarette and made a distressed hacking noise before fading off again. An hour passed and Kyle hadn't called. He sent over a text message asking about the car. "I'm at the diner by the gas station," he typed and added an emoji of a little coffee cup. Outside, the rain continued beating the windows in a hypnotic rhythm. Another hour passed as his anxiety grew. It was getting late and Vince was expecting them. Surprisingly, he didn't even have Vince's number stored in his phone. Kyle did. He was always texting with Vince. Perhaps he had already sent a message about their little breakdown. Maybe, just maybe, Vince was on his way to pick them up.

Suddenly, he heard a strange noise out in the distance, a mournful wail somewhere beyond the diner. The pitch was feminine and painful sounding and fatally brief. At first, Danny had thought he had imagined it. He was peering out through the window, the storm having just passed, but saw nothing but empty space and the roads stretching down towards the mechanic's garage. Then, he heard it again, this time closer. It was a scream, a brief terrible scream almost instantly silenced.

"What are you freaking out about?" Vera said. She was giving him a queer look.

"You heard it, too," he said with a gasp. "I think someone's in trouble."

Vera laughed. "It's a fox. That's the sound they make when they're in heat."

The countryside was a strange place. He stared back out through the window, thinking of the vixen they had stumbled upon earlier that day. She had babies with her. It couldn't be the same fox.

Half an hour passed. He did not hear the noise again. He sent another text message to Kyle, this one just a series of question marks.

Suddenly, Betty's hand slapped against the counter top like thunder. "We're closing soon," she said and dropped off the hand-written check. "Station stays open all night, but I'm closing. You need to pay up." Her face was a cruel creased map, and then he noticed the twitch in her right eye. A small layer of film coated it, the pupil slightly discolored.

"Of course. I'm sorry," he said. It was only six dollars and some change for all the borrowed time. He went to the ATM and tried Kyle's phone again. This time it rang twice before hanging up.

"What a bitch," he mumbled.

"Uh-oh, trouble brewing?" Vera called out.

The rain had stopped and the late afternoon had set in. With each step forward, the town got darker. A few porch lights were illuminated, but there were no street lamps. Somewhere ahead, he was certain he had seen a small animal, perhaps a cat or a small dog, dash across the road.

On the other end of town, the tire shop's lot was empty, the Beetle safe inside and presumably fixed. The same duo of mechanics milled out front, each drinking from a beer bottle. They were staring long before he came into focus. "Is my car ready?" Danny blurted out and they pointed towards the office. Kyle was not there.

The receptionist closed her paperback and plucked her glass off. "Glad you made it," she said with a half-yawn. From under the counter, she withdrew a clipboard with his keys attached. "Your total is at the bottom. Please sign here. Cash or credit?" Her voice sounded like an automated machine.

"My friend is supposed to pay for this," Danny said. "Do you know where he is?"

The woman made a point of peering over the counter and inspecting the empty waiting room. Half of the chairs were folded up against the far wall. "Nope, can't say that I do."

Danny held his breath, half-expecting Kyle to jump out of some hiding spot and yell, "Surprise!" Nothing happened. He stood there with a blank stare and the desk clerk smiled presumptuously because it was his turn to speak. All the gears in his head quit turning and restarted themselves. "I'll be right back," Danny stammered.

"Sure thing. I'll be here all night."

He returned outside. The wind had picked up. He called Kyle's phone and this time it went straight to voicemail. He peered around the building. The mechanics rose from their seats, emitting a string of curses as a minivan wobbled in on another deflated tire. A family of four crawled out, looking tired and disheveled.

And then, there he was: the mechanic from earlier, the one with the ponytail. "Hey. Have you seen my friend?" he asked.

The man turned to him with a blank expression and then shrugged before turning back to measure the tire.

"Hey! The guy I came here with. You were talking with him earlier. Where is he?"

The other workers let out a snort, nudged each other. One of the mechanics mimicked Danny's voice with a coarse falsetto. "Where is he? Where is he?"

"Dude, I don't know who you're talking about," the mechanic said. At first, he seemed annoyed, but then stood with a sense of bravado, as if he decided to appear intimidating. "Let me do my work."

There was a tense silence. The family scurried inside to the front office, glancing back over their shoulder, and Danny worried he was making a scene. He backed away slowly and dialed Kyle's phone, again cutting directly to voicemail. All the mechanics seemed to ignore him and yet eyed him fiercely.

Back inside, the temperature had dropped a few degrees. The clerk was setting up a space heater when Danny barged in and she scampered back behind the partition. "Are you alright?" she asked, though her voice was flat and uncaring.

"No, I'm not. My friend is missing. He was here with me earlier and now he's vanished." His voice was surprisingly loud. The family flinched and the woman took a defensive stance, both hands buried from view behind the counter. Someone else shuffled around behind her in the back office. Danny dialed Kyle's number again, this time speaking loudly enough for the whole room. "Kyle, it's Danny. It's time to go. If you don't call me back soon, I'm calling the police." He hung up, thinking of the ridiculous message. If the police did show up, what would he tell them? There was nothing right about this trip at all. He had no business being there.

From the back office, the manager emerged. He was a pot-bellied man with a trimmed white beard, skin coarse and scarred from years of harsh weather. While the clerk openly scowled, his face was calm, almost paternal. Despite his grim complexion, his eyes were deeply penetrating and intelligent.

"Son, you're making a lot of noise out here," he said. He had wandered out into the center of the waiting area, pulling up one of the folded chairs. "Sit down here," he said. There was a subtle violence to his tone, one that was felt but not heard. Everyone was looking at him now: the manager, the clerk, the family of four. He felt his face burn red, but did as he was told. "Alright," the manager continued. "Now, what's going on?"

Danny gripped the edge of his seat. His foot dug into the layer of dirt on the floor. Within a few swift motions, his shoe scraped against raw wood underneath. The lady behind the counter cleared her throat but he kept staring down at his feet. While his mind flooded with everything that needed explaining, his voice had dried up. After a few moments of frustrated rambling, he managed to say that he'd been trying to contact Kyle for hours, that Kyle had wandered off with one of the workers, that he wasn't answering his phone and that Danny was scared because it was getting late and he wanted to go home. The family edged their way to the door, braving the cold outside. He didn't want them to leave.

"Mary, would you please bring Zack in here?" the manager asked and the woman left the waiting room. "Do we need to call somebody for you? Your parents, maybe?" Danny told him that wasn't necessary and then lied and said he already had. The clerk, Mary, returned with the man with the ponytail. His coat was different, no more ugly green fatigues, but now a brown bomber jacket. He held a socket wrench. "Zack, we have some things to talk about," and the manager recounted Danny's story in a concise manner.

"Oh that kid was talking to me during my smoke break," the mechanic said. "Asked me a whole bunch of questions and then wandered off. Haven't seen him since."

"That's not what you said outside," Danny snapped.

"Be quiet!" the manager yelled and Danny tensed up in his seat. Then, the old man turned soft again. "Now son, obviously Zack here doesn't know where your friend is. I know you're upset, but I'm not sure what you want us to do. Is there someone we can call?

He sat quiet for a moment. "Call the police. Something's happened to him." He willed his voice into a calm sound and then flushed, wondering how ridiculous he sounded. And then he remembered the backpack, all of Vince's party favors.

The mechanic let out a low mean chuckle. "Get back to work," the manager snapped and Zack moved back into the garage. "Alright now, if that's what you want to do, then we can do that. But it's getting dark out. I'm sure your friend will be back at any minute."

Danny nodded. "I think I can wait a little longer."

The manager smiled lightly. "Alright. Now, in other matters, your car is ready. And we need payment and you're making a scene and disrupting my workers and bothering my customers." Danny peered back at the entranceway, knowing full well the family was lurking outside in the cold. "No, no, no—eyes on me," the manager continued. "It's getting late and we should be closing up soon."

"But, I can't leave without Kyle."

"I know. But right now, we have performed a service for you and you are past due on payment. Now if Kyle ran off with all your money, then yes, I think we should call the deputy down here right away."

Danny tensed up. He had cash and a credit card. And once he paid, he'd be expected to leave. "That won't be a problem. I can pay up right now."

The manager smiled and called him a good boy. Behind them, the woman returned to her register, her ill-fitted boredom resumed. She printed off a bill and he handed her his check card without even looking at it. He exhaled a long sigh of relief when the receipt printed without any further delay.

Once again, the manager hovered over him. "Now that's settled, if you want to go looking for your friend, maybe Zack would be willing to show you around. You'd have to ask nicely though."

Danny squeezed his car key in his hand. It felt warm, like a magic ward against evil. "I'm not going anywhere with that man."

"Fair enough." The manager patted his shoulder before turning to the clerk. "Mary, why don't you call Vera down at the gas pumps and see if she'll put him up for a bit. Maybe Kyle is down there waiting for you right now. Probably thought he could get out of paying that way."

Mary got on the phone and kept her voice low. After a few minutes, she gave an assertive nod.

"You see, everything's going to work out just fine. You have a warm place to hang out a bit. We'll be here another hour or so. If Kyle shows up, I'll make sure he calls you. He has your number, right?"

"Yes." In that moment, Danny felt like a child, an admonished child, one who had behaved very badly.

The manager led him into the garage, following close behind, a hand gently hovering on his shoulder as if to steer him in the right direction. The Beetle was in full view, the new tire practically glimmered. The receipt guaranteed it for twelve months. When he sat down, he locked the doors, the entire staff all on the outside with their tools, looking in at him.

It was dark outside. Danny's foot pressed down on the accelerator which caused him to skid recklessly through puddle after puddle. Almost all of the houses were lit, but with the shades drawn over every window. As he reached the gas station, he almost forgot to stop, hitting his breaks hard enough to prevent him from crashing into the pumps.

Vera was waiting, poised in the doorway. He rolled down the window and she called out, "Honey, what's wrong? It sounds like pandemonium down there."

"Is Kyle here? Have you seen him?" he called out. She shook her head. "I need to gas up real fast," he said.

Vera gave him a pleasant smile. "Sure thing, honey. I'll turn on the pump and then you come inside. I've got a fresh pot brewing."

Danny flicked his check card in and out of the slot and started fueling. Again, he called Kyle's phone and it went straight to voice mail. For a moment, he imagined him sitting in one of the diner booths, eating peach cobbler out of a dish with ice cream, a fresh Parliament dangling from his lips while a roll of cash burned a hole in his pocket. Then, he imagined Kyle wandering back up to the tire shop, stoned out of his mind, another terrible scene with the manager would happen. No matter what, even if Kyle did suddenly call, he wasn't going back there for him. Kyle would have to walk and meet him at the diner. The gas pump dinged and the receipt spit out. Danny glanced up and there was Vera's silhouette, almost hidden through gas station's window. Two fingers were separating the blinds enough so she could peer out. And when Danny caught her, they closed again.

He got back on the highway, where the evening was changing into an endless sea of dark, where the white lane dashes on the road became a string of waves. He thought he'd pull off at the very next exit, but didn't. He was set on Proctor, where Vince was probably tapping his foot impatiently. Danny would tell him about the town and the tire shop and insist they go back in the morning. One thing was certain. Kyle had been correct, the wheel was perfectly fine.

A short time later, his headlights caught two shapes dashing across the highway: a deer in close pursuit of a fox. The deer made dangerous leaps, as if aiming its hooves for the center of the fox's back. The Beetle swerved onto the shoulder lane, though the animals were too far away for a collision. The curve in the road looked familiar, and though it was unlikely, Danny wondered if this was the very spot they had originally stopped, where all their troubles began and he felt the grief of it linger about like a fog. But his eyes were still scanning out past where the headlights could reach, trying to see if the fox had made it to the safety of the brush. They were like ghosts, a quick flash of movement and color, and then both animals had been lost to the darkness.

Come back.

OMAHA

Michael H. Ward

Pat Kelly, standing paralyzed on the empty street corner, was willing himself to cross when a carload of teenagers, careening past the stoplight, spit at him and screamed, "Cocksucker!" It was Saturday night, late July 1963, stiflingly hot and humid, even at eleven o'clock. Pat had been trying all summer to make himself walk into the Ron D Voo Lounge, a sleazy bar tucked into the corner of the old Regis Hotel. With no cars in sight, he thought, "God help me," and ran across the street, ducking into the entryway beneath the pulsing neon champagne glass.

Inside, men were packed together in a dense cloud of cigarette smoke. The bar was small and the air smelled faintly sour, like a locker room. Older men, younger men, men dressed as women. An obese black man in a bright orange caftan and blond wig sat at a piano surrounded by patrons singing show tunes. Above him hung a glittering silver banner: "Tiny Cherokee—LIVE!" Shouted conversations competed with an enthusiastic chorus singing "Oklahoma!" The noise, jostling, and laughter made it feel like a circus. Pat wanted to run but a burly man in a plaid shirt shouted, "Don't block the door, honey. Fire laws!" and pulled him into the melee. He saw a small open space in the far corner by the fire exit and threaded his way toward it. Pressed against the wall, he struggled to breathe normally and appear relaxed. He was terrified that he'd be discovered to be underage, or worse, that he would be recognized, easily identified by his copper-colored hair and the deep dimple on his chin. His height and broad shoulders made it hard to disappear into the crowd.

As if by magic, a young man materialized from the crush and handed him a cold bottle of Budweiser. Smiling, he squeezed in next to Pat and said, "You look terrified. At least pretend you're having fun."

Pat was speechless. He had fantasized about this moment hundreds of times, and here was his dream guy: a little shorter than himself, olive skin, dark eyes, a black crewcut. Pat's heart gave a little lurch. He nodded his thanks and smiled.

"I'm Lenny," the man said. "You?"

"Padraic," he replied, fumbling in his shirt pocket for a cigarette. "My friends call me Pat."

Lenny smiled and, bringing his lips close to Pat's ear, said, "Very happy to meet you, Pat."

They tried to make small talk, but it was nearly impossible to hear. After a few moments Lenny got them a second beer and, moving in front of Pat, pressed back into his body, laughing at Tiny Cherokee's antics at the piano. Pat wanted to rest his chin on Lenny's head but felt self-conscious. He hoped Lenny couldn't feel his erection against his butt. He was embarrassed by how powerless he was to control his body's response to Lenny's proximity and the saturating heat of the bar. Next to them a drunken drag queen, teetering on impossibly high heels, fell heavily against the man in front of her, who started cursing and shoving. Lenny grabbed Pat by the arm and yelled, "Let's get out of here!"

The cool air and the quiet of the city at night were a welcome relief. Pat suddenly felt shy, wondering what to say to this good-looking stranger. Lenny released Pat's arm and suggested they get something to eat. The streets were nearly deserted as they walked the four blocks to the Greyhound bus station, the only place left open. Pat asked if the bar was always so crowded and rowdy.

"A couple of weekends ago," Lenny said, "two drag queens got into a hair pulling contest. In minutes wigs were flying in all directions. Miss Cherokee climbed up on her piano bench and screamed, 'Throw those bitches out! I'm the only diva here, and I'm in the middle of my set!'"

Pat laughed, enjoying watching Lenny's face as he talked, struck by how much he looked like one of his coworkers at the Coca Cola plant. There was nothing that seemed gay about him except what he was talking about. He was so at ease.

The waiting area in the bus station was seedy, people sleeping on wooden benches or sitting huddled with their luggage, waiting for early morning transportation to Rapid City or Des Moines. Pat and Lenny took stools at the counter in the diner, which was empty except for an elderly woman dozing in a booth in the corner. The short order cook came out from the kitchen. "Gentlemen!" he said, looking speculatively from one to the other. Lenny sat back on the stool and said, "Popular spot at this time of night, huh?"

The cook smiled. "Best time for me. The drunks haven't come in yet and the whores are out looking for business." Without looking at Pat, Lenny said, "My buddy and I'll have bacon and eggs. And coffee." Pat liked the way Lenny took charge.

"Okey dokey," the cook replied and set out paper napkins, silverware, and glasses of water before returning to the kitchen. To fill the silence Pat began talking rapidly, about his family, his summer job loading trucks at Coca Cola, his hopes of escaping the Midwest when he graduated from college. After several minutes he was breathless and stopped as suddenly as he had begun.

Lenny just continued to smile.

Taking a sip of water, Pat spilled a little down his chin and wiped it off with the back of his hand.

"You OK?" Lenny asked. "You seem a little nervous."

Pat thought he was probably teasing but the question did little to calm him down. "Enough about me. Tell me about you."

"I was an army brat, born in Texas, raised on bases in Germany and Okinawa." The cook brought out two mugs of coffee and Lenny stirred in milk. "I joined the Air Force just out of high school. I'm a Sergeant First Class with the glorious Strategic Air Command in Bellvue." He said this with a little smile and Pat couldn't tell if he was proud of it or making fun.

"What about your family?" Pat asked.

"Mother and father, two younger sibs, Greek and Italian background, all in Montana now." He took a sip of coffee and looked at Pat appraisingly. "You're Irish, right?"

Pat laughed. "It's hard to miss this hair."

Lenny said, "And the freckles and the blue eyes." After glancing around the room, he reached out and briefly touched Pat's chin. "And that dimple gives me a hard on."

Lenny's touch was a shock, so intimate. The cook came through the swinging doors and set their plates down on the counter, and the men straightened up. Pat realized he was having fun, and he wished he could laugh out loud, make some noise to get the tension out of his neck and shoulders. They set upon their bacon and eggs and ate in silence. Pat noticed the rumbling of a motor as a Greyhound pulled into the bay near the waiting room.

Lenny looked at his watch and said, "I have ten minutes before the last bus leaves for the base." He turned on his stool to face Pat and, almost imperceptibly, rubbed his right knee against Pat's. "Or we could get a room at the Y." Pat felt a moment of panic, unable to respond, but Lenny held his gaze, continuing to gently rub his leg. After a moment Lenny said, "I'm going to take your silence as a yes," and stood up.

Pat had taken swimming lessons at the Y as a ten-year-old and remembered only how cold the water was and that he'd felt strangely excited in the locker room to be undressed in front of strangers. A lot of the men walked around drying themselves and talking to each other, unselfconscious of their nakedness, and Pat couldn't help noticing how big their penises were. Once a man caught him staring and grinned at him, which made Pat's face redden.

The neighborhood was run down even back then. The seven story cement block building looked desolate this late at night. The lobby was as dingy as the bus station, with cracked tile floors, walls yellowed from years of cigarette smoke, and a scarred wooden counter separating the night clerk from the guests. The clerk, an elderly man with a grizzled beard, opened the battered room register. Lenny pulled out his military ID and laid it on the counter. Matter-of-factly he said, "We drank too much at the girlie bar and missed our last bus to the base. Do you have a room?"

The clerk chuckled. "OK, Sergeant, I'll put you and your buddy on the sixth floor. Stay away from the fourth floor. That's where the queers are."

Pat startled, wondering if somehow they had betrayed themselves, but Lenny laughed and said, "Thanks for the heads up. We'll be careful."

Room 606 was stifling, with an iron bed and a scarred desk with a wooden chair. They opened windows wide and faced each other, alone for the first time. A breeze blew into the room and Pat could feel the sweat begin to cool on his body. The mild high from the beer was evaporating, his courage waning. Lenny moved close, unbuttoning Pat's shirt and running his fingertips over his curly red chest hairs. Pat's nipples stiffened but his body was rigid.

"Relax," Lenny whispered, stroking Pat's cheek. "I'm not going to bite you." He caressed Pat's shoulders and arms, which were heavily muscled from a summer of loading trucks. "You have a great body."

"I have to tell you something," Pat said, moving away toward the window. He fumbled again for a cigarette. "I've never done this before."

There was a momentary silence. Lenny said, "You're kidding, right?" He shook his head in disbelief, then laughed softly. "How old did you say you were?"

Pat looked out the window, crossing his arms over his chest. "I told you in the bar that I was twenty-one. But I actually turned nineteen last week."

"Lucky me. Come here, pretty boy." When Pat didn't move, Lenny went to him, flicked Pat's cigarette out the window, and kissed him gently. Turning to the bed, Lenny pulled his tee shirt over his head, then unbuttoned his jeans and kicked them off. He was lean and muscular, his chest and flat belly nearly hairless. Pat followed suit, still uncomfortable, but his sex responded with a mind of its own. "You're beautiful," Lenny said, moving slowly against Pat, kissing his eyes, mouth and neck. The smell of stale beer and cigarette smoke from the bar lingered, but Pat had never been close enough to a man to know this new smell, a mix of sweat, fatigue, and desire.

They fell on the bed in a tangle, arms and legs, tongues. Pat had diligently made out with his girlfriend in high school for hours without feeling much of anything. And the few times he'd fooled around with other guys in seventh grade, he'd felt intensely turned on but filled with shame afterwards. This experience with Lenny was entirely new. It was awkward to figure out how their bodies fit together, but feeling Lenny's erection against his own was electrifying.

When Pat came the first time he felt like his whole body was erupting. It was as if he'd been separated from the world by a spun glass shell, invisible but impenetrable, and in that first orgasm with a man, it shattered. Pat found the experience disorienting in its intensity. Then he wanted to try everything he'd ever imagined, and all at once. Lenny moved with assurance, evoking responses in Pat that made him tremble. After Pat went down on Lenny, Lenny laughed and said, "OK, now I believe that this is your first time." Pat sat back, but Lenny, seeing his face, said "Hey, I was just kidding!" and drew Pat to him, rolling on top of him and tickling him until he squirmed with pleasure. Within seconds Pat was lost in desire.

After their second orgasms, bodies spent, the young men flopped back against the pillows. The bedding had become completely undone, and their clothes were strewn on the desk, the chair, the floor. The lampshade nearest the bed was askew. The room looked as if there'd been a frat party but without the beer keg. Bashful, Pat asked if he could curl up with his head on Lenny's chest. Lenny complied with a grin, pulling him in close. Pat loved how smooth Lenny's skin was, and for the first time felt the thump of another man's heartbeat against his ear.

Lenny said, "When I first saw you come into the bar, I thought you were an undercover cop. You looked so serious, so like you didn't want to be there. Then I thought of the young recruits at the base and figured you were just scared, and anyway too young to be a cop."

He shifted slightly and Pat asked, "Am I too heavy?"

"Oh no, sweet boy. You're perfect." He absentmindedly stroked Pat's hair. "I can't believe you waited so long to have sex. I was experimenting when I was thirteen."

"My family is very Catholic," Pat said softly. "*I'm* very Catholic. I told my feelings about boys to our parish priest in the confessional when I was twelve, after I was in a circle jerk. He said, 'You'll go straight to Hell if you do that. That's the worst sin, the worst.'"

Lenny kissed him on top of the head. "Well, Padraic, he was wrong about that. And he was probably a closet case." He yawned and reached for his watch on the lamp table. "Listen, I've got to get the 7 o'clock bus to the base. I'm on duty at 8:00. I need to get some shuteye before I face my squadron commander." He stretched and shifted Pat's weight to the side. "Will you stay until I have to leave?"

Pat smiled a big smile. "Of course." Lenny rolled over and, yawning loudly, was instantly asleep.

Pat slipped carefully off the bed and retrieved the crumpled pack of Marlboros from his shirt. As the sweat dried on his body, he sat on the wide window ledge facing east, relishing the simple pleasure of being naked, and lit a cigarette. He was never naked at home, except in the shower. Modesty was the rule, which included him and his little brother wearing underpants and tee shirts to bed, even in the sweltering summer heat. His two sisters wore nightgowns. Despite there being only one bathroom, the six Kellys maintained an ironclad propriety in keeping their bodies covered. Pat felt deeply relaxed as he viewed the faint, pale gray light beginning to show on the horizon, the Missouri River becoming visible less than a mile from where he sat.

The worst sin. How could that be, he wondered? He had never felt so alive. He hadn't slept in nearly 24 hours, but his mind was alert. Even his skin tingled.

"Queer! Faggot!" The words had been bandied about the locker room after baseball practice, but never directed at Pat. He had felt disturbed nonetheless. He'd wondered early in high school if he was homosexual. During a Catholic retreat for the sophomore boys, the director, a hypermasculine priest who chummily referred to their girlfriends as "the ladies," expounded on the kinds of sin that their "baser instincts" might drive them to. He smirked his way through masturbation, proceeded with a baseball metaphor involving female body parts and bases earned, and with no transition shifted to the word "bestiality," which made the boys squirm. Finally he moved on to homosexuality, as if it were a near relative of sex with animals. Looking suspiciously at the boys for a long moment, he said, "Homosexuality is so disgusting, we won't even talk about it here."

Homosexuality, Pat had thought, *Oh, dear God, please don't let this be true. I love my girlfriend. Isn't that enough?* But he had known in his heart it was true. Those furtive but exciting encounters in seventh grade had meant more to him, in the end, than it seemed to have meant to the others. Once the kissing parties started with girls, the other boys had lost interest in fooling around, and Pat willed himself to go along. But the desire had remained.

Pat was suddenly drawn back into the moment when he heard a sound: Lenny gently snoring. He felt a rush of tenderness as he looked at this man, so innocent in sleep, his arms wrapped around a pillow. *I'm so lucky you were my first,* he thought. Pat had one gay friend at college that he'd met in a poetry class, Justin, who had filled his head with stories of drunken parties and "wild sex," whatever that meant. It was Justin who told Pat about the Ron D Voo Lounge months before. It had taken him this long just to walk in the door. *And look at me now!* He almost laughed aloud.

After checking the time, he went to the bed and gently shook Lenny, who said, "No, no," clutching his pillow tighter.

"If you want to get that bus, you'd better get your butt up," Pat said.

"Since when did you get so bossy?" Lenny asked, rolling off the bed and stretching. "Ugh, you're right. I've got to get moving." Pulling on his clothes, he looked at Pat for a long moment, then said, "You have to be cautious, Padraic. This gay thing is tough to manage. Be careful who you hang out with. There are a lot of sharks out there."

Pat suddenly felt bereft. "Won't I see you again?"

Lenny was frowning as he dressed. He looked at Pat sitting on the edge of the bed and his face softened. "Sweet boy, my schedule is so unpredictable. And you live at home. How are we going to connect?" But he grabbed a pen from the desk drawer and scribbled down a phone number. "If you can talk privately, call me around noon on Tuesday. It's the pay phone at my barracks. If someone else answers, hang up."

That didn't seem like much of a guarantee to Pat, but he was buoyed up by the hope that Lenny might see him again. "Go," he said. "You'll miss the bus." Lenny kissed him once, hard, and was gone.

The room was very quiet. Pat sat on the rumpled bed and picked up the pillow that Lenny had held close. Burying his face in its softness, he inhaled deeply and was certain he could identify Lenny's scent. Still holding the pillow, Pat turned back to the window and brightened. Eight long blocks led down to the Missouri River, and the densely packed buildings of downtown Omaha took on the colors of the sunrise, hundreds of plate-glass windows glistening peach, then rose, then crimson.

Fixing Uppers

Maureen Brady

S cuse me," said the woman with the camera as she stepped in front of me to get a good angle on the bride and the bride. Sylvie and Bean were both in tuxes, which I thought did not bode well. I wanted to tell them before they went to the extreme of getting married maybe they should seek more contrast on the butch/femme scale. But I suspected I was just being cynical, trying to find reasons for my lifetime relationship to have crumbled before my eyes? Fortunately, my ex had not been invited to this wedding.

"Sure," I said, my eyes on the photographer's back. It was solid, substantial, a salt and pepper ponytail trailing down its center. Appealing, I thought, as she clicked away, shooting the brides as they stood under a canopy of trees in their side yard, the Hudson River flowing in the distance. Around my age, was my next thought, even though I had sworn off any sort of involvement for as far as I could see into the future.

I was antsy and wanted this ceremony to come to a close so they could break out the champagne, which might help me settle down and enjoy the party. But the mothers were taking turns giving little, or not so little, speeches. The only thing little about their speeches was the stingy amount of recognition they gave to what they were here for—the union of their daughters. Instead, they went on and on about themselves. Sylvie's mother started it with how pretty the budding trees were, and how she had always wanted to be an artist, and at least now Sylvie might get to try her hand at being one, since she had a secure job as a paralegal. (What kind of a non-sequitur was that?) Bean's mother ended it with, "This is not the wedding I always imagined for my Beatrice, but we'll see. You all seem like very nice people."

Sylvie looked pained. Bean scowled and rolled her eyes toward the river, and I thought, and hoped she could hear me thinking it: "Right, let's take these two mothers down there and toss them in."

The tenor picked up after the first toast, even though the bride and bride were AAer's and half the folks there were toasting with some sickeningly sweet nonalcoholic pear juice, but it must have contained enough sugar to raise them up with the rest of us, because the mood changed to festive. A line up to congratulate the brides, finger foods delivered by a couple of slim, gay waiters, refills on the drinks, and the freedom to take a stroll down by the riverside, which I did with a couple of the guys I'd met at Bean and Sylvie's house before.

Returning from the river, I passed by the gifts lined up on one side of the wraparound porch, mine a weed whacker with a large bow around its handle—one of the many practical items they had listed on their Lowe's registry—and searched out my nametag on one of the tables before I went to replenish my drink. I needn't have bothered doing that as I was seated with the drinkers and our wine glasses got re-filled at a reliable clip. I remember less and less as the lunch went on, but I know our table laughed a lot, and when we had our visitation from the brides, I leaned over and said how sorry I was about their mothers using this platform to make the wrong speeches, and when Bean's face dropped, I realized my bringing up their mothers was completely gratuitous; that a nasty part of me had seeped out, wanting to kill their happiness at their great day by reminding them of their evil mothers.

Ever since the break-up with my ex I hadn't been able to keep down the feeling that a person who was me and yet not me was lurking just beneath my skin, judging everything we came up against in a super sarcastic way, and making me want to break out and deliver a punch, or stick out a foot to trip an unsuspecting victim. I was annoyed at having to listen to her slant on things but figured I'd better, because it seemed like, in an obnoxious way, she was trying to protect me. After all, the more innocent me had journeyed right up to a major betrayal by my ex without any notion such an offence might be in store.

I gulped down another glass of wine, hoping to obliterate this extra voice, at least for now.

At the roadside, where only a smattering of cars remained, I fumbled for my keys. Unaccustomed to carrying a purse, I turned out its contents onto the hood of my car. They weren't there, of course, because they were under a wad of tissues in my jacket pocket. One by one I put back the wallet, the change and my cell phone and zipped the purse up again.

"You okay?" a voice said behind me. It was the photographer.

"Don't force me to walk a straight line," I said, "but otherwise I'm fine."

She tilted her head and seriously considered me.

"Get some good photos?" I asked with a slur.

"Sure did." She paused, then added, "I thought the two of them looked lovely, and it was such a nice wedding."

"Guess so," I said, and then felt compelled to add, "I'm not all that much for the institution of marriage, but I guess it's okay for those who feel they need it."

I stepped away from where I'd been leaning against my car and nearly lost my footing but caught myself before I went down.

"Whoa," said the photographer, helping to right me. "No way you're going to get behind the wheel."

"Sure I am," I said. "I'll be fine."

Was it possible she didn't hear me? Because she shifted her large camera bag to her other shoulder and took a firm hold on my elbow and guided me a couple of cars further up the hill, where she planted me against the driver's door while she loaded her stuff into the back seat, then walked me around and deposited me on the passenger seat as carefully as she'd deposited her camera bag in the back. "But…but my car," I protested weakly.

"I'll bring you back to get it when you're sober," she said squarely, leaving me without a choice.

Next thing I knew we were in her driveway. Cute '50s style one-story bungalow with a closed-in porch across the front. Was she single? Did she live alone? My head spun. Had we introduced ourselves earlier? If so, I couldn't remember her name.

"Um…Is this your house?"

She nodded.

"I don't even know you," wobbled out of my mouth. "Or your name."

"Jackie," she said.

"Oh."

"Yours?"

"Ginger," I burped.

"Okay, Ginger, let's get you some coffee," she said then, and before I could struggle my way out, she came around and helped steady me. As she walked me up the bluestone path, the warmth of her hand passed into my elbow. It felt so good I missed it the instant she let go to manage her keys.

At her kitchen table, one of those enameled metal tables with side leaves that pulled out to widen it, I blew on the hot coffee, steaming my face. At the first sip, my head straightened up enough to make me realize how much I had overdone my drinking at the wedding. When? Well, it had gone on for such a long time, starting with the champagne…It was that waiter, refilling the wine glasses whenever they were half full. One of the ways I tried to control my drinking was to count glasses and slow down if I got to three. Damn him. I had no idea how it had gotten to be nearly ten o'clock at night.

Jackie's green eyes were upon me, watching as I sobered up a fraction. "Drink up," she said. "And we'll put you to bed."

The room suddenly took on a charge. Put me to bed! Was she going to bed me? I tried not to show my reaction, though I was secretly thrilled that she might lie down beside me. I half drained my cup of coffee in a gulp and said, "I don't usually drink coffee after noon because it will keep me awake."

"I doubt anything will keep you awake this evening," she said with an eye roll.

Next thing I knew we were in her bedroom and she laid back one side of the bed as if this were a fancy hotel. "Here," she said, tossing me a long, well-worn T-shirt with a faded P'town sunset on its front and turning back toward the door. "You can use this for sleeping."

"Wait," I said.

"It's okay," she said.

"What's okay?"

"You're sleeping in my bed. I'll pull out the couch in the living room."

"Nah, I can sleep there."

"No, go ahead and change."

"At least come back and say good night, then," I said.

She looked at me as if I were a plaintive child who wanted to be read to sleep, shifted her stance from one leg to the other and finally said, "Okay, I'll be back in a minute," before closing the door.

I lay back in her T-shirt, inhaling the pleasant odor of laundry soap, possibly sunshine—did she dry her clothes on a clothesline? In between moments of nodding out, my head still seriously swirling, it occurred to me that her whole lifestyle seemed like a big draw. Here I was lying in her bed thinking maybe I wanted to be her!

When she came back, still fully dressed, she brought a tall glass of water to the bedside table.

"Oh," I said, "so nice of you."

I patted the other side of the queen bed. "If I move over, I don't really take up that much space," I held my arms tightly against my sides to show her how narrow I could make myself.

She smiled but only shook her head. "Go to sleep. I'm fine in the other room," quietly exiting and pulling the door closed behind her.

My heart flipped. I inhaled the odor of the pillowcase again. Well, I wanted to at least be someone more like her.

I lay there thinking of times I'd been sick as a child—measles, mumps or even severe sunburn—and my mother had arrived to give me special attention. Breakfast and/or lunch on a tray and a new coloring book she had hidden away to save for such a time, or a storybook, from which she would read as she sat on the side of my bed, creating a downhill for my body to spill towards her. She was a nurse, my mother, and sometimes worked night shifts and struggled to get even a minimum of sleep during the day, which made her impatient with my childish demands. Except when I was sick, and then I rated at least as high as her lowest patient.

I was surely just as sick now, but from my own indulgence. I pressed my fingers against various spots on my skull, trying to counter the iron bar that seemed lodged in the center of my brain. I didn't deserve Jackie's bed, but I was so glad to have it. Dizziness overtook me and I couldn't tell whether it was the alcohol messing with my cerebellum, or I was swirling with a crush. I was actually glad that Jackie had refused my offer to make room for her in the bed. I was horny as all get out, yet suddenly the knowledge that sex was not going to solve any of my problems seemed to float up like something close to wisdom.

❖

She was cooking bacon when I shuffled out to the kitchen at 9 AM. Eyes bleary, mouth fuzzy, that iron bar still present, but as long as I didn't move my head too much, it sat more or less dormant.

Bright-eyed and fully sober, she extended her arm to offer me a seat, then poured me a coffee while asking how I was.

"I've been better," I said. "But I've also been worse...like last night."

She nodded and smiled. "I'm sure," she said.

"You're pretty perky," I said.

"Why wouldn't I be?"

"Sleeping on the couch. Giving up your bed?"

"I was perfectly comfortable. And I hope you were, too."

I nodded, then drummed on the metal table with my fingertips and took a look around. The cottage was '50's inside and out, but Jackie or someone had painted the tacky paneling a refreshing light mauve with a satin finish, creating a shiny bright kitchen. "Cute house," I said.

"Thanks. I love it."

My eyes roamed to the large picture window in the living room that looked onto a short back yard bordered by a stand of maples.

She asked me where I lived and I told her I was living in my latest fixer-upper.

"Oh," she said with a quizzical frown.

"It's what I do," I said. "Like you photograph weddings and things. Do you make a living at that?"

"A slim one."

I nodded and discovered that I shouldn't have, as the motion brought my headache into focus again. "Me, too, but I have to live in most of my fixer-uppers to make a living at it. I do the painting and the simpler carpentry myself, and then, just when it's looking like a place one might like to live in, I sell it and move on to the next one."

"Must be unsettling."

"Not too bad. I grew up in the military. I keep a bunch of suitcases handy. Hard on a partner, though. My ex didn't want me to sell anything, just keep on buying. But it doesn't work that way."

"Is that what happened to the relationship?"

"Maybe, one factor…Too simple, though. As my therapist says, 'There's more than one story to every breakup.'"

"That sounds true," said Jackie.

"What about you?"

"I'm a homebody. Like to stay put."

"I mean have you had any bad breakups?"

Jackie closed her eyes and dropped her head and her small but distinctive features I was growing attracted to—fine lips, turned up nose—seemed to fade. "I lost my partner to breast cancer when it came back around the second time," she said quietly.

I shook my head. "I'm so sorry."

"It's okay. It's been almost five years now."

"Still," I said, "that's tough."

Jackie went silent as she lifted the bacon from the frying pan and placed it on paper towels, soaked up the grease and tossed in the eggs to scramble. I listened to the birds chirping outside and tried to think of something else consoling to say but nothing came to me. It certainly wasn't time to tell her about how my supposedly devoted partner had gone off on a one-month temporary job on the West Coast and fallen prey to the seduction of a silly woman, whom I considered my inferior in every way.

"I hope you're not vegetarian," Jackie finally said. I sniffed the air responsively and gave her a big smile.

"Omnivore," I said, as she plopped eggs and bacon onto the plate in front of me.

She had a knack for cooking. I could tell from the way she got the eggs scrambled perfectly medium and the bacon crisp but not burned. We munched away while I complimented Jackie's cooking and enjoyed filling my fitful stomach while sitting across from her, breathing in more hope than I'd felt in a while.

"So tell me something about yourself?" she said, her face back to lively.

I shrugged. "Like what?"

"Like what excites you?"

"Finding a good house to turn around excites me," I said. "The funkier the better. I'm scared of mold, bad smells, rotting sills, termites, even though lots of that is manageable, but it's so much easier to get rid of funk. When someone's just lazy about upkeep and lets a place go…

it's like a relationship you forget needs maintenance as long as you're living in it, so you go blind as to how you're neglecting it."

Encouraged by her curious look, I rambled on. "That's what I did with my ex. Got happily self-satisfied with my creative house projects and felt like saying, 'Well, where's your life? Get something going for yourself.' So she did! But with another woman. I hadn't meant that." I paused and Jackie just held the silence, so I continued. "This seems to be a fault line in me. With a house, I can see it; with a relationship, I can't."

I shut my yap then, saying, "TMI."

"Well, it's interesting," Jackie said, raising her eyebrows. "So what happened?"

"You really want the whole gruesome story?"

"I'm listening," she said, flashing an impish grin.

So I told her about how after week-one of the month-long gig, the California woman had invited my ex to her home for dinner. My ex claimed she didn't even know this woman was a lesbian and expected there'd be others at the dinner and maybe she could make some friends to get her through the month away. But it turned out the woman lived alone and steered her to the bedroom to show off how her bed was covered with teddy bears. My ex tried to tell me it was sweet to see all those teddy bears and get a tour of which ones had been carried forth from childhood and where she'd acquired the rest of them. I said she sounded like someone missing a few brain cells, but my ex said she was smart, that she'd been doing all the financials for the project they were working on. 'Smart with numbers,' I said. 'And with what an easy mark you are.' She asked me what I meant by that. 'You know, no impulse control,' I told her.

"And then, when she got quiet, well, I knew they must have moved the teddy bears aside."

"I'm sorry," Jackie said, "that sounds awful."

"Devastating," I said, my hands automatically coming up to cover my heart with the memory of that brutal moment when I learned of the affair.

Jackie looked as if she could feel my pain from the way she pursed her mouth. But, wanting only to leave that dreadful day behind, I didn't go on. Instead, I concentrated on finishing off my bacon and asked about her deceased partner.

"Nel, she was a sweetheart," Jackie said. She bit her lip. "She could be tough, though, especially at work."

"What kind of work?"

"Parole officer."

"Oh." I nodded, beginning to form a picture.

"We met at the county building, when I was still a social worker."

"Hard work for both of you," I said.

"It was hard," she said, "especially dealing with the bureaucracy. So when Nel couldn't stay home alone any more, I took a leave of absence and became her caretaker. And when she died, she left me enough so I can make it on my photography, long as I live simply. And I never returned."

"Well, that's good, anyway, that you can do work you like."

"Yeah," she said, but sounding as if she might cry.

"I'm sorry again," I said, still unable to bring up any other words.

She shook her head and smoothed her hair back toward her ponytail. "We were trying to get pregnant when she got the diagnosis. Turkey baster method."

"Who was going to have the baby?" I asked.

"She was."

We sat in silence broken only by the cackle of birds outside, and for a moment, I felt a bit of her heartbreak rather than my own.

"It would be so good if the earliest attempts had taken. Then I'd have a little person here that looked like her. Probably a daughter."

"What makes you think that?"

"Well, upside down is supposed to improve the odds of making a girl. So Nel and I would get the sperm and bring it home in a cooler, and after I'd inject her, she'd do something like a shoulder stand with her legs up against the wall at the top of the bed, and we'd kiss and get sexy while we waited for it to take."

I laughed at the picture she'd created, and finally she gave a little chuckle.

"Sad to have to give up a dream like that," I said.

She picked up my plate and stacked it on hers. "It is," she said, "but am I really living if I'm thinking like that?"

❖

Back in my fixer-upper, I lay on the queen bed and stared at the ceiling, bright white Benjamin Moore ceiling paint, two coats, slight pink tinge to the walls, only the trim left to be painted. It was a spot of peace, while the rest of the house was still a mess.

I contemplated the empty space beside me. Not that I minded the silence in the room in the middle of the night. Not that I minded sleeping under the covers of my choice, making me not too cold and not too hot. My ex had been both a snorer and a sprawler, sending me to what seemed like a small corner of the bed. Still, the touch of a warm foot before falling asleep. That had been deeply reassuring and I wanted it again.

After sleeping off my hangover for several hours, I got up and contemplated making a thank you call to Jackie. "At least give her enough time to let her think you have a satisfying life," I chastised myself. So I went in and worked on the paint job in the renovated bathroom where I'd changed out the crappy beige toilet for a bright white one and installed a new sink. I draped everything carefully, then rolled on a high gloss pure white, took pains with where the wall met the floor and was back in the kitchen cleaning out the paintbrush and roller when the phone rang. When I looked at the call number, my heart sang.

"I was about to call you," I said. "To thank you for saving my ass from trying to drive home and escaping whatever calamity might have ensued. And for the great breakfast, too."

"No problem," she said. "You sound like you're feeling better."

"Sure am," I said, thinking especially now I was. "I just finished painting a bathroom."

"Oh."

"Yeah. In my latest fixer-upper. Living room's still a mess but that's next. Then I'd like to have you over."

"O—kay," said Jackie, emphasizing both syllables of that word.

The vibe of her hesitancy set me off, wondering what? Had I come on too strong? Or misread how sweet she seemed?

"I...I..." I didn't know what to say. I couldn't afford a rejection and my tough girl side seemed to have departed for the moment, leaving me to feel how thin my skin was. I was close to tears and all she'd said was a hesitant "O—kay."

"What's the matter?" she asked, after my unfinished sentence dangled in the air for an inordinate amount of time.

"Nothing. Just…I wasn't sure if you meant you wouldn't want to come see my temporary home."

"Sure," she said. "Sure I'd like to. But I was calling to see if you might like to come over and rehash the wedding. I got some good pictures of Bean and Sylvie, even got the sourpuss mothers."

That made me chuckle.

"A couple good ones of you, too."

"Oh, yeah," I said, wondering if they would serve to display the sloppy state I'd been in.

"Want to come over later and see them?"

Jackie was waiting for me to answer. I bit my lip. Of course I was going to say yes. But…but what? Was I doomed always to be on the fence when I liked someone?

Like Bean and Sylvie, Jackie was sober. I knew she hadn't been in an inebriated state at the wedding, but it hadn't occurred to me she was one of those drinking the pear stuff, yet of course that made sense. She herded me out to take a walk on the dirt road that started just past her house, to star-gaze! What a novel date, if that's what this was. Our shoulders touched a few times and I wished I'd had a couple of drinks before coming, to embolden me enough to take her hand, but that didn't happen.

Back at her cottage, Jackie offered me coffee again.

"Have anything stronger?" I asked.

"Nope. But my coffee's plenty strong."

I opted for herbal tea, hoping to calm my nerves.

"Nice aroma to the coffee, though," I said, as she filtered hers at the stove.

"Yeah, that's half of it, the great smell," she agreed, splashing more water on the grounds.

Was it the rich French Roast aroma, or a flash forward of imagining I might one day risk growing close to someone again that suddenly threw me back to the couch where I'd been seated with a cup of coffee the day my ex disclosed her affair. I heard the words as they had freakishly streamed out of her mouth, saw her guilty eyes squinting as if to protect against whatever I might throw at her. I'd gone stone cold, and my legs had turned to rubber, making it impossible for me to get up. My mind had blurred with memories that spanned our years together in a kaleidoscopic manner.

I came back to the present when Jackie started to pour the hot water into an adorable teapot that looked like a pumpkin in front of me. She put the cover on the pot, sat catty-cornered and fixed a questioning look on me, letting me know she had seen me sail away.

"I'd thought the ex and I were going to be forever," I said, shrugging. "It seemed like we both fell so deeply in love, and then we just went along, good periods and not so good ones, but nothing horrendous. Nothing I couldn't get over, until this."

"Did you try to work it out?" Jackie asked.

"Of course. After the initial shock, we went for couples counseling and made a deal. Her part was to terminate all contact with the 'other woman,' which she convinced me she had done. Mine was to try to warm my heart back up enough to forgive her. So far, so good, right?

"Then, along came her birthday and the delivery at our door of a grand bouquet of California type flowers—huge open-mouthed Venus fly traps—the kind that seem to say they've come to eat you up. They were accompanied by a card, which, since she was out, I took the liberty of reading."

"And?" Jackie leaned forward.

"It said that this woman, who was supposedly having nothing to do with my ex, was yearning for her madly."

"As if those mouthy fly traps didn't speak loudly enough," Jackie said with a mischievous smile.

"Right," I said, and began to chuckle. Then we both broke out into hilarious laughter as Jackie gestured with both her hands, making them into Venus fly traps closing in on their prey.

I laughed until I had to bend over because my stomach was sore. A minor form of hysteria, perhaps, but it released a lot of shame as well as a ton of endorphins, and made it seem like I might be capable of starting over some day.

Jackie raised her coffee cup, gesturing a toast. I was drawn toward her delicate and agile hand, though still wishing for something stronger than this herbal tea I had been given at her behest. Then I remembered the very fact I was here suggested I might be in trouble. That Jackie had spared me from driving home way too inebriated. That there might be quite a few more cups of tea in my future.

I poured from the pumpkin pot and raised my cup to hers.

"Cheers," I said, with as much cheer as I could muster.

"Good riddance to the ex and the teddy bear woman," Jackie said, bumping my cup.

"Indeed," I agreed, bumping back and giving her a wide smile.

"And here's to us," Jackie said, lifting her cup higher, "fixing ourselves up."

STONES WITH WINGS

Louis Flint Ceci

Cyprion was pollinating the okra when he heard Father Marten approach. The Father Receiver did not interrupt. He waited while the young oblate twirled a fine brush inside each tight blossom. When he straightened up, Father Marten said, "You don't like okra, do you?"

"No, Father Receiver," Cyprion replied.

"Nor do I. Yet you tend to them as lovingly as the other plants."

"It has to be done. Without pollinators, the garden would be barren."

Father Marten shook his head sadly. "We balanced the world on tiny wings, and they broke."

"They didn't break by themselves, Father. We panicked. We sought to stop the blight, and poisoned the world instead. From the First Collapse to the Second, it was our hand."

"And all the Powers of the Earth could not stand without their aid. Perhaps more gentle hands may bring them back."

Cyprion shrugged. "As the Rule says, 'Our hands must be in service to Creation till Creation is restored.'"

"Till Creation is Restored *to the Creator*," Father Marten said, completing the verse.

Cyprion looked away—not in chagrin, but to hide his smile. The Father Receiver often probed him like this. "I am grateful for the protection of the Hermitage, Father, but—"

"But you are not yet ready to join the religious. Yes, I know. I shall give up on you some day, Friend, but not today." He looked across the rows of plants. "Is it going well?"

"The tomatoes need only a brisk shaking to set. Some hybrids even produce seed. Over here," he walked over a row, "are plants grown from last year's."

Father Marten bent over the hairy-stemmed plants. "There are blossoms."

"There were blossoms last year, too. But no fruit."

"At least the seeds sprout. That's more than the companies left us. Your cross-breeding regime has done wonders."

Cyprion shook his head. "We can't eat wonders. We will soon be out of patent seed. If these don't set fruit…" He trailed off.

Father Marten straightened up with a sigh. "I hate to think I've eaten my last tomato." He gave Cyprion a half smile. "Though the end of Brother Mallek's okra gumbo would be less mourned. How are the chickens?"

"The chicks are improving. Most can walk, though the wings are useless. To get them to the point where they can range on their own, I fear, will take more than we have on hand."

The Father Receiver tilted his head. "You mean we need a sturdier cock?"

Cyprion blushed, though he knew Father Marten meant the resident rooster that woke the community before the first office of the day. "I'm afraid Saint Vigil has done all he can for us."

"It may be that Goodman Mack has what we need. I would like you to visit him."

Cyprion did not hide his distaste. Mack was a goodman farmer like himself, but he overworked his livestock and treated them cruelly when they did not bend to his will. Cyprion had seen him kill a horse with a single blow from a maul because it refused the bit after a day of plowing. No sooner had the poor creature thudded to the dust at their feet than Mack turned to Cyprion and asked what price the Hermitage would pay for fresh meat. The memory still turned his stomach, though in the end the monastery had made the trade.

"Must it be today?" he asked. "Our hens are in no hurry."

"No, but soon would be helpful. There is another reason to visit Goodman Mack. Will you walk with me?"

The two of them strolled through the rows of vegetables that supplied the Hermitage of San Lucca and the village below with fresh produce, dried beans, and compost. Father Marten was silent. Usually cheerful and forward-looking, he dwelled less on the deprivations brought on by the First and Second Collapse and always spoke of the Restoration as if it were already underway and certain to succeed. Cyprion had less faith. He knew how thin the thread of life could be, how starvation still hunted the land, and how narrow his own escape had been. He also knew that a soul could be starved of more than food. A journey to the village would stir those memories again. He preferred his breeding charts and plants, and spent many days as silent as any eremitic monk.

Father Marten, on the other hand, was usually voluble, so his silence marked a difficulty. "Goodman Mack's tally is still in our favor," Cyprion ventured. "He cannot charge us more than he owes."

Father Marten laughed. "No, but he's certain to try. Look at the books with Brother Ishaak to be certain. But tallies are not the reason I wish you to visit Mack." The Father Receiver halted where okra gave way to cucumbers. "A wild boy has been found on Mack's farm. In the woods actually, between his land and ours. It's not really clear where he comes from, but Mack has him now and I have…concerns."

A chill lodged in Cyprion's stomach. "A wild boy? Wild, how?"

"Naked. Mute. Likely starved. Probably more starved now, since Mack has him."

Cyprion nodded. "I'll go today."

Cyprion tallied what Mack owed the hermitage for seed and manure and considered what he might demand for lending out a cock to stud. Promising Brother Ishaak he would make it balance, he tucked a hen under his arm and headed down the mountainside. The path was steep and rocky, and parts had washed away in the winter rains. Ball alum and blue dicks poked above the still-green wild grasses. The blooms would wither soon and the grasses sear beneath the sun.

The land was difficult to farm, with arable plots only in narrow shelves between the mountains and the sea. The Hermitage of San Lucca lay along one such strip. Years ago, inland visitors had flocked to these folded lands for their scenic wonder, but when agriculture collapsed in two catastrophic slumps, roving bands of desperate families streamed to the coast, looking for food. They soon wore the land bare. The Hermitage had escaped seizure only by virtue of its charter with the village below: the monastery would take in the old and infertile, people the village had no use for and therefore no obligation to feed. In return, the hermitage shared its harvest from garden and orchard and got to keep the sanctuary of its cloister.

The year he turned thirteen, Cyprion's family had crept south along the shore. Picking seaweed on the rocks below San Lucca, he slipped and broke his ankle. His family left him there. A villager found him on the sand, too weak to fight the incoming tide. He was dumped into a cart and hauled up the mountain and left at the hermitage gate. A stone of silence had settled on his heart then, a stone that seemed part of the cloister walls.

In the years since, Cyprion had gradually taken charge of the gardens and hens. Like all oblates, he slept outside the walls, but the community sheltered and fed him—a thin meal, but sustaining. Even now, as the path down the mountain leveled out through a clutch of stunted cypress, he was looking forward to the journey back. He resolved to finish his business with Mack as quickly as possible.

Mack's farm sat at the edge of the village. As Cyprion entered the muddy yard a blast of oaths came from the barn followed by a whip crack. Fearing the worst, he rushed in. "Goodman Mack!" he shouted, thrusting the startled hen forward with both hands.

The farmer and his eldest son stood beyond the light cast by the open door. The son was crouched as if ready to spring on a cornered animal. His father squinted at Cyprion. "What yer doing here?"

As his eyes adjusted to the gloom, Cyprion saw a third figure dressed in sack beside a tumble of hay. Both hands gripped a pitchfork. His eyes were wide with terror. If this was the wild boy, he was tall for his age. His skin glowed against the dark recesses of the barn, his black hair nearly disappeared.

Cyprion caught his breath. "I've come to…I'd like to offer…"

"I can take him," the son said, eyes fixed on the thin figure.

"We're busy, monk," the elder Mack said. "Come back another time." He turned and raised his whip.

"Wait!" Cyprion stepped forward, clearing the rectangle of light from the door.

The wild boy gasped, dropped the pitchfork, and took a halting step toward him.

The son sprang forward with a grunt and slammed the boy to the ground. "Gotcha, ya little bitch!" He writhed on top of the boy, pinning his arms above his head.

The commotion caused the hen to squawk and ruffle her neck. Cyprion cooed her to silence as he approached. As soon as the wild boy made eye contact with him, he went still.

So did Cyprion. He swallowed. "Is this the wild boy?"

Goodman Mack spat. "Boy my ass. He's some rich fuck's plaything that's run off."

"Why do you say that?"

"Well, he's obvious been fed, ain't he? But he's never done a lick of work in his life. Look at those feet, them hands."

Look at that face, those eyes, thought Cyprion. "You mean to work him?"

"If he eats, he works."

"Has he eaten today?"

Goodman Mack shifted his whip to the other hand. "What yer here for, monk?"

To some, everyone on the mountain was a monk. Cyprion didn't bother to correct him. "I'm here for…for him." He nodded at the boy. "We heard up the mountain you had an extra hand—"

"Extra! Hah! He's more trouble than he's worth. Can't talk. Won't listen. Can't even pitch hay."

"We need an extra hand in the gardens. It's pollen time."

Mack looked at him and set his shoulders. "He was found on my land."

"I heard he was found in the woods, but it doesn't matter. I'll pay for him."

"Da!" the son wailed from the barn floor. "You said I could—"

"Shut it!" his father commanded. "Pay what?"

Cyprion held out the chicken. Mack snorted. "She's well-fed," Cyprion said. "Hermitage feed."

"Fuck your crippled chooks," the son muttered.

"I said, shut!" Mack boomed. He eyed Cyprion narrowly. "How does this tally?"

Cyprion drew a breath. "It tallies even." He was going to have some explaining to do with Brother Ishaak.

"You'll need this," Mack said, throwing him a rope. The son

groaned and rolled off the boy, who rose slowly, never taking his eyes off Cyprion.

"What for?" Cyprion asked, handing over the hen.

Mack wrapped his huge hands around the bird, which immediately began squirming and squawking. Mack grinned at it toothily. "There's some meat on this one at that." He looked up and jerked his head at the boy. "For that. He'll run off otherwise."

Cyprion held the boy's gaze. "No he won't," he said.

❖

"How can he declare himself if he doesn't speak?" Brother Ishaak objected to Father Marten.

"He is too young to declare himself, even if he could speak," the Father Receiver replied.

"It's another mouth to feed."

"He may be another mouth," Cyprion said, "but he is also another pair of hands and feet."

"He is more than his parts," Father Marten noted. "There is something else there. You see it in his eyes, don't you?" He looked from the brother to the oblate, but neither spoke.

"What if he proves..." Brother Ishaak glanced at Cyprion, "disruptive?"

"He won't," Cyprion said firmly. "He'll be too busy in the orchards, the garden, and the coop."

"The garden is inside the cloister," Ishaak insisted.

"But the orchard isn't," Father Marten replied calmly. "And the henhouse abuts the exterior wall, a few paces from Cyprion's cabin. Do I remember correctly, Friend, that there is a store room at one end, walled off from the roost?"

"There is, Father."

"That might be a suitable place for—well, what shall we call him? We can't keep referring to him in the abstract. He's far too real for that."

Ishaak snorted. "You might well ask, but you'll wait for an answer."

"Palom—" Cyprion blurted out but stopped when they stared at him. He shrugged. "Paolo."

"Paolo it is," Father Marten said. "I'll enter him in the rolls, but on promise of discernment, not as a received member. In particular, Friend Cyprion, he is your charge. If he proves disruptive, he cannot stay. He will have to be returned."

Cyprion gasped. "But surely—"

Father Marten raised his hand. "Let us not worry about the future until it is discovered." He turned to Ishaak. "Thank you for your counsel, Brother. We will be alert to your concerns." He pulled the leather-bound Enrollment Book from a side drawer and laid it on his desk.

Brother Ishaak bowed and left, scowling.

Cyprion turned as well, already thinking about what needed to be done to make the storeroom habitable.

"A moment, Cyprion." Father Marten rose and approached him and clasped his hands in both of his. Cyprion felt heat bloom from his chest and rush over his face.

Marten said, "I know this touches your heart. I know it touches more than your heart."

"I will not return him to Mack."

"But if he has to go?"

"I will go with him. I will not leave him undefended. He deserves a life free of fear, free from cruelty."

"So do we all, I pray."

"He should have a normal life."

"In a hermitage? Did you?"

Cyprion looked the Father Receiver in the eye but did not answer.

Father Marten tapped the Enrollment Book. "Paolo will be given the opportunity to declare himself. If the community agrees to receive him, he can remain here the rest of his life. But before that, he must reach discernment. He must make a choice." He looked up. "A choice I fear you were never given."

"I have always had a choice. I chose to stay."

"Because you had nowhere else to go? A monastery is not a place to hide away from the world, but a place from which to engage it. I think we have done you a disservice, sheltering you here. Your plants, your numbers, your charts—they keep you to yourself. But keeping to yourself keeps you *from* yourself, your full self. I hope this boy, this Paolo, can change that. You may serve each other."

Cyprion did not understand. Marten was talking about love, he knew that much, but what kind of love? What was Father Receiver giving him permission to do?

Father Marten seated himself behind the desk. "The choice to stay or go must be his own, once he can voice it. Not yours, not ours. You must promise me that, Cyprion, if you undertake this charge."

Now he understood. He could put all his heart into the boy, but he had to be willing to give him up if the time came. But what choice did he have? To give him up now would be to throw a wingless bird into the howling, hungry world. "I promise," he said.

Paolo became a frequent sight inside the cloister, and not just in the garden. He was ideal for delivering meals to the eremitic monks. He would move silently from cell to cell, stopping at each door to open the outer cabinet, remove the soiled plates, and insert the day's meal, never seeing the contemplative inside. If he did happen upon one, his lack of eye contact with anyone but Cyprion and his continued muteness guaranteed the monk's inner journey went undisturbed.

He had the opposite effect on Cyprion, who narrated everything to the boy, whether he was candling eggs or charting hybrids. He read the Songs to him each evening, a practice one of the older monks pronounced "ancient, profound, and approved." But the Songs did not lead Cyprion to deeper spiritual truth. He knew he was using the recitations to keep the heat of Paolo's presence in his room past compline. His hypocrisy humiliated him.

One night, with Paolo seated on the cot beside him, Cyprion found the words of the evening's Song hollow and lifeless. Unwilling to end their time together, he opened the book to the index and said, "This is how I learned to count. It can be very calming. You start anywhere." He closed his eyes and jabbed his finger at the page. "Here. Song Twenty-six, page 122. Add the digits together, one, two, and two, that's five. You go down five to Song Thirty-one, page 127. This time, you sum the digits and go up. You alternate up and down, tracing a path. Sometimes a Song repeats, and when it does—" He looked up, expecting boredom or bewilderment on Paolo's face.

What he saw instead frightened him.

Paolo's fathomless eyes were wild and the pupils twitching. He rocked back and forth, his hands clutching the air.

"Paolo!" Cyprion cried, fearing the boy was having a seizure. He dropped the book and hugged him to his chest. The trembling stopped and he heard a deep indraw of breath, like a drowning man surfacing. Cyprion drew back. "Are you all right?"

Paolo took several more breaths. With each his lips would contort and his tongue move, but no sound came out.

"Are you trying to speak, Paolo? What are you trying to say?"

Paolo took several ragged breaths, then let out a long sigh. He hung his head and tears dropped from his eyes.

They still embraced. Paolo's legs were draped across his. Neither moved.

"Did I upset you?" Cyprion whispered. "I upset you. You wanted to hear the Songs and instead I played my silly game. I'm sorry, Paolo, I won't ever—" He stopped. Paolo was touching his lips very softly, very gently. The room thundered with silence. Paolo picked up the book of prayers and opened it. He took Cyprion's hand and placed it on the index page. "Again?" Cyprion asked. "You want me to do it again?" Paolo gazed into his eyes.

Cyprion started the formula again, reading aloud as he followed it. Whenever he looked up, Paolo was still looking deep into his eyes. After one particularly long sequence, the pattern led him back to the Song where he started. "There," Cyprion said, smiling, "it repeats." He looked up. Paolo was asleep.

It must be halfway to prime, Cyprion thought. He should carry Paolo back to the storeroom. But the boy was exhausted and suddenly so was he. He laid Paolo down on his cot, pulled the woolen blanket over him, and considered his options. There was little room in the cabin, just enough for the cot and table and rows of potted plants. He could sleep in Paolo's room, but the smell of feathers and manure would keep him awake. He could spend the night in the chapel, perhaps reading the Songs in earnest, finding the deeper wisdom the monks assured him was there. The one thing he could not do was join Paolo. The boy hadn't a whisker on his face, while Cyprion's beard, though short, was full.

In the end, he took a spare blanket from the shelf over the door, moved a row of plants, and lay down beside the cot. He used the Book of Songs for a pillow and was asleep before another thought could enter his head. He slept so soundly neither Saint Vigil nor the morning bell woke him.

❖

Paolo's appetite for numbers grew. Cyprion fed him sequences, magic squares, triangles. Each night, the boy grew more expressive, more eager, and more reluctant to return to the coop. Cyprion, too, was feeling the tug of that reluctance. But still the boy did not speak.

One afternoon Cyprion was tending a graft in the orchard when a deep voice below him said, "Friend." He glanced down and gave a start at the sight of a tall, bald priest with enormous gray and black eyebrows and a full beard. He scrambled down the ladder. "Father Soledad," he said, hastily wiping pitch from his hands. "What is it? What's wrong?" He couldn't imagine what could have prompted the hermit to break his silence.

"The boy," Soledad said. "In the garden. He insists." He turned and started down the path.

A thousand fears flooded Cyprion as he followed. Had Paolo been injured? Been attacked? Taken ill? This was just the sort of disruption Brother Ishaak had warned them about! And what did Father Soledad mean by, "He insists"?

They entered the cloister through the back gate. A small group of brothers and oblates ringed one side of the garden. Father Marten was hurrying toward them from his office. In the center stood Paolo, a hoe in both hands like a staff, ready to ward off attack.

"Oh, no," Cyprion muttered. It was worse than the encounter in the barn.

"He called you," Father Soledad said. "By name."

Cyprion gaped.

"Well?" Father Soledad's heavy eyebrows lifted. "Go to him!"

Cyprion pushed his way through the knot of people to Father Marten. "I am so sorry, Father Receiver. I don't know what—"

"I think Paolo has something to show us. He won't let anyone near, though. He insists on you."

"Cyprion!" Paolo whispered hoarsely.

Cyprion stepped forward, searching Paolo's face, his hands, the ground for some clue. He had been hoeing between tomato rows and stopped half way. "What is it, Paolo? What's wrong?" He reached out to stroke his face to calm his breathing, to get that wild look from his eye. But Paolo shook his head and pointed a trembling finger at the plant beside him.

Cyprion knelt down and looked. Then he glanced up at Paolo. The boy's breathing had eased, but Cyprion's was beginning to tighten. He stood up and checked the next row over, then the row Paolo had pointed to.

"What is it?" Brother Ishaak asked impatiently.

Cyprion embraced the boy with both arms. He didn't care who saw.

"Friend Cyprion?" Father Marten asked softly.

He turned to them, beaming. "A tomato. Among the hybrids. A tomato from seed."

"Excellent progress," Father Marten said as they strolled around the perimeter of the cloister garden. It was six weeks since the sighting of the first tomato. Now there were over two dozen, and the first were beginning to show a blush of red. "Your methods have begun to bear fruit."

"The real test will come next year," Cyprion said. "Then we'll see if seed from this cross will also produce."

Father Marten smiled at him. "I wasn't speaking only of the garden." He nodded to Paolo's gangly, broad-shouldered figure carrying the mid-day meal to the cells. "He makes eye contact. He greets the brothers as they pass. He has even been known to smile."

The sun felt warm on Cyprion's head. "I can't take credit for that. He grows in his own way."

"As do you, I think. You, too, have been known to smile lately. But there is one thing I have not seen Paolo do."

"What is that?"

"Play. It cannot all be weeding and pruning and tending the hens. A boy should play."

Cyprion watched Paolo move from cell to cell. "I don't know how to do that."

"When were you last at the pond?"

Cyprion frowned, trying to remember. "During the winter rains, perhaps, to check the pipes."

"It's summer now."

He couldn't imagine what Father Receiver was getting at. "The rains were good. The reservoir should last well into autumn." Father Marten was silent. "Do you want me to check?"

Father Marten sighed. "If you must, Friend Cyprion. But the water should be quite warm by now, especially near the shallow end. Warm enough for swimming, I should think."

Cyprion stopped, his mouth slightly open. Paolo was returning with the empty bowls, wiping his brow on his sleeve.

"Think on it, Friend," Father Marten said, moving off. "But do not think on it too much."

They climbed the hill to the holding tank above the hermitage that afternoon and followed the pipe to the pond. They stopped at the shallow end where muddy footprints marred the bank. Cyprion could feel Paolo's eyes on him, but he stared out over the shining water as if it were an obstacle course. "Well," he said at last, "I guess..." Then in swift movements, he lifted his smock over his head, shucked his sandals and undergarment, and strode into the pond without looking back. He took a few splashing strokes and felt for the slippery bottom with his toes. A rustling behind him followed by more splashes told him Paolo had followed his example. He dove under the water to avoid looking. When he surfaced, Paolo was beside him looking anxious.

"Gone!" Paolo said. His dark pupils showed a spark of panic.

"No, no. I just held my breath and went under for a bit. See?" He took an elaborate breath, made a show of clamping his mouth and nose shut, squeezed his eyes, and went under again. When he surfaced, Paolo seemed to relax. "It's fun. Try it."

Paolo frowned so Cyprion demonstrated again, this time keeping his eyes open. Under the water, he could see the full length of Paolo's naked torso. The water was murky, but he was close enough to make out details. It was obvious from his development that Paolo was at least as old as Cyprion. It was the lack of facial hair and his original scrawny state that had made him seem younger. His legs were solid white columns disappearing into the swirling mud below, and his muscular arms—his muscular arms were reaching for him. Cyprion gasped and came up sputtering, Paolo gripping his shoulders.

"Don't!" Paolo cried. His grip tightened as water poured from Cyprion's nose. "Don't go."

"I won't," he coughed. He grabbed Paolo for emphasis. "I won't ever go from you."

Paolo searched his eyes, then pulled Cyprion to him and hugged him fiercely. Cyprion returned the hug, water dripping from his beard down the lad's back. With each breath, they relaxed until they were breathing in unison, the sun warming their heads, the water cooling their backs, the summer insects flashing their wings over the water.

Insects, Cyprion thought incongruously. *More than last year.*

He felt something stir against his groin, and as soon as he realized what it was, his own member began to swell. *This is not the sort of play Father Marten had in mind*, he thought and pulled away. The water rushed between them, cooling his belly and deflating his arousal. He didn't look to see if it had the same effect on Paolo. "Maybe we should go back."

Paolo shook his head. "Hens can wait."

"Well, back to shore, then." Cyprion took him by the hand and waded back to the spot where their clothes lay. His were in a heap on the muddy bank, but Paolo had thought to drape his over a bush lupine. Waves from their frolic had soaked Cyprion's undergarment and half his smock. "You were smart," he said, pointing to Paolo's dry clothing. "You can put yours on right away."

Paolo picked up Cyprion's wet things and spread them on a bush next to his. He turned, smiling. "Stay."

Now they were both naked in the bright sunlight. Water glinted in the hair at Paolo's crotch and ran down his legs. Cyprion could feel the water drying on his back and wicking from the hair on his chest. Paolo took a step forward and touched his beard with his fingertips. Cyprion swallowed. "You'll have one, too, someday."

Paolo shook his head slowly. "No. Never." He dropped his hand and turned away.

Cyprion shivered. He wanted to call back the sunlight of Paolo's smile but didn't know how. He picked up a stone, smooth in his hand and warm from the sun, and threw it at the pond. It skipped a few times before sinking.

Paolo gasped. He looked at the ripples spreading over the pond's surface and turned to Cyprion in bright excitement. "Again!"

"What? The stone?" He picked up another one and flung it at the water. This one skipped much further. Cyprion smiled. "Not bad, huh?"

"Stones fly!" Paolo exclaimed. He grabbed a handful of stones and threw them at the water. They sank.

"Wait," Cyprion laughed. "You have to pick the right stone. A smooth one."

Paolo picked up a stone and inspected it. "Smooth stones have wings?"

"Well, not exactly. We give them wings when we—" Paolo threw his straight at the water where it disappeared with a *splunk!* He turned around with such a furious look that Cyprion laughed out loud. "Here, let me show you."

They chucked stone after stone until finally Paolo flung one that seemed to skip forever. They counted seventeen hits before it sank, then whooped for joy. Cyprion clapped Paolo on the back.

"Aeii!" he cried, wincing.

They had stayed uncovered for too long. Both were badly sunburned. They dressed, hissing in pain as the rough cloth scraped against their reddened shoulders. "I have some aloe juice," Cyprion said. "It may help, but I'm afraid neither of us will sleep tonight."

"Why?" Paolo asked.

"It'll hurt, that's why."

"No." Paolo pointed to the water. "Why?"

"Why the stones?"

Paolo nodded, his eyes shining. "Stones fly. How?"

Cyprion looked at the pond. "I never thought about it. I guess…" He looked at Paolo's eager face. "I guess it could be calculated. The weight of the stone, the shape, the angle."

"Yes! More."

"More? The surface tension, I suppose. Viscosity. Air friction. All those affect the number of skips, the length of the run."

"But *we* are the wings. *We* make them fly."

"Oh. Yes, of course. How hard we pitch them, but I don't see—"

Paolo leaped forward and kissed him hard on the mouth, then danced down the path, shouting, "We are the wings! We make them fly!"

They did not sleep that night. They filled every scrap of paper and wooden plank with Cyprion's calculations and Paolo's drawings. Saint Vigil sang and they did not hear. The bell rang and they did not go. A rap at the door made Cyprion look up and realize it was day. He opened the door to find Father Marten and Brother Malleck.

"Friend Cyprion, have you seen—?" Father Marten broke off when he saw Paolo leaning over the table. "Ah. Brother Malleck was wondering if Paolo would be collecting the eggs this morning?"

"And the morning meal grows cold in the refectory," Brother Malleck added. "He missed yesterday's evening delivery entirely."

Father Marten smiled. "We've come to rely on our young friend, I'm afraid. Perhaps we've taken him for granted."

"I'm so sorry, Father Receiver," Cyprion stammered. "We were up at the pond—"

"Swimming?" Marten asked hopefully.

"We started out swimming, yes. But then this question came to us, about stones and how they skip across the water and, well, you see…" He gestured to the table and the surrounding floor littered with their work.

Father Marten took a step into the room. Feeling Brother Malleck peering over his shoulder, he turned and said, "Brother, perhaps one of the other oblates can deliver the morning meal?"

"There's mid-day prep as well."

"Paolo will be there to help you—" He looked at Paolo, who was scrutinizing his drawings, a knuckle in his mouth. "—directly."

Brother Malleck nodded and left.

Father Marten approached the table and picked up a sheet of figures. Paolo grinned at him and nodded. "You go for a swim and come back with calculations," Marten said. "You have a strange notion of fun, Friend Cyprion."

"It *is* fun!" Paolo exclaimed. "Stones fly! We are the wings!"

Father Marten put the paper down carefully. "Yes, perhaps. But the hens need tending to and Brother Malleck needs help in the kitchen. Friend Cyprion, you have tasks too, I believe?"

"Of course, Father."

"Good," Marten said and headed for the door.

"Father!" Paolo blurted out. Marten and Cyprion turned to him. "I have—" He rubbed his hands together. "I have decided."

"Decided what, Paolo?"

"I want to stay. I want to stay here."

A broad smile spread over the Father Receiver's face. "You are declaring yourself, then? You want to be part of our community?"

"Yes, Father, I do!"

Marten turned his smile to Cyprion. "See what a little play can do? We'll have to settle on a cabin, or clean out one of the unused cells."

"No!" Paolo exclaimed.

The smile died on Cyprion's face. He longed for and dreaded what he knew was coming.

"Here," Paolo said. "I want to stay here. With Cyprion."

"Oh." Father Marten looked from the boy to the oblate. "That might prove...disruptive."

"It will not, Father Receiver," Cyprion said immediately.

"You have already missed morning offices. Twice."

"That will not happen again."

Marten looked around. "It will be cramped in here."

"It is cramped in the henhouse. He is a growing boy."

"Nearly grown, I should say." Marten turned to him. "Paolo, do you understand? You are asking to be part of our community, but we religious keep to separate cells."

"Cyprion is not religious," Paolo answered.

Cyprion's heart skipped a beat. Father Marten cleared his throat. "No, he is not. He is an oblate. But he follows the rule and the offices, and is under my authority."

"I understand, Father Receiver."

"Hmm," Father Marten said, unconvinced. "Can you eliminate these night-owl arithmetics and keep to our schedule?"

Cyprion looked at Paolo. Did he understand? Paolo's eyes were clear, no trace of wildness. "I can, Father," Paolo said.

"And attend all offices?" He glanced at Cyprion. "Whether Friend Cyprion does or not?"

Paolo smiled. "I will, Father."

Cyprion felt a stone lift from his heart.

"Good." Father Marten turned to go. "The community must still consent. I will bring the matter before them at the charter meeting next month. Until then, you remain in your room beside the henhouse, is that understood?"

"Thank you," Cyprion and Paolo said together.

Marten paused at the door and looked at them. "Stones with wings," he said shaking his head.

❖

Father Marten seemed determined to keep them busy at opposite ends of the hermitage that month. Cyprion was put in charge of rebuilding the village path. Paolo continued his rounds delivering meals, but surprised both Cyprion and Father Martin with plans for a greenhouse inside the cloister, which he set about building. They saw each other only at offices, but whenever Cyprion looked up from the Songs, he invariably met Paolo's eyes across the aisle, dark as night and bright with life.

At the mid-summer charter meeting, Paolo was received as an oblate into the Hermitage of San Lucca. That night, he moved into Cyprion's cabin.

The cabin still smelled of earth from the plants Paolo had moved to the greenhouse. There were two chairs, a table, a lamp, and two cots set against opposite walls, but Cyprion couldn't see anything but the tall young man before him.

Paolo took him by the hand. "There are two cots," he said evenly.

"Yes," Cyprion said, unable to think.

"They are narrow."

"Yes."

For a moment, Paolo said nothing. Then he wrapped his arms around Cyprion and pulled him close.

Cyprion felt light, as if he might float away. "This is…disruptive," he murmured.

"No," Paolo said.

"It is too soon."

"No." He pulled his work smock over his head, then gently lifted Cyprion's and stepped into his embrace. His skin was as smooth as water, as warm as a stone in the sun, a stone with wings.

FLAWED

Felice Picano

I'd be amazed if the little shop were still there. It's not really convenient to go back and check, so I'll probably not know for a while. But back then even that scuzzy part of San Francisco was giving in to the gentrification that had begun taking over the city.

At the time, the shop was surrounded by small, ethnic, countertop diners, a tumbled-down tailor shop and a cigarette store cum tiny grocery for the cripples and drunks and layabouts whenever their monthly welfare benefits arrived.

The only reason I even looked in the shop window was the owner, an oversized man, with ginger mustachios almost out to his ears and ginger whiskers down his front, with a shiny bald head, dressed in black leather, heavy with chains and gewgaws, including one dangling skull and crossbones earring. "A club act" I would call him if I'd noticed him while alongside my friend and she would smile. He was striking: meant to be as colorful as possible. Typical in the city. Less so as an antique store owner.

I was also drawn by the profusion of mirrors.

It was unclear whether this was a mirror shop or an antique shop. I stopped at the window after getting the opera house tickets and figured I'd amuse myself for ten minutes by going in. The owner ignored me, involved in a conversation on antique puce Princess phone, adding up invoices on a pocked, old IBM desk calculator.

To my surprise it wasn't just a store front; smaller rooms extended deep into the block, where surrounding shops still had living quarters.

I ended up looking around in the room furthest from the front door. Suddenly, Mr. Black Leather arrived, stuck out a meaty hand, and said, "Hans Olthen." Just then we both heard jangled bells signaling someone entering the front door. "Back in a sec," Hans offered, flirtatiously adding, "Anything or one particularly interest you here?" Before I could answer, he pointed to three floor-model mirrors I'd stopped at and said, "Half off, half off, and don't bother with that one, it's flawed." He flounced off to the front of the store and I heard "*Ach, Gretel! Wunderbar!*" followed by rapid German.

So, of course, I looked at the three mirrors.

Looking glasses is more like it, since they appeared to be vintage 19th century. Two were faux-Federal style, late in the century with obvious attempts at copying the more prized earlier style with its distinctive architrave top. The third was a puzzler. It too had the faux-Federal style of arched top and double wood sides; but it also had what seemed to be East Asian carvings, finely done, almost hidden on the very dark wood of the two sides. I couldn't make out the wood used. The other two mirrors were maple and cherry, but while dark as mahogany, this was grained wrong for that and so, enigmatic. It was also larger: almost seven feet by four feet wide and leaning right on the floor, while the others had doubled bottom pieces and one had lion-claw legs.

The discounted two were placed direct to the passing viewer, and their glass was clear if a little blurry at the beveled edges, but without any crazing. The third, larger one was faced away from the viewer. They were all surrounded by Craftsman-Era, fake zinc-shaded lamps set on brown-as-dirt matte ceramic bottoms, which rested on out-of-the-70's four-foot high stereo speakers. I had to twist myself into a corner to get a good look inside the supposedly flawed mirror and even then, I made out nothing at all. No reflection, never mind a flawed one.

Wait! There it was! A dull reflection of the doorway behind me and my body in the camel-hair overcoat I'd unbuttoned in the warm back room. Despite the lack of sharp reflection, I didn't see a flaw, until I looked closely, top corners first, then down, and left corner, all of them fine, but wait! There it was. A twist or turn of the glass? In the lower right.

When I knelt to look to see if it was the fault of the glass, suddenly it was clear, quite clear, but instead of reflecting back the closet door like the rest of the glass, it was reflecting green: light green, medium green, even a few deep greens, and as it clarified in front of me, it was *reflecting* green leaves, branches, portions of a bush and in some motion too, as though it was a video or live action film.

I almost fell over. I did stumble into the closet door. When I crept forward and looked again, the flaw had spread. The entire right side third of the glass was reflecting what looked like part of a forest.

I was trying to make up my mind to call Hans and discuss this with him, when he burst into the room, and said. "It was nothing," shaking his head, then added. "Silly woman. She can see, no, how completely Gay Gay Gay I am! Interested in the womankind not one bit." He'd spun about with his words and landed even closer to me than I found comfortable. "But you!" he added. "You, I have definitely seen before."

"I don't believe we…"

"No. No. Don't tell me. You were not so well dressed as this, I think. So maybe that is what off me throws." Touching his large pink brow as though to recall, "Black or Navy blue tee and maybe, yes, it vas motorcycle boots."

"You must be kidding."

"No, no, Hans, that is incorrect," he lectured himself. "But somewhere…I am so sure."

"I am not that kind of…"

"No insult intended. I have nothing but respect for…"

"This mirror!' I interrupted him by changing the subject. "Unlike the others it has no price on it."

"Because it is flawed."

"Then, the price…out of curiosity's sake," I explained.

"I told you. It is flawed and haunted, yes?"

"Yes. Well, as least about the flaw. I see very fine markings here. What's the provenance?"

"Provenance is very fine. From upper Nob Hill. Very large house next to Spreckles mansion. Well, on same street. Estate sale. All quite legal."

"I meant before that? Is it Asian or what?"

His big meaty hands came out and folded in space. "Wish that I knew."

"Because it might easily go with the dark wood colors in the library of a lady I know."

Hans peered at the delicate stylized chrysanthemums, and was that an open fan pictured too? "Cannot help. Hans takes notes at estate sales. Not this time. Siamese?" he hazarded.

"Or Javanese. And the flaw?" I turned to touch it on the right side. "Where's the flaw?"

Because as I looked at it, the green vanished and the glass was clear and shining too.

"Is there!" Hans asserted without even looking. "Take my word. You bring it to that lady. She throw you out the door!"

❖

"It's been months, maybe years since Diane has looked so well. She's positively glowing."

We were in the lobby of Davies Hall during the interval. MTT was conducting Mahler, a specialty of his, so it was full. I was just beyond the main floor bar, speaking with a blonde of a certain age named Conchita with seven other names, most of them, my friend, Diane, had intimated, husbands she'd divorced or outlived.

"She's a lovely woman," I agreed. "Lovely tonight. As are you."

"Do you think?" she preened. "It's vintage Balmain. I can't pull off those new designers. What do they always say, the older, the softer the lines and darker the skin, the more pastel the hues? Back to Diane. May we hope that there will be an announcement soon?"

"An announcement?" I asked, flummoxed.

"No announcement is forthcoming, Conchita, except the symphony will begin, now that we've had the overture and song cycle as appetizers and a bit of bubbly."

Diane slipped a beringed hand through my arm and smiled with her eyes at me, so that we were sharing something at the older woman's expense.

"But really Diane," Conchita began, aggrieved. Then we all heard the chimes.

I wasn't sorry that Diane began to lead us away.

"But wait, darlings. You haven't told me yet that you'll both be at Keith and Enrica's?

Diane waved. We filtered through the orchestra crowd to our fifth row center seats.

"Don't pay attention to Conchita," Diane lightly urged. "Listen only to me."

"Don't I always?"

We sat and the first violinist appeared on stage and Tilson Thomas himself appeared and the audience settled down. That haunting post-horn motif tore through the silence with its plangent call from afar. I thought about what they had both said. I had made more progress than even I'd expected.

I turned to Diane and she to me and we smiled at the sonic wonders to come.

❖

"What did you mean when you said that the mirror was flawed *and* haunted?"

"Is that what I said?"

"Yes, exactly those words."

Hans was wearing a variant of his usual dead cow: a vest covering his torso save for his very hairy nipples and his equally hirsute navel. He was certain I'd come to see him and my asking about the mirror was an excuse. He played along or at least pretended to do so.

"Specifically, what did you mean when you said it was haunted?"

He had a feather duster and was dusting all around himself—reminding me of those balletic hippopotami in *Fantasia*.

"The mirror was wrapped in canvas sheet when I saw. Someone, I don't remember who, a servant or housekeeper, said it was kept wrapped many years. Wrapped tight and bound tight with cord. No one unwrapped since it was delivered. I think she said it was of danger." He shrugged.

"Because it was haunted?"

"It's superstition, is it not?"

"It was of danger if it fell on your toes, because it's so heavy?" I asked.

He emitted what romance novelists term a "mirthless laugh."

"What is important—is distorted. Because of flaw."

"And yet I like it very much," I said. "If it is so awfully flawed and distorted why not sell it to me at a discount? As damaged goods?"

"Well...I haven't put it up for sale yet."

"Does that mean you wish me to name a price?" I asked.

"That would be too much of a disregard. Is how you say it?"

"Insult, I think you mean? Too much of an insult?"

"Yes, insult is the word I look. But why talk of flaw things when there are so many perfect things?! For your lady friend, you said." This last phrase spoken so archly, I could have struck him for his insolence!

"Now you are insult. Subtleties I am aware, yes, but do not exactly understand," Hans admitted. "I still believe we have met before. Other circumstances. Yes! I believe."

"I *don't!* Now, shall I look into the mirror today?" I asked.

He didn't protest.

"Where exactly is this confounded flaw of yours?"

He danced a little on tip toes. "Now you *not* see it," Pointing to lower righthand corner.

"When *do* you see it?"

Hans shrugged.

"Have *you* seen it?"

Hans shrugged again.

"And the haunted story? Fake, I suppose, to jack up the price."

He handed me a small pad and a chewed up looking stub of lead pencil he kept in his vest pocket. "You make price you want here. Put it on desk when you leave."

That's when I knew he hadn't paid much, or perhaps anything, for it. That it had been part of a general sale of furnishings.

I wrote a price and put it into my pocket.

As though in synch, the front bells jangled and he excused himself and exited. From where I stood, I heard his greeting, "So, Antony. What shall it be today? Perhaps this *escritoire* they say from Fontainebleau?"

I looked at the mirror again, and there was that green I'd seen before.

I wedged myself in such a way that I could look at it directly, touched the mirror and I'll be damned if the entire mirror didn't then clear enough to show that scene. I could make out forest, tropical, perhaps even Amazonian, given all the orchidaceous flowers and lianas. All the while I was thinking "I can see it, yet Hans couldn't? Or did he not even try?"

The leaves moved and sometimes a twig or branch jerked. As I stood entranced, I began seeing not so much movement as the tiny consequences of small, not visible things moving. I remembered there was a magnifying glass for sale a room away and longed to get it. At the same time, I was afraid to move away from this extraordinary sight for even a second.

I heard sounds coming too, faint at first, what might have been the far-off cries of primates or birds. I'd just absorbed that, when a hummingbird darted into the scene. It went for the inside of an orchid-like bloom of cream spotted with red, hovered and sipped nectar; in profile so that I could make out its bronze and green throat and front feathers. It was about to move out of the picture when it suddenly turned full face and stared.

"It can't possibly see me, can it?" I asked.

Perhaps in reaction, it darted forward, right to where I thought was the front edge of the glass. Astonishing. I was even more astonished when it darted forward another inch and I would swear its beak—nothing else but the beak—broke that indelible surface.

I must have gasped out loud and fallen back because faster than the eye it darted away and out of sight. I fell into the wall and struck the side of one of the other mirrors there and had to move quickly to keep it and myself from falling.

"Are you okay?" I heard a voice. A distinguished looking African-American man—Anthony?—must have been in the room next to this. He rushed forward to aid me. I thanked him.

"Oh, my!" he said and looked around. "He's been hiding these from me."

I moved in front of the "flawed" looking glass but he only had eyes for the smaller ones. "Hans!" he called, then smiled at me saying "That scamp!" I could hear him saying as he went toward the front, "Hans, you naughty, naughty man! You've kept these lovely Federal mirrors from me," the voice diminishing as he went away.

I checked inside the big mirror and thought, I have to know for sure, and closed my eye and stuck a hand in. Opened them to see my fingers right at the branch end of some flowering bush. I grabbed it and snapped off the end. Hearing the other two approaching the room, I pulled my hand back, in time to see the scene in the mirror beginning to dim again. I stashed it in my coat side pocket and strolled as casually as possible toward the front.

I met Hans and Antony coming at me. As they passed I turned and said to Hans. "My offer will be on your desk."

❖

"You're all right with all this, aren't you?"

"All this" being the open front courtyard of the Legion of Honor set up with café tables and chairs, portable torch heaters, a string quartet playing, delicious food, and Mumm's and Prosecco served by waiters so smooth they might have been on roller-skates.

I might have answered satirically. Instead I said, "You're joshing, right? I *love* all this! I love the place. I love the Vlaminck and Derain exhibit inside. What's not to like?"

She smiled "When we met, I wasn't sure you were as much of a culture maven as I am. God knows, Harley wasn't."

Harley: her dead husband. Worth who knew how much, exactly. Diane didn't.

"I am as much of a culture maven as you are. I just haven't been able to afford it like this before. You know, front row seats at the symphony, boxes at the opera, fund raising galas with five-course dinners."

"That's the other thing I have to ask you," Diana suddenly sounded serious. "Are you all right with someone else...you know, treating you to it."

"I'm fine with it. I'm delighted with it. But only because it's you—and not anyone else —who is doing the treating. I feel like we are in this together."

"We are! We are!"

She became pensive.

"You won't suddenly get all masculine proud on me and feel vulnerable about it?"

"I don't think so. Did Conchita say I would?"

"Several of my women friends have had more...more experience in these things, to be completely honest. I've always been sheltered. By my parents. By Harley. So I'm reduced to having to ask. So, no qualms?"

"My only qualm is what your friends think of you bringing me everywhere."

"Do you care?" Diana asked.

"Me? No. Not really. I know that makes me a terrible person."

"Me either. And, no, it doesn't make either of us a terrible person."

"I think it helps that we're not too different in age," I offered.

"It helps even more that you are well-read, knowledgeable, and intelligent on most of the subjects my friends are likely to..."

"Quiz me on?" I tried.

"Now you are being terrible."

"But yes, thank you." I agreed. "Except, of course, finances. I'm not very good at that."

"Thank the Lord," she laughed. "That's all Harley *thought about!*—finances."

A *Romanza* by Schubert originally written for the piano was now glittering over our conversation, just as the dessert, a towering Bananas Foster, arrived.

"I couldn't possibly eat that monstrosity, could I?" Diane said.

To the waiter I suggested. "Why not leave *one.* We'll share it."

"You really are a mind-reader," Diane said. "I'll taste yours. But no more."

"Well, maybe *two* tastes!"

Just then the transplanted-from-Atlanta heiress named Alexis-something-or-other flowed into one of the recently vacated chairs, followed by her far-too-young new husband.

"Well, darlings. Did you discuss it?" Alexis said stealing sips of the other guest's bubbly.

"We were working our way to it," Diane tried shooing her friend away. "Go away!"

"Working our way to what?" I asked and gulped what seemed to be too much dessert.

"The round the world trip!" Alexis said.

"Come with us!" Paul, the new hubby, said to me. "It'll be fun."

"It'll be terrific fun if the four of us go," Alexis agreed. "You know it will!"

"Well, now that you've opened your big mouth, Alex darling, and let the feline out of the Prada," Diane said humorously. "You two had better go away and let *us* discuss it. Before the poor man chokes on his bananas and ice cream."

As they were leaving, Paul turned and I saw his lips move to "Say yes!"

Diane began: "I always wanted to go. Now Alexis has tickets. There's an itinerary at my place. Nice hotels. Super cruises. But we'd be gone a year and two months. I've always wanted to go and never could with Harley. We'll have separate rooms all the way, because well, we're just good friends, right? Don't want to spoil anything by being anything more than that."

"Will Alexis and Paul have separate rooms?" I asked before I could stop myself.

"Given how poorly she sleeps. I'd say yes...I'm sorry to spring this on you!"

I thought of Paul, so handsome, so young, so apparently willing. I thought of luxurious week-long cruises up the Nile and two weeks down the Danube. I thought of four-star hotels in Monte Carlo and Biarritz, Cartagena and Shanghai and all of it with this charming, sophisticated lady. Could I possibly bear it? You bet I could! "When do we leave?!"

But before she could do more than be radiant in response, I said, "But I've got a gift for you, for your house actually. For that downstairs billiard room that no one has used since 1918. You cannot say no."

"Then I'll say yes," and Diane leaned across the arc of table laden with crystal and porcelain and sterling candlesticks and set a perfect little kiss on my forehead.

"Now I'm off to the Ladies. I'm grabbing Alexis on the way so we can scream like twelve-year-olds over how happy we are. Why don't you sit with Paul and keep him company?"

❖

The flower I'd picked out of the forest was *Licula*, from the Ingei Forest outside of Sarawak. The leaves I'd grabbed belonged to another flowering plant, *Thrixspermium Eryhisbron*, again from that forest in Borneo. At least, that was the conclusion of the researcher at the Botany department at Berkeley I'd brought them to. He'd been "thrilled" to see them and so I left them with him, taking only his detailed report, which added, "This forest contains over 1,175 species of flora and fauna, much never seen elsewhere. Both of these plants grow near the so-called pitcher plants, *Nepenthes*, also known as the Venus Flytrap."

Next step was the most daring: to go through the mirror all the way.

I guessed it led only to that forest. I'd seen nothing indicative of a building or construction of any sort, and so I would need a knife or sharp edge to mark exactly where the entryway lay in the forest. Prepping for that meant dressing down from the formal clothing I'd worn whenever I went into the shop—to be able to say to Hans that he didn't know me and had never known me.

A lie, of course. He knew me from my bartending days South of Market in one or another motorcycle bar. Or from my work before that as assistant manager at a sex club. "Manager with extras," my friends called it. Meaning I visited client's rooms for pay. True, I looked different. Gone was the long hair, the full beard, the eternal brown glass aviator glasses, though I'd kept souvenirs, especially the leather vests I'd stretched across my tanned, muscled, at times oiled, torso. My hair was short now and salt and pepper; my face bare of hair; gone now were the small tattoos on my neck. And, I was always clothed now. More than clothed, well clothed, thanks to a friendly woman at a certain snobby Episcopal church donation room who had a maternal interest in me and so saved nicer things for me. It was there I'd encountered Diane, who saw me in good clothing and who'd assumed I was donating, like she was. That led to chat. Chat led to a coffee date. That led to a dinner date and…

But Hans could still screw it all up. So Hans must be dealt with. Which meant I would have to make certain he was out of the way before the trip around the world began. For that, I needed to go in.

Hans closed early on Thursday. I slipped in when he was busy over-gesticulating, secreted myself in the back room of the shop behind the mirror. As soon as he locked up, I turned to the mirror and touched it to clarify. Shortly it did. Same scene as before. The broken twigs were those I'd taken. I took many deep breaths, then tried a finger, a hand, an arm, and I stepped through and spun around, took out the knife and marked the four upper and lower corners of the way I'd come through onto tree trunks and by arranging twigs on the ground. It was astonishing: I really was there. I needn't cut too much ahead to get out of this copse. Perfumes and odors assailed me. But the immediate area became quiet, noting my arrival. I kept turning to mark my path back, cutting many landmarks.

Ten minutes of walking ended when I heard voices. Suddenly above me there was a whoosh and the cry of an animal. I saw the little monkey struck by the arrow fall to the ground. Three young male New Guinea natives wearing only penis sheathes and headdresses hustled into the area and picked it up, celebrated with each other and took off again. They were too excited by their prey to stop and look around and perhaps notice me, crouching, silent, half-terrified. Seeing them was all I needed to know.

I found the mirror re-entry only after some searching and some panic. What if I couldn't get through again? Or only later? It hadn't been long. Maybe twenty minutes.

I found it, and closing my eyes, I pushed a hand through. Yes!

Then I went about destroying those careful signs I had made to find it. And stepped through to the other side. It was dark in the room where it had been twilight before and I held my hand out before myself and didn't crash into anything. I let myself out and locked the shop door behind me.

❖

"Aren't you glad you listened to me and put the mirror up for sale." I paused for effect. "You're a hundred dollars richer and you got rid of something you never expected to sell." Before Hans could reply, I said, "Here's the address I want it shipped to. It's up Nob Hill a few streets from where you found it. By the way, since I did pay for the shipping, they'll be here in a half hour at the most to wrap it and take it; I'll remain—if you don't mind."

Hans still looked surprised as he pocketed the cash I'd given him and marked the bill 'paid.' "I don't understand why you want," he sounded aggrieved. "It's flawed."

"I happened to discover it's flawed in a particular way. Which makes it marvelously valuable. Would you like to see?" I teased.

He followed me to the back room and together we took hold of it and faced it forward. Anthony-Whatever-His-Name had bought one smaller glass, so there was room now.

I knelt. "See! Right here!" I touched the surface and as I did it began to clear, and then become green. I heard Hans grunt in surprise behind me. "Now look closely!"

The surface gradually cleared and it was the same New Guinea forest scene from before.

I heard him grunt again behind me. "But what is? A painting under?"

"Better than a painting, Hans. It's a doorway."

He grunted again. I touched the surface and my hand went right through.

"This cannot be!"

"It gets better!" I said in my best Abracadabra voice. "Watch!"

I stepped through the surface into the forest. He made a loud noise. When I turned, I could see him dimly, fallen against the far wall. I swatted at an insect and plucked a *Licula* off its branch and then stepped through into the shop again.

"It's trick of some kind!" Hans asserted.

"You don't believe me," I said, waving the pink and white flower at him.

"It cannot be."

"But it is. And now the wondrous magical mirror belongs to me."

He hesitated then he reached forward and touched the surface and watched his finger go through. He turned to me with a childlike grin on his face.

"Go on. Why stop there?"

"Oh, no!" He backed away.

"Suit yourself," I said, unconcerned. "But when the deliverers come…This really will be your last chance."

"You have gone through? It continues?"

"I have gone through. It continues. I've stayed an hour already. But once I have it for myself…no one else will be able to go in."

He'd been slowly inserting all five fingers and then a hand through. By this time his hand has reached a twig. He snapped it off and pulled it through. Wonder on his face.

"It's real."

"Of course, it's real." I began polishing the wooden frame with a dust cloth I'd carried in my overcoat.

"So...Maybe I can go in for one minute?" Hans asked.

"It's now or never."

It took him a while to get up his nerve, then he cautiously entered the mirror. He found himself on the other side and suddenly there were hummingbirds all around him. He was like a child again. He moved forward, then turned and could see me dimly, and then he went forward.

When I could barely make him out, I touched the mirror at its top right corner as I'd learned to do and swept my hand down through on a diagonal to the lower left. And then from the lower right to the upper left again, until it was solid glass again.

Then I took the hammer out of the inside pocket of my coat and slammed the mirror as hard as I could.

I expected it to smash. Instead it rang like a giant bell. At least in the little back room it did. I don't know what noise it made on the other side. But the mirror didn't shatter, as I'd hoped. Instead it fogged over completely.

Not a minute later the front bells jangled and I went to let the shippers in. I'd already begun wrapping the mirror and they took over swiftly and efficiently. They wrapped it tight, sealed it with tape and carried it to the truck. I went with them and met Diane's housekeeper at the door and we placed it in the downstairs game room.

Nineteen months later, after our trip—and our official engagement—Diane suddenly had to see "her gift." I was afraid she would be disappointed. I was prepared to make excuses about the shippers' mishandling it.

It was unwrapped without ceremony and before I could step to the front to look, I could see utter delight on Diane's face. "It's a beautiful painting, Darling! Remarkable! Almost three dimensional. I feel like I could reach out and touch one of those hummingbirds!"

"Wait!"

Before I could stop her, she did touch it. She touched glass. Solid glass.

"It's too nice for this dingy room. We'll put it upstairs. But where?"

"How about the mantel in what we are now calling my library?"
I suggested.

"Perfect. Then I can visit it every day!"

That meant I can look at it every day.

I do.

Sometimes I think I see a hummingbird wing flutter. At other times I've almost convinced myself that I can see the very edges of Han's ginger moustachios behind a clump of *Thrixspermium* bushes.

THE GROVE OF MOHINI

J. Marshall Freeman

The offer was weird—possibly illegal—and Sid wasn't sure why he'd accepted. Maybe because he had to waste three nights on the hookup app for every hookup that actually happened. Guys ghosted on him all the time. Others were openly racist in that polite Toronto way: "No offence. Just a preference." So he'd said yes to Friday night's first offer, even though it went against his instincts. After all, what had his instincts gotten him so far? Isolation, lies, following someone else's script in the drama of his life.

And that was why he was standing on the sidewalk while the lights of the city winked on, and everything quivered on the brink of a midsummer weekend. Sid peered down the street, willing his ride to arrive. What if one of the neighbours he barely knew spotted him and asked what special plans he had for the night?

"I'm being paid $250 to be a nymph in an enchanted grove," he would probably admit with his unhelpful reflex for honesty. He looked down at his decidedly un-nymph-like outfit: sky-blue polo shirt, white chinos, and flip-flops with plastic straps in popsicle-orange. Arthur, the mysterious stranger on the app, had said to wear sandals; the rest would be provided.

The bubble tea shop across the road was a glowing fishbowl of movement and colour in the deepening twilight. A cluster of friends exited into the night, laughing, slurping from their big plastic cups, leaving behind just two guys, sitting at a corner table. They were in their mid-20s, a few years older than Sid. The taller one was white, a cloud of auburn curls falling to one side of his head, the other, black, with an elaborate architecture of dreads. They held hands. They leaned in close. The white guy lifted their interlinked hands to kiss the black guy's fingers. Sid watched them for clues, trying to recognize himself in either one, until a silver SUV pulled up and blocked his view.

The van's back door slid open, and a young guy with a diamond nose stud said, "Are you NewInTown99?" He looked Sid up and down with an uncertain expression.

Sid put on the same big smile he used in family barbecue pics. "Hey, yeah, that's me," he said and climbed in. There were two other guys inside, not including the driver who didn't acknowledge the new arrival. The boys were all twinks—skinny and white, in shorts shorter than Sid would buy. One wore a tight Nicki Minaj t-shirt, one a striped crop top, and the third, the guy with the nose stud, wore a semi-transparent, sleeveless black shirt. Sid could see his nipples, pierced and ringed. The boys were pretty in a way that left him vibrating with a mix of desire and unease.

"I think I'm underdressed," he told them, laughing awkwardly.

The boy in the crop-top tossed back his bangs and said, "There's always room for a J. Crew queen!" The other two giggled. Sid had no choice but to smile.

It grew darker outside, and Nicki Minaj rolled down the window. "Leaving Oz. Next stop: who-the-fuck-knows."

"We're on the Rosedale Valley Road," Sid explained as they sped along between the trees, but the boys weren't listening.

"Darryl," said nose-stud. "Are you sure we're not being serial murdered?"

"Or sex-slaved," added Nicki.

Crop-top shook his head. "No, I hooked up with Arthur before. He swore on his mother's Hammacher Schlemmer catalogue that we wouldn't have to do anything but prance around and drink cocktails while a bunch of old guys discussed, I don't know, their mutual funds and the cost of Viagra."

Nose-stud snorted. "I don't mind bending over for some sugar daddy if he promises to pay off my student loans."

They were heading up the Bayview Extension, the Don River dark and silent to their right. Sid imagined jumping from the van the next time it stopped. *Shut up!* he berated himself. *You're not a child.*

He would handle whatever came his way. Maybe he too would find a new daddy to pay for university, one whose money came with fewer expectations. The daring thought made him smile, and he turned his face into the shadows so the others wouldn't see.

The twinks were staring into their phones, swiping and texting, while Sid looked out the window, keeping track of their route. The van turned left onto Eglinton West, and then right into a quiet suburb, winding around and around through courts and crescents, until he'd lost all sense of direction. The houses grew larger and farther apart, brooding judges with wrought iron eyes and cobblestone tongues, their grand wigs the canopies of ancient oaks and maples that curled above them into the night sky. When the van slowed and pulled up to the curb, Sid's stomach clenched.

Leo was lost. Gavin had said to use the GPS on his phone, but Leo insisted on jotting down directions on the back of an envelope. Old School. Now his neck hurt from peering up at street signs, half-obscured by abundant foliage. Reluctantly, he turned on the GPS.

"Speak, O Sybil!" he told the phone, and its thin, bossy voice responded.

"At the first opportunity, make a u-turn."

Leo sighed, grinding the gears as he threw his 15-year-old Corolla into reverse. The evening had barely started, and already he felt like a loser. Tonight, a coterie of A-gays would gather to *ooh* and *ahh* at Gavin's grand new residence. They'd network and ask who did the catering and the gardening, and hate on each other with Botox smiles full of whitened teeth. Meanwhile Leo, who taught introductory communications at a community college, would stand in a corner, compulsively straightening the curled collar points of his fading "good" party shirt and remind himself not to drink too much.

He hoped to hell Stefan would show up. Stefan wasn't really of the A-gay world, but he knew how to navigate its currents. Leo, Gavin, and Stefan were all that was left of their old group. Leo had been barely 18 when they all met at a protest following the 1981 bathhouse raids, and Stefan was still his best friend after all these years. Stefan had ridden the wave of a new media in the 90s to become the head of his own "media group," whatever the hell that was. Leo, on the other hand, had never quite finished his PhD in patterns of global mythology.

"You're smarter than most professors I know," Stefan had recently scolded. "You could have tenure by now."

To which Leo retorted, "I don't need the meaningless approval of academia." But he didn't convince either of them.

"You have reached your destination," Sybil proclaimed.

"So be it," he answered. He peered through his dirty window at the edifice that rose into the hot night—a mini-Versailles, lit like a national monument.

"Oh my God, Gavin Keenlyside," Leo said. "You probably bought it just to spite me."

He tried not to feel humiliated when the valet drove his accidentally-vintage car off to join whatever climate-conscious hybrids and midlife-crisis sports cars the other guests drove. He was just relieved he hadn't been mistaken for the pizza delivery boy.

As he climbed the steep driveway, a van pulled up to the curb, and four young men hopped out. Three of them, in a laughing knot, were the newest generation of gay scenesters. Probably they'd been out to everyone at 14, oblivious to the history that made their freedom possible, to all the ones that died along the way. The fourth boy, a sober South Asian, followed behind, pushing his glasses up his big nose and eyeing the house with astonishment.

From the shadows to the side of the three-car garage, a no-nonsense woman in a neat white polo shirt and black khakis called out, "Boys! I'm Jeannine, the stage manager. Come around to the side door and check in." Catching sight of Leo, she said, "Good evening, sir. The front door is open. Have a nice time."

Leo gave her a mock salute and immediately felt like a fool. Climbing the wide stone steps, he pushed open the massive wooden door, which was so perfectly balanced, it seemed to drift under his touch like a cloud. He stepped into the enormous foyer, and a waiter handed him a drink even before he had time to be appalled by the sheer quantity of marble and tea-stained hardwood. Gavin was coming down the curving staircase like Gloria Swanson—though in chequered seersucker, not organza—giving orders to a man in a salmon summer suit who jabbed at an iPad and hurried off. With no small amount of theatricality, Gavin *noticed* Leo and sashayed the rest of the way down the steps.

"Good evening, Leo the Lion," he said, planting a demure kiss on Leo's cheek. "Leave it to you to be early."

"It's almost nine o'clock, Gavin. You called the party for 7:00."

"Oh, please! Only my parents came *that* early. They're already in the kitchen with a bottle of sherry and two glasses, playing cribbage. Anyone who's anyone won't arrive until 10:30." He leaned one hand on the marble newel post and raised the other in the air, indicating… everything. "Do you love it?"

"I want to run screaming," Leo answered, sipping the champagne which he knew damn well was a hundred times the price of his usual New Year's purchase. "Soon you'll be alone in the middle of the night, wandering room to room like the ghost of Ian Curtis."

"No dear, unlike you, I know how to enjoy life. I shall fill every room with cut flowers and uncut boys. You know, jealousy brings out the colour in your cheeks."

Leo couldn't help smiling. The rhythms of their conversation, 35 years in the making, were as comforting as they were taxing.

"Fuck you, dear," he said. "I suppose a tour is unavoidable?"

As Sid entered the cavernous, half-empty garage behind the twinks, an earlier group of guys was being ushered deeper in the house. How many hot young men had this Arthur recruited? Sid was last in line as they signed in one by one with an older, severely thin man in leather jacket and pants.

"Which one are you?" The man showed him a list with their profile handles down one side. *Hung+Yung, JustDave, YasKween…*

"I'm NewInTown99. That's me here."

"Real name?"

Sid froze. "Oh, you need that?"

"Liability. Otherwise we can't pay you." When Sid didn't respond, the man narrowed his eyes and drawled, "Don't worry; I won't let your mother near this list."

"It's Siddharth Sadangi." He spelled it. They filled in the rest of the blanks and Sid signed the form. Still bent over the table, he looked up at the man and whispered, "I don't think I should be here."

The leather man raised one grey eyebrow. "No?"

"The other guys...They're all really beautiful. They know how to dress and...and be *properly* gay. I'm..."

"New in town, I get it," he responded with a smile like a lemon twist. "You need to relax, kid." He took Sid's hand and slipped something into it. He pointed over his shoulder. "Through that door to costume and make-up. You'll be paid on the way out if you fulfill all your duties and don't piss on Mr. Keenlyside's azaleas."

Sid peeked discreetly at the jolly, red gummy bear the man in leather had slipped him. He brought the candy to his nose and smelled the sweetness of artificial strawberry and the thick pong of weed. Before he could tell himself it was a bad idea, he popped the whole bear in his mouth and downed it after only a few chews.

Sid stepped from the garage into the house just as the boy with the nose stud emerged from a door to his left, pirouetting into the hall like a bad ballerina. He was naked except for a brief yellow bathing suit, which showed off his junk to fine advantage, and a leather harness with clear-plastic insect wings attached to it. His hairless body twinkled with a dusting of gold glitter, and a pair of black antennae poked through his curls.

"Buzz!" he told Sid, his wide eyes dramatically ringed in black and purple, before running down the hall, following a line of signs with printed arrows.

Someone inside the room called, "Next!" and Sid entered obediently.

"Another bee?" asked the heavyset woman in black sweats and black tee, oversized red glasses, and rainbow hair tied in pigtails. She didn't bother suppressing a yawn. "Or maybe a dragonfly."

"I'm bored to tears with insects," answered a man standing behind a chair in front of a big mirror topped with bright lights. His hair was a fire-engine red bowl cut, and he was straightening out his makeup kit, cleaning a large brush. "Stand up tall, boy, let me look at you."

He approached and cupped Sid's chin in a hand whose liver spots and wrinkles belied the surgical smoothness of his face.

"Remove your glasses," he said, and Sid did as he was told. "This one is clearly a satyr."

"I can do that," the woman answered and began pulling costume pieces from a large duffel bag.

She undressed him so fast, Sid had no time to resist. He was fitted out in a leather vest and leopard briefs; iridescent stripes of gold were painted on the brown skin of his exposed torso. He didn't even realize he had been given curved horns of white bone until he sat down in the makeup chair before the big mirror.

The makeup man contemplated his living canvas for a moment, then began. Sid saw the dull square shape of his face grow contours under the flashing brushes, the jaw line softening, the cheek bones rising to prominence, until he was both delicate and dangerous. His eyes were curved out and up, and his hair whipped into waves like the sea.

The reflection Sid saw in the mirror made him gasp. It wasn't that he was unrecognizable; on the contrary, he knew this untamed creature as someone long banished. It was the child he had been—a wild, free animal, mostly, but not altogether a boy. But how could that be? That young innocent had not survived. And yet, staring back at Sid was the very child. Somehow, in this mirror world, it had lived to be dipped in the miracle waters of puberty, to emerge fully formed—a perfect beast of the night—lithe, sensuous, and rich with lust. Sid stood up from the chair, leaning forward on the makeup table to stare deeper into the mirror. His image seemed to throb before him, the long frame with its black hair, its grace, the weight of the bulge in the leopard shorts. And the eyes! Victorious and amused, they seemed to say, *You thought you could crush me, didn't you?*

Appearing behind his shoulder, the makeup artist sighed and cooed, "Mama, I'm pretty…I'm a pretty girl!"

Sid turned and snapped at him, "I'm not a girl!" and hurried out of the room. His head was spinning as he followed the arrows on the wall deeper into the house, toward the domain of the beast.

Leo was already sorry he'd signed up for the tour, sorry he'd not stayed at home with the new remastered Blu-ray of Max Reinhardt's "Midsummer Night's Dream." Instead, he nodded mechanically as Gavin droned on and on, attaching a price tag and contractor horror stories to each "exceptional detail" of his new house. The home theatre, the crafts room, the wine pantry…And they'd only covered the ground floor. Leo sent up humble thanks when they again crossed the foyer, because at the moment, the great door swung open and Stefan entered.

"Steffer, come!" Leo yelled as he lurched forward and grabbed his friend's wrist. "Gavin is giving the most fascinating tour!"

That inevitable look of the lost lamb crossed Stefan's face. His peach jacket was cut like a morning coat, and from the breast pocket, a cerise handkerchief lolled like the tongue of a Labrador. Stefan never seemed to age. The grey was hardly visible in his soft, careless blond hair; his face wasn't so much wrinkled as traced with fine cracks like antique porcelain.

"Great," Stefan said, and piled a tiny plate high with hors d'oeuvres from the offerings of two passing waiters. Sober six years, he waved away the proffered champagne, and Leo made himself resist another glass for his friend's sake.

Gavin swirled his heavy crystal tumbler of whiskey in apparent distress. "Maybe I should start the tour again."

Stefan crossed to Gavin, planting a kiss among the sparse hairs on his scalp. "Just pick up where you left off. I'll get the rest on the next round."

Gavin perked right up. He pointed at a huge, soulless painting on the wall and said something about "expressionism" and "resale value."

Leo whispered to Stefan, "He's unbearable."

"Only to you."

"I'm an excellent judge of character."

Gavin spun around. "You're literally talking about me behind my back."

"It's a beautiful house, Gav," Stefan enthused.

"Oh, you haven't seen *anything* yet!" Gavin marched them up the sumptuous curve of the staircase and down a wide corridor which thrust through to the back of the house like the grand concourse of an ocean liner. The corridor ended at a huge picture window that revealed a terraced backyard, stepping down and down into the ravine below. The patio, where guests were filling plates at a buffet, was just below them, lit by *art nouveau* lampposts. Down a level was a lawn and long beds in full flower. Further down, another lawn melted into the shadowed forest of the ravine. The trees reached into the night sky, swaying ghostly in the glow of spotlights.

Leo noticed figures at the forest's edge, flashes of pale skin caught by the electric moonlight.

"What the fuck?" he said. "Have you recreated a cruisy Queen's Park summer night, circa 1985? How nostalgic! If I go down there, will I find leather men from Burlington on their knees?"

Stefan laughed. "You could give them your old safe sex speech, Leo."

Gavin rolled his eyes. "Oh yes, everyone *loved* you interrupting their 3 am fucks for an impromptu condom lecture."

"I saved lives," Leo snapped back. "More than you can say."

But Gavin had lost interest in their squabble. "Look!" He pointed as two boys in slutty faerie costumes ran out onto the lawn, skipped a tandem circuit, and disappeared back into the trees. He chortled with pleasure. "I hired nymphs! You know, Leo, from all that mythology you love." Gavin leaned against the walnut railing and explained to Stefan. "Nymphs were like the geishas of the Greek gods."

"No they weren't," Leo objected, even though he knew he was being teased. "They were minor gods themselves, worshipped and revered as aspects of the natural world."

Gavin downed the rest of his whiskey. "Isn't that basically what I said?"

"Shall we continue the tour?" said Stefan.

Sid stood at a door at the back of the house. His head floated free like a balloon, somewhere above his body.

"Are you okay?" Jeannine, the stage manager, asked.

"Great," he told her, trying to access his best job-interview face.

"So, mainly you'll stay at the edge of the forest, peeking out from behind trees. Try and let the lights catch you. And look seductive if you can. But don't climb the trees; we won't be liable if you fall out of one."

I can be seductive, thought Sid, loosed by his transformation and by the magical gummy bear. *I am the bear in rut, stumbling through the forest in search of a mate.*

Jeannine was still talking, and he tried to focus. "There are two food and drink stations, and yes, there's alcohol, but remember you're here to do a job."

Sid peered out around the doorframe. There were a lot of guests—mostly on the patio, but some in the garden below. A bat flew through one of the spotlights, and Sid startled.

"Just remember," Jeannine said, "you've been hired as an actor. It's not your job to perform sexual favours for the guests. If anyone makes you feel uncomfortable, you come and find me."

"Unless I want it," said the bear, and Sid raised an embarrassed hand to his lips. "I'm sorry."

"Jesus Christ," Jeannine muttered. "Why did I take this gig?" She gave him a little push out the door, and his momentum carried him down the steep stairs toward the lower yard and the forest beyond. His flip-flops went slap-slap on the steps.

Sid remembered running, remembered like it was yesterday. The long, blue towel had been a superhero's cape, but also—more secretly—the long sash of a prince's royal garb, and most secret of all, a princess's sari, straight out of the stuttering Bollywood tapes his mother watched on her ancient VHS player. Eight year-old Siddharth ran the length of the beach, rail thin and swift as a greyhound, the towel and his long black hair flying behind him.

His mother was under their faded family umbrella, talking with a woman Siddharth didn't know, both wearing bright one-piece swim suits. His father sat on a beach chair with a medical journal, stubbornly sweating it out in the sun. Siddharth circled around the two women in a tightening spiral before collapsing, breathless and dizzy with pleasure, beside his mother. He could feel the cozy heat of her bare, brown thigh against his side.

"And is this your daughter?" the strange woman asked in her big, friendly, American voice.

Siddharth sat up in panic and immediately caught his father's disapproving glance, eyes cold as steel over the top of his journal. Siddharth's shame put him back on his feet, and he dragged himself away, all his lightness gone. Like a bad bit of math, the pieces of him didn't add up. His heedless pleasure was a problem to be solved. It put him in danger—maybe endangered them all. No matter the cost, the equation would have to be balanced.

A throbbing beat, chill but insistent, rose from speakers in the garden, propelling his memory forward eight years.

Age sixteen now, Sid stared with satisfaction at his image in his bedroom mirror. With good grades, dull clothes, and a vicious grip on the reins of his sexuality, he had vanquished that fey waif of a boy, the one who cried when he wasn't chosen for a team, the one whose hands and hips were too mobile when he was excited. He had forged from the stuff of himself a young man of wide shoulders and serious demeanour. Beloved Dadi—his tiny, round grandmother—said her Siddharth would soon make the young ladies swoon.

But deep down, he knew he wasn't a real man. He wasn't like his brother's friend, Lucas, who never had to restrain himself. The masculine ease with which he inhabited his body, whether horsing around with his male friends or flirting with the blushing girls, made Sid furious with envy, stunned him with lust. And there was no strategy to deal with these feelings but to pull the reins tighter, bind himself without remorse until he breathed only once a day, late at night, alone in the dark of his room.

Sid's drifting mind returned to itself. He was deep in the forest, though he couldn't remember leaving the path. He leaned back to peer up into the tree canopy—black it was, with shadows blacker still— and immediately felt dizzy, circling down on folding legs until he was sitting on the dry twigs and cushiony moss. He laughed at this private slapstick show, and his laughter conjured two of the glistening nymphs. They ran the woodland path before him, lit by an inner grace. Sid had no choice but to rise and follow.

He found them in front of a bar, set up at the base of a broad and virile oak tree.

"Crantini, please," said one nymph.

"Stoli and lime," said the other.

The bartender answered, "I have Molson Canadian and white wine in plastic cups."

Sid was staring deep into the indigo eyes of the beautiful bartender, who turned and asked him, "And what can I get for you?" The question seemed hilariously loaded.

But Sid just said "Wine," and before he could form any romantic banter on his thickening tongue, Jeannine was among them, shooing them out to pose at the forest's edge.

❖

Now the house was abuzz with guests, and Leo asked Gavin, "Don't you have to go play host?"

"I'm waiting to make a grand entrance," he said, checking the lacquered lay of his thinning hair in a gilded hallway mirror. "And there's one more room on the tour, one that only my two oldest friends will appreciate."

They came around a corner into a short stub of a hall with a single door.

"Welcome," Gavin said with a hand on his heart, "To the Hall of Memory." He held the door open for them, and Leo and Stefan stepped inside.

The first thing Leo saw was an old, white yachting cap, hung on the wall like a hunting trophy.

He gasped. "You have Marco's hat!"

Stefan came up beside him, and Leo could feel the tension before his friend even spoke. "Gavin, we wanted to bury him in that hat. You knew that. You watched me freak out at the hospital, blaming the nurses for losing it, but it was you who took it!"

Gavin clenched his fists like a child about to have a tantrum. "Marco was my lover. I had a right to take whatever I wanted!"

Leo watched Stefan's eyes fill with angry tears. It occurred to him that anger could be a defence against pain. Because even when an ache is familiar—thirty years and counting, in this case—it still hurt.

In its heyday, their group had comprised sixteen beautiful and horny young men, laughing, drinking, and dancing their way through Toronto's gay community. Leo remembered them marching on police headquarters together, part of a throng 4,000 strong, blocking traffic, chanting, demanding reform. After being raised in shame, they were claiming a place in the sun for their queer brothers and sisters. Then barely a year later, the first confirmed death in Canada from "the gay plague."

Stunned, they had watched each other vanish like the shrinking guest list in an Agatha Christie play—one senseless death after another, no time between for the shock to abate. Sixteen friends, and all that was left were the three in this room, the only ones granted the time to lose their youthful beauty and contemplate a more prosaic death.

And there they were before him. All sixteen hanging on the wall of Gavin's shrine: Jimmy, Jae, Alphonse, Kitty, Marco—smiling or blowing kisses, each 4X5 portrait in its own neat grey frame. All of a sudden, Leo understood the grotesque plan of the décor.

"Gavin! What have you done?" he said.

A tall and narrow bookshelf, festooned with artefacts of their youth, stood like a monolith in the middle of the wall. Hung to one side were thirteen pictures. On the other side, three. The living and the dead, separated by a tower of protest buttons, butt plugs, and glitter-strewn drag gear. A vertical river Styx, rising to silence any question of who was cold and gone, and who still warm.

Now it was Leo's turn to wrap his grief in anger: "Gavin, you asshole, you…you've atomized us! Where are all the group pictures? The picnics on Hanlons? Where's the one where we're marching up Yonge Street together singing 'Power to the People'? That's who we *were!*"

"We were individuals too," Gavin protested. "I'm honouring each and every—"

Leo shouted over him. "It's a goddamn score board! The ones on that side lost, right? And we're the winners. Why? Because we're still alive?"

"Yes!" Gavin shot back. "The three of us are still here and I feel good about that! I'm sick of fucking survivor guilt, okay? We cared for them, we watched them rot before our eyes. We fucking buried them when their families wouldn't. Well, I'm still alive! I'm successful and I have a fucking house overlooking the ravine!"

Leo could see tears in Gavin's eyes. He didn't care. Stefan was still in front of the yachting cap, his long fingers touching it with a tender reverence.

"You broke up with Marco when he got sick, Gavin," he said, his voice rising. "You couldn't handle it. Remember? That was six months before he died! You have no right to this hat!" Leo almost screamed as his usually serene friend ripped the relic right off the wall, tearing the hook and a piece of drywall out in the process, and ran away down the hall. Leo took a quick look into Gavin's wounded, unbelieving eyes and ran after Stefan, the two friends flying down the grand staircase together like fugitives.

❖

The forest had ceased to make sense to Sid. He stumbled along the paths, taking gulps from his second glass of wine and running into the same ancient tree over and over. With its wide, welcoming boughs, it was like a parent who always pulled him back into its embrace, simultaneously comforting and stifling. Then Sid was out on the lawn, waving back at the men hooting and beckoning from the gardens above. But the spotlights in his eyes were too bright, so he hurried back to the dark embrace of the forest. There was fog at the edge of his vision, and a creeping sense of being watched by forces older than he could imagine.

He'd misplaced his wine somewhere, but the forest in its beneficence brought him back to one of the bar stations. He stuffed a handful of chips into his mouth, their salty perfection another gift of the night, and partook of more wine.

Sid was ready to go deeper, indeed had no choice. In the arched boughs of a tree, he found a suit jacket hanging from a branch. He passed through the arch into a grove where a fat older guy, pants at his ankles, was fucking one of the nymphs—the one who had worn the Nicki Minaj tee in an earlier incarnation. The man's sweating face was lit by the pale glow of his phone as he filmed the penetration in close up.

"Sorry," Sid murmured and fled.

He ran on and was relieved to find his friends, the bee with the nose stud and the crop top boy, who might have been a squirrel. They were kissing languidly, dicks out of their briefs, jerking each other off. Sid's cock swelled in sympathy, and his mouth grew dry. He swallowed the rest of his wine and moved to join them, groping himself.

But when he was close enough to smell their sweat and body spray, the bee turned to him with a wince.

"Yeah, sorry, it's not you, but I'm not into brown guys. Just a preference, okay?"

Something was happening to the world; its edges were getting smaller and smaller. Sid's body was suddenly in revolt.

"But I'm a good person," he told the bee. "I'm…beautiful."

Then he was crashing through the trees, trying to coordinate the movements of a body that no longer seemed his own. Running and running, changing from boy to prince to princess to satyr, he heard the sound of water ahead and steered toward it. He wanted to wash himself clean, drink deep, dissolve.

❖

Leo and Stefan stood in the foyer, not sure what to do next.

Leo, more out of breath than his fit friend, moaned, "Ow, I buggered my knee."

"What did I just do?" Stefan said, clutching the hat to his chest.

Leo looked around nervously. "We better get out of here before security drags us into a back room and…does things to us."

Stefan laughed. "This isn't a Tom of Finland cartoon, you idiot." He pulled out his handkerchief and mopped Leo's sweaty brow.

Leo began to giggle and soon the two of them had fallen into each other's arms, howling with laughter. Leo took the hat from Stefan, and a tenderness twisted his heart.

"Look at the charms Marco hung off the band. Stars and moons and mermaids, like an 11-year-old girl."

Stefan touched the peak. "And sweat stains, three decades old."

"I'm shocked Gavin didn't have it dry-cleaned." The familiar ache squeezed at his heart. "That room, Steffer…God, I remember them all like it was yesterday."

"I know. And you slept with most of them."

"Ha. Half the time, I just lay there while they cried into my chest hair."

"Everybody's teddy bear."

"When I really wanted to be their hungry butt boy." They laughed again, and Stefan put an arm across Leo's shoulders and kissed his cheek.

"Danny and I will have you over for dinner next week," he said.

"Okay. I'll bring wine. But text me a suggestion; I don't want Danny to think I'm clueless about the finer things."

Stefan withdrew his arm and gave Leo a sharp look. "Everything you say is self-criticism. It drives me crazy. Even when you're calling Gavin names, you think he's better than you."

"Shall we compare my shit stain of an apartment to…this?"

"Leo, I'm going home. If you're not having fun, you should too."

"And give Gavin the victory? No way, I'm here to enjoy myself!" He plunked Marco's hat on his head, pecked Stefan on the lips and strode out into the backyard.

He circled the patio, sampling everything on the buffet tables. He smiled and waved at half-familiar faces, but the music was too loud for him to make out what they were saying. He pirouetted once for someone who pointed admiringly at the stained yachting cap. Grabbing a dewy bottle of Czech beer from an ice bucket on the bar, he wandered down the stone steps into the garden.

The music was vaguely familiar. Rihanna or something. Did Gavin really keep up with the charts, or was everything here—from the food to the music to the house itself—a trendy decision he paid someone else to make?

He crossed the lowest lawn and stepped into the forest. The dark unknown of the woods at night had always thrilled him. Camping as a kid, he would give himself delicious frights imagining monsters hanging above him in the trees. You'd only survive the walk to the bathroom by feigning bravery, maybe whistling.

But the only strange creature the forest produced that night was some bourgeois fool, tucking his sweaty shirt into his pants and zipping up his fly as he breezed past Leo, barking into his phone, "Tell him if he can't match that price, we'll find another supplier!" Leo stuck his head under the arching branches and found one of Gavin's hired nymphs, looking very fucked and counting a stack of bills.

"Hope you're on PrEP," Leo told the kid, who scowled back.

"Mind your business, old man."

"All praise to Bacchus," Leo responded, saluting the kid with his beer before pushing deeper into the forest. The music was muffled now, and he could hear the splash and trickle of water to his left. Changing course, he saw eyes among the trees. More nymphs? Maybe real ones this time, true spirits of the forest from a time before the Europeans.

The ground grew slippery, and Leo almost fell down the steep slope. He had found the creek. Winding through a clearing, a thousand reflections of the moon glittered on its tiny swells. And by the bank lay a satyr, one foot in the water, groaning, a hand grasping at the air.

"Hey, you okay, guy?" Leo asked, putting down his beer and kneeling beside the young man.

"I don't know…everything's turning. I can hear my blood rushing in my ears."

"That's just the creek. Here, sit up." He looked the boy over. "You on something?"

He grabbed Leo by the shoulder and looked deep into his eyes. "I ate a bear."

"What? Oh, you mean gummy bear? Okay, probably just THC. Might have been strong, and if you're not used to it…Did you drink too?"

"Wine," the boy said with a sad nod. "Am I going to die? They can't see me like this."

"Who?"

"The police. My parents." Lit by the moonlight, his dark eyes filled with tears.

Leo pulled the boy's head against him and cradled it. "You're not going to die. You're just greening out. Breathe deep and relax. I've got you."

Sid felt his fear slowly melt away as the older man held him. He was handsome, with a big kind face and warm green eyes. Not too old to be attractive. The top buttons of the man's shirt were open, and Sid could feel coarse curls of chest hair against his cheek.

"I'm Leo," he said. "What's your name, Mr. Satyr?"

"Siddharth."

"I like your costume, Siddharth. Most of those boys look ridiculous, but you have enough mythic heft to pull it off."

"The makeup guy, he thought I looked like a girl." Sid imitated the high voice. "'I'm pretty, mama. I'm a pretty girl!' Why did he say that?"

Leo laughed. "It's from 'Gypsy.' He's just an old musicals queen. You don't look a girl. I mean…you look…you look like this forest. Masculine like the trees, feminine like the stream. Are you from a Hindu family, Siddharth?"

"My parents. My mom mostly."

"Because gender is pretty fluid in Hindu myths. The Ardhanarishvara was a manifestation made of Shiva and Parvati together. And then there was Mohini, who was a female form that Vishnu once took. His girlfriend figured out who he really was by jerking him off."

Sid liked Leo's voice, liked the way it rumbled through his chest. "So, I can be a mostly boy but a bit girl? That would be okay?"

"It's 2019, kid. Gender is what you make it." Leo stroked the boy's head, dislodging a costume horn that had already lost its twin. Siddharth's makeup was streaky now, but his eyes were breathtaking.

"Let's get you out of here" Leo said and helped him to his feet, watching the beautiful body unfold until he stood several inches taller than Leo.

Back up on the lawn, nymphs were dancing to the thumping music. Three or four of the guests had stripped naked and were running around the lawn howling, object lessons in the benefits of well-tailored clothing.

The stage manager was sitting on a lawn chair, drinking a beer and shaking her head at the spectacle.

"Rough night?" Leo asked as she took in Sid's unsteady gait and clucked her tongue.

"I'm quitting the theatre," she said. "Joining Doctors Without Borders and doing some good in the world."

"You *are* a good person," Sid told her with great sincerity.

Leo laughed. "Where are his clothes?"

"Go through that door up there. Arthur will probably pay him despite his condition. Better hurry; I think Mr. Keenlyside's new neighbours called the cops."

The valet brought Leo his car, and he helped Sid into the passenger seat. In his street clothes, with remnants of makeup still on his face, he looked like a mighty forest spirit escaping into the world of mortals.

"You can sleep at my place," he told Sid. "You'll be fine in the morning, and no one will be the wiser."

As they started their journey, Sid grabbed the captain's hat off Leo's head and put it on.

"Can I fuck you?" he asked, and Leo almost lost control of the car.

"No," Leo answered. "You need to sleep."

"But I want to cuddle."

"Maybe."

"And then I'll fuck you," said the young satyr, and began quietly singing the song that had been playing when they left. Something about *waiting on that sunshine boy...*

Leo, wise in the way of myths, knew the dangers whenever gods and mortals mated. Anyway, sex was out of the question—Siddharth was too drunk to consent. And tomorrow, sober, the beautiful young man would have no interest in the decaying ruin of his host's body.

Still, Leo was hard as they drove downtown, and his erection was a beacon, a better GPS to follow into the night.

SHOPPING FOR OTHERS

William Christy Smith

Marshall Higgins had to get out of the house. Even though he lived alone, he needed somewhere outside in the open, where he could be by himself and digest the news. He'd held it in all afternoon.

He crossed Elysian Fields and hurried through the cast iron gates into Washington Park. He plopped down on one of the concrete benches, underneath the live oak trees and crepe myrtles, in front of the aspidistra. This was the place to sit down, take a deep breath, and try to figure this out.

Just five hours earlier, he'd walked out the doors of Godchaux's Department Store on Canal Street, the ones on the side that employees used, to go to the clinic at Tulane University Hospital. It was his lunch break, a mere thirty minutes, and he was going to get the results of his HIV test. Marshall had decided he should finally get tested, mostly as a formality. He'd only been with three partners in his entire life and no one recently, and he was fairly certain he couldn't have been infected.

Marshall had remained silent, sitting at a table in a small office, while a white-haired, bespeckled physician who looked to be in his seventies or maybe eighties entered the room and took the chair across from him. Marshall noticed that he was a plodding man, moving in slow motion, adjusting his glasses as he read Marshall's chart. He'd probably retired already but was called back into service because no other physicians wanted to deal with AIDS patients. The doctor introduced himself, extending his arm limply to Marshall's, a liquid handshake. Could the doctor move a little faster and get this thing over with?

The doctor opened a yellow folder without fanfare. Inside was a piece of paper that he scrutinized before passing it to Marshall. There wasn't much on it but the message was clear. Marshall stared at the paper in disbelief. There they were—three little letters followed by a plus symbol.

"Are you okay?" the doctor asked.

"Yes, I'm fine," Marshall answered. But he wasn't. He was melting inside. He was about to protest, to say that the test couldn't be correct, but knew it was pointless. He didn't want to be rude to the gentlemanly doctor, but he wanted out of the room as soon as possible.

He stood to go, and he could tell it alarmed the physician.

"Are you sure you're ready to leave?" the doctor said. "I can stay and talk with you if you'd like."

"No thanks," Marshall said. "I'm okay. I'd have been more surprised if I hadn't tested positive."

It was a lie, of course.

"Do you have a friend you can talk to?"

Marshall had to think about that one for a moment. "Yes, I have one."

Marshall was referring to Will Parsley, a colleague and former head of the ladies shoe department at Godchaux's. He had been Marshall's closest friend at the store and outside it. While Marshall was low-key and kept to himself, Will was flamboyant. Sometimes he embarrassed Marshall with his exuberant personality.

"Is he someone you can talk to about your status?" the doctor asked.

"Yes," Marshall said, but he wasn't sure he could locate Will.

"I'd be happy to stay with you."

"That's okay. I have only a half an hour for lunch, and I have to get back to work."

As he sat in Washington Park, he wondered if he'd been too abrupt with the doctor and speculated about his attention span with the customers he'd helped in the afternoon. He contemplated what to do next. Get another test to verify the results? That would probably be a waste of time. Change his diet and go on an exercise regimen? Good idea but unlikely. Max out the credit cards with trips to Europe and expensive clothes and jewelry? That didn't seem right.

Eventually, he decided the best solution was to sit tight and do nothing. Put some distance between him and the events of lunchtime. It was Friday. He would go out and get plastered, something that happened rarely, and when he recovered from the hangover, he'd go out and do something he had always wanted to do—make some friends. He was going to need them.

❖

Marshall Higgins had worked at Godchaux's his entire adult life. He'd secured a position at the Canal Street store just a few weeks after he graduated from high school, and he knew it was the place he would be for the rest of his life. He made great money at the classiest department store on Canal Street.

Marshall liked to joke that he started at the top and worked his way down. He began on the fifth floor in Records and Stereos. Within a year, he was working in Linens and the Bath Shop on the fourth floor. He liked it there because of all the candles. It smelled like vanilla, apple, cinnamon, and cloves.

After another year, he was in China, Silver, and Glassware on the third floor. His managers were uniformly happy with him, and after just five years with the company, he was asked to take a sales position on the main floor—skipping the second floor completely—serving the notoriously difficult women who shopped in the jewelry, cosmetics, gloves, and handbags departments. He loved it, and didn't consider it work at all.

Eventually, he became a personal fashion consultant, serving the Uptown ladies and the secretaries of the men who worked in the Central Business District. He focused mostly on clothes, but had the freedom to advise customers regarding any department in the building. When new merchandise came in, he called his ladies and informed them that new frocks were going out on the floor the next week, but he could get them a preview if they wanted one. He scheduled appointments in the beauty shop. Helped daughters navigate the Junior Shops. Guided sons through sportswear and shoes. He could find anything for anyone. He had created a network of managers in the Godchaux system and buyers outside the store that he could go to for advice. If someone needed something that was hard to find, or that needed to appear quickly, Marshall could track it down.

He came to the rescue when birthdays or anniversaries were forgotten. He was discreet and had learned how to keep the secrets of the men who had more than one woman in their lives and the women who went over budget. He made deliveries when necessary. He went above and beyond the call over and over. After a couple of years, Marshall knew the cream of the crop of New Orleans society. He'd developed a massive Rolodex that consisted of New Orleans' movers and shakers.

He earned a straight nine percent commission, when many other employees were making seven, and he also earned generous tips from his customers and products from manufacturers and suppliers who were grateful for his recommendations. He liked the money, but it was the satisfaction of helping others that made him tick.

Part of Marshall's success was that he was non-threatening, and he could sell to both men and women. He wasn't overtly effeminate, though he suspected many of his clients assumed he was gay. Marshall was plain. He had a small frame and wispy movements, but he wasn't frail or dainty. He moved with grace except for the occasional flap of the wrist. Marshall had a soft presence, with short, shiny brown hair and a small nose. He didn't have an athletic bone in his body.

His legs betrayed him first. The nerves in his feet and lower extremities had become damaged and started to send incorrect stimuli to his brain. He had begun to feel unexplained pains in his lower extremities, and gentle touches resulted in throbbing and discomfort. He was on his feet all day. He couldn't go on if they wouldn't cooperate. Assholes, he cursed at his feet. Just when he needed them most, they were giving up.

"When you say 'numbness,' what are you talking about?" Dr. Lindsey asked. "Tell me where it is." By now, Marshall was seeing a specialist in infectious disease. Robert Lindsey was a tall man, with an abruptness that made him seem callous. He had a sense of humor; in fact, he constantly employed it when working with his patients. It wasn't the kind of humor that produced big smiles. His eyes laughed more than his mouth.

"At first, it was tingling in my feet and I didn't think anything about it, but it continued," Marshall said. "Then I began to feel pain and sometimes I can't feel anything."

"What do you mean?" Dr. Lindsey asked.

"Sometimes I can't feel anything in my legs."

Dr. Lindsey prodded Marshall's legs while asking him if he felt anything. Sometimes he did and sometimes he didn't.

"Have you heard of neuropathy?" Dr. Lindsey asked.

Marshall said that he thought he had but he couldn't define it.

"It means that you have raised levels of blood sugar and that can damage nerves in the extremities of your body, especially your legs. Over time, your nerve endings can be destroyed, and you lose your ability to sense things like pain and temperature."

Marshall nodded.

"We're going to talk about some things you need to do," Dr. Lindsey said. "We'll start with diet and exercise, and see how things go from there. We've got to get this under control if we can because it can develop into something very unpleasant. Okay?"

"At least I know what it is now," Marshall said, trying to put a pleasant spin on the visit.

"Keep up that attitude," Dr. Lindsey said. "Because with this diagnosis, you're no longer a person who is HIV positive. You are officially a person with AIDS."

❖

"I heard the news. Thought you might need me."

It was Will Parsley, his voice clear as crystal in Marshall's ear as he lay on his bed. He'd been listening to a relaxation cassette tape in his Walkman and had fallen asleep with the earplugs still in his ears.

"Where have you been?" Marshall asked. "Wait. Don't tell me. You've been to Paris to see all the sights and shops, haven't you?"

"Not even close," Will said. "Besides, I was waiting for you so we could do those things together. We were going to walk arm-in-arm up and down the Champs Elysees and have romantic dinners. Remember? That's what we promised each other."

"Well, I wish you were here right now."

"Me too."

Marshall paused to collect his thoughts.

"I'm not doing so hot. I have neuropathy. I can't feel my legs half the time. I'm having trouble walking. But the worst part is that my doctor thinks the HIV might have made its way to my brain."

"That's not good."

"It's horrible," Marshall said. "Confusion. Speech problems. Vision problems. Balance problems. And dementia. That's what I get to look forward to."

"If you get dementia, I hope you'll be one of those guys who does funny things that make people laugh. Not the kind that becomes violent."

"I'm worried about my job. It's the one thing I love more than anything. Shopping for others."

"You might love it, but those people you serve, they take you for granted. They think you're just another nelly retail queen."

"You might be right."

"I know I'm right. The moment they find out you have the gay plague, they'll ditch your sorry ass. Every single one of them."

Marshall sighed because he knew it was the truth.

"Maybe you're right, but what can I do about it?"

"I think you should get even."

Marshall popped to attention.

"What do you mean, get even?"

"You know a lot about the very unique shopping habits of many of the city's upscale citizens." Will said it with a sneer. "What if you wrote it all down? An exposé? Something to leave to the world. 'Confessions of a New Orleans Fashion Consultant.' A modern cautionary tale."

Marshall wanted to say no, but a little part of him liked the idea. "I don't even know how I would go about it."

"Ahh," Will said. "You do know how. You saw the notice about the writer's group forming at Skylark, the one for guys who are HIV-positive. The purpose of the group is for them to write down their experiences. It's a social thing too. You might meet someone and become friends. Plus it's your favorite restaurant."

"Oh Will," Marshall sighed. "I don't even know if I can walk to Skylark."

"It's a wonder any of us can walk at all, we carry so many dead on our backs," Will said. "You'll find a way. Don't let the world make this our shameful secret. We are not the ones who should be ashamed."

❖

Marshall Higgins was one of the last persons to arrive at Skylark for the meeting of the writer's group. Even though it was the middle of October, the temperature was scorching, the last remnants of summer. He had wanted to go sit inside a cool theater and watch *The Last Emperor* but he couldn't find the money. His savings had dwindled to nothing. He could stay at home and watch TV. The first episode of "thirtysomething" had aired the previous month and he liked it.

Marshall didn't want to be early to the meeting. He wanted to see how many other people were there, though it was unlikely he would know a soul. He never went out any more.

He regretted being there the moment he sat down at a table. What in the world was he going to write? What possessed him to come here?

But he stayed. If the class petered out, he would stay and have dinner. No harm done.

He could charge it if he could find his credit card. The leader of the class was a young man who was full of enthusiasm but he'd have to work at controlling this crowd, small as it was. When he was asked to introduce himself, Marshall surprised himself by not only stating his name, but that he worked at Godchaux's as a personal fashion consultant. He said he wasn't sure what he would write. Deep down, he wasn't sure he would ever come back.

When the session ended, he prepared to leave, but a man who sat at the table behind him introduced himself.

"You should write something about being a fashion consultant," he said. "You could tell tales of the things the wealthy folks buy and what they do with their money."

Hmm, Marshall thought, where have I heard that before? Marshall's mind went immediately to one of his most loyal customers, Molly Collins. She had a fondness for expensive lingerie and exotic perfume. "If the walls of your home could talk," Marshall had once said in jest, wondering if he'd crossed a line.

"Honey, if the walls of my home could, they'd defer to the bed." She was salty and did not hold her tongue on any subject. He missed her. He hadn't seen or spoken to her in months, and he wondered how she was doing. He had called her, toward the end of his tenure at the store, but she hadn't returned his calls.

He thought of Rachel Narcisse, who threw spectacular dinner parties for her husband's oil and gas cronies, and for whom he had ordered numerous dresses in which she entertained. He recalled the women who lived near Coliseum Park, three sisters who always visited the store in a small pack before going into the Quarter for lunch. He wondered about the man who ordered lady's undergarments—for himself, and all the wealthy Uptown women who still purchased clothes for their sons who were well into their twenties and thirties.

"I don't know," Marshall said. "A personal fashion consultant must be discreet. I don't know if I could betray any confidences."

To his surprise, a circle formed around him. He shook hands, made small talk, and joined some of the men at the bar for cocktails.

As he was departing, the other men shouted out, "See you next week."

Was it just a toss-off comment, one of those things said when someone leaves. Did they really mean it?

Marshall could have predicted what would occur. In a city where things are known even before they happen, his diagnosis had become news to his coworkers and his clientele. He tried to keep it secret, and had taken pains not to inform anyone at work. Even though it was expensive, he filled his prescription for a new drug, AZT, on his own, bypassing the insurance company which would have alerted the human resources department. He went with one of the pharmacy chains instead of the smaller family-owned businesses where many of the moneyed people did their business. This bought some time, but eventually his health status was part of the Godchaux's grapevine.

He didn't bother too much with trying to figure out how it happened. Perhaps he was careless and left a receipt from the pharmacy somewhere. Perhaps a coworker heard him asking for AZT in the pharmacy and made a logical assumption. Perhaps a receptionist at the doctor's office knew someone at the department store and blabbed what she knew.

For the first time, Marshall began to use his sick days. He had experienced several infections in his legs and feet, and it made walking more difficult. He developed an unnatural stride that many of his coworkers noticed. About six months after his diagnosis, Marshall developed Bell's palsy, which caused the left side of his face to droop into a frozen mask, making communication difficult, but he regained most of the control over his facial muscles within two months. The most embarrassing event occurred on the day before Christmas, always a day of huge crowds and manufactured stress, when he lost control of his bladder near the end of his shift. It happened in the storage section of the Better Half Store where he was trying to track down a wool suit for a client. He couldn't believe what was happening to him, but knew he was in trouble.

He met with Human Resources the Monday after New Year's Day. He didn't want to go. The two people who ran the department were there. They were kind and understanding, he thought later, but they didn't give him much choice. He was given a generous severance package, and he'd have insurance for a while, but when it ran out, he'd have to pay for it. If they could find anything at the store for him to do, he'd be the first to be contacted.

No one ever called.

❖

Marshall was resting on his couch when Will checked in.

"You had to know what a bunch of two-faced backstabbers they were," Will said. "They like to describe us as one big happy department store family, but it's all a myth."

"Still, after all the years," Marshall said. "I was expecting more."

"Maybe a gold watch?" Will snorted.

Marshall adjusted his head on the pillow and lowered the volume on the remote control. When Will settled in, it could be a while.

"I just don't want to sound too judgmental," Marshall said. "That would be too much like them."

Will stifled a guffaw. "Judgmental? Girlfriend, we worked in the city's finest department store. We were retail queens of the highest order. We were judgmental to the max. In fact, it was our duty to be judgmental. How else were those people going to learn?"

Marshall smiled. "We were a little judgmental, weren't we?"

"Absolutely. We spent our professional lives promoting the purchase of things. We were shills for consumer products." Will was practically shouting now. "We were fools for capitalism."

"And we were good at it," Marshall said. Will's speech had

energized him. He sat up in bed, clasping his hand to his throat as if clutching pearls he had once sold to his wealthy clients.

He was out of breath.

"How do you feel?" Will asked.

"I feel fine," Marshall replied. Then he remembered who he was talking to. "I'm not so fine. You know that. I can't catch my breath, and I feel like my mind goes off and takes little excursions without me. I was trying to save my energy for the writing class."

"How's that going?" Will asked.

"I like it," Marshall said. "The guys are very kind to me. I think they know I'm losing it. They keep telling me to write down all my experiences at the store."

"Are you?"

"I'm trying, but it's difficult to remember it all. It's so hard to concentrate."

"Are you too fatigued to go on an adventure?" Will asked.

"What kind of adventure?"

"Someone in your apartment building is a supporter of David Duke," Will said. "There's a package down by the mailboxes that contains some bumper stickers for his campaign."

"Who's David Duke?" Marshall asked.

"Oh my," Will sighed theatrically. "It's worse than I thought. David Duke is the ultra-conservative white supremacist who's running for president. He's from Louisiana."

"Oh yes, now I remember," Marshall said.

"Do you still have a directory of your former colleagues at the store?" Will asked.

Marshall's eyes lit up immediately.

How long were these tests going to go on? Marshall had spent most of his morning being examined for signs of dementia, which he knew he didn't have. Dr. Lindsey said he suspected the presence of hallucinations and paranoid delusions. He'd also discovered hand tremors, decreased balance, abnormal eye movements, and an overall lack of coordination—all subtle signs of dementia. He chided Marshall for withholding information about his condition.

"I've been asking you for months if you'd had any of these symptoms and I wish you'd told me about the confusion earlier," Dr. Lindsey said.

Marshall kept his head down like a chastened schoolboy. "I didn't want to brag," he said, but then he realized that a flip answer might be recorded as yet another symptom of his alleged dementia.

Dr. Lindsey doctor sighed. "At least we can keep you out of the pokey with this diagnosis."

Marshall giggled and was surprised when the doctor laughed too. "Where did you get those bumper stickers?" Dr. Lindsey asked.

"Someone left them on my doorstep," Marshall replied, but he knew the doctor wouldn't believe it, thinking that there must be an elaborate story as to how and why Marshall had managed to get his hands on "I Support David Duke" bumper stickers.

"At least you have a great sense of humor, unlike some of the people who found them plastered on their cars, thanks to you."

Marshall had been caught, but not before he'd planted several dozen bumper stickers on the autos of his former coworkers. He wouldn't be charged. Everyone involved decided to throw up their hands and call it a prank pulled off by a disgruntled employee. But they didn't want it to be repeated.

"Well, if I'm crazy, how can I promise that it won't happen again?" he asked the doctor.

"Let's try to not have it happen again," Dr. Lindsey said in a tone of understanding mixed with sarcasm. "You're beginning to develop dementia but I don't think you're a danger to yourself or to anyone else. Not yet. But I am concerned that you're not eating well. You're skeletal. Can you assure me that you'll start eating more?"

"When I leave here I am going directly to the grocery store," Marshall said. When the doctor looked skeptical, Marshall assured him. "The Schwegmann's on Elysian Fields. It's on the way home."

It took Marshall almost ninety minutes to walk from the medical center to the Schwegmann's Store—fourteen blocks through the Quarter and another five to the store. When the automated doors opened and the cold air rushed around him, he felt a surge of relief. The walk had drained him. He grabbed a grocery cart instead of a basket, mostly because he could lean on the cart and it would keep him upright.

He began to cruise the aisles slowly, trying to make a decision about food, what he would eat that night. But he wasn't interested. Nothing looked good.

Out of the corner of his eye, he spied a familiar face. It was Rachel Narcisse. He wasn't surprised. It wasn't a chance meeting because he'd known she shopped at Schwegmann's on Wednesdays. She was so predictable, a creature of habit. She was the opposite of him, who was now so unpredictable.

Rachel Narcisse was a petite and very fit dark-haired woman, a stay-at-home wife who attended aerobics class religiously. She was very serious about the way she ran her household, the way her children were educated, the way she lived her life. Her most notable feature was the large, pair of black glasses that covered most of her face. They gave her an overly studious expression that made her appear like a modern-day Ninotchka.

Rachel Narcisse had purchased many items at his suggestion—shoes, jewelry, and little black dresses. He remembered that her most recent purchase was a cocktail dress and a small clutch purse for a dinner, something that honored her husband for his charity work.

She flitted back and forth to various aisles, working off a list, grabbing items to place in the cart, then replaced some of the items to their shelves before grabbing something else. She looked determined, like a worker bee. Her cart was loaded down, probably with healthy food for better brain stimulation. A small child, probably no older than two years, was strapped into the cart's kiddie seat, his chubby legs sticking out of the slots.

Marshall watched Rachel as she moved from aisle to aisle, shelf to shelf, reading labels and checking items off her list. When she looked up once, he waved his hand. Did she see him? She had to have seen him. But she didn't wave back, didn't acknowledge that he was there. It made him sad, then he became annoyed.

When Rachel pushed her baby-laden cart to the meat section, Marshall decided he would help her with her shopping, just like he had before. Marshall walked over to the hams. He was surprised there was such a large selection, and he began to claw through the refrigerated bin in search of the biggest one. He found one, a thirty-pound beauty at $2.99 a pound. Why was it so expensive? Oh, because it was spiral-cut. Very nice.

Rachel was off on one of her manic excursions to a nearby aisle.

Marshall remembered to lift with his legs and not his back, a mantra in the world of retail. The ham weighed a ton. He cradled it in his arms, and lugged it out of the bin with difficulty, legs bent to support the treasure, back swung out so he could maintain his balance. It took all his strength to get it to Rachel's cart, and he heaved it in, damaging a box of whole wheat crackers and squashing a small tub of yogurt.

Marshall huffed back to his own grocery buggy, still empty. He had his back to Rachel's cart, and he could hear that she had returned, but she didn't appear to notice the new item that now occupied her cart. Off she went on another excursion to another aisle. Marshall rolled his empty cart a few feet, in front of the case with lunchmeat and hot dogs. He grabbed a package of bacon and then zinged it through the air to the cart, whizzing past the boy and landing in the cart.

"You didn't see that," he mouthed to the child.

Marshall turned away, headed toward the aisle with the soda pop and snacks. He was happy that the bacon hit the target the first time around. Could a truly demented person pull that off? But he was disappointed with Rachel. People really shouldn't leave their children unattended.

❖

For weeks now, the guys in the writing group had been encouraging Marshall to write his Godchaux' memoir. The stories he could tell would make a great comic novel. If he wanted, he could write a wonderful self-help book for people who hated to shop and needed some helpful pointers to make their treks to the store less threatening. But Marshall still wasn't ready to break his confidences.

"I think what I'd really like to do is write some erotica," he said. He thought erotica sounded better than the word "pornography."

At the next meeting, Emile Abadie presented him with a bag full of pornographic magazines and a giant jet black latex dildo that belonged to George Morrison, a group member who'd died a few months earlier. Emile had made a sweep through George's apartment to get rid of the more salacious items before his mother arrived to bury him. He gave the items to Marshall for the purposes of "research."

Try as he might, Marshall failed at his attempts at erotica and pornography.

"I just couldn't get it down on paper," he told Emile. "I think it's because I have such limited experience. I've only been with three guys and it was all pretty vanilla stuff."

"What?" Emile stated. "Only three guys?"

"Yes," Marshall said.

Emile stared at him, wide-eyed. "You mean to tell me that I've been with more guys in one night than you've been with in your entire life?"

"Evidently," Marshall murmured.

"Give back your Gay Membership Card," Emile said.

"Very funny," Marshall replied. "But I will give back that big black dildo you gave me. That thing is just gross." He couldn't believe that someone could actually have a sexual experience with something of that dimension. It had to be at least fifteen inches long and four or five inches wide. Plus it had the nauseating smell of latex. It made him cringe when he looked at it.

"Your loss," Emile replied. "You can bring it back. I bet we can find a home for it."

Marshall stuffed the monstrosity into an old Gucci gym bag that he'd been carrying around, intending to visit a gym for a workout. After he went to Dr. Lindsey's, he'd reunite the odious item with its owner. If he could remember.

❖

"It looks like you're having some balance problems," Dr. Lindsey said. "And what about your ability to remember things? It seems like you are floating off somewhere while you've been sitting here. Does your mind wander off a lot?"

Marshall didn't want to answer. "No more than usual." He silently congratulated himself on providing a somewhat true but vague response.

Dr. Lindsey didn't blink once. "Are you having some difficulty with your gait? I'm thinking you might have vacuolar myelopathy, or spinal cord involvement with HIV, and it's making you less coordinated. When you sit, do you find yourself leaning off to one side or even falling?"

"Yes," Marshall conceded.

"I think it's because you don't have adequate postural support," Dr. Lindsey said.

That's how it went for Marshall, a series of questions followed by incriminating answers, a gigantic afternoon of defeat.

"I'm sorry, Marshall," Dr. Lindsey said when the exam was finished. "I know it's difficult. Do you want me to call you a cab to get you home?"

"No, I'm going to walk," Marshall said. There was no money for a cab. He stooped to pick up his Gucci bag.

"Is that heavy?"

"No, it's just fine," Marshall said, and he grabbed the bag before the doctor could pick it up. That was all he needed was for Dr. Lindsey to find out what he was carrying. He'd probably speculate that the reason Marshall had a poor gait was due to the fact that he was carrying around a bag with a giant dildo inside that caused him to list off to the right. He considered telling the doctor that he intended to use it as a crutch. It seemed big enough.

Marshall made it out the doors of the medical building and onto Canal Street, toward the river. Then he'd cut through the Quarter toward home.

When he made it to Baronne Street, he thought he heard a familiar voice calling to him. Was that Molly Collins? It had to be. She was getting out of a cab in front of Immaculate Conception Church. She must be going to noon Mass. There were a lot of people on the sidewalk. He moved closer to the church. The sign welcomed parishioners for Good Friday and Easter services. That's why there was a crowd. It was Good Friday. Marshall decided he'd join the crowd.

Why was Molly Collins here in this church? Possibly she was chasing a man. Perhaps she'd found religion. No, it was more likely she was chasing a man. Molly had been one of Marshall's most reliable customers for years. He'd found many an outfit for her, and in the process, he'd listened to her raucous stories, told in her deep cigarette-cured and whiskey-soaked voice. She'd gossiped and joked, and once even offered to set him up with a distant relative, the son of a politician from Baton Rouge. He hadn't seen her since his days at the store.

He wondered where she'd gone after calling out to him. The church was crowded, but the worshippers were beginning to sit down since the service was about to begin. He should be able to spot her now. Then he saw her, sitting in a pew just a few rows from the front.

Oh no, he thought. Now she needed his advice more than ever. Too much animal print. He recalled that he'd warned her about this before. And the slit in the back of her blouse—too much. Visible bra straps were never acceptable.

He slid into the same row and sat down a few feet from her.

"Molly," he whispered. She turned her head, then recoiled when she recognized him. She jerked her head back to the front.

"Molly," he said again. This time she shushed him. When he scooted closer, she turned to him and whispered, "I don't want to see you. I'm sorry."

Marshall couldn't believe what he'd heard. She'd been a friend. He'd coached her through many a potential social catastrophe. Now she wouldn't talk to him.

As he sat in silence while the service continued, he realized that she was like all the others, another person who'd abandoned him. Why did they do that? Why couldn't they help him now when he'd provided so much help to them? He had his head down, almost in prayer, steaming.

The parishioners had begun to collect in the aisle and walk to the front to receive communion. Molly stood and joined the line, but she didn't look back to where he was sitting. She'd left behind her purse, a giant white satchel with a large center patch and intricate stitching. She hadn't changed, lugging around a purse as big as a boxcar. She must have everything in there but the kitchen sink. Then a thought crossed his mind.

While everyone held their heads down in prayer, Marshall unsnapped the clasps at the top of the purse and opened it. He reached into his own Gucci gym bag and brought out the monster dildo. He stuffed it into the purse with the top of it lolling over the edge like a dead eel.

He got up to leave and managed to hobble down the side aisle, more than halfway back from the front of the church. He heard a bark-like screech, followed by a thud on the floor, then gasps from the church-goers. He imagined that she'd seen the purse opened and had begun to open it further to see what was lying inside. When she found it, the dildo was launched into the air with a shriek. He was happy he'd come to church, gratified that his load had been lightened.

❖

"Hey Marshall, how are you? Do you want something to eat?" It was Bella, and then Ruby, who joined him at the table at Skylark.

"No thank you," Marshall replied. "I'm not hungry."

"You are looking mighty frail," Ruby said. "Are you sure we can't get some food into you?"

"On the house," Bella said.

"No thanks," he said. "It wouldn't stay down anyway."

"Sure?" Ruby asked. "I could make some macaroni and cheese for you. That might do the trick. Whatever you need, sweetie."

"No thanks," he said. "I love the macaroni and cheese here but Will tells me that it gives me bad breath."

He gave a little self-deprecating chuckle.

"Will?" Bella said. "Who's Will?"

"Will Parsley. We worked together at Godchaux's. You remember Will Parsley, don't you?"

"Of course," Bella said. She raised an eyebrow. "When did you talk to him?"

"Just a couple of days ago," Marshall replied.

They just stared at him, exchanging quizzical looks.

"Marshall, we haven't seen Will in a few months," Ruby said. "How did he look?"

Marshall thought for a moment. "Fine, I guess. I just talk to him. Usually my eyes are closed."

He stood up and took several steps to where Emile was sitting. Emile was going over a short story that was going to be critiqued that night for the writer's group. As Marshall was leaving, he could hear Bella and Ruby whispering that Will Parsley had been dead for more than two years. That couldn't be right. They'd be talking later tonight.

"Hey Emile, how are you?"

"I'm great. Marshall," Emile said. "You look a little down. What's going on with you?"

"I'm not going to stay for class tonight. I'm too tired. I just stopped by to let you know that I intended to bring back the large, black you-know-what but I don't have it anymore. I ran into an old customer at Godchaux's and I gave it to her."

"Really," Emile said. Marshall could tell he was waiting for more information but he was too tired to explain it all.

"It's a long story," Marshall said.

"I'll bet it is," Emile said.

"It was the only job I ever wanted. It was the only one I ever had. I was good at it. Why did this have to happen? Why did they all turn their backs?"

Emile nodded his head. It was clear to Marshall that he didn't know what to say.

❖

"Are you ready?" Will asked.

"Ready for what?" Marshall responded.

Will Parsley heaved a deep sigh.

"We're going shopping," he said.

Marshall sat up on the bed. He felt as if a little bird had awakened inside his chest and it was cautiously spreading it wings.

"I don't have any money."

"We don't need money anymore."

"I don't have any credit cards," Marshall said. "Well, I have them, but they don't work anymore."

"We don't need those either."

"This must be a special trip," Marshall said.

"It's very special," Will Parsley said. "We are going on the shopping trip to end all shopping trips. Forget Canal Street. We're going to start in New York, and then we're going to London. And it goes without saying that we'll be hitting Paris."

Marshall couldn't believe his ears, but like everything else, it sounded too good to be true. "I can't go, Will. I've got so much to do."

"Name one thing," Will said in a holier-than-thou tone.

"I thought I might finally begin to write down some of my experiences at Godchaux's. There are a lot of funny stories. But I don't want to name names or betray any confidences."

"When will you stop being so protective of them?" Will said.

"Stop shopping for others. Let's shop for you."

"I don't really need anything."

"Yes, you do. Come on, Marshall. Let's go."

Marshall thought he felt himself rise but he couldn't tell anymore.

"Are you coming?" Will asked.

"Yes," Marshall said. "I'm coming. Wait for me."

And without Marshall's numb feet ever touching the ground, they were off.

SOLID GOLD SATURDAY NIGHT

W.L. Hodge

My grandfather Burton was forever trying to get me laid and he loved to dispense advice. "If you can't be good-looking," he'd tell me, "be excellent." He'd go on to explain that demonstration of mastery communicated to females that a male would be a good maker of babies. Burton didn't exactly demonstrate mastery—he never made any babies—but he told me he didn't need to be excellent. (In fairness: he looked, and looks, like Paul Newman.) He said I, on the other hand, needed all the excellence I could get. But I don't know. I've always thought I looked okay…in a dress. Burton was also forever trying to make me a man and it was as pointless as trying to get me laid—his wife Carmen raised me Catholic and I've known I was a girl inside since I was three years old, when I wrapped my bunny blanket around my waist like a skirt and shook my hips in the mirror while singing my favorite song (at the time): "Can I See You Tonight" by Tanya Tucker. I was in love with Tanya Tucker. Burton said there was hope for me yet.

Most of his advice was wrong (he said chicks liked it when you stared at their titties…and when you called them titties…and when you called them chicks) but, regarding excellence, Burton could not have been more right. Excellence works spectacularly…on *me*. I fell in love with the most excellent female ever tonight. My God, did she demonstrate mastery.

❖

My companion tonight: Connecticut immigrant Rev. Josie Becker, the new rector at All Saints' Episcopal Church in my "hometown" of Caledonia, Texas. Her likes include knitting, opera, and holding my hand while I cry. Her dislikes include anything I liked when I was 21. Or so I assumed. "Where can a couple of lesbians get into trouble around here?" she asked me. It was a bit disconcerting, hearing this from a priest in a sensible skirt and Keds. The lesbian-priest thing was still all so new to me.

As was the being-called-a-lesbian thing—though I, too, was wearing a sensible skirt and Keds. Excuse me: a sensible dress and Converse. "There's a Starbucks," I said. "It's inside a Target. But it's still a Starbucks."

"Not enough trouble, Asa. I feel like getting stupid."

It was six in the evening. "Getting stupid starts after your bedtime," I said. Her new job starts tomorrow at nine-thirty. Tomorrow is Sunday.

"I don't have a bedtime anymore," she said. "I'm forty years old."

I've been forty years old since I was four years old and I've never had a bedtime. I'm an architect—which means I don't sleep, period—and when I was a kid I routinely stayed up until three in the morning as Burton spent weeknights in an RV on his jobsites and Carmen worked six nights a week managing a honky-tonk in the Fort Worth Stockyards called Waltz Across Texas. Carmen was also an alcoholic and I'd stay up to make sure she made it home. To keep myself awake I'd tape songs off the radio and recreate them on the piano. Malcolm Gladwell said it takes ten thousand hours of practice to become an expert at something and…let's just say I got my ten thousand hours in. I was expert enough to land a gig playing cover songs at Ike's Ivory Bar across the street from the Austin Convention Center. I played Billy Joel's "Piano Man" at least ten times a night. I had to. I needed to pay for architecture school. I played covers for model supplies. I am not proud of this.

I am also not proud of this: I listened to oldies when I was a kid. I had to. I needed to eat. Burton went to work with Carmen on Saturday nights (for free drinks and cheap women) so I'd walk sixty-five feet west to my Tía Juana's house, her living room thick with the aroma of her famous enchiladas and her nephew Eloy (my second cousin), whose method of attracting females consisted of dousing himself in the Brut cologne he shoplifted from Winn-Dixie. Eloy's father Tío Teo hadn't been seen for a while and his mother Tía Teresa never ate. Instead she'd sit at the table with a pack of long brown More menthol cigarettes, a cordless phone, and a portable radio tuned to the local oldies station. She had three goals in life:

To put a bullet in Tío Teo's brain;

To prevent Eloy from putting a bullet in someone's brain; and,

To penetrate the switchboard at *Solid Gold Saturday Night* and request her favorite song of all time: "Love Will Keep Us Together" by the Captain and Tennille.

At press time, none of these goals has been achieved.

I once asked her why she loved that song so much. "It's not just the music," she said. "It's the memories." Tío Teo insisted that "Love Will Keep Us Together" be the first song played at her wedding reception... or so she said. I can't remember. I was there but I was six months old. Tía Teresa owned a record player and I once asked her why she didn't just play the song on 45 whenever she wanted. "It's our code," she said. "It means Teo and I still love each other."

Fast-forwarding twenty-five years or so: Josie and I weren't anywhere near code status.

We'd known each other less than forty-eight hours and, aside from a kiss in the turnstile at Caledonia High School's Homecoming last night, our chemistry had always been strictly platonic. That kiss was less a profession of passion than a protest against heteronormativity—a protest she initiated, not me. Falling for her would be (and is) pointless. I'm going "home" to Austin tomorrow after I watch her do her job like I said I'd do—and after I do the job I came up north to do. My birth certificate is locked in Burton's closet and he threatened to kill me if ever I went inside it—but he's somewhere in the Stockyards right now trying to get laid and, as such, I'll be popping over to *chez* Burton just as soon as I finish this journal entry. My therapist Dr. Woo is making me journal my feelings. It's pointless but we often do things that are pointless. Things like falling in love with our therapists. I call it love. Dr. Woo calls it transference.

Rewinding to six this evening: I was dying. My nutritional intake in the previous forty-eight hours had consisted of one museum-café sandwich and two More menthols. I told Josie I didn't want to get into trouble on an empty stomach as getting into trouble for me entails drinking and I do stupid things when I drink. An empty stomach gets me stupider much quicker. "Then let's eat," she said. "But you didn't answer my question. Where can we get stupid around here?"

Caledonia is dry and Fort Worth wasn't exactly the kind of place where a couple of forty-year-old lesbians could get stupid when I was a kid. "Well," I said, "there's always Denton."

Denton, sweet Denton: thirty miles from Caledonia and a world away, a parallel universe populated by slackers and sinners where the drumbeat of time staggered along at half-speed like a 78 RPM record played at 33. Nobody cared in Denton. It was legal to drink alcohol on the courthouse lawn. Correction: it was illegal but the law wasn't enforced. Nobody cared.

You can still drink on the courthouse lawn—or you can have dinner across the street at this nouveau-Southern-comfort-food place where the cornbread is locally sourced and the menu has no prices. (Think Waffle House meets Alice Waters.) Josie insisted on going inside. "This place is adorable," she said. "This *town* is adorable. Honestly, this is what I thought Caledonia would be."

Caledonia is what most people from Connecticut think Mississippi is. Denton used to be what I thought Austin would be. Austin is San Francisco—and not San Francisco in the Sixties (free love and cheap housing) but San Francisco now: tech bros and gentrification. I arrived in Austin and six hours later I wanted to leave. Twenty years later I still haven't quite gotten around to it. I'm not in love with packing.

I've always been packing but, in Denton, nobody cared. "Josie, you should have seen this town way back when," I said. "Denton was the Castro of the Dallas-Fort Worth Metroplex."

"Oooh, tell me more."

"Well, maybe I'm exaggerating a bit. There was only one gay bar," I said. "The bar was called The Industrial Zone." I believe I started tearing up a bit.

I know I'm tearing up now. I went back to Denton…and my gay bar was gone.

Besides my best friend (and other second cousin) Otilia (and me) there were exactly two other known lesbians in Caledonia: my middle-school gym teacher Debbie Armstrong and her "roommate," Otilia's high-school soccer coach Rachel Martinez. Coach Martinez told Otilia she could just call her Rachel. She also told her about a place in Denton where girls and other girls were at liberty to get busy in the bathroom. The place of which she spoke was a dingy warehouse on an unpaved, unnamed gravel road across the railroad tracks from the factory that made Corn-Kits instant-cornbread mix. No sign told you it was The Industrial Zone. You just *knew*. You walked up to this random-looking dude blocking an unmarked door, you waved your ID, and you whispered the passphrase. You only had to do this once. Whisper it once…and you joined the club. It was a place where everyone knew your name. Not your birth name. Your *real* name.

Everyone who's ever felt the need to walk into a gay bar for the first time has a story. Some say it's like a release from prison. Others say it's like coming home. For me, it was all these things…and more. It was like entering the promised land. The Industrial Zone was exactly as promised: dank, dark, and devoid of anything remotely resembling a heterosexual. Smoke and a mix from "Camelot" to Creedence filled the air, there was pool (not my thing) and dancing (not my thing, either), and there was exactly one bathroom which for some odd reason was always occupied. In short: it was what a gay bar is like when there's only one gay bar in town.

But Otilia and I didn't drive thirty miles through the land of Canaan (also known as North Texas) every weekend to go to a bar. For one: The Industrial Zone was barely a bar. There were exactly two kinds of beer—Bud and Bud Light—and only in cans. For another: I have never liked beer. But for a third: The Industrial Zone was more than a bar. It was a place to bask in the warmth of one's kind and work through the indignities of life amongst (yet apart from) the Canaanites. It was a place to check in and check on one's friends—and once you whispered that passphrase, you were a friend. And it was a place to take comfort.

The Industrial Zone showed you there were others in this world who were thinking and feeling what you were thinking and feeling—who were going through what you were going through—who talked like you and acted like you and (even in my case) looked like you.

Except she didn't look like me. I wouldn't have fallen for her if she'd looked like me. I wasn't in love with myself. I'm still not. But I was head over Keds in love with *her* and I went to The Industrial Zone to smoke, to admire, to worship. That bar was my one true church and I celebrated my Sundays on Saturday nights.

Her name was Lauren and she was the bartender.

She told me her story over a pack of More menthols. She'd emigrated to Denton from Baxter Springs, Kansas to study art at North Texas State. Art school hadn't paid off—there were about ten million other BFAs in Denton—and her previous position as a security guard at the Corn-Kits mill hadn't worked out. But she'd seen the milling about across the railroad and wondered. One night she crossed the tracks and she, too, said it was like crossing the Jordan. It just so happened that the previous bartender had quit the night before and Francine, the owner, was doling out cans of Bud her own damn self. Lauren's job interview consisted of mixing Francine a Manhattan. She'd been tending bar at The Industrial Zone for ten years when I first walked in the door.

Lauren was ageless, lithe and graceful, quick to crack a joke and quicker to snap you with her bar towel (her method of expressing mock displeasure). She was pharmacist, therapist, and (in my case) finishing-school madam. She was blunt. I'd been doing everything wrong: my makeup, my voice, my outfits, my shoes. But she was gracious. She liked my blonde hair, she said my hazel eyes were pretty, and she agreed with me that the best way to deflect others from the truth about one's facial features was to wear a cute pair of glasses. But she was merciless.

She forced me to switch from Keds to stilettos and walk in circles around the bar until I could do it a hundred times without wobbling. She made me do voice exercises, right there at the bar, to pull my voice out of my chest and my Adam's apple and up into my sinuses. And she made me talk with my hands. But I hate my big ugly man hands, I told her. "It's not the size of your hands," she snapped back. "It's what you do with them." I acquired mastery but she was honest: no matter how fabulous I looked, I was going to get dick-shamed at some point. She told me to suck it up, put up my dukes, and defend myself. She said I had it in me. I asked her once why she tried so hard with me, why she cared. "Because I love you, honey," she said. "Also, my birth name is Lawrence."

Her efforts were wasted. Austin didn't just have multiple gay bars—it had dedicated lesbian bars—and six hours after I came to town I walked into one and asked for my favorite drink. The bartender comped my Smirnoff-and-tonic. "Keep on keeping Austin weird, my *man*," she said. I slid off that stool, slinked out of that bar, stuffed my girl stuff into an apartment-complex dumpster, and spent the next twenty years unlearning everything Lauren ever taught me.

(In case anyone's wondering: Josie's birth name is Josie.)

Back in the present-day at *chez* Waffle, she looked up The Industrial Zone on her iPhone. "Here it is," she said. "On Fry Street." She showed me her phone and tittered. "Lookit, honey," she said. "Fry Street dead-ends into Scripture Street and it's two blocks east of Normal."

I blanched. In my day, Fry Street was light-years from normal: hippies strumming guitars over cans of loose change, grunge people moping over pitchers of beer, and artsy types spouting philosophy over cups of coffee much better than that shit at Waffle House. And absolutely everyone was smoking. But I made the mistake this evening of driving by for old times' sake.

Reporting damage: Fry Street is now located smack-dab in the middle of normal. *Hetero*normal. Frat boys and sorority girls getting shit-faced off jello shots, tech bros with MacBooks monetizing their social media presence, and exactly zero people were smoking. "You know, we could go to Dallas," I said. "There's tons of gay bars in Dallas." My grandfather built one of them: a place in Oak Lawn called Daddy's. He told me he had to dead-lock his RV every night for fear of being gang-raped by homosexuals. He insisted he was not into homosexuals. He did not use the word "homosexual."

Josie looked up Dallas on her phone. "That's thirty miles from here," she said. "Thirty miles from Connecticut is New Jersey." She signed the credit-card slip and plopped her napkin on her plate. "Come on, honey," she said. "It'll be fine."

"Fine" can mean any number of things.

❖

The doorman at the new Industrial Zone was young enough to be my kid and he made sure I knew this. "No need for ID," he told me. "You're good, ma'am." At least he called me ma'am. Funny, though— he didn't call Josie ma'am (she hates being called ma'am; it's as if he knew her) and he carded her. She giggled when he did it. It was a bit disconcerting.

The new Industrial Zone was more than a bit disconcerting. There was nothing industrial about it. Nothing about the place said Gay Bar except the rainbow-flag theme that threaded through everything from the rainbow-encircled neon Miller Lite sign to the rainbow-outlined neon clock in the shape of Texas. And the marquee advertised live music. ("Live music" at the old Industrial Zone entailed singing along to "Greatest Love of All" at closing time.) The place was packed— but with a clientele that wouldn't have been caught dead at the old Industrial Zone.

I saw straight people.

The Industrial Zone had been gentrified by heterosexuals: straight guys with beards who looked too mild to hate-crime me and straight ciswomen with X-ray vision out to dick-shame me. The straight guys were unobtrusive but the ciswomen congregated in a giant floating fire-ant ball of intertangled twenty-somethings in strappy sandals, skinny jeans, and matching low-cut T-shirts that (literally) said She's Taken but I'm Available...except for the queen bee, who wore a tiara. Bachelorettes, for fuck's sake, and they were blocking the bar. I gripped Josie's hand. "We could go to Fort Worth," I said. "There's probably gay bars in Fort Worth now."

"Fort Worth's just as far from here as Dallas," she said. "It's eight o'clock already and I've got work tomorrow." A song came over the PA and she put her arm around where my waist would be if I had one. "Lookit, honey," she said. "They're playing Cher. There's still some gay here, yet."

"That's such a stereotype," I said. "My grandfather Burton loves Cher. His favorite song is 'Gypsys, Tramps, and Thieves.' But it's because he says it was written about our family. He loves Cher. But he's way into females."

"That's the grandfather who's hiding your birth certificate in his closet?"

"The same."

Josie giggled. "When you finally get in there...let me know what else he's hiding."

I got her drift. "Not possible," I said. "He called me the f-word so much, I thought it was my birth name."

"Again...let me know what he's hiding."

We were unable to breach the line of bachelorettes so instead we found an empty two-top and a waiter with a beard informed us that the new Industrial Zone featured 37 beers on draft.

I've never liked beer and I was the designated driver so I asked for a Coke. Josie finally decided on one of the 37 beers and signaled her disapproval of my drink choice. "Smirnoff and tonic for her," she said. She knew my favorite drink. It was a bit disconcerting.

What I saw next transcended disconcerting. "Look over there," I said. "In the corner."

She looked. "A piano," she said. "So what?"

"This place is now a *piano bar.*" I shook my head sadly. "Give a bar a piano," I said, "and that piano will need someone to play it. That someone will be forced to play 'Piano Man' at least ten times a night. Don't get me wrong. Billy Joel's great. I mean, 'Allentown' is why I started playing the piano. I heard it on the radio when I was five years old and I said to myself: *I have got to make that music.* But...forgive me, Reverend, but I fucking *hate* 'Piano Man.'"

"You're forgiven." She reverted to her typical role in our relationship: that of my therapist. "I feel like this is coming from somewhere deep," she said.

"Very deep." I lowered my head. "I worked in a piano bar," I said. "Ike's Ivory Bar. Across the street from the Austin Convention Center. I am not proud of this." I buried my face in my hands.

She unburied them. "Wow," she said. "I'm impressed."

"Don't be." The waiter brought our drinks. Josie sipped her beer. I downed half my Smirnoff-and-tonic in one gulp. "It paid for architecture school...until it didn't," I said. "One night these tech bros came in. There were eight of them. That's key here. Anyway: you didn't just shout out a request. Ike had a system: you got a laminated card with a list of songs, you marked it up with a china marker, and you gave it to your server. Ike would tally up the requests then give me a list of songs to play. Well, tech bros are into disruption and these tech bros disrupted the system. They started shouting, 'We got a request! We got a request!' I kept playing. But they kept shouting. Started yelling. Finally, Ike came out of the office and tapped me on the shoulder. I stopped playing. 'These gentlemen have a request,' he said. I was like: whatever. I leaned into the mike and more said than asked: uh, what's your request. They rose, as one, and held up their cards, each of which featured but one single letter, which spelled out a word. Correction: two words. Eight letters. You do the punchline."

"'Piano Man!'"

"Bingo. So I played 'Piano Man.' Except I didn't play 'Piano Man.'"

"What'd you play?"

I giggled. "'Allentown.'"

"How'd that go down?"

"This might surprise you, but tech bros aren't in love with songs about the human impact of economic disruption," I said. "I damn near started a riot. Ike fired me on the spot." I knocked back the rest of my drink.

"That's too bad."

"No, it's not," I said. "I played covers to drunk people for tips. You, on the other hand: you sing opera. Opera. Now *that's* what I call music."

"I don't sing opera. I *sang* opera. Until I had to wear pants while singing it."

"I'm not in love with singing in pants, either," I said. "Or doing anything else in pants."

Josie took a rather large sip. "So, I'm a contralto," she said. "There's a saying in opera: contraltos get stuck playing witches, bitches, and britches. I was a witch in *Macbeth* and a bitch in *Aïda*. Then along came *The Marriage of Figaro*. I was like: oh, fuck, here come the britches. And here they came. I wanted to be Cherubin*a*. But they wanted me to be Cherubin*o*." She took another considerable sip. "It wasn't like it was some last-straw moment," she said. "I'd already decided to become a priest. And opera wasn't all I knew how to sing." She giggled. "I didn't have the world's most active social life in high school," she said. "Let's just say I had my weekend evenings all to myself. I used to lock myself in my bedroom with the radio and listen to—I can't believe I'm telling you this—*Solid Gold Saturday Night.* Pathetic, right?"

"Not as pathetic as listening to it with your great-aunts like I did."

"Wow, that *is* pathetic," she said. "But I can top *that.* I used to *sing along.*" She took another sip of beer. "There was one song I loved to sing above all others. Guess what it was. Hint: you mentioned it earlier."

"My family anthem, as sung by Cher," I said. "My grandfather would love you, Josie. But he'd love you anyway. You're female. He's way into females."

"Is he now."

"Funny," I said. "Back in the day, at the old Industrial Zone—the *real* Industrial Zone—you had to say a passphrase to get in. The first line of a Cher song. Guess which one." I sighed. "I first whispered that passphrase before half these people were born."

"Tell me about it." She finished her beer. "I'm going to the ladies' room," she said. "Wanna come with?"

The new Industrial Zone had a ladies' room. "I'll pass," I said. Texas state law says no girls like me in the ladies' room. There is no knife sharper than the gimlet eye of a bachelorette at a bathroom mirror and nobody dials 911 faster than a gentrifier.

Josie got my drift. "I'm sorry," she said. "It's just...you're always a woman to me." She was just being gracious. "I'll be back, honey. Don't leave home without me."

"I won't leave without you. But it's not home anymore."

She squeezed my hand. "I'm with you, honey," she said. "I'm with you."

And then she wasn't with me. I was alone, drifting in a sea of straight people, fair game for bachelorettes with eyes like infrared scopes. I tried to distract myself from myself by focusing on the movements of guys in shirts that said Staff around the piano in the corner—but my head was starting to swim. I'd barely touched my locally-sourced cornbread at dinner. It tasted like it'd been sourced from a box of Corn-Kits. I was on the precipice of inebriation, on the cusp of stupid. I do stupid things when I drink.

❖

Marx said that history repeats itself: first as tragedy, next as farce. Karl Marx would have loved "Allentown."

Josie hadn't been back at our two-top ten seconds before a voice came over the PA. "Denton, we have a problem," it said. "[Tonight's featured performer] is running late. We'll keep y'all updated." Groans arose from the bachelorette section and the room got uneasy. Five minutes later the voice came back over the PA. "Update," it said. "[Tonight's musical guest] is stuck in traffic." Bachelorettes started booing and I noticed a migration of men (both straight and gay) towards the opposite side of the room. The ciswomen started chanting We Want Music, We Want Music and from the corner of my eye I saw guys with shirts that said Staff securing glassware. The voice on the PA returned. It sounded afraid. "Question," it said. "Anyone here know how to play the piano?"

"She does! She does! She does!" It was Josie, screaming and waving her arms like a GI flagging down an incoming chopper. "She plays the piano! She plays the piano! She plays the piano!" She started jumping up and down and she's six feet tall so this is saying something. "Over here! Over here! Over here!" The woman is *a forty-year-old Episcopal priest*, for fuck's sake.

My heart dropped into my Converse. "Don't do this to me," I said.

"Come on, honey! This will be fun."

The crowd parted and a guy with a beard approached us. Gayness unclear. "Who's the musician?" he asked. He was the voice on the PA.

"She is! She is! She is!"

"Inside voice, Josie," I said. "He's standing right here." I turned to the guy. "I believe my companion's mistaken. I'm not a musician."

"She worked in a piano bar."

"Like I said: I am not a musician." He eyed me. "What bar?"

"Ike's Ivory Bar across the street from the Austin Convention Center." The woman has a memory like a steel trap.

He stroked his beard and nodded his head in approval. "Been there," he said. "Good times." He leaned in. "So, I just need you to help me keep things at a low boil until the talent arrives," he said. "I can't afford another bachelorette riot. Last one cost me five grand in glassware." He was the new Francine. "Can you sing?" he asked me.

Thank God: my opening. Or rather: my closing. "Can't sing worth shit," I said.

"But I can." Josie put on a pleading face. "Please, Mister Manager. Please let me sing." He eyed her like she'd tackle him if he said no. She was big enough, for certain.

"Fine," he said. "You can sing."

"But I'm not going to play," I said.

"There's a hundred bucks in it for you."

"I'll play."

"Thank God," said the owner. "Follow me, girls." The crowd parted again as he led us to the piano. He took the mike. "Ladies and gentlemen," he said. "While we wait for [whoever it was] to arrive, please welcome..." He turned to Josie and asked, "What's your name?"

She leaned toward the microphone. "Cherubina."

"Please welcome Cherubina." He put the mike on a stand. "Don't fuck this up," he muttered. "If there's a riot, you girls don't get paid."

I surveyed the crowd: gay and straight guys in the front, bachelorettes in the back—and crickets. Absolute crickets. I took my seat, lifted the key cover—and blanked. I forgot why the black keys were black and I couldn't find A. I wasn't going to kill. I was going to be killed.

But Josie.

She gripped the mike stand, adjusted it...then started to sway, her skirt softly swishing, her armies assembling, her mojo rising. She took the mike off the stand. "You came here tonight to see someone else," she said. *"And I came here tonight to make you forget they ever existed."* She turned to me. "GT&T," she whispered. That song starts on an A. I found A. She turned back to the audience. "This is a song," she said, "about a gal in trouble."

This is the same woman whose property it is to knit baby cardigans: She didn't sing that song. She died to it. She died a forty-year-old priest from Connecticut in a sensible skirt and Keds and was born again as a barefoot sixteen-year-old Southern girl in a low-cut dress with a night job and a bun in the oven. She drove that song like a freight train, all forward motion, barreling through every bar, rising to every high note, sinking to every low. She didn't sing that song like she'd sung it before. She sang that song like she'd lived it. *Like she was living it.*

I might have been playing. I can't remember. All I remember: is falling in love.

I wasn't the only one. The front of the room erupted. "Thank you," Josie said. She turned to me. "What next?" she whispered.

"You choose. You're the star."

"What can you play?"

Something arose in me: the desire to demonstrate mastery. "Baby," I said, "I can play anything."

She grinned. "That's good," she said. "Because honey…I can sing everything."

We were right. The crowd wasn't just into Cher. They were into Chaka Khan, too (Josie's pitch-perfect rendition of "I'm Every Woman" just *slayed*) and when she sang Adele's "Hello," there wasn't a dry eye in the place. (Except for the bachelorettes' eyes.) There was a dry throat, though. Josie asked for something to drink and *no fewer than ten men* ran to the bar where they almost came to blows competing over who would get to carry her water but then they made up and they all carried it, presenting it to her on bended knee like she was the queen of The Industrial Zone. Which she was. Then we played Queen. "Don't Stop Me Now" brought the house down and Burton would've loved it. He likes Queen. He'd love Cherubina. He's way into females.

The Queen was gracious. "Want to pick the next song?" she asked me.

"You choose. You're the star."

"No, you pick."

I pondered this. The song list at Ike's Ivory Bar was heavy on the Elton John. My second-most-requested song (after the dreaded PM) was "Rocket Man"—but I'm more into Sir Elton's slow, sad songs like "Harmony" and we'd already done slow and sad. "Bennie and the Jets" would have been a good way to start the show but we'd already started the show and guys with shirts that said Staff were starting to roll equipment into the room. It was time to end the show. I wanted Cherubina to go out on a high note—literally.

"Josie, you said you can sing everything."

"I did."

"But can you sing 'Greatest Love of All'?"

She took a deep breath. "Yes," she said. "Yes, I can."

Yes, she could—and yes, she did—and yes, by the second verse the entire room was singing with her. (Minus the bachelorettes.) Even I was singing and I can't sing worth shit. We sang that song like it was the national anthem. *Our* national anthem. Our family anthem. *We were family.* A holy spirit descended from where holy spirits descend if you're into that stuff and a love filled the room, a love that felt like it would explode through the walls of The Industrial Zone and expand to encompass the universe. I hadn't felt such universal love since Burton and I went to the victory parade after the Dallas Cowboys won Super Bowl XXVII.

That parade ended in a riot.

The Queen was gracious. "I sounded so much better once you guys started singing with me," she told the room. She took the mike off the stand and stepped into the audience. "Sorry to disappoint you," she said, "but I don't do this for a living. I'm a priest. That song says it's important to love yourself. And it is. Each and every one of us is worthy of love. But *this* is the greatest love of all: the love of God. We *do* achieve it. Each and every one of us. Friends, you are loved. God loves you. Just the way you are."

The queen bee, the bride-to-be, spoke up or shouted: "Shut up and sing, lady!"

"Funny. That's what my congregation says." It was funny. The front of the room agreed. Josie looked at her watch. "Ten o'clock," she said. "Past my bedtime. If you like what you heard tonight—either what I said or what I sang—you're in luck. I appear every Sunday at All Saints' Episcopal Church at 1519 West Broadway in Caledonia. You'll have to wake up early—show starts at nine-thirty—but there's no cover and the wine is free." She had that room so wrapped around her finger, they laughed at a joke about the *Eucharist.*

The queen bee hadn't drunk the Kool-Aid. She'd probably been drinking jello shots instead. "If you're not gonna sing," she yelled, "then shut up and let's hear from your *boyfriend.*"

The Queen was not amused. "That's not nice," Josie said. "Apologize. *Now.*"

She's so sweet. She holds my hand while I cry and she defends me in public. But I was sick of being defended. Lauren told me I had to defend myself. She said I had it in me. "Thanks, Little Angel," I whispered, "but I got this." I leaned into the mike on the piano. "Bride-to-be, do you have a request?" I asked.

She yelled, "Ladies…what do we wanna hear?"

They rose, as one, and screamed at the top of their lungs: "'PIANO MAN!'"

Then I did something stupid. I do stupid things when I drink.

The song list at Ike's was heavy on the Elton John. The tenth-most-requested song was "The Bitch is Back." It was popular with women celebrating divorces. It seemed like an appropriate substitute for "Piano Man" tonight but the guitar riff at the start of "The Bitch is Back" is a bitch to play on the piano. It requires loose fingers. And…I don't know, something Josie said in her sermonette stuck with me: the title of a song, another Billy Joel song, a song about a love unconditional, a love unceasing, a love that required no changing. And Josie had that room eating out of the palm of her hand tonight. She connected. "Allentown" was the last straw for Ike. It wasn't the first. He said I lacked a connection with the audience—but I had nothing in common with tech bros and conventioneers. I didn't want to connect. Excuse me. I wanted to connect exactly once: with the contingent of smoking-hot females in glasses who wandered into Ike's from a librarians' convention back in 1998. We *connected*. They asked nicely if I'd play them a song. The name of that song was "Piano Man." I played them that song and I played it and played it. I'll do anything a female in glasses tells me to do.

Josie wears glasses. "Be nice, sweetie," she whispered. She called me sweetie? She'd always called me honey.

"Being nice." I leaned into the mike. "One 'Piano Man' coming right up."

"Wait." It was the bride-to-be. "We got another request."

"Thank God." Right?

"Ladies," she yelled, "what do we want to see?" The bachelorettes had already risen. "HIS DICK!"

There was something in how Josie had handled her heckler: with aboveness, with humor, with grace. The grace of God, if you're into that stuff. She did not do unto others as was done unto her. She went high when others went low.

I ain't Josie.

Lauren always said I had it in me. "Bless your heart," I said. "If I showed you my dick, you'd cancel the wedding." Even Josie thought this was funny. She tried to not show it. She failed. "I'll play you a song, you ex-wife-to-be," I said. "But it ain't gonna be 'Piano Man.' See, I had this gig in a piano bar back in college. Played covers. Requests. I played 'Piano Man' at least ten times a night. I'm almost as sick of that song as I am of Disney princesses like you and your brat pack invading our territory and blocking the bar."

"Amens" and hoots of approval. I'd connected with the audience. Most of it, at least.

"I'll play you a song," I said. "No. I'll play *us* a song. This song is for *us*. For those of us who remember when you people wouldn't get caught dead in places like this." More "amens." "This song," I said, "is for those of us who remember when places like this were the only places we could be ourselves without getting killed." Even more "amens." "This song," I said, "is for those of us who listened to people like you and hid our true selves from ourselves and the world. This song," I said, "is for those of us who've had enough of being told who to fuck, who to marry, and where to go to the bathroom." I stretched my fingers. That song requires loose fingers. "I once was lost," I said. "But when I walked into The Industrial Zone twenty-one years ago…I was found. But then I lost myself again. But now I'm found again. And bitch, I ain't ever going back." I cracked my knuckles. "Speaking of bitches and back: the name of this song is 'The Bitch Is Back.' Please rise for our national anthem."

But the room had already risen.

It wasn't the size of my hands. It's what I did with them.

I played them that riff and I played it and played it. The room didn't wait for the second verse to start singing along. The *whole* room. The bachelorettes were singing the loudest. Then some of them jumped on top of the bar. They started kicking glassware. That's got to hurt in strappy sandals. Guys in shirts that said Staff started trying to pull girls off the bar. The girls didn't like that. They started kicking faces. That's got to hurt in strappy sandals. It's not a bachelorette party till the cops arrive. The cops arrived. It wasn't a bachelorette party. It was a bachelorette riot. We didn't get paid. I was banned from The Industrial Zone for life. Cherubina was asked to come back next week.

❖

The Queen was gracious. "Of course I'd never go back without you," she told me as we walked back to my peach-colored Beetle. "I sounded so much better when you were playing with me." She took my hand. "We had something good going tonight," she said. "Something great. My nipples were hard. Honestly, it felt like sex. I feel like I need a cigarette."

"Funny."

"I'm not joking. Be so kind as to spot a girl a cigarette, would you?"

Again: Episcopal priest. "Josie, you can't smoke," I said. "You have a reputation to uphold. Someone might see you. You'd be inciting others to sin. It'd be scandal." Also, I had only two More menthols left.

"I suppose you're right," she said. "It would be scandal."

I stopped walking. "You know what else would be scandal?"

She bit her lip and smiled. "Tell me."

I smiled back. "I'll show you instead." I tiptoed, took her face in my hands, and we opened each other's lips like cottage doors on a snowy evening, our tongues like little girls with new puppies at Christmas. It wasn't protest. It was passion. It was pointless. I have to go back to Austin tomorrow…but we often do things that are pointless…and I do stupid things when I drink. Things like journaling in a moving car. Things like letting Josie drive. And things like falling in love.

Washington's Retreat

Stephen Greco

Joey brought the tofu just as Anthony was unloading the cart at the checkout counter.

"Oh, that's the firm, Joey, see?" said Anthony, looking at the package his little brother was proffering.

"Isn't that the kind we usually get?" said Joey.

"We get extra-firm because I thought you liked it. But we can get this, if you want."

"No, I want extra-firm. I'll get it." Package in hand, Joey headed back toward the refrigerated case where they kept the tofu.

The girl at the checkout counter, tattooed and pierced with a mess of blond and blue hair, smiled wanly as she continued to tally the items Anthony was pulling out of the cart: Cans of chick peas and black beans, bags of jasmine rice and faro penne, bunches of carrots, celery, kale, and leeks, a jar of half-sour pickles. Fresh Fantastic didn't carry meat—despite the store's promise to "expand your horizons, enhance your palette, and explore the limitless potentials of food, so that you, too, can find your edible love"—so they'd have to pick up the steaks they'd been talking about over at Fleisher's in Park Slope, maybe the next day.

"He your helper?" asked the checkout girl.

"Yeah," said Anthony.

"Cute. Son?"

"No. Brother."

"Oh."

Anthony knew he looked older than his age, which was sixteen, but really—old enough to be Joey's father? His fake ID said twenty-one, and he could pull off that age flawlessly, but even so, what kind of world did this girl live in? Then again, Anthony thought, why would anyone be paying close enough attention to him and his brother, who was eleven, to see the truth? And anyway, what kind of world was this actually—Clinton Hill in the era of "Brooklyn USA"—in which two black-haired, blue-eyed boys in basketball clothes shopped for a week's worth of organic food, conspicuously without a mom or dad? Dickens' orphans were no more self-sufficient. A sharp observer might have noticed something nuanced at the checkout counter: the gently parental kind of patience with which the older boy dealt with the younger; the practiced, adult kind of teamwork with which the brothers went about this necessary weekly chore; the decidedly grown-up kind of sexiness with which the older boy casually showcased his dark good looks with a baggy, black nylon tank top and coordinated shorts, worn with black-and-white striped Adidas shower slides.

It was a warm Saturday afternoon at the end of May. Joey's school would be out soon, and Anthony would have to figure out the summer. July would probably mean summer school, since P.S. 287 offered a history program that Joey was excited about. Maybe in August they could go upstate again, to hike in the Shawangunks. It was just the two of them now, and they'd made a pact that this was the way they were going to keep things, so they could remain calm and safe and together. During the previous year their mom had died of a heroin overdose, after being repeatedly roughed up by a crazy boyfriend, and the boys had been forced out of her place in Fort Greene, basically onto the street. Anthony found a new place on Craig's List in an old building on Washington Avenue near the Navy Yard, a row house that had been converted long ago into industrial space and then into a den of artist's studios. Their mom's brother, who reluctantly came up from Miami for the funeral, had been convinced to co-sign the lease, while dismissing the new place as "the ass end of Brooklyn." The landlord was a painter, who lived and worked on the ground floor. He asked no questions about two boys living together and probably wouldn't do so, Anthony knew, as long as the rent got paid on time.

"Here," said Joey, reappearing with the tofu.

"Thank you, sir," said Anthony.

That was the last item. As they left the store, laden with bags,

Anthony suggested they treat themselves to fruit smoothies at the store's little sidewalk stand. Joey had a Berry Blast—blueberries, strawberries, raspberries, and raspberry sorbet—while Anthony opted for Mango Madness—mango, strawberries, pear, and pineapple juice. *Such a good kid*, thought Anthony as he watched Joey slurp away contentedly, sitting there at the picnic table. *He deserves the best.* Anthony had made it a priority to see that Joey stayed in school and not be derailed by domestic chaos. Next year the boy would be in the sixth grade and his prospects were good, excelling as he did in social studies and an advanced program called Go Math! The less Joey dwelled on the darker side of his mother's death, the better they'd both be, Anthony thought. It was sad to be without parents, but there was plenty of love in their tiny family and plenty of room for Joey to develop individuality that, who knows, real parents might squelch.

As for Anthony, there was plenty of room for something to develop too, but he wasn't sure what. He had no friends, really, except for the guys he saw at the gym. He'd never been particularly hemmed in by his mom, except during her periodic attempts to clean up and get respectable, but it was certainly easier now, without her inconvenient-though-never-very-convincing objections, for Anthony to go on dating the older men who paid well for the company of a handsome youth with good manners and a conversational nature. This was something he'd fallen into—fine. It was paying the bills now—fine. Whether or not he'd ever find the time to develop a real boyfriend or girlfriend, or go to college, and whether or not what he called his art was going anywhere, time would tell.

The sculptures he made with junk he found in the street—small stuff at first, when they lived with their mom—were getting bigger now that they had more space. "Assemblages" are what his landlord called them, when he first got a look at them, with encouragement that thrilled Anthony. The landlord even said that he might include one of Anthony's pieces in a fall show he was organizing in Bushwick of so-called "outsider art." *Keep going*, said the landlord. *It's all about discovery.*

What Anthony had discovered in the previous year is that he and his brother were indeed outsiders: they'd become that, they'd been made that. The trappings of middle-class life, as defined by trapunto-covered sectionals and matching graphite-steel washers and dryers—that was for their mom's parents' generation, not for them. Born into Tudor Revival splendor on a fancy street on the "good" side of the Sunset Highway in Bay Shore, Long Island, their mom had been squeezed, after the death of her parents, into a narrow, less-than-middle-class margin of barely dignifying material comfort that she scrambled to inhabit for as long as she could. She'd been a dancer, which was never a workable life plan. Now her boys were well below even that margin, let alone the Oz of glass towers that New York was quickly becoming, and Anthony had no plan yet either, except for him and Joey to survive.

Instead of a plan, he aimed for a kind of realistic vision about life for him and his brother, an unillusory view of the terrain they inhabited—akin to the one Joey expressed when he came home from school one day excited that the topography of New York that had been so important during the Revolutionary War was still discernible today. They had been studying the Battle of Long Island.

"There are these hills," burbled Joey, "called the Heights of Guan, and between them these passes where the British tried to get to the Americans. And they're still there, in parks and stuff—you can see 'em on a map. And right *here*, Anth, where we are, in 1776 was all forest and farmland, and a block away in the river is where the British kept Americans imprisoned on ships…"

Anthony was proud of his brother's interest in history. That could help point the way forward. So, Anthony thought, could his own understandings about the city. This was indeed the ass-end of Brooklyn, and very soon it, too, might be more Oz. So the boys would have to remain alert, flexible, ready.

A few hours later they were home.

"Ramen OK?" asked Anthony, from the kitchen counter.

"Sure, I guess," said Joey. He was at the table, busy with his iPad.

"I'm thinking the usual thing—mushrooms, scallions, tofu."

"Shitakes, please."

"Oh, right—we got some. So like in twenty?"

"OK," said Joey.

The meal was one of their favorites, and an added benefit was that it cost no more than a dollar per serving. Anthony would have a bowl with Joey and see the boy settled in for the evening, before going off on his date—dinner with a Londoner named Matthew, a media executive who visited New York often on business and liked to see Anthony for dinner and then for an hour or so in his hotel room. For this Anthony would earn $3500—more than enough to cover the next month's rent, utilities, health insurance, and a lot more ramen and kale. When Matthew had texted to see if Anthony was available, he said he wanted to try a new, upscale Japanese restaurant that offered kaiseki cuisine. Anthony googled the place. It charged $375 a head for the traditional multi-course Japanese dinner "presented with the elegance of tea ceremony," and $90 each for the sake pairing that Anthony knew that Matthew would order.

We're having a little ceremony of our own right here, thought Anthony, as he brought over a full portion for Joey and a small one for himself. The boys ate at a massive, antique wooden table that was in place when they took the apartment—a possession of their landlord, who let them use it in exchange for continuing to store it there. Their home was simple: rough wooden floors and rickety old windows; a few Ikea pieces mixed with the perfectly good "previously owned" items they'd found in the street, like a bench-like sofa that would not have been out of place in a doctor's office. Anthony had made it a point to buy new beds and bedding.

"How's the pageant thing going?" asked Anthony. It was Joey's end-of-year social studies project: a Revolutionary War pageant to take place outdoors, in Fort Greene Park, on the steps of Prison Ship Martyrs' Monument.

"It's going," said the boy. "Are you still coming?"

"Sure I am. Next Friday, right?"

"Yeah."

"OK. Do you know what they'll do if it rains?"

"I don't know, they didn't say. I guess we just keep doing it. You know it was very rainy when Washington made his retreat."

"Fine, but what about the audience?"

Joey mugged a look of comical alarm, which made them both laugh.

"We're so soft nowadays," said Anthony. "Hey, need help with your lines?"

"I only have one, I told you."

"Let's run it."

"Oh…," said Joey, balking.

"C'mon, Joey," said Anthony. "Let's have it."

The boy took a moment to compose himself, then declaimed, "Good God, what brave fellows I must this day lose!"

The line hung there in the air, for a moment.

"Wow, awesome," said Anthony.

"Ya think so?"

"Yeah, Joey, absolutely! Again, please?"

The boy shifted his position to get more into character.

"'Good God, what brave fellows I must this day lose!'"

Anthony shook his head in admiration.

"That's great what you do with your arm—that gesture!"

"And I have a three-cornered hat and a spyglass!"

"No way. And a wig?"

Joey laughed.

"They said wigs were too expensive," he said.

"So you're Washington."

"Yeah, I'm Washington and it's August 22, 1776, and the British have him cornered in Brooklyn Heights, and in the middle of the night he evacuates his army across the river to Manhattan. So it's a British victory and a loss for Washington, but it's a necessary loss, so he can keep his army intact and go on to win the war."

"Wow, A-plus, buddy," said Anthony. "Or wait—they don't give grades in your school, do they?"

Joey grinned.

"I'm between 'major documented progress' and 'documented mastery,'" he said.

"Oh," said Anthony.

"Between nine and ten out of ten."

"I see."

Three hours later, Anthony was sitting cross-legged on the floor of a rustic teahouse in the corner of a quiet garden on Manhattan's lower West Side, not far from the Meatpacking District. He was with his date Matthew, in one of seven such teahouses that comprised the restaurant

Wabi, where the hostess had greeted them at the door and walked them through a hallway and out onto a stone path, through the garden to the six-tatami-mat room that would be theirs for the evening. From there their server took over—an elegant, kimono-clad lady of a certain age who'd already served the first few courses, after each of which she knelt for a minute at the service entrance, to make sure the men were enjoying their food, before slipping out and sliding the shoji screen shut.

"I almost feel we shouldn't be talking," said Anthony.

"I know," said Matthew. "There's such a lot of contemplation to be doing."

So far they'd had four courses, starting with an *amuse bouche* of deviled egg with lobster, truffle, and ponzu jelly, served on a green ceramic leaf—Matthew seemed to know all the ingredients. Then a trio of appetizers, conger eel rolled with burdock root, broad beans and mashed taro, and octopus with vegetables dressed in vinegar and miso, served in three precisely formed ceramic bowls—hexagonal, circular, and paisley-shaped. Then a second appetizer of fried trout and bamboo shoot in dashi sauce with wakame sea weed, served on a squarish platter glazed with a sketch of irises clumped on a rivulet, surrounded by fireflies. Finally a sashimi course, served on a wooden plank. From outside the teahouse, whose shoji screens to the garden in front of them remained so far closed, came only the sound of a trickling stream.

"Do you think we could be the only ones here tonight?" asked Anthony.

"That's the way these restaurants are," said Matthew. "Very private."

"The presentation is amazing," said Anthony. The wooden plank for the sashimi was carved in a subtle wavy motif.

"They use vessels that harmonize with the food being served, which itself is themed to the season."

"Harmonize?"

Matthew pointed to the platter.

"Fish, rippling water," he said. "Springtime, green leaves, insects coming alive…"

"Oh. Nice."

"Those three bowls, very severe and geometric?"

"Uh-huh?"

"A bit of visual wit."

"I see."

"You're not enjoying it."

"On the contrary, I'm enjoying it a lot." Anthony was speaking with what he thought of as his twenty-one-year-old voice.

"Good," said Matthew. "I want you to."

"I was just thinking today at the market how I needed more ponzu jelly in my life."

Matthew smiled peacefully. Then another silence—not awkward; more aesthetic in nature, as they continued to contemplate. Also, possibly the effects of the sake were kicking in. Matthew was in a grey suit, an open collared shirt, and black socks; Anthony was in neat slacks and a black silk shirt that was unbuttoned enough to expose a good portion of his smooth, well-formed chest. He was barefoot, having decided it would be elegant to wear his new Prada loafers without socks.

"How was your day?" asked Matthew.

"Oh, you know—I worked a little on a piece, I went to the market, I helped my brother prepare for his school's social studies pageant."

"Oh?"

"Yeah, apparently George Washington withdrew his troops from Brooklyn near where we live and saved his army from total defeat by the British."

"Lord."

"We live right near the river where some of His Majesty's ships were parked to store prisoners of war."

"I see."

"Apparently lots of dead Americans were thrown overboard and washed up near our street."

"Some people will do anything for attention."

"Do you mean…the British or the Americans?"

"Fair point."

"He's obsessed, my brother."

"A budding historian."

"Could be."

"Thank goodness we're not at war now," said Matthew, giving Anthony's big toe a little wiggle and tug.

The attendant called out gently to announce her presence, then slid open the shoji screen and served the next dish: kinmedai—which Matthew explained somewhat helpfully was a fish known as alfonsino—smoked with pine needles, presented with a tempura of wild mountain vegetables and shira-ae mousse—mashed tofu. After which came lidded bowls with lobster steamed in smoked onion soy milk with herbs, presented with beet purée; and then a mini bamboo bento box of seared duck with avocado miso and fresh greens.

Observing the efficiency of their server became more thrilling with each course, while from outside in the garden now came the sound of other parties who'd arrived and, sometimes, footsteps near their tea house. It was after the server had delivered a palate cleanser—basil sorbet on a dish shaped like a chrysanthemum blossom—that she made a small gesture inviting their approval and then slid open the shoji screens in front of them. Revealed was the spring garden at night, a lush verdancy graced with a little stream and illuminated by lanterns, discreetly populated with other rustic tea houses glowing around the garden's edge.

"Very pretty," said the server, almost to herself, as she retired and left the men to their sorbet.

"Did she just tell us what to think?" asked Matthew. He was joking, as by then they were both in love with the lady's unassuming grace.

"She was quietly overwhelmed by the beauty," said Anthony, "as she always is, night after night."

"Imagine that," said Matthew, taking a tiny bite of his sorbet. "Staying alive to the shock of beauty, time after time."

"At her age, too," said Anthony.

"How old do you think she is?"

"Hard to tell. Not young, though."

"No."

"Age can be so difficult to assess."

The point was an impish jab at Anthony, who was at least forty years younger than his companion.

"Matthew, I…"

"Sorry. I know you're sensitive about your age. Perfectly understandable in someone who's twenty-one."

Anthony cocked his chin toward the garden view.

"It's amazing to think this exists in Manhattan."

"It's amazing, frankly, that you exist." Matthew was staring not at the garden but at Anthony.

"Now, you know I'm way too young to get married," said Anthony, playfully.

"Actually, no, you're not," whispered Matthew, growing serious for a moment. "I just want you to know how much you're beginning to mean to me. I know you have to go home tonight, but I hope the next time I come over, probably in September…"

Anthony tried to formulate a response, but couldn't think of anything, so they both just sat there.

A rough-edged platter patterned like bark, bearing wagyu beef shabu-shabu and green asparagus, with wild rice arrived. A round lacquer platter, orange like the sun, framing an artful dessert presentation of fresh nashi pear, grapes, persimmons, grapefruit, and pomegranate, with vanilla custard and quince jelly. A pot of tea that Matthew called "matcha."

"So you worked a bit on a sculpture today?"

"A thing I'm doing with a bicycle wheel I found."

"Sounds interesting."

"We'll see."

"Does art run in your family?"

Anthony laughed.

"My mother was a dancer and a drug addict. My grandfather was a neurosurgeon and a gambler. All of those things are out, for me. I don't know much about my father."

"Is art what you want?"

Anthony thought for a moment.

"I don't know that my wanting anything would help it happen, so maybe why bother?" he said.

"Awfully dark for twenty-one."

"Matthew, I'm really sixteen." A pause, and then: "By rights, I should be skateboarding under an elevated highway about now."

Matthew took another sip of the daiginjo sake that had been poured for dessert.

"I know what you mean," he said expansively. "So am I, in a way, sixteen—you know? We all are. It's something to hang onto, if we can."

Anthony sighed.

"Amen," he said.

"I'm just saying you deserve the best," said Matthew, turning toward Anthony. "And Vincent, if there's anything I can do to help you get to the next level...if sculpture is your thing, I can introduce you to some people."

"Thanks. We'll see. I really appreciate it, Matthew. But fate is part of this, too, you know, and that shit is strong."

"Absolutely. Without question. No judgment, Vincent, but I've seen guys like you go on to do great things. Sometimes you have to go a little backwards, in order to start going forward—even if you don't know where the direction of forward is."

"From where I stand it's a little hard to see what's forward and what's backward."

"Fair point."

On Friday it didn't rain and the school pageant was a big success. With the help of loudspeakers and recorded music, the sweep of the entire American revolutionary effort was summoned passionately by a very committed cast of five-to-twelve-year-olds. The event, which took place on one of the terraces below the Prison Ship Martyr's Monument in Fort Greene Park, drew at least a hundred people—parents, family members, other school children, and passersby who happened to be in the park that day. And following the pageant's sketches and tableaux was an informal potluck picnic.

Anthony wouldn't have missed the day for the world—though he did have to turn down a date that would have brought him at least another $3000-4000. *No worries*, he thought. There were several things lined up for June, and Matthew was texting about the idea of flying him over to England to look at some gardens or something.

"You were awesome, buddy," said Anthony, giving Joey a big hug when the boy ran over to him, a bottle of orange juice in hand.

"Thanks, Anth. Did you see the American prisoners?"

"I did. They looked like zombies."

"Yeah, they were supposed to! My friend Martin's dad works on Broadway and did the makeup."

"Very convincing." Towering above them was McKim, Mead,

and White's 150-foot-tall Doric column with a bronze urn on top—an eternal flame honoring the thousands of American Revolutionary soldiers whose remains are interred in a vault at the column's base.

"Oh, and Anth—people want to thank you." At which point Anthony noticed that all the students who had taken part in the pageant were gathered around.

"The kids wanted to say thank you for the wigs," said Joey's social studies teacher, Henry, whom Anthony had met at the beginning of the school year. "They really added a realistic touch and the kids had such a blast wearing them."

"Thank you, Anthony," came a chorus of happy little pageanteers, many of whom were wearing, under their three-cornered hats, the white and brown wigs Anthony had bought for them, with tight side curls and bowed queues in back.

"Thank you, Anthony," said the fifth-grade Jamaican girl who'd played Admiral Howe.

"Oh, you're very welcome," said Anthony. "You guys did such an amazing job. Congratulations!"

"Really, we're very grateful," said Henry, as the gang ran off to their families and friends.

"It was a pleasure to be able to do it," said Anthony.

"Joey's a real star, you know."

"Broadway calling?"

"That too, but I meant in school. We've all got our eye on him. He's very special and has lots of potential. May I ask if you've thought about secondary schools for him?"

"Isn't it...early for that?"

"Not at all. The reason I bring it up is that I've got connections at Lehman—they have a high school of American Studies there—and at Brooklyn Latin, which is closer."

"Oh."

"If you'd like, I could put in a word. Or we could discuss it further, at your convenience."

"Thanks," said Anthony. "Yeah, I guess we should. Appreciate it."

"Good," said Henry, "here's my card."

Anthony took the card and studied it, and Henry continued.

"You *are* his guardian, aren't you?" he said.

"Oh, yes," said Anthony. "I am."

"Great, yeah. I mean…you seem a bit younger than most of our adults."

"I know, I know."

"And listen, don't let the financial side worry you. I mean, maybe it's not an issue, but if it is, there are great scholarship programs that were made for kids like Joey, no matter what their deal is."

"Good to know," said Anthony, "though that probably won't be an issue."

"I mean, there are even good places abroad. I know that Cambridge, for instance, has a terrific history program that's open to American students."

"Do they?"

"Positioning Joey for that would be very possible."

"Hmm," said Anthony. "Well, then we should talk about that, too. I, uh, happen to have some business that takes me to England now and then…"

SALVAGE

Karelia Stetz-Waters

They are just girls really, these newly enfranchised conscripts in my shop. Seventeen maybe. Not demanded conscripts, I'm guessing. They were born after the war. At least as children they raced past sagging fences made of stretchers and the hulls of drones, yelling out their own dreams. Then they chose this life, the one they wear now as clearly as if they were still in uniform. I can see them eyeing me, lingering in the doorway. Their hair is cropped close as is required by their order.

The boldest comes toward me.

"We turn toward the rising sun," she says.

It's a challenge she doesn't have a right to make here.

"I honor the sun with my pure heart," I say, covering my heart with my hand.

I know men who have lost an arm for not repeating this liturgy.

The girl taps her fist to her heart. "Self-conscript, eleven."

Self-conscript. She does not see the paradox. Perhaps there is no paradox for her.

"Brother, demanded conscription. Sister self-conscript, nine. Father first-demanded-conscript, three years."

She continues with the litany: age of entry for the living, years of service for the dead. Her family has affirmed their dedication. She finishes and looks at me. She knows I am salvage. On the street corner, this would give her the right to spit at me, but not in my shop while her friends are scanning the window for patrolmen, the wall for the images they want. They feel it: that age-old yearning to decorate the body, to alter, to amend.

I will not tattoo them. I could lose my shop or worse, but I enjoy watching their struggle. I liked the conscripts better during the war. They were vicious, but they had more integrity.

The images are hung on little plaques hooked to the wall, and the boldest girl turns toward the wall and picks a half-sun rising over a black line. Of course she does. It's not enough that the image is emblazoned on the uniform I know she should be wearing. I consider pulling down the metal grate that separates my work area and bed from the storefront, but I don't.

"How much, salvage?" the bold girl asks.

She hates me for I contribute nothing to the Front. I own: my body, my tools, my shop, myself. There are many ways to become salvage. I defected before the Front could shove a weapon in my hand. I thought if I slept on a grate beneath the city streets, I could escape the war. Not even the feral dogs that feed on dust and sunlight escaped the war.

Through the hot, dirty windows I see a figure moving purposefully across the street, coming toward the door. She is a conscript too, but high ranking, for her hair is pulled back in a braid. She opens the door. I wait for the girls to notice her, but she enters without a sound, without a shadow. She is about my age, I guess, but she looks younger, with the aggressive cleanliness of the Enlightened Liberation Front. A perfect seed-bearer. I am salvage; I'm not blind. I look away.

I should be afraid. If the woman thinks that I am delaying for her benefit alone, that I will catch the girls' eyes and later they will come back with tanks of gas and bullets to trade, she has the right, by law, to execute me. That does not happen here in the north where salvage outnumber the conscripts, and the Front needs so many men to decommission the great war-tankers. It is like carving up a city. I know some who have spent their whole life on one ship, climbing its gutted flank, searing off pieces with a blue flame. They sleep with their acetylene tanks. Still there is more metal than there are men.

"I honor your sacrifice," I say to the bold girl. "I cannot defile the body of the rising sun."

The girl steps closer to my counter.

"You don't get to refuse me, salvage. And we're not paying." She tosses her shoulder, almost coquettish. "You owe us your life."

The world is safer now, after the war. Perhaps I owe my life to the Front, not to this child but to others. There were those who welcomed the first conscripts, waving the Front's flag as the conscripts marched down the flowering lanes. I think we all know now. There is one regime, then there is another. In between is the war.

The woman behind the girls—I guess she is their sergeant—is seething, but her anger only moves in her eyes.

"You have already committed your life to the rising sun. You do not need this," I say to the bold girl. I hold up the card with the rising sun. "Take it. A souvenir."

Another girl puts her card down on the counter: an image of an octopus drinking from a bottle. A few drunken bubbles rise from its lips. I think she must have pulled it from the wall without looking. She is nervous. I tilt the plaque upward slightly so the sergeant can see. She looks from me to the girls to the card.

"Really?" I ask the girl. "Conscript, why?"

I think I see a smile flicker behind the sergeant's rage.

"I…" the girl stammers.

The stern, clean lines of the sergeant's face soften. She shakes her head.

"Perhaps your friend would like to comment on this choice," I say, nodding toward the sergeant.

The girls turn. The sergeant's eyes meet mine. I think the girls know we have been watching each other.

The sergeant's tirade is stern and by-the-books. *Purity. Integrity. Transparency. To defile the body of a conscript is to cut the flesh of the people, to defile our peace and our redemption.* The girls blush hot red, and one starts to cry. I don't move. I am no longer afraid. I am not old, but the war stays with you. I can see that in the sergeant's eyes. She will not demote the young conscripts or send them to the mines. She loves them, and she's tired. I can see that too.

I pull down the grate after they leave. I leave the front door unlocked. I am not surprised when the sergeant returns, dressed in a narrow suit that is all angles and lines, the kind women wore in movies before the war. She has painted her lips a dark red. I can still see the sun rising, but it is a good disguise. On the street, she would look like salvage, one of the few who has made a fortune off the decommissionings. Most salvage die with nothing but their tattoos. But I am proof there is still room among our ranks for a few to rise, to bargain, to keep something of our own. We are worthless, but, in some ways, we are freer than the conscripts with their rations and their clean hair.

I am sitting behind the counter reading. It is summer. It is always summer now. It's hot, and I've taken off my shirt like the men do. It doesn't matter. My breasts are as lean as a boy's chest, and anyway, decorum is for the conscripted. She looks at the lines that cover my body, from the fine lace on my hands, up over my first tattoo: the lamb. My ribs bear an anatomical representation of the bones within. Many of the drawings I have inked myself for practice. Some were drawn by my lovers. The effect is not beautiful. It is not meant to be. We left beauty behind with the war.

The sergeant moves into the space with the quick efficiency of a patrolman securing a corner.

"Lock the door, would you?" I say, carefully placing a slip of paper between the pages of my book.

She moves the metal bar across the door and presses the alarm. A red light blinks to life outside, but that is all it does. Who would come if an alarm sounded? I lift the grate so she can step under. It is like lifting the sheet of a bed.

"We turn toward the rising sun," I say.

She says nothing.

"Your conscripts..." I say. "I assure you. They were not defiled."

She dismisses my assurance with a wave of her hand. Her nails are perfect seashells. Her skin is smooth.

"How long have you been here?" she asks. "In this shop?"

I remember this street when it was lined with cafes twinkling under strings of lights. Could we have passed each other on one of those nights when the wind carried the smell of anise and the sound of guitars?

"Ten years," I say.

She asks me about my art. I shake my head. There is no art after the war. We circle around this and other truths.

Finally, she says, "Is there anywhere where you can...where no one would know?"

If she has followed the edicts of the Front, she knows less about her body than she should. *Pure of purpose. Pure of body. Pure of heart.*

"It would be almost inside you," I say. "Only your medic would see, and I can make it look like a birth mark or cancer. I can't make an image. They could find an image."

"That doesn't matter," she says.

I know men who have lost an arm for not repeating the pledge. *We turn toward the rising sun.* I would not make that sacrifice, but I understand. I say the pledge when it benefits me. Words are words. But I cannot resist this woman's rebellion and her fatigue, although I could lose more than an arm for what I am about to do. I release the heavy burlap curtain that screens the space behind the grate from the shop's dusty windows. I light a small lamp. I wipe down the chair in which so many salvage have lain.

"You'll need to…"

Her skirt is so narrow, the fabric so unyielding she cannot lift it over her hips. I take her hand. Gently, I unzip the back of the skirt, encircling her waist, so close I could touch my lips to her face. It has been years since I undressed a woman. Something deep inside me stirs like it does when I walk down to the port and listen to the free sailors whisper stories of a city in the south where a just man rules, and there is no salvage, only men and women farming yarrow in sunny gardens, and at night there are cafes.

I fold the sergeant's skirt and set it aside. She is still wearing the tight, corset-like undergarment the Front calls her "gown." The stiff fabric leaves red impressions in her skin. I draw my thumb across one of the marks, soothing her skin back to its natural smoothness. I think she's trembling. I settle her back in the chair.

Carefully I prepare my instruments, narrating as I go. How I clean the gun. How I take the sterilized needed from the jar of thimerosal and chlorine. How I boil the ink over a small flame and then cool it. Before the war I used a new needle for every customer.

"Will it hurt?" she asks.

If she was conscripted during the war, she has suffered more than even I can imagine, but I say, "Yes. It will hurt."

I take out a piece of cotton and soak it in the disinfectant.

"Open your legs," I say.

Her body smells of clean salt, nothing like the death's head oysters the men pull up from beneath the tankers.

I am surprised the Front has not required the removal of her hair. Fine, curly hairs cover her pubis, but I suppose it doesn't matter. Except for washing and elimination, her body is sealed inside the plastic-fiber casing of her inner garments. I look at her. Her labia are curled inward, compressed by the garment, like a moth still in its chrysalis. It seems wrong to stick my fingers into that privacy, to wipe her down with the disinfectant and startle that shy, soft part of her body with the sting of a needle. She reminds me of a beautiful creature curled in on itself to sleep in darkness.

I don't think anyone really sleeps anymore.

I stroke her very gently with the tip of my finger, watching her face as I do. I know where her clitoris is buried although I cannot see it. I want to touch her there, to massage her, to coax pleasure out of her slumber.

"Here." I part her labia and open her. "I will make a small mark. It will look like a freckle. Sometimes women have marks like that."

I am holding her labia between my thumb and forefinger. I can see a sheen of moisture at her center. I can feel her body stiffen, but I don't know how to speak the question our bodies are asking. I take my tattoo gun and the good clean, cool ink and the newest needle. The familiar buzz of the gun inks a tiny spot of black onto her inner labia. I know it doesn't hurt—not like that—but she gasps.

"That's it," I say a moment later. "Stay here."

I retrieve a tiny foil package of antibiotic cream, a luxury I do not waste on regular customers. I tear the foil and rub a little onto the new tattoo. She closes her eyes. I know I should stop, but I keep stroking that tiny spot.

"How old were you when you were conscripted?" I ask.

She says, "Fifteen."

Child soldier. We've taken the sting out of that term now that half the Front self-conscripts before age ten. They know no other world. At least the old men on the tankers still look toward the horizon.

"Have you born seed?" I ask.

"No."

"Has it been suggested that you do?"

"Suggested, yes," she says. "I cannot make that dedication. It's not in my nature."

"It is not in my nature either." I move my fingers down, circling the opening of her body. She's wet. I have lost track of what punishments would befall me were this crime discovered. "Your tattoo is done," I say, still touching her.

I transfer the moisture from her body up to her clitoris which is now visible. Tiny. Red. Erect.

"If that is all you've come for...the patrol will be changing soon. It is a good time to travel," I say.

Her eyes fly open. She is older than I realized. I can see that. But her startled, frantic eyes tell me she is unpracticed in this art. She understands what I am doing, but she does not know how to ask for more.

"Not all my family are conscripts," she whispers. "Before the war...I had a sister who lived in the south. It was different there."

Her voice is strained.

"Should I stop?" I ask, rolling her clitoris between my thumb and finger like a pearl.

"No."

I move my fingers above her clit and rub deeply. In the little pool of light cast by my lamp, we are the only two people in the world.

"There are rumors," she says. "I've heard the admirals say that the Front is losing power. They say there are places in the south. They say we may be the last city where the Front still holds power."

"There are always rumors," I say. There are always rumors of hope. It is in our nature.

"They say the Front checks the ships for messages," she whispers although every ethanol-drunk sings that same story on the piers. "That is why we don't know. They say no one who sails past the meridian may return. They say the Front leaders are afraid. There is no need for the Front in the south."

"Stories," I say.

"But if they were true?"

If they were true? I stroke her sex gently. She is sighing now, breathing heavily, lifting her hips.

"They have churches and music and gardens." Her eyes are closed and her hands grip the armrests.

I want to dream with her. A cottage with a garden, nasturtiums. But I know what dreams do. I've seen it in the sailors' eyes.

"This is all there is," I say.

Her hips strain against my hand.

"There has to be something…" She moans as I squeeze her clit. "Something else, something more."

I keep my touch light. She squirms. We stay like this for a long time. I draw her closer and closer to release. I am dreaming of yarrow and anise. I love the sergeant's dreams, her suffering, her innocence. Finally, her soft moans take on an edge of desperation.

"Oh, God," she whispers. "I can't…please."

Her body knows how this must end.

I kneel down. It is the only thing I can do. I kneel down, and I take her whole sex in my mouth. I plunge my tongue into her until I find a rhythm, a port, a compass. She is crying now and her hands are in my hair, pulling me to her, urging me on. When she comes, her body arches up and freezes, electrified. I can feel the pulse of her release against my face. I think somewhere in the distance I hear gulls crying.

That night I lie in my cot, listening to the gulls, thinking about the sergeant. Before she dressed, she told me she had received a letter from her sister…a year ago. But, still, that is not so long compared to the war.

"She's waiting for me," the sergeant said. "Come with me."

I think about the sailors. I've never tried to leave the city. People do. Some wash up dead. Some disappear. I cannot sell my shop. The Front reclaims all salvage property brought into commerce. But the sergeant has resources, and I know the dark pathways beneath the docks. You can charter a boat if you have the means.

I slide my hand beneath the band of my loose canvas pants and find the same bright spot I found on her. I draw my pleasure out as long as I can. When I come, I feel as though a thousand stars have pricked me, like a needle yearning beneath the skin. The sound of gulls. The first crude brushstroke on a cave wall. Her blood. Our sex. She says she knows other officials who have left. The tales of old men. The war took everything. She says she will come for me. She says we will leave together. Better to lie beneath the tankers than to hope.

Still, I rise before dawn. I take out my gun. I do not clean the needle I used on the sergeant. Instead I mix her blood with my ink. I draw a black line along my wrist, up my arm, into the tender skin. I trace the whole vein, then shade it, give it substance. I color it the blue-red of live blood. It crosses other images. My art. My hope. She says she will come for me. I wrap my instruments in clean muslin. I know men who have died for less.

TRICK HEARTS

Michael Graves

I bark at the cheerleaders. "Hit the bricks! We were here first!" Skittering away, their hair ribbons flounce.

Reed tells me, "You don't have to be an asshole, Dusty."

Today, on this Saturday, our donation can is stickered in S.A.D.D. logos. Students Against Drunk Driving. While Reed fidgets, coins ting about.

I tell him, "The UNICEF kids better not show up either. They're mega pushy."

Reed sighs and says, "It's not like it used to be. Maybe people know that we're full of shit."

"Just keep smiling, but in a sort of sad way. We need enough for a twelve-pack or this party tonight is pointless."

My phone thrums with a message from Benji. I glance down and see yet another photo of his brutish cock.

"I'm starving," Reed says.

"Same. Maybe I'll go in and steal more Halloween candy."

A woman with white sneakers and two brawling tots approaches. She tells them, "Stop with your crap or no friggin' treats."

The children swat at one another.

"Morning, Ma'am," Reed says. "Would you like to donate to S.A.D.D.?"

"Huh?"

"A donation? To Students Against Drunk Driving."

The woman sighs. "Shit. I don't know if I got any change."

"We'll take dollar bills too," I tell her.

One child slaps the other's cheek. Crying erupts.

"Ugh. *Fine*," the woman says. "Here's a buck." She stuffs the currency into our can, almost wincing.

I say, "Thanks for helping to keep drunk students off the road. Have a *stellar* day."

❖

I dump coins into the Credit Union's seemingly magical sorting machine. I tell Reed, "I hope it doesn't get clogged. That always happens. And the tellers get so pissed. Especially the fat gay one."

Our money clinks, churning through the apparatus.

"How much do you think we got?" Reed asks.

"No clue."

Reed grins. He unwraps a throat lozenge and places it on his tongue.

"Are you getting sick or something?"

"Uh, no. I just like the way these taste."

"Cherry, huh?" I say and smile.

Despite his wayward, ink-black hair and his face, pimpled like a box grater, Reed often looks handsome. Lonny wouldn't turn him away.

He asks, "What should I dress up as tonight? My cousin gave me a lion costume. Is that gay? Is that ghetto?"

I shrug.

"What are you gonna be?"

"Every Halloween since I was like, seven, my mom has forced me to do drag. I wanna be scary. Maybe I'll just wear a stupid zombie mask. I don't know."

❖

I often wish my mother could somehow become a supermom or a mama bear or a martyr mom, but she is far too busy being selfish. In truth, she is quite like a friend I only enjoy for an hour or so.

Right now, my mother holds a vial up to the light. Shaking it, she glares at the debris that swims round and round.

"What even *is* that shit?" I ask. I'm slouched at the dining room table, sifting through my childhood photos.

"It's some kind of pricey gel. Injectable. FDA approved," she says. "Technically, it's expired. So, they had to get rid of it. But Jenny said it still works."

House music begins whomping from the parlor where Glory, Dorchester's second most famed drag performer, stomps to the beat. Her wig flaps about, neon nails laser-like.

"Julia!" Glory yells, "Come dance. *Now!*"

My mother muscles open a box of syringes and smiles at me. "So...*I'm* going to be a doctor. I'll plump patients up, make them look sexy and young. The money will be fabulous!"

"You're gonna kill someone," I say. "And then you'll end up in jail."

She lowers her soot-colored eyes. "I'm really trying here, Dusty. You make more money than me these days. The electric company owns us. And the landlord too. This way, I can pay some things off. Like maybe even the Dell bill. Where did that computer end up?"

I chuckle softly. "In the basement, probably."

"Well, *you* killed it with porn," she says and giggles. "Hey, I just got a hundred and fifty bucks! I did Mrs. Harris' tits!"

"Aren't they big enough already?"

"That's what I said. But she's a paying customer. So I obliged."

I finger a naked photo of my six-year-old self.

"Maybe if my business takes off, I can finally get my '74 Cutlass. I already have the floor mats, Honey Pot." My mother slurps her third glass of Pinot. She thrusts her face close to mine. "Me and that Cutlass are destiny. I *know* it."

"Whatever, Doctor," I say, almost tittering.

Glory calls, "Dusty! Come out with us tonight!"

My mother says, "Yeah. You used to love Jaques. It's the Witches and Bitches Ball."

"You'll dance yourself dead!" Glory shouts.

My mother cackles and the goblet tumbles from her lazy grip. Shattering, glass chunks fling to and fro. One large splinter skates across the floor.

"Oh, shit," my mother says. She begins to softly cluck with sobs. "Don't move! Don't get up!" Her body is quaking.

"What in the fuck?" Glory plods in.

"It's just…that was scary. I'm sorry." She cups her mouth. "What a scary sound…"

❖

Reed and I strut past a Jedi, a crayon, and five whores. Spiderman argues with Jesus about Percocet while the cross-country jerks force a kitten to drink rum.

My costume, a high jacked Pinterest idea, was fashioned by my mother just this afternoon. I'm wearing a hooded sweatshirt fastened with several mini cereal boxes. Franken Berry, Count Chockula, Boo Berry. A plastic knife impales each breakfast treat.

"Do you like my costume?" I ask Reed.

He squints and replies, "Um, yeah. Yes. I don't get it, though."

"I'm a cereal killer. See?" I stab a box.

Reed shrugs, yanking on his lion whiskers.

My phone vibrates and I see that Lonny has sent me another text message: *"Where r u cutie???????? Don't even think about fucking me over. CALL Me!!!!"*

"I'm gonna find Benji," I tell Reed. "Don't put the fuckin' beer in the fridge."

"Gross. It'll get skunky."

"And don't put it down," I say. "Kids'll start to scrounge."

❖

Black and white make up smear Benji's face. He smells like weed and already dons a dopey grin.

"I wanted to be Paul Stanley," he says, "but I couldn't figure it out. So, fuck it. I'm Ace Frehley."

"Kiss sucks," I say. I yank a wad of money from my sock and pitch it into his lap.

"Jesus," he says, grinning. "How many videos did you do?"

"Anything about your mom's transplant?"

"Not like we can afford it. Her kidneys are toast by now anyway."

I can feel my face soften.

Benji says, "They suck out all her blood and then give her new blood. Someone *else's* blood." He pulls on his groin. *"Lupus.* Ain't that a gross name? Even for a disease, I mean?"

I shuffle toward him and stroke his skinned head. "I wish you weren't so fucked up."

"Yesterday, she said she can't wait to die since she already feels dead. And I kinda hope it happens. Ain't that the worst?" Benji says.

"I wouldn't want to feel dead either."

Benji peers at me and says, "Hey, does that kid Reed like you or something?"

"He's my friend. We go canning together."

"Whatever," he says and half-snorts. "Bet he's a total bottom anyway."

I long for the former Benji. I wish for my summer boy heartthrob. During June, I felt as though the public basketball courts had been paved for only his lay ups, only his cackles, only his sunset hand jobs. Benji had stolen me a bouquet of dimpled balloons from King's Motor Lot in July. During August, we bore the heat, sleeping forehead to forehead, almost naked in the bed of his dead uncle's pickup truck. Whatever the summer day, he would always say something like, "I love when you blink for me. Them long lashes are like spider legs. Daddy long leg lashes."

Benji now asks, "Can we fuck real quick?"

I sigh. "Did you bring a rubber?"

"Awwww," he complains, "I'm out."

"Then stop using them on her."

He shrugs. "Jenna can get pregnant. You can't. At least I don't think," he says with a chuckle.

I swill my discount ale.

Benji begins to drum his fingertips on my hip bone. "You beg me to be nice to you all the time. Why can't you be nice to me right now?"

I tell him, "We shouldn't have to try so hard."

Benji unbuttons his corduroys. "Hurry up, though."

Two Trumps wrestle and one underclass girl, refusing costume, remains plopped beside Reed and I. She continues passing us beers. I have seen her before, perhaps at the grocery store or the drug store or the shoe store.

I jab Reed's shoulder. Even though he is directly by my side, I send him a text message:

I think this girl is a sophomore. Sophomores are vile.

Wut's that meen? he replies.

I'm stifling laughter.

It means nasty. Gross.

Oh. K.

She probably wants to suck your dick.

Reed sinks deeper into the couch. He, replies: *THAT is VILE.*

Aloud, I say, "I'm gonna go soon."

"Naw. It's fun." He squeezes my hand. "Stay."

"Benji can give you a ride home. He said he wants to ask you something."

Reed stares at me for seven seconds. "What for?" he asks, sour-faced. "That guy's pretty much an asshole. Everyone knows you two mess around. You in love with him or something?"

"I guess I'm trying not to be." I snap open a brew. "Did you know he has a mega learning disorder? It's kind of hot…but kind of sad."

Reed laughs. "Morons don't give me a boner. Look, I'm going with you. You're my designated driver. S.A.D.D., remember?"

❖

It's Sunday and I have slept beyond noon. Easing downstairs, I bat away my erection. I see Glory, wigless, slumped at the kitchen table. My mother slides a needle into her brown cheek, plunging fluid inside her flesh.

Glory says, "I guess zombies *do* rise."

My mother asks, "What happened last night?"

"I didn't even get that wasted," I say, yawning.

My mother jabs the syringe toward me. "But Benji…"

"Let's not talk about him."

"Honey Pot…He crashed his car. He died. He's…dead."

I can feel my entire self quickly wring out like a soapy dishrag. Any shred of comprehension floods free.

My mother explains, "Cop Carmichael called. I guess Benji ran off the Pike. He…hit a tree. Shit. You probably don't want to hear this…like this. Ugh. Fuck."

"It's okay to cry, baby boo," Glory says.

"Dusty doesn't do that," my mother explains. "Even when he was an infant. The doctor said it was creepy." She turns to me. "I'm sorry about your boyfriend, Honey Pot."

"He's not my boyfriend. I don't even think we were friends really."

"Are you gonna be okay?"

I shake my head and say, "Probably? Thoughts and prayers, I guess?"

I have puffed away all of my weed and *Sleepaway Camp 2* plays on our pirated cable. As trick-or-treaters crow and squeal on the street below, I can smell my mother's never-ignored Sunday dinner. She is dicing, roasting, seasoning, and I permit myself to be fooled some. Coiled in my bed, I almost feel cozy.

There is a faint thud on my door. "What?" I moan.

Reed squeezes through, his hands stuffed in his pockets. He says, "It got fucking cold out. Like winter. All those little bastards are gonna freeze for their loot tonight."

"I hope my mom turned off the lights."

"You wanna dress up and give it a try?" Reed asks. "We still got baby faces. Might be your last chance for a Krackel bar."

"No way."

Reed sheds his coat and sits at the foot of my bed. He reeks of the frigid Dorchester air, my favorite scent. "How about Benji? Pretty fucked up, huh?"

I lean against the headboard. "He's a tard. Was too fucked up. Got himself killed."

Reed's eyes dart around, from the ceiling, to the slasher film, to the endless mounds of laundry strewn about. "You know, it could have been me too. What if I went with him? Then I'd be dead right now."

"It was a freak accident," I say.

Two teens begin shrieking for their lives on the screen.

Gently, Reed plucks up my pipe and sets it back down. "Maybe it wasn't an accident. It's like, I was thinking, what if God's the real boogey man. Worse than Freddy or Jigsaw or Jason. Maybe he's out to get us."

"God probably doesn't care that much. I'm pretty sure we're all killers in our own way anyhow."

"I thought you would be upset," Reed says. "So…are you?"

Sighing, I say, "We're really broken up now. It's totally final. I'm supposed to cry, so I'm waiting for that to happen."

"Don't worry. I'm gonna stay with you." He pulls back my quilts like a tender bayside tide. "Come on," Reed whispers, "Let me in."

He slides beside me, thrusting his chest against my back.

Once the threat of trick-or-treaters subsides, my mother piles plates with roast beef, corn, and mashed potatoes. Reed spits out his cough drop and we eat on my bed, before both falling asleep to the soundscapes of B movie murder.

❖

I hustle north on the Mass Pike.

Reed says, "Slow down, Dusty."

Just after Exit 32A, I pull over. There are bushes mown down and busted tail light chunks gleaming in the cold sunrise.

"Fuckin' spooky shit," Reed whispers, tipping back an extra-large Dunkin' Donuts coffee cup.

I glare at this place, the place where Benji's organs, like factory cogs, ceased movement. I've decided that his death is really quite simple: if a child carelessly breaks his toy, it stops working and becomes useless. Still, I cannot shed the idea that, perhaps, death was Benji's final slight.

Already, a pathetic highway memorial is planted nearby. There are photos tacked to trees, scented candles and small sugar pumpkins. Jenna, I'm sure, was quick to construct this.

Reed turns to me. "Should we get out and say a prayer or something?"

"It won't do any good, I don't think."

❖

Lonny resides in a Canton split-level. He is often boasting about the improvements to his finished basement. Despite new needle holes that polka dot his arms, Lonny co-owns Maymark Furniture Stores with his stepfather. I sometimes see the commercials between horror movies.

With a leering smile, Lonny says, "Dusty! Thought you disappeared on me. You didn't forget about our little loan, did you?"

I follow him down to the basement. "I do have homework and tests and shit like that, you know?"

"Double lives. I have one too," he says. "But porn is my passion, my paradise."

I begin to peel off my dungarees, yet they become snagged and I almost topple to the plush carpet.

"Careful, sexy boy," Lonny says. "Ya lost weight like I said. Want some coke?"

"No," I reply. "Thanks, no."

"You feeling loose? Relaxed?"

"Sure."

Lonny locks the legs of his tri-pod. "How's your mom doing anyway?"

"The same, I guess."

"She finish law school yet?"

I nod. I pass him my naked childhood photos. "I want three-hundred for these. I know you've got friends that'll want them."

Lonny thumbs through the first three pictures and then, quickly, slides them in his rear pocket. Smirking, he motions to the sofa. "You like that couch?"

"It's nice."

"Got it for almost nothing. The distributor sent the wrong color. Dumb fucks."

"Oh," I whisper.

"Okay. Get on it and, like…spread your legs…"

I obey his commands.

I ask, "Six-hundred more, right? Then we're square?"

"Boy scout promise," he tells me. "You think we should do a theme? Like a doctor's office theme? Or a sports theme?"

"I guess if you want."

"Ah, fuck it. Themes are too much work. Alright, sweetheart, now look bored. Nice."

I glance away from Lonny's lens and see fabric swatches in the corner. I also see one automatic rifle.

He says, "I bet you suck off all the boys after gym class, huh?"

"Not so much."

Lonny sidesteps, zooming, clicking, pinching at his groin. "Now, take out your cock. Show me what you got."

"Lonny?"

"What, sexy boy? You freakin'?"

"No," I say and shrug. "I'm fine. But what if I brought a friend sometime? So we can be done, you and me."

Lonny's expression looks somewhat like a frown.

A spray of smashed jack-o-lantern chunks freckle the pharmacy parking lot.

One elderly woman scuffs toward us. Despite the dingy heavens, she wears a visor.

I say, "Care to donate to kids with leukemia?"

She frowns. "Naw. No, thanks. I need to know where my money is spent."

I reply, "Well, it goes to help all those kids with *leukemia*."

The woman gropes her pockets, finally threading a tissue free. She swabs her nose. "I know my quarter will probably go towards address labels or bumper stickers. They'll make calendars with it. My money!"

Reed interjects, "Everything in this can...it goes straight to the kids. Every penny."

She steps closer, grips her purse. "What do you care anyway? Shouldn't you be chasin' girls and smokin' drugs? You got leukemia?"

"No. I don't," he says. Reed shakes the can nervously. It pings, rattles.

"He doesn't, but I do," I say. "And he's my best bud in the whole world. And he just wants me to get better. It's like, some days, I already feel dead."

When I return to my bedroom, I find Benji's perfectly trimmed obituary waiting on my bedspread. This is my mother's attempt to appear concerned. Glaring at the blotted print, I see the Telegram has used his official yearbook photo. The newspaper claims Benji had "died suddenly," leaving his mother and two brothers. It states that he "excelled at many sports, particularly basketball."

I strip and begin stroking my dick, squinting at his senior smile.

While we lay in bed, Reed skates his fingertips across my shoulder blades.

I ask him, "What do you wanna to watch?"

"Whatever you want," he replies.

"*Nightmare on Elm Street 2?*" I suggest. "*So* gay. *So* good."

Reed rolls onto his back, stinking of throat drops. "Is your mom pissed I'm here so much?"

Shrugging, I say, "Who cares? But don't your parents miss you?"

"I text my mom like, a million times a day," he says. "She just wants to make sure I'm happy. But it's better if I stay here. I like staying here. I feel safer. With you, I mean."

"Why?" I'm snickering.

"If we were in a horror movie, you'd be the good one." Reed chuckles. "And the good one always lives."

Since breaking my left arm in a sixth grade shoplifting scheme, I have not felt my tears aching to pour free as they do now. Perhaps, if I allow them to flow, I won't feel so capsized every second of every minute.

I tell him, "I'm bad, Reed. I'm not good. You don't know lots of things about me 'cause I lie…all the time I lie."

"Why?"

"I don't know. I guess because I like you."

"I like you too," he says.

"He uses my real name for the videos. He told me he didn't have to come up with anything else because I was born with a slutty name."

Reed's face grows pinkish. "I know. I've seen a few of 'em."

"Isn't that sort of sick and sad and pathetic?"

Reed presses the tip of his nose to mine. "All I know is you're good, Dusty. So good."

❖

I pad downstairs in just boxer shorts. Knuckling my eyeball, one renegade lash grates my pupil, causing a teary haze.

"Hi, Dusty." Jenna, Benji's girlfriend, sits on the sofa.

"Why is this happening?" I exclaim, squinting at her exceptional blonde ponytail.

"I just came to see your mom. You know, for a little makeover."

"Bigger tits won't bring Benji back."

Jenna glares at her cell phone, scrolling and scrolling. "I'm trying to cheer myself up. It's been a hard couple of days. And I want to look nice for the funeral too."

"You're...so...*sweet*." I sit across from her, spread my legs and stare.

Years ago, I decided that Jenna is much more intelligent than everyone else because she's decided to simply act unaware of the obvious. It must be simpler and truly, she probably achieves what she's aiming for.

Jenna taps her phone. "Will it hurt?"

"Will what hurt?"

"The needle, silly. Your mom said I won't feel anything, but a needle is a needle."

I plunge my hand into a nearby candy dish. I begin raking through the dusty, clumped Halloween corn.

"She told me I'd be fine," Jenna says, "but I really, really hate shots."

"I don't believe a lot of things my mother says. Did she tell you she's a lawyer?"

Jenna looks up at me. "No. Is she?"

Rising, I yank on my groin and turn toward the staircase.

"Look, I don't hate you or anything," she says.

"Oh, good."

"I'm just...I'm glad I don't have to feel jealous anymore. Like... we would talk about you...even when we weren't talking about you.

He blamed it on taking Accutane and Adderall, but I think Benji wanted to be with you most of the time."

I glance at my phone and see that it is after 2:00 AM.

I ask Reed, "Should I go to the funeral?"

He unwraps another lozenge and clicks off *I Know Who Killed Me*.

"If I don't go, will people think I'm an asshole?" I ask.

"I'm sure plenty of kids already think you're an asshole." Reed is chuckling now.

"Shut up. Fucker," I say. "What if Benji's watching? And maybe I can get some crying done there. Then I'll feel a little better at least."

"I'll take you," Reed says. "Anyway, we better go so we don't piss off God and end up goners."

Glory howls, weeping on the front steps. She wears a blistered, ballooned face. "I texted you, bitch! Look at me! You done fucked me up!"

"Holy shit," I whisper, aghast.

My mother reaches out, petting the air. "Sweetie, sweetie. Just calm down. And please *be quiet*."

"What's happening?" Puss dribbles from Glory's bulbous cheeks.

My mother says, "I told you, just give it a few days and you're going to look fierce. I promise, sweetie."

"It burns, Julia! My face is hard. Like a rock."

"It's fine, totally fine" my mother says.

Glory moans, "It hurts to talk!"

My mother begins closing the door. "Like I said, do not go to the doctor. Cause it's gonna die down and…it's gonna be okay. You'll be ready for the stage. Just wait."

Glory growls like some fabled beast. Her snarling soon recedes, further down the block.

I snatch my mother's arm, saying, "She *better* be okay."

My mother jerks away. "She will be! I know what I'm doing, Dusty. Jesus Christ in heaven."

"I really wish you had gone to law school. You might need that degree."

I ignore the syringes bleaching in the sink.

In one hand, I grip a broom, in the other, a wine glass. I will attempt to summon my sadness. Almost begging for tears, I long to feel different or new or reborn. I recall listening to Benji's heart thump, too slow as it always did. I conjure images of his shredded, limp corpse. I think of morticians pumping Benji's body with brightly colored chemicals. I let go. The glass drops and shatters on the floor.

"What the fuck?" my mother says, entering the kitchen. She carries a large box. "Ugh. That sound."

My cheeks remain dry. "Sorry. What's that?"

She beams. "You're going to freak. I bought some leopard seat covers for the Cutlass."

My shoulders sink and I begin sweeping up the wreckage.

"Come on, Honey Pot. I've been working so hard and I had to treat myself. There are some appointments tomorrow. I've got a handle on things. I guess I better buy some new wine glasses, though."

Like every child, I have contemplated running away from home. To Toledo, to Niagara Falls, to the Poconos. I knew, even at age seven, that my mother could never survive without me. My younger self would always unpack the rolled coins and candy bars and wait for her next scam.

St. Anne's Church is spattered in Halloween egg prank remains.

I tell Reed, "I bet the ground is already frozen. He can't be buried."

"It has been pretty cold," he says.

I hike up my slack, creased trousers.

Reed asks, "Then what will they do with him?"

"Put him in a freezer until April, I guess."

"Vile," he says.

Mourners stream through the parking lot. Male classmates wear chinos, slicked hair and smoke-drenched hoodies. The females mostly look like sluts with short black skirts and smears of makeup never suitable for chemistry class. Three elderly women hobble by us.

Reed asks, "You think God is watching right now?"

"Well, it is church. Don't worry. I'll protect you."

A lumbering goon lurches closer. Tattoos of some kind ring his wrist. "You Dusty?"

"Why?" I ask.

"You were pals with my brother. Benji said you helped him out." The boy stinks of discount vodka and he carries a necktie.

"We had some classes together," I say.

"No," he replies, cackling. "You helped him out. Now that he's gone, just so you know, you can help me out too."

A woman charges toward us. She nabs the boy's arm and tows him backwards.

"Ma? The fuck?"

She turns to us and says, "Boys, thank you for coming. It's very… polite. You must have nice parents."

Reed says, "I'm sorry for…everything."

She smiles for only a moment.

"Me too," I say. "I'm sorry. Benji talked about you all the time. I'm glad you felt well enough to come and, like, say goodbye."

She begins shaking her head. "I guess he told you some of his stories too. I've been finding out that I'm all kinds of sick. Apparently, I've got cancer and Lupus and MS. I've got a real mean trick heart too. Never knew."

Reed and I arrive home with two large Dunkin' Donuts cups. We plan to smoke weed and watch *Shivers*.

"Cop Carmichael called!" my mother hollers, scrambling from the kitchen. "Glory must be talking to them. We gotta get all this shit outta here. Like now!"

Instantly, my mother and I gather vials, stuffing plastic CVS bags.

Reed picks up a calking gun. "What about this?" he asks.

"Yeah. That too," she replies.

"Unbelievable," I say, almost spitting.

My mother drops used syringes into an Amazon box. She pleads, "No one get pricked or jabbed. Fucking be careful!"

"What are you going to tell them?" I ask.

"Just…that she's a liar and that I don't do that and that they can search me and that…she's…I don't know…delirious from all her HIV meds…"

"Is she even going to be okay?"

"I don't know," she whispers.

"You can't scam everyone!" I hear my own voice climbing, cracking. "She's your friend, mom. She's our friend."

"I can't afford to have friends." She glances at Reed. "And neither can you."

My chest is jacking. "I never thought we'd get this bad…"

"Dusty, I don't have time for your drama…Now, take all this. Drive to some suburb and find a dumpster. When no one is looking, get rid of it all."

"What if I say, 'no'?" I whisper.

"Then maybe you'd be guilty too." My mother kneads the air. "Go."

Beyond the frosted windows, Dorchester whizzes by. I see a slashed recliner among the sidewalk trash, waiting for retrieval. I consider the number of Christmases, Super Bowls, and Halloweens that chair has been part of. A knit cap hugs Reed's head, one giant pompom bounding with every neglected pothole bump.

I say, "If you want, I can drop you off."

"No way," he says. "I'm not letting you go by yourself."

I produce a slight, faux smile. "I've tried to change our lives. I've tried to fix our lives. You know, what we do. I just can't figure it out. It's weird."

"It's going to be okay, Dusty," he tells me.

"I don't know what okay is. Hey, would you try something for me?" I ask.

Reed bobs his head. "Okay."

❖

We've already stashed everything behind Maymark Furniture's central location.

I tell Lonny, "Another advance. It's just…rent is due…"

He flaps his hand toward Reed. "He got a big dick?"

I shrug. "I don't know. I need at least a thousand, though."

"Maybe start by saying, 'please.' Let's just see how far you two go, okay?" Lonny clicks on his deluxe sound system. "St. Elmo's Fire (Man in Motion)" begins to throttle, epically. "Want some coke?"

"No," I reply. "Thanks, no."

We zip off our hoodies and sit on Lonny's prized sectional.

"Just tell me if I'm doing it…wrong or not like you like," Reed whispers.

Lonny begins air fisting to the 1980's beat. "All right, cuties. Whenever you're ready."

I poke my left eye. Another lash has fallen away, searing, tormenting my pupil.

"I don't know if I can do this, Dusty." Reed places his hand on my chest and drives his face toward mine. "I mean I want this. I really want this, but maybe…not like this?"

"You'll be great. I know it."

"But like, the internet is forever."

"It's okay," I whisper. "You're gonna feel so good."

My sight blurs and I attempt to blink away tears.

"I knew you could do it. See, you cry just like everyone else," Reed says. "You're thinking about Benji, huh? Or your mom?"

"I think I'm thinking about me. And about you too," I tell him.

THE IMPORTANCE OF BEING JURASSIC

Daniel M. Jaffe

B ill understood Quinn to be whispering "dirty," but in the raspy, heavy brogue, the word came out as "dehrty": "Yer a dehrr-ty, dehrr-ty man," Quinn flicked out his tongue and sucked it in, frog-like. With a thurping sound: "You're a dehrr-ty, dehrr-ty man." Thurp thurp thurp.

This encounter was moving beyond anything Bill had anticipated, yet he found the strange intimacy seductive. He was excited.

A journalist for the *Boston Globe*, Bill had arrived in Dublin this morning to write a human interest story on the upcoming gay marriage referendum. Polls anticipated Ireland becoming the first country to authorize gay marriage by public vote. Traditional, Catholic Ireland.

Not having slept on the plane—and his body reminding him that he was older than he used to be—he spent the day napping in his Jury's Inn Christchurch hotel room, studying local newspapers and webzines, making notes and listing questions for his article. He supped in his room on take-away from the "great wee chipshop" around the corner, Leo Burdock Fish & Chips—greasy, salty, thick-crusted smoked cod accompanied by more fries than he could possibly consume. Later on, he trimmed his grey beard, donned jeans and a button-down blue shirt that showed off his squarish pecs without appearing too obvious—his decades-old uniform whenever scoping out a new city's gay life. Bill always enjoyed these forays most of all, surveying the terrain before his newspaper's photographer arrived and hovered, thereby preventing Bill from conducting his most enjoyable background research.

Passionate encounters with locals were the secret to Bill's success as a human interest story writer. Even in his late 50's, he could still get laid with fair enough regularity, especially as an exotic foreigner. Few journalists' articles contained the under-the-skin insights Bill's did, revelations feeling like disclosure to a trusted confidant. Bill's interviews read like intimate pillow talk because that's precisely what they were.

Bill put little stock in ethical baloney about maintaining journalistic distance: if you want to get an inside story, you need to get inside. Repressed countries were Bill's specialty because they burst with scared horny locals who had few other bed partner options. Want a journalist to cover police harassment of Russian gay activists? brutality against gays in Iraq? death-threats against gays in Uganda? Send Bill with a pack of condoms to ferret out the under-cover(s) scoop. Only a matter of time before he'd win a Pulitzer. He sure was having fun trying.

Bill headed out in the cool evening for George, the nightclub touted on all Irish gay websites as Dublin's primary gay hangout. He'd undoubtedly find some trick to "interview."

Strolling down Dame Street—odd, he thought, how historically grand the word "Dame" sounded in Ireland, whereas in American ears it came across as outdated Al Capone cheap. He walked the narrow sidewalk past restaurants, pubs, cafés, repeatedly bumping shoulders with those walking toward him until he realized that the Irish walked the way they drove—on the left, unlike on-the-right Americans: head-on collisions were inevitable.

A scan around the cobblestone courtyard of Dublin Castle, a mix of red brick Georgian palace, grey medieval fortress, and white-grey Gothic revival chapel. A quick look-see at City Hall with its white-grey granite columns and triangular pediment. On the corner of South Great George's Street, a main shopping avenue, he faced an enormous mural covering the entire side of a grey building: two young men, one in white sweater, the other in black, snuggling in romantic embrace. Larger-than-life gay love, four stories high. And tacked to a lamppost on the corner beneath it—a bold, green-lettered "Yes For Marriage Equality" poster sporting a rainbow flag. All this smack in the center of Catholic Dublin. A more in-your-face public display than he could recall having seen in Boston.

That must be the place, with the rainbow flag over the entrance and a thick bouncer staring into Bill's eye. He nodded at the guy and stepped inside. A low-lit cavernous space with stairs to the right—the upper level looked closed…well, it was a Sunday. The music was fast-paced and louder than he liked. Bill walked to the far end of the long bar with men and women in their 20's chatting, noted the stage behind the bar, empty now of the drag acts he'd read about. He grabbed a black leather barstool, asked the muscular barman for a pint of Guinness, one of those touristy must-do's. He savored the thick molasses foam, the mix of bitter and heavy sweet, then turned to the lean young man beside him, a handsome fellow with close-cropped blond hair, and introduced himself, knowing that his accent would lead at least to a where-are-you-from conversation. Bill slapped on his personae of naïve visitor: "All I basically know about Ireland is leprechauns and four-leaf clovers."

"And all I know about America is that you all carry guns and shoot black teenagers when you're strung out on crack."

"Point taken," said Bill, impressed by the cleverness, sour as it was. He switched strategies. "Of course I also know Shaw's plays and Beckett's, Joyce's *Dubliners* and *Portrait of the Artist*—as a teenager, I even won an award at an oratory contest for declaiming the fire and brimstone sermon."

"A literate American? Who'd believe it? No doubt you've read *Angela's Ashes*, too, loving every page that confirmed your image of downtrodden Ireland."

Not unusual for younger men to be disinterested in bars, but hostile?

"And," continued the young man, "surely you were self-righteously appalled by that movie, *The Magdalene Sisters*?"

"The one about Irish nuns enslaving unwed mothers? Of course I was appalled."

"Makes you feel all superior, doesn't it? Like you Americans don't have pedophile priests and other such."

Bill held up his hand like a stop sign. "Didn't mean to offend by my mere existence."

The young fellow dropped his head. "Three pints and I turn jackass. Sorry. Guess I'm pissed because I'm out of commission." He grabbed his own crotch.

Should Bill ask?

"A fucked-up piercing in San Francisco a year back," volunteered the young man. "Every now and again, my Prince Albert splits the head of my dick. The healing takes weeks, so all's I can do is look and drink and grouse."

"On behalf of all guilty American piercers, I apologize." Unusually frank for a first conversation. Is such openness typically Irish?

The young man extended his hand. "Declan."

Firm handshake. "Bill. I'm here on assignment for a newspaper. To cover the gay marriage referendum. I'd love to know your thoughts. It's a remarkable turn of events."

"Because we're such backward Papists?"

Bill stared at him.

"Sorry. I'm being a dick: yah, it's damn exciting."

"It's always the legislature or the courts authorizing gay marriage, never the people themselves."

"Never thought I'd see it. Ten years ago, I'd have said you're daft. Even five years ago. In a perverse way, the Magdalene sisters and child-molesting priests are to thank."

"Really?"

"They lost the Church its authority to order us around on moral issues. This is a bit of a backlash."

An observation that would make its way into Bill's article for sure.

"You're not bad looking, you know, Bill, with your fuzzy grey beard. For them that goes for daddies."

"Do you?" Flirtation was fun even if it couldn't lead anywhere.

"A bit of vanilla with a cuddly Da would be good for a change. Too much fetish play, and I can only get hard with extremes."

Bill raised a naughty eyebrow. "Why do you assume all daddies are vanilla?"

"Ahah…you like some smacks with your cuddles eh, Da?"

Bill winked.

"If only I were healed," said Declan with a sigh. "You might go to the Boilerhouse, back in Temple Bar across from City Hall. The baths. If you don't mind drunks. There are two gay Irelands: us lads under 40, comfortable in public. And the over-40's—mostly closeted, grew up squashed under the Church's thumb. They need half a dozen pints before they can bring themselves to grope around in the Boilerhouse dark room."

"Quite the recommendation."

"Or you could just try Jurassic."

"Where?"

"You don't know it? Next door. Jurassic Park, we call it. A quiet bar for the few out older gays and young lads that likes 'em."

"'Jurassic,' huh? Flattering."

"It's just our way—playing with names. The James Joyce statue off O'Connell, himself with a cane, we call 'The Prick with the Stick' because he was a randy bastard. And the needle statue there—it's the poor part of town, you know, immigrants and such—we call it 'The Stiletto in the Ghetto.' Fun knicknames. 'Jurassic.' Right through them doors at the back of the bar."

"Join me?"

"Nah, one look at me by your side and nobody else'd dare approach. I'm too good looking."

Bill laughed.

"If I were healed, old Da, I'd fuck ya sure."

"A true romantic."

Bill chugged the last of his Guinness, swiveled off the bar stool, gave Declan a peck on the cheek, sauntered over to the double wooden doors and through.

Immediately calmer—softer music. A small, cozy, long narrow room, wooden floors, chipped grey-green paint on the walls, large gilt-framed mirrors. Bill sidled up to the dark wooden bar in desperate need of polishing, scanned the dozen beer taps, ordered a Tuborg from the young blond barman in a "Staff" black tee shirt. He then stepped over to a corner seat against the wall, from where he could survey everything.

Bill noticed a short tubby in his late 60's with a young fellow tugging on his arm now to get him to leave—hustler or daddy's boy? Only three other patrons, in their late 50's. One, hunched on a barstool—black-framed glasses, thick grey hair, a bit of a paunch—gave a quick rabbit glance. The shy type were often the hottest once you loosened them up. The conversation with Declan had gotten Bill worked up. Besides, business had its demands, too: pillow talk with a man his own age could offer helpful insights, especially after what Declan had told him about the over 40's.

Bill took the lead in the standard bar stepdance: he stared stiffly until the hunched guy met his eyes and darted his own away; then Bill looked aside to give the hunched guy a chance to size Bill up; then both met eyes, momentarily stared, looked away; then both met eyes, stared, held gazes long enough for one of them—Bill—to risk rejection and smile. The hunched guy returned a sheepish half-nod. Bill walked over, extended his hand for the as-expected limp-fish shake.

"Hi there, I'm Bill."

"Quinn," the fellow said. From the heavy aroma of beer on his breath, Bill knew he'd been drinking a while. "An American, are ya?" A heavy brogue.

"My accent give me away?"

"That and yer boldness."

"Not too bold, I hope."

"No no. Boldness is quite welcome, actually."

Bill gave Quinn a light kiss on the lips. Quinn cringed, pulled himself back.

"Sorry," said Bill. Too bold. Come to think of it, he hadn't seen anyone kissing in the larger room next door.

"What one might shun in public," said Quinn softly, "one might enjoy in private." His eyes darted around the small room.

"Ah. Got it. No PDA for you."

Quinn's eyes scrunched.

"No public displays of affection."

"By no means." Quinn's hand reached out and gently grasped Bill's forearm. "However, if yer up for it…it's a pleasant walk to my apartment on a cool night such as this."

Bill smiled. "Now who's the bold one?"

"Well," said Quinn, grinning shyly, "the evening's getting on, and I'll need to wake early…"

"And you've got no other prospects," Bill teased.

Quinn squeezed Bill's forearm. "I've always been partial to them with beards. Besides, yer smile radiates needed warmth."

Bill was a sucker for honest vulnerability. He clapped Quinn on the back. "I'd love to come to your apartment."

Quinn said little more than "this way," on the walk down the street in the direction of Trinity College, simply hunched his head tighter into his shoulders, a turtle drawing into shelter. Bill respected the discomforting silence, noticed that as they turned onto Nassau Street and proceeded along the university's outer perimeter, Quinn's quick gait slowed. They passed shop windows displaying now traditional woolen vests and caps, now unsold pies and scones that would be of questionable freshness tomorrow morning, and red brick Georgian era buildings recalling a wealthier past.

Quinn hesitated at a building on a particular corner, pointed at the wrought-iron-fenced park across the wide avenue. "Merrion Square." He then glanced up to the building behind them, typical with its white-grey stone first floor façade and upper story red brick, glanced at a round plaque too deep in shadow for Bill to make out, crossed himself, continued walking, took out his keys, hobbled up a few steps, fumbled, let Bill into a white-walled vestibule and up to the second floor apartment. The moment the door shut behind them, Quinn breathed in deeply and stood tall, as if having stepped out into fresh country air. "You are very welcome to my home," he said. "A refuge of safety because…" Leading Bill by the arm to the living room window, he pointed. "There."

"Merrion Square?"

"Inside the fence. The corner."

Across the wide avenue, beyond the park's fence and shrubs, Bill made out a huge rock supporting a reclining male figure. "Is he real?"

"At one time he was most surely. A statue now. My patron saint."

"St. Patrick?"

Quinn chuckled, freely. "Tourist cliché. No." Quinn turned Bill by the shoulders and faced him toward a photograph hanging over the bricked up, white-manteled fireplace. "Here: A photograph I took. A close-up of Himself on the rock across the street."

Bill examined the replica thin, sunlit man reclining on a rock, legs spread wide with left knee propped up, right hand saucily holding red lapel of green smoking jacket, wavy hair covering ears, long face offering a wry smile. Totally recognizable. "Oscar Wilde."

"Himself. Born and raised just a few doors down this very block, on the corner. It's American College now. They don't allow tours. At least there's a plaque where one can pay respects. Every morning and evening I gaze out my living room window at the patron saint of all Irish homosexuals. And on Sunday mornings—early before others are about—I sneak over, reach up and caress his feet in those black Oxfords. He suffered for our sins, did poor Oscar. Imprisoned and shamed. But now eternally young in resurrected state. Watching over me, showering me with ever grace. And permission."

This guy was more than a little strange. Creepy even. Bill hoped to lighten the mood. "Quite the coincidence getting this apartment."

"Coincidence? For 10 years I struggled to find a flat in His Holiness's aura." Quinn slipped his hand into Bill's, brought it to his lips, kissed it, slid Bill's index finger into his mouth, rolled his drooling tongue around it, slipped it out. "You wouldn't be wanting another Guinness, would ya?"

"I don't know," said Bill, retracting his hand and wiping it on his jeans. "I—"

"Not to be rushing, but…tomorrow I must wake early so as to reach school before students and faculty." He dropped his voice to a whisper. "I'm Vice Principal, ya see. Discipline is my bailiwick. Rules and regulations. Moral order." He turtled into himself again, looked out the window. "If one shows up late or bleary-eyed, there'll be questions. Mustn't give reason for questions. No suspicion of any kind. Not any." He brought right thumb and first two fingers to mouth, pressed them against lips while whispering, "No suspicions. If they find out, they'll sack ya, and then where will ya be?…Shamed before the community. Utter humiliation. Penniless. Living on the streets you'll be, and then—"

Maybe this was a mistake. Unless…could this be Irish normal? Bill lacked perspective. If only he could ask that younger fellow, Declan, who seemed normal enough. Bill should shift gears, turn this into a simple interview, then make his "I've got a headache" excuse and leave it at that. "The school would fire you?"

Quinn snapped his head and straightened up as if coming to.

"They'd fire you for being gay?" pressed Bill. "But the country's about to approve gay marriage." Contradictions, inconsistencies, and injustices made for dramatic newspaper stories.

"I'm Vice Principal in a Catholic voluntary school, ya see. The Church is the last venue where it's legal to fire a sinner. That will never change. I fight temptation best I can, but…the Devil's a strong one, he is."

Yes, a great angle for his article. But Bill should definitely forget the sex—the poor guy was traumatized. Bill took a step backward. "Listen, I know I was pushy at the bar. My American way, that's all. I'm really just looking to meet some folks and get to know Irish life a little better. How's about we sit and chat…Unless you'd rather I just leave."

"No!" exclaimed Quinn, reaching out into the air between them. "Do stay. I welcome yer forwardness. I need it. If ya must know...I rarely risk visibility in Jurassic, but tonight...tonight I..."

"Tonight you were lonely."

Quinn looked up into Bill's eyes. "It's been half a year, ya see. How long can a body go without? The headiness of the upcoming referendum...the posters all over town and the news every night on the telly with handsome young couples hugging their embraces... well...my excitement got the better of me, ya understand. Just to be in Jurassic, to sit amongst my fellows, imagining possibilities with this one and that. Possibilities I could take home after, to fill the imagination and...and my hand, if you'll excuse the crudeness. Not that I expected actually to engage in suggestive conversation with a stranger, let alone invite one into my home. But you...an American..."

"You mean, a non-Irishman."

"Yes, a man not from these parts."

"No risk I'd interfere with your life."

Quinn nodded. "For 25 years I lived with a partner and they never suspected, the fathers at school. Half a year ago, Seamus died from a blood clot in his leg that went to his brain. I told them the sudden loss of my 'brother' addled me, so they let me take off half a year to get my head in order—they know compassion, ya see, those fathers, in their way. Tomorrow's my first day back."

Bill pursed his lips in sympathy, took a tender step close. Quinn reached up to Bill's shoulders, stepped in for the kiss Bill intentionally gave him. With their lips pressed together, Quinn released into Bill's mouth a high-pitched, beer-scented whimper. Quinn's tongue probed Bill's mouth, as if frantically searching.

With a tenderness rare for himself, Bill used his lips to guide the kiss from desperate to gentle. Of course Bill had no genuine interest in this disturbed man, but he'd long been a believer in the solidarity of the oppressed. In compassionate brotherhood. In the moral duty of out men to nurture less fortunate closeted ones. This wouldn't be his first sympathy fuck.

Without loosening his grasp, Quinn sidled Bill to the brown sofa opposite the fireplace, lay back pulling Bill on top of him. Quinn kissed and tongue-thrusted and clutched at Bill's shoulders, at his back, grabbing tight as if to merge Bill into himself.

Bill lifted his head. "Whoa, boy. You gotta let me breathe. You're a hottie."

Quinn grinned so broadly that upper lips retracted over gums, revealing crooked upper eye teeth. "I'm nasty, aren't I?"

"Yeah, you sure are."

"Say it. Ya must say it. Talk dehrty to me with yer American porno movie accent. Hot hot."

"You're a nasty nasty boy." Bill found himself getting turned on. So maybe this wouldn't be as much sympathy as quirky pleasure. "You're the nastiest boy I ever met."

"Yessir, yessir. I am. Nasty nasty." Quinn wriggled with delight. "Tell me what ya want, my Da," Quinn hissed through clenched teeth. "Say what ya want from yer nasty boy."

Yeah, Bill could get into this. He slid off the sofa, kicked off his shoes, removed shirt and jeans as Quinn stood and tore off his own. Both men naked, Quinn fell to his knees, took Bill into his mouth, grunting.

"That's it, nasty boy. Like that."

Quinn moaned.

"Take your Daddy like that."

There was no charity now in Bill's reaction. He grabbed the back of Quinn's head, pulled so hard that Quinn gagged and gasped, yanked himself back, stared up at Bill with eyes that gleamed nearly red. Bill shuddered, looked away, his gaze falling onto the sofa wall, onto a painting of the Sacred Heart of Jesus—the Savior's hair wavy to the shoulders, his bleeding heart vulnerable on the chest and exposed.

Quinn grabbed Bill's hands, pulled them down onto his thick nipples. "Squeeeeeeze yer boy's titties, Da. Squeeeeeeze me."

Bill did.

"Harder. Harder...Aaaah," moaned Quinn. "Yess. Yess." He flicked his tongue, murmured in raspy whisper, "Wi-ckehhd...wi-ckehhd. So wi-ckehhd."

Bill yanked the nipples taut.

"Ohh," moaned Quinn. "Dehrr-ty...dehrr-ty. Ahh...Yer a dehrr-ty dehrr-ty man...Yes...yes...fil-thy." His tongue repeatedly flicked and slurped. Thurp thurp thurp.

Quinn shoved Bill onto the sofa and spat on him, sucked him deeply in and out, over and over, then lifted Bill's legs and plunged his tongue deep, pulling back to whisper, "Perfec-tion." Lick lick. "Oh, the taste of dehrty perfec-tion." On and on in a trance-like state, all as Bill himself felt entranced, eyes rolling back. Quinn's tongue thrust. "Please, Da, please let me join in yer perfec-tion..." Probe probe. "Our perfec-tion. Christ's perfec-tion."

Bill shoved Quinn back, leaned in and bit his nipples hard as Quinn moaned, grabbed Bill's middle finger and yanked it behind himself, begging Bill to "put it where it belongs, where it belongs. Make me perfec-ted. Perfec-ted. Take me, Jesus, for I am yer own. Impale me, sacrifice me on yer holy cross, pierce myself as Yerself were pierced, make me holy, yer devoted slave in eternity, forever burning in the hellfire of the undeserving and wicked."

Bill slid his finger into the moist tightness. "Yes!" said Quinn. "Now feed me yer host." Suck suck. "Give me blessed cum-union..." Suck suck. "Give me! Give me!"

Bill couldn't hold back, shuddered, clutched Quinn's head to himself as he spasmed and grunted.

Quinn gulped and moaned.

Then he held Bill in his mouth softly.

Then he slid Bill out with a kiss.

Naked and still on his knees, Quinn gazed up at the Sacred Heart of Jesus hanging above Bill, clasped hands in prayer, murmured, "Forgive me Father, for I have sinned."

Bill leaned forward and held him while Quinn continued to murmur prayer with the solemn calm of the confessional.

After Quinn finished, they sat side by side on the sofa, Bill holding Quinn's hand. "I don't know what to say," said Bill honestly, agenda-less and somewhat sad.

"I thank ya for that," said Quinn, his face relaxed. "For yer indulgence."

"I should be thanking you." Bill kissed him on the cheek. "Would you like to talk? Maybe tell me about your...your late partner?"

Quinn withdrew his hand from Bill's. "I've got to wake early." Quinn stood, reached to the floor for his clothes, the universal signal to tricks that it's time to leave.

They dressed in silence. Bill again hugged Quinn, who stood with arms limply at his side. "I don't feel right just leaving," said Bill. "Will you be okay?"

"Saint Oscar watches over me."

Bill stroked his cheek. "Quinn, your openness…what you shared of yourself…I'm a little speechless."

Quinn gave a weary grin. "I'll remember you, my American porn star."

Bill gave a light kiss on the lips and lingered, Quinn allowing him without encouraging.

"Take care." Bill left, headed down one flight to the white-walled vestibule, heard the apartment door click closed behind him. Deadbolt.

Outside, in a bit of afterglow haze, he crossed the avenue and paid momentary homage over the iron fence to the statue of Oscar Wilde, recalling snippets of his plays and wit, his imprisonment on account of love that, for good practical reason, had dared not speak its name.

In a series of cool breezes, Bill walked toward his Jury's Inn Christchurch hotel, replaying the evening's encounter. What had he just experienced? In a matter of minutes, that strange man had revealed so much of himself to Bill, depths Bill would never have expected to be permitted to see.

The journalist in him wanted to describe this experience, to show Americans the Irish pain Bill had just witnessed, whether singular or universal, Bill couldn't know. Yet he must respect Quinn's privacy.

No breeze now, just stillness in the bruised-blue night sky. Solitary grey clouds.

Bill shivered in the dry chill.

Muffled sounds of drinking buddies as he passed this pub, and that.

By the time he reached the imposing Dublin Castle whose cobblestone courtyard, he'd read, would host hundreds of revelers awaiting the marriage referendum tallies in a mere few days, Bill felt a surge of writerly inspiration, and began structuring the article he'd traveled here to write: he would present lengthy descriptions of the referendum process, of course, and the historical struggle to achieve marriage equality. He'd recite obligatory vote tallies and exit poll statistics, would include extensive quotes from ecstatic young couples about to tie the knot and from joyful parents whose children will have just gained social legitimacy. He'd even try to include diplomatically phrased quotes from shocked and dismayed priests. And then, in honor of Quinn, yet without referring to him except in thought, Bill would conclude the article with a rally to awareness that, as glorious a harbinger of future freedom as this marriage referendum truly was, it had arrived too late for centuries of couples living fearful hidden love, too late for widows and widowers grieving in silence alone, too late for lonely individuals knowing romance only in safe imagination recesses, too late for women and men suffering damage beyond repair, for people like Oscar, living carefreely only after death and only now, in rock-bound effigy.

ARUNDEL'S NAME

Jamieson Findlay

SAVE OUR TREES

Can you imagine Camp Fortune robbed of its trees? Can you conceive that magnificent amphitheatre of hills of which Camp Fortune is the centre, and in which the members of the Ottawa Ski Club take so much pride, left unsheltered, stark naked, in all the ugliness of its bare, windswept rocks?

What can we do about it?

We could buy the land with the trees on, and keep it as such if we had the money.

We are launching a tree-selling campaign so that every one of our members may have a share in this good work... One tree of any kind, with the exception of maple and pine will cost you 25¢. A maple will cost you 50¢ and a pine $1.00. Buy a tree and you will receive a numbered certificate...

From *The Ottawa Ski Club News*, Ottawa, Canada, February 1928

Arundel. The name was a jump spark between the major chambers of Connor's worn heart. He couldn't explain its effect on him. He knew nothing about the woman, but her name was that of a gypsy queen, or a girl-god from the pagan past, or a flamenco-dancing contessa, or one of the female daredevils who rode the diving horses off Atlantic City's Steel Pier, soaring fifty feet into the water, and doing so with such tight form that neither girl nor horse suffered so much as a scratched cornea (usually).

And he had come to know her name only because she bought a tree.

Connor had become involved in the tree-selling campaign of the Ottawa Ski Club. Why, he couldn't exactly say. A transplanted Southerner, a refugee from Prohibition, he figured he somehow had to make a home out of this city of ice and snow. Selling trees seemed far preferable to actually going outdoors on skis. Since he had access to a printing press at the American Legation, where he was posted, he was put in charge of making up the certificates of tree purchase. A tall limber widow named Lilly Standish ran the campaign—Lilly the ski jumper and society lady. She collected the money for the tree sales and gave Connor the names of purchasers to put on certificates. And when the buyer happened to be female, Lilly always insisted that the lady's full name be inscribed.

"Women always have to take the last name of their husbands," she told Connor. "Why should they give up their first names, too?"

And so, when Connor printed off the certificate for tree purchaser no. 37, it was made out not to "Mrs. Basil Grey," but to "Arundel Grey." Arundel Grey, princess of fire, siren out of the water, fisher of men's souls from her moon-ship! And he'd be able to give her the certificate personally—Lilly had insisted on it.

Imagine his wan and disenchanted face when, at the next ski club tea, he sought out the woman and found her to be as drab and uninspiring a matron as ever made Christmas cake without the cognac.

"Thank you for saving our woods, Mrs. Grey," he said stoically, handing her the certificate.

In her heavy tweed skirt and sensible wool cardigan, Mrs. Grey looked plush and protected. No mythological fire shone from her soluble blue eyes, no hint of a horse diver's pearlescent light. She seemed the sort of woman who would devote herself with minimal complaint to the interminable care of an elderly relative. Her cheeks were full and her mouth decorous; she had a small heirloom chin and the imminence of another. Connor could not guess how old she was—maybe early forties. Whatever her age, she had probably looked like this for years.

She glanced at the certificate and flushed.

"Something wrong?" said Connor.

"It's just that you put my...Christian name on it." She hesitated over "Christian," as if that wasn't quite the right word.

Connor blinked. "Yes?"

"I usually go by my married name."

Connor nodded; she looked as irredeemably married as a woman could look.

"That was Lilly's doing," he said apologetically. "You know Lilly."

Mrs. Grey reddened again and looked around the room. Connor wondered if Lilly's suffragette leanings made her uncomfortable.

"I'd be happy to change it if you want," he added.

Mrs. Grey quickly slipped the certificate into her handbag. "No, that's all right. It's just..." She looked around again. "...Only my very close friends know my Christian name."

"Well, more people *should* know it. It's a beautiful name."

She gave a small folded smile. Her face changed subtly when she smiled: dimples appeared, a meander of light went through her eyes, and she lost for a second her air of dowdy wholesomeness. Connor wanted to see this effect again, and so added: "It sounds like a name with a story behind it."

"I suppose everybody's name has a story behind it," she said.

"But your name sounds like it comes from a myth or a...*chanson de geste.*"

She breathed out a timid laugh, and Connor caught the faintest whiff of mint—a clear scent, not fusty like everything else about her. "Well, it's just...my name. Anyway, thank you, Mr. O'Flynn. Your accent is very unusual."

"I'm from New Orleans." *N'ohlins.*

To Canadians, Connor's phrases often seemed to dip and rise as if riding a magnolia breeze: "one of a *khand*," he would say, or "a fine *cord-yawl* man."

"New Orleans!" she said. "And you're a *skier?*"

"No, no, I'm too warm-blooded. I just help out with the certificates. And you?"

"I'm taking the Saturday lessons for married ladies at Dome Hill."

The married ladies, thought Connor dolefully. According to Lilly

Standish, who taught the group, they thoroughly enjoyed themselves without their husbands.

"You're a wild bunch, I hear," said Connor.

Again Connor caught an eddy of light in Mrs. Grey's eyes, like a brandy flame in a darkened room. "I'm learning so much," she said, and flushed again. "You really should take up skiing yourself, Mr. O'Flynn. It's so healthful."

"Yes, well…enjoy your certificate, Mrs. Grey."

To think that her name was such a gush of raw beauty! In her cardigan she seemed no more breasted than an Easter Island idol.

❖

The next night, surrounded by souvenirs of home—parade doubloons from Mardi Gras, an old straw hat, a small cap-and-ball revolver once owned by his Confederate-soldier grandfather—Connor poured himself a glass of bourbon and picked up the latest issue of *The Ottawa Ski Club News*.

> News from the Eastern Lodge: On Saturday night, Stobie Milhouse ate 11 Italian sausages, downed 5½ beers and then stole 2 ski poles—because somebody stole his! If you took Stobie's poles by mistake, please contact…

Connor leaned back, eyes half-closed. Arundel Grey. She wore so many clothes; she smiled in such a folded way. If only she could get in touch with her true name, her true nature. A *chanson de geste* was indeed hidden there, under that winter caparison of wool, under that whalebone corset…for he was sure she wore such a thing.

> Don't forget our Wednesday night ski hikes to Dome Hill Lodge, which is as good as Yankee Stadium with ice cream, soft drinks, and a big orthophonic to play your favourite dancing records. Also a hot dog stand.

His thoughts fell away from the page; the bourbon worked on his creative faculties; and there was Arundel Grey standing before him, wearing the same amount of clothes, but with eyes half-lidded and humid-soft, like a hot August sky.

Want to try some parlour skiing, Mr. O'Flynn? she said.

He got up from the armchair, wobbling slightly.

Parlour skiing? he said.

Yes, it's perfect for beginners. And the great thing is…it doesn't require many clothes.

Smiling, she turned around so he could unbutton her gingham dress. Very quickly she was out of it, and underneath (as expected) he discovered a corset—the elasticized kind, not whalebone after all. Black stockings were attached to the corset with garters. He stood still in wonder: she had a body. A bit Rubenesque, but really not bad at all, in a seventeenth-century way.

He suddenly wondered what she would think of his body: whenever he caught a mirror glimpse of his naked torso, he felt he had all the musculature of a coat hanger. But she took his hands and put them on her hips, and with him standing behind her they practiced what she called "the jump turn" amid bouts of giggling, lowering themselves and swiveling clumsily, and pausing to take frequent sips of bourbon. She had drawn up her hair at the back, and at her nape were impossibly fine, light-tawny hairs; they made him think of the tiny lines on old maps that indicate wilderness, or the steepness of mountains. He began kissing her neck passionately.

If I were Rodin, he said, I would not sleep or eat until I had sculpted you. (At home, bourbon in hand, he would often practice saying soft tickling things to women.)

Oh, *push*, she said lightly. Help me get this off.

She unclipped her stockings while he began unlacing the corset, and after a minute they had wrestled it off.

What a contraption! she laughed, tossing it aside. She kept the stockings on, clearly conscious of their arousing effect. Next came the camisole, which had a single dainty tie at the front; she undid it while keeping her amused gaze on the bulge in his trousers. He kissed her breasts: each was a pearled overfullness, like a water droplet on the underside of a leaf, and blessed with a larger-than-usual nipple.

He heard her murmur something about a transformation, but he didn't catch it—he was too busy kissing everything he could.

❖

People think that the world is dead in winter, but actually it's dead in late fall. With the snow comes a quickening; valleys and hills begin to take on light; and flesh turns sleepwalker at all hours.

In the days that followed, Connor found himself constantly sliding into reveries about Arundel Grey. He was bewildered by their intensity and frequency. He could be riding the Sparks Street tram, or printing forms at the American Legation, or composing another dreary diplomatic invitation, and Arundel would be there, sweet water from the brackish wells of the day. Sometimes she came just to talk, but mainly she came to have sex. As she told Connor, these interludes were an escape for *her*, too.

Sleeping, he was bravo and barnstormer. They did the usual dream activities like flying, with some wild harlequin twists. Once he found himself in a tandem ski jump with her, standing on the back of her skis while they soared through the air, both of them naked except for witch-elk ski boots and grey woolen socks. Fifty feet below them, the spectators clapped and cheered. Arundel's curved warmth cleaved the streaming cold around him. I know I'm dreaming, he thought, but...wait, let me see. In mid-air she bent at the waist, as ski jumpers do, and his penis slid inside her briefly. Maybe it wasn't a dream after all! He heard her laughing very naturalistically as his penis popped out. When they landed, she edged one ski ahead of the other, his foot moving with hers, and they both managed to keep their feet. Definitely dreaming, he thought. But the realization liberated him, and before they came to a complete stop, he managed to enter her again. The crowd cheered wildly.

He was certainly moving beyond the theory of skiing.

But he wanted to see her again, and that would mean getting out on skis. The best place for an innocent encounter would be Dome Hill, where she went for her weekly lessons. *Oh, hello, Mrs. Grey. So nice to see you again. Yes, I'm on skis—I guess you inspired me!* On Saturday morning he wrestled his eleven-pound hickory ridge-top skis ("Made in Canada by Scandinavians") into the streetcar and rode with the other skiers to the Dome Hill stop. Disembarking with his equipment under his arms, he marveled. The valley was brimful with light, the sky a startle of blue like a flock of hyacinth macaws. It took him five minutes to do up his bindings. Clutching his bamboo poles, he moved off in the laborious stamp-shuffle of the beginner. He studied the easy swing of passing skiers and strove to mimic it, but his skis wouldn't go smoothly over the snow. Small children passed him nonchalantly. The heel strap of one binding kept creeping up to the edge of his boot. At one point he took off his skis and studied the bindings balefully: metal toe flanges to keep the foot in place (bent), straps for the toe and heel (ineffectual) and a boot plate (coming loose). Shouldering the skis, he began walking but kept sinking through the crust. Eventually he had to put the medieval things back on. He got to Dome Hill at 10:30, almost missing the lessons for married ladies.

From the shadow of Dome Hill Lodge he scanned the hill. Lilly and Arundel stood together at the top; the other women must have already left. Lilly was streamlined as usual in men's ski slacks and flight jacket; Arundel was wearing a dirndl skirt and cowl-neck sweater. He shuffled closer. Arundel snow-ploughed cautiously down the hill, Lilly following easily, and then they both wrapped their skis with something (waxed sealskin, he found out later) and tramped up again. At one point Arundel toppled over, laughing: Lilly helped her up and they stood side by side, Lilly's arm around her student's waist, while she gestured in explication to their skis.

He watched them for half an hour, growing colder and colder. Arundel seemed transformed. He felt shy now about approaching the two skiers; they seemed cocooned in their own sky and snow. At length he turned around and began slogging home. Who was Arundel? Why did her name have this talismanic power? Was she the first wife of Adam? A miracle-working Irish queen? The secret consort of Jesus?

That night, she asked him if he read poetry. Naked, she had turned herself around and was lying on top of him. She'd seen it on a French postcard, apparently.

Tell me if you like this, she continued—

> Lovely the swift
> Sparrows that brought you over black earth
> A whirring of wings through mid-air
> Down the sky.*

It's glittering Aphrodite, she said, riding in her chariot drawn by sparrows. Beautiful, isn't it?

Grasping his penis firmly, she pressed her tongue against the moist slit, parting it slightly.

All right, she said, your turn.

Waking alone in the morning, he knew what he had to do. He would find out the source of her name. He would unearth the lost story of Arundel.

❖

He had barely embarked on this quest, dipping into Bullfinch's *Mythology* and *The Nuttal Cyclopedia of Universal Information*, when he was completely thrown off the rails by an encounter with Arundel's husband.

Basil Grey was a small man with caret wrinkles above his eyes and a sad, moral face—a non-skier, apparently. Ordinarily he would be just another of Ottawa's pleasant, innocuous inhabitants with whom Connor had nothing in common. But given his fantasies about Mr. Grey's wife, Connor was very curious about the husband. When they ran into each other one day at the drugstore, Connor was both uneasy and intrigued. Basil Grey didn't seem to notice.

"You're the tree seller," he said, trying to summon interest.

"That's me," said Connor nervously. He cast a surreptitious eye over Mr. Grey and saw nothing more than a child wintered by time. Three kids, apparently. A modest job as a bank clerk. Hair growing out of his ears. Surely this man could never love a woman like Arundel.

"I understand you're giving out certificates for the trees," said Basil. "I think my wife was too shy to ask for one."

Connor opened his mouth and closed it again. Obviously Arundel had said nothing to her husband about the certificate. He began to sense he was inside a story that went deeper than he thought.

"I'll...make sure you get one," he said and, casting around for misdirection, added quickly, "Mrs. Grey tells me she is enjoying her ski lessons."

"It seems that way." Connor detected something in the man's voice—disapproval with a note of wistfulness. No, this man could never love Arundel. But he probably did love Mrs. Basil Grey.

"Are you a skier, Mr. O'Flynn?" said Basil.

"No, no." Connor forced a chuckle. "I mean…I did it once but I think that's going to be the last."

This confession seemed to break down some of Basil's reserve.

"My wife wants to try the craziest things now," he said in a low voice.

Connor felt a barely perceptible dislocation, as if a magnetic field had reversed itself deep inside him.

"I beg your pardon?" he said.

"She just started lessons this year, and now she wants to do *ski jumping*."

"Ski jumping?"

"Absolutely daft." Basil Grey shook his head. "I don't know where she gets these ideas."

❖

At the next ski club tea, Connor watched her restively from a corner. Was it his imagination, or did she look more animated, more alive, than before? He waited until Basil had left his wife's side, and then, gathering his courage, sidled close.

"Hello, Mrs. Grey," he said.

She turned on him her eyes of faded blue. "Hello, Mr. O'Flynn," she said placidly. "How are your trees selling?"

"Like hotcakes. Hot as…hotcakes." He didn't notice any particular nuance in her look, anything to indicate a sharing of dreams. "How are the ski lessons going?" he asked blandly.

She looked pleased. "I think I've lost some weight."

"I'm glad." He pushed ahead clumsily; he didn't know when her husband would return. "I've actually done a bit of skiing myself. At Dome Hill and…at home."

"At home?" she said.

"Yes—I do parlour skiing. I think I've got the jump turn down."

He watched her face for any flicker of knowingness, but she just stirred her tea and looked across the room. "That's nice," she said absently. "Well, I'd better see what's become of my husband."

"Mrs. Grey," he said urgently, lowering his voice, "can we meet sometime?"

"I beg your pardon?"

"Can we meet? Somewhere private?"

Her eyes narrowed. "Why?"

No, he couldn't say it; he couldn't even hint at the recent adventures of his soul. From her look he might have been an insurance salesman or a peddler of Prohibition rum. Could all those rich fantasies just be his alone? In desperation he blurted out: "Because…I've discovered the story behind your name."

Connor was completely unprepared for her reaction. The blood drained from her face.

"What's wrong?" he said. "I'm sorry, I didn't mean to—"

She had come closer; the fright in her eyes had given way to anger. "What have you discovered?" she hissed. "Tell me!"

"Just…the origin of your name," he faltered. "Remember I said it sounded like a name from a story? Well, I know the whole story now."

She blanched again. "What is it? Tell me!"

"Well…I can't. Not here."

"Why not?"

"Because…" He was flailing badly but not quite under the waves. "There are too many people here. You have to hear it in private."

She continued to gaze at him with eyes of flint. "Very well," she said. "I will meet you."

"Thank you," he gasped.

He couldn't understand what had just happened; he couldn't understand anything about this strange affair. She glanced around quickly to see if anybody was in earshot.

"Tomorrow, Ogilvy's is having a sale," she said. "I'll be in the tearoom at the back. Two o'clock."

"Yes. Thank you."

She turned away, but almost immediately turned back.

"Please," she said in a low voice, "don't tell my husband."

Connor blinked. "What?"

"It'll mean the end of my marriage. The end of me."

"I'll tell nobody," said Connor vehemently.

She gave him a last tormented look and fled across the room.

❖

Connor was mystified. Clearly she believed he had discovered some intimate secret about her. Well, he would set her mind at rest. He'd explain that he had discovered nothing about her, no story about her name; he'd been babbling like a half-wit. Babbling in the hope that he could see her alone. He'd be dirt in her eyes, but at least he'd be acting honourably.

And yet, he did have a story about Arundel—their story, the tale of their secret selves meeting in his fantasies. Dare he tell her about that? God, no, that would make things worse. Maybe he could come up with some harmless little story about her name.

And then he thought of Lilly Standish. He was sure the married ladies confided their secrets to her; she might know what Arundel wanted to hide. But he'd have to tread carefully. He could never let Lilly know that he was interested in Mrs. Basil Grey, she of the hair nets and thick calves.

Connor could not tell whether Lilly actually liked him, or was just amused by him—by his quaint Southern lilt, his hothouse melancholy, his straw hats. But when he called on her that evening, she cheerfully ushered him into her parlour and told him he looked pensive.

"But then," she said, pouring him a brandy, "you always look pensive."

Lilly had the dark waterbird beauty of a Man Ray model—high cheekbones, a cupid's-bow mouth, night-fluent eyes. She had, in fact, once appeared in one of Man Ray's *cinépoèmes* (this was in Paris, where she had fled after the death of her husband) and had apparently done a dance routine with Kiki of Montparnasse. Man Ray's photos could be found scattered throughout her house—all of women, their faces and torsos patterned with light and shadow. Tonight she was wearing a burgundy lace dress with a slanted hemline and a fashionable corsage at her hip. She was forty years old and as supple as a dryad. On the ski trails she was a master of the *geländesprung*, in which a skier would plant both poles, bend low, and leap into the air over an obstacle. She could have had any man she wanted but seemed only interested in skiing and photography.

"Speak your troubles, dear man," she said.

Suddenly assailed by misgivings, Connor decided to say nothing about Arundel Grey but to sketch out a hypothetical situation.

"There's this person I know," he said, "and she's got a very unusual name. I think I fell in love with her name before I even met her. That happens with us Southerners sometimes."

Lilly selected a cigarette from her case and sat with one arm supporting the elbow of her cigarette hand. It took a moment for Connor to realize she was waiting for a light. He struck a match and she leaned forward, cupping his hand. He saw a flesh-tinted shadow between her breasts and thought: what a shape-shifting marvel. On the ski slope she had the lineaments of an adolescent boy, but here, in that dress, she could have made an elderly Anglican minister go off like a roman candle.

"The thing is, this person seems very...protective of her name," he continued, waving out the match. "As if it had some secret attached to it."

Up till that moment Lilly hadn't been paying close attention, but now she paused while inhaling and fixed him with her noctilucent eyes.

"And somebody else said to this person that he knew the story behind her name," he continued. "But he didn't know it at all; he just said that. He was being an idiot. And now this person is furious at the other idiot person. It's almost as if she thinks he's going to *blackmail* her with her own name."

Lilly averted her face slightly to exhale, never taking her eyes off Connor.

"There's more to it than that," he said uneasily, "but that's basically where it stands now."

Lilly languidly drew on her cigarette. Her eyelids fell and her lips parted; a curling wafer of smoke appeared between her tongue and upper palate. She straightened to exhale—chin tilted, mouth in a languorous "o"—as if she had just felt the touch of a lover's tongue between her shoulder blades. She was the picture of careless indolence, but Connor got the strange feeling she was thinking hard, grappling with an unexpected problem.

"Tell me more about this person with the unusual name," she said easily.

Connor turned towards the coal fire. "I can't."

"Why not?"

"Because, Lilly, it's...complicated. Anyway, the question is— what do I do?"

Lilly placed her cigarette in an ashtray and leaned back, crossing her legs.

"You know, Connor," she said, "Among some tribes of the world, it's the custom to have two names—a public name and a secret name. And you don't tell your secret name to anybody because it's actually your soul. You guard that name because it's you, and you don't want anyone to hear it who could harm you. Evil magicians, for example."

"That's exactly it!" said Connor excitedly. "I fell in love with her secret soul, I fell in love with—"

He almost said it: *Arundel.* He had even formed the "Ar"—had Lilly caught it? He kept talking to cover himself: "And the thing is, I've arranged to see her tomorrow, and I don't know what to say to her. I'm going to look bad whatever I say."

"I agree with you," said Lilly. "Tell me—have you been intimate with this woman?"

"Intimate?"

"Yes, Connor, intimate."

Arundel leaned over in Connor's mind and her breasts took on form, filling a more slender space, trembling slightly like a soap bubble on a wand when a child breathes it into fullness.

"Not in so many words," he said dispiritedly.

"What?"

"*No.*"

Lilly nodded. "And you haven't discovered anything secret about her. Anything that could be used for…blackmail purposes."

"No! And I would never—"

"Yes, yes, I'm sure you wouldn't." Connor thought he detected relief in her voice. She stubbed out her cigarette and stood up. "I must go."

"Wait a second," said Connor. "You're not just going to walk out on me?"

"I have a very pressing engagement."

"But…I thought you were going to *help* me, Lilly. What about all those tree certificates I did for you?"

"I can't help you if you don't tell me everything."

"I'm protecting the woman, Lilly. I'm protecting her good name."

He followed her out into the vestibule and stood watching while the maid helped her on with her coat.

"Well, thanks a lot, Lilly," said Connor bitterly, when the maid had left. "I hope I've amused you for five minutes."

She turned. "Oh, Connor, *stop.*"

He blinked. "Stop what?"

"Stop being so pensive. I'm not going to help you if you're going to look pensive." She threw her scarf over her neck with her usual theatricality. "Very well, I'll give you some advice. When you meet this woman, tell her the truth. Tell her that you don't know any secret about her. Tell her you had no intention to blackmail her. Tell her that you just wanted to see her again. And then maybe you'll find out who she really is."

"Who she really is?" he echoed.

She reached out and put a hand on his cheek. "You know what you've done, Connor?" she said sympathetically. "You've just created a woman out of a name—the way the pioneer in the old story made a wife out of snow. It's no crime. We've all done it at one time or another."

Riding the tramway to Ogilvy's Department Store, Connor was as nervous as he had ever been. His erotic reveries had ceased completely, and now he could only see Arundel as furious and afraid.

Ogilvy's was filled with Ottawa housewives looking for bargains on rayon stockings, "ski togs," and Regal Ware pots and pans. Arundel was dressed as she had been when he first met her; she was just another dowdy matron, taking a break at the small in-store tea room.

"Hello, Mrs. Grey," he said fearfully.

"Mr. O'Flynn," she said, with no trace of disquietude. "Please sit down."

Connor understood that he should get right to the point.

"I felt that you hated me yesterday," he said. "You seemed to think we were enemies. But we're not."

"No," she said. "I know that now."

"You do?"

He wondered what had changed, why she seemed so calm now; but just then the waiter brought more hot water for her teapot, and they were both silent.

"And you don't know anything about my name," she pressed, once they were alone.

He shook his head. "I just thought that Arundel was a beautiful name and that it should have a story."

He had the strongest feeling that she guessed everything—that he had fantasized about her, made for himself (as Lilly said) a woman out of snow. His face burned. But she didn't seem contemptuous or sorry for him; she just nodded and stirred her tea.

"Is Arundel your secret name, Mrs. Grey?" he asked conversationally.

She took a placid sip of tea. "You could say that. My secret name, my magic name—my true name."

"But what does it mean?"

"Different things. It comes from the French word for swallow, *hirondelle*. It means 'dell of eagles' in Old Norse. It's the name of a town in England. It's the name of Bevis's war horse—Bevis of Southampton—in the old poem. And so on." She smiled. "I like a name with lots of stories inside it."

Connor frowned; the etymology of the name shed no light on why she should want to keep it a secret.

"It was my lover who gave me that name," she added, poised as ever.

"Your lover?" repeated Connor hoarsely.

He had sat up straighter at "lover," but one glance told him that she wasn't referring to him.

"Lovers do that, don't they?" she said. "Take you out of your ordinary name and into your magic one."

"But your husband"—Connor was working hard at unravelling it all—"he doesn't know your secret name?"

"He knows me as Arundella, or just 'Della.' But neither of them is me." She looked straight into his eyes. "Because 'Arundel' doesn't really have a sex, does it? It could be a woman's name, or a man's. It just depends...on the story."

Connor stared at her for a long moment and then removed his bewildered gaze to the refuge of his teacup. In his confusion he vaguely remembered a story about the Eskimos, who believed that at a certain time in your life, you needed to take on a new name, to re-inspire yourself…Should he reply with *that*? Anything to get him over this very awkward moment.

"So now you know the story behind my name, Mr. O'Flynn," she said, crumpling up her napkin. "And what I want to know is…is my story safe with you?"

What story? he thought, but said soberly, "Until death."

"Good. Because my name is very precious to me." For the first time she smiled at him. "Goodbye, Mr. O'Flynn," she said, getting to her feet.

But Connor remained sitting. "Mrs. Grey, do you read poetry?"

She looked down on him curiously. "Why, yes, I do. What about you, Mr. O'Flynn?"

"You asked me that question before. Do you remember?"

"I'm afraid I don't." She dabbed imperturbably at her mouth with her napkin.

"You quoted me some lines about sparrows towing Aphrodite in her chariot. Or maybe it was swallows."

Now she seemed to lose a bit of her poise: she turned her face away slightly, as if in disbelief. "I quoted that to you?"

"Yes. You know the poem?"

"Of course; it's Sappho. But I really can't remember quoting it to you. Not to you."

Connor caught the emphasis and smiled ruefully. Arundel, you don't know the power of your name, the power of your transformation. He had been like a tuning fork brought close to one already sounding: he had begun to resonate in sympathy—and at the same pitch.

"Well, it doesn't matter," he said, getting to his feet. "Good-bye, Mrs. Grey."

"Good-bye, Mr. O'Flynn," she said, still bemused.

"And thank you."

Arundel's secret would be safe with him—he was a Southerner, after all. Still, he felt he'd had a narrow escape. He really had no desire to know more about the stories inside Arundel's name. It was all a foreign country to him: snow, ice, skin-flaying winds, strange feral stars and women who seemed to share the qualities of those elements. He just wanted to forget this latest rococo episode and keep grinding away at life. For that was how he lived now: grinding away at the days while the days ground away at him.

And yet, the next Saturday afternoon, he loaded his skis onto the Wrightville streetcar, got off at the end of the line, and thrashed his way to Lac des Fées. He came no closer to imitating the easy swing of the other skiers, but at least his bindings worked (his friend Win had done some repairs), and this time he remembered to take a full flask of bourbon. When he got home, he felt he was improving.

And one day at Dome Hill, tramping doggedly up, he happened to glance at the northern slope, where skiers had built a good-sized jump out of hay bales. He saw a skier racing toward the jump and recognized Lilly Standish, wearing her usual black slacks and flight jacket. Even an expert like Lilly was wobbling a bit with the bumps, but she maintained her speed. Her knees were bent, her chin raised, her ski poles tucked under her arms.

Connor watched as her skis went up the slope of the jump. Straightening from her semi-crouch, she leaned forward at the waist. Her toque came off but she kept her form beautifully. For a second she was embayed in the blue, a woman held up by a strange power—as if, hidden high in the sunlit air above, streamed a vast cloud of small harnessed wings.

*From Sappho, *Selected Poems and Fragments* by A. S. Kline (translator), © 2005

THE UNIT

Aaron Hughes

For
"Navy Simon" & "Fireman Rick"

[Australian Defence Intelligence Organisation (ADIO)]
[Branch: Royal Australian Navy (RAN)]
[Investigation re.: Leto, H. Commander]
[Clearance: Level 7 Only]
[Interview held at: [Redacted]]
[Interview Subject: Prusa, N. Chief Petty Officer]
[Date: 23 February 2016, Monday]
[Time stamp: 17:00]

My name is Nester Prusa. My rank is Chief Petty Officer. I am a Navy Clearance Diver. My Service Number is [Redacted].

I was there that night. I saw everything. Or nearly everything. What I didn't see, I pieced together later from talking to the other guys in the unit.

I can talk about it now. Because you can't touch him. His reputation is so strong now that *nothing* you can say will tarnish it.

And soon, it won't matter anyway.

❖

They call me "Nessie."

I suppose it's a play on my first name, Nester. And because I'm a scuba diver. And, somehow, that fucking Scottish water creature, which kind of looks like the double-snake emblem of our unit. Who the fuck knows how these nicknames really start? All I know is that they stick like shit to a blanket. And they stick for *life*.

Commander Heracles Leto saved me. I don't mean that he just saved my life in the field; countless times at that. He saved me in all the other ways that matter, too. He saved *all* of the guys in our unit. Well, we all know that's not true: it turns out he couldn't save everyone. But those of us who are left, we're alive because of him.

Heracles—Herc—was second-in-command of one of the Navy's CDTs [Clearance Diving Teams] in Sydney. It was a good team, but he wanted better: he wanted his *own* team. At some point, Herc accepted who he was, and he'd made peace with himself.

So, he decided he would establish a team of like-minded guys. He made discreet enquiries with the other teams. He'd heard rumours across the service about men in the other units. Some of us were in New South Wales, but most of us were in units across the other states. Many of us were from some fucking wog or ethnic background or another. He sought us out.

I was a Leading Seaman at the time. My career was going nowhere fast. So was I. I drank too much. I partied too hard, even by Navy standards. I slept around, too. Not with other sailors—even I wasn't that far gone—but I'd become a slut. I'd even barebacked with a couple of guys, just for the thrill of it. I was a fucking idiot. I was lucky not to catch anything serious. Well, apart from that one really fucking bad case of the crabs.

Herc travelled across the country seeking us out. Like him, I was in Sydney at the time. One night, he followed me to a seedy back-room leather bar. He bought me a drink; actually, he bought me six. He struck up a conversation. I knew who he was straight away, though. But I listened. He made a good case. He did with all of us. He spoke well, like a leader, someone you could trust. His reputation didn't disappoint. None of us turned him down.

Looking back now, I wished a couple of the guys had said no. Maybe things would have turned out differently.

Have you met Herc? No? I didn't think so. I guessed you hadn't interviewed him yet. Do you have any idea of the man? What sort of a presence he is?

Herc is big. I mean, seriously big. Navy divers are usually smaller guys. Because it's easier to get in and out of tight spots in and under the water if you're leaner.

Not Herc. Six foot three. A-fucking-mazing tattoo down the length of his long back; two snakes, intertwined, winding down and around his body, ending along the line of his pelvis. Mind you, the tattoo looks a bit worse for wear these days, given all of his scars. He's a fucking Greek man-mountain. So fucking hairy, he gives one of the mincing homos near our base a wet dream once a fortnight when he gets the faggot to wax him. Otherwise, he'd never have been able to get in and out of his dive suit without an entire fucking tin of talcum powder. He chose the rest of us against type, too. None of us are less than five foot ten. He wanted a team of guys who *looked* like they could kick arse, and who could actually *do* it, too.

But that's just the physical. You won't know who Herc really is until you meet him and talk with him. You'll get a real sense of his strength then. I'm not saying he's a fucking saint; none of us were, are, or ever fucking will be. Especially Phemus. No one who goes to war comes back quite the same. But Herc's a real leader. You don't see many of them in the service anymore. His mojo got all of us to trust him—I mean *really* trust him—and it got us all into his new unit.

Herc'd had unofficial approval from his CO [Commanding Officer] to make enquiries. Once he got all the guys lined up, he went back and put in a request for a new team. Do you know what sort of respect he commanded, even back then? To be able to head-hunt guys for his own team?

The transfers all went through, quickly and quietly. For various reasons, some units—like mine—were all too glad to be rid of us. One at a time, we shipped into Sydney.

We turned up on the Monday for "hell week." Which is just what we got: ten days of pure, un-fucking-adulterated hell. We'd all had diving experience. Otherwise, we wouldn't have been there. I'd even sobered up a bit for it.

But it wasn't enough. Herc knew that for our unit to work—to get any sort of respect—we had to be tougher sons-of-bitches than all the other teams. So, he set about breaking us down, then building us back up again. In that week alone, we were put through nearly forty staged dives; ten more than the other units. It was brutal. A couple of the guys couldn't keep up. The rest of us made it through. But that was only the start.

Over the next six months, we worked harder than any other unit. We trained, we dived, we worked out, we studied. We stacked on the physical and mental muscle to be the best.

And yes, the rumours are true: we were all fags. There you go, it's on the official record now. Who gives a fuck, though? Everyone in the upper ranks knew. No one cared. We did our fucking job. Better, usually, than anyone else. Herc gave us a diamond-hard focus.

You're probably thinking: it was like a fucking faggot porn movie, yeah? Bunch of muscled up meat-heads, high on testosterone? Sucking and fucking each other senseless all night, in our bunks, in the barracks, in the water? Dream on.

There was *none* of that.

Herc had made it crystal clear: don't shit where you eat. Besides, we had to rely on each other to survive in combat. We were tight, but not that tight. There's a difference between fucking a guy's arse, or taking his cock, and saving that same arse and cock in combat. Herc made sure we knew the difference. At least that's how it started in the beginning. But there's always one exception to every rule.

Me, I saw it from the first day Petty Officer Hylas Driope walked in the door. Eventually, everyone did.

You could feel the electricity in the room, between him and the boss. They both ignored it at first. As a result, Herc was harder on the Jew-boy than the rest of us. He pushed him something fierce. But Hylas took *everything* Herc dished out and he still came up smiling, although sometimes grimacing.

Hylas was beautiful.

I mean, yeah, he was handsome, but he was fucking beautiful. Long of limb; "coltish," I heard him described once. A ranga with pale skin so white you could see the blue veins running underneath, especially when we got out of the ice-cold water after a dive. And those fucking curls. The rest of us had short, back and sides. Hell, like Heracles, most of us shaved our heads because we were in and out of the water so much. Not Hylas. Yeah, he had short hair, but he kept those Shirley Temple curls. Made him look even younger than he was, but not like a girl. He was too much of a man.

Hylas became the centre of the unit. He was easy with a joke. He'd be the ear for your problems. He'd help you with your studies when you struggled. He'd push you in the gym when you flagged. He listened when, in the early hours of the morning, you felt like a fucking imposter and a failure. And when you were shaking from sheer exhaustion, fucking frozen from being in the cold water for hours on end, he'd help your fumbling fingers with your diving gear. There was nothing he wouldn't do for the guys in our unit.

❖

Case in point.

Not long after he'd arrived, we were prepping for a night dive. My hands were shaking. I was having the DTs from all of the alcohol I had tried to replace my blood with over the last couple of years.

Edgy and jittery, I was speeding through my pre-dive check. I'd thrown my equipment on and was about to dive in.

Hylas grabbed my upper arm none too gently. I spun around, ready to deck him. He had his goggles and mouthpiece on already and could only point.

I looked down and realised I hadn't clamped off one of my tubes. It would have taken awhile under the water before I'd realised my air mix was off.

Maybe I would have realised in time. Maybe I wouldn't have. Maybe down under the water in the dark, where it gets so cold that your dick shrivels and your nuts escape up into your chest, I would have just fucking surrendered. At that time, I didn't have much of a reason to live.

And if I had, maybe I wouldn't be sitting in front of you fuck knuckles today telling you my truth.

I kid you fucking not: Hylas was there for me, for all of us. Sometimes he saved us. Sometimes he helped us save ourselves.

After our first tour of [Redacted], we realised what it meant to lay down your life for another guy in the unit. But, somehow, Hylas went beyond even that. He was really *there* for all of us. He was fucking beautiful, and I don't care how much of a fucking pansy knob-gobbler I sound when I say it, either.

❖

It took a while, but Herc saw who Hylas was, too.

He came to realise that Hylas was the glue of the team. He encouraged it, but Jesus, he was hard on the kid. Hylas was no idiot. He knew what the deal was. Herc was hard on him because he cared. He *really* fucking cared for Hylas. He cared for *all* of us, but there was something special about Hylas. Sometimes you see it in combat, when a guy shines in the heat of battle.

Have you needle dicks ever seen that? Have you ever seen a soldier light up in the field? Have you ever seen a man fucking *blaze*? I didn't think so.

That's what Hylas was like. It was like those—what do you call those fuckers, androids?—in that fucking sci-fi movie that Phemus, our comms guy, used to watch all the fucking time: "The light that burns twice as bright, burns for half as long."

That's the light that Hylas had. We all saw it. Herc saw it.

Later—too fucking late—I realised that Polyphemus, or Phemus as we called him, had seen it, too.

Over the next year, we watched the sparks fly between Hylas and Heracles. All through our first tour together in [Redacted]. Man, what a fucking year that was! Then when we got home, we kept watching them. We knew the deal and we respected it. We understood the rules. But somehow, like I said, we all knew that some rules are meant to be broken. It just took a while for both of them to realise it, too.

I saw it when it happened, you know? As far as I knew at the time, I'm the only one who did. You can hear it first from me.

I was supposed to be in town with some guy's ankles up around my ears that weekend. But my hire car had broken down. Fucking Jap. piece of shit. I had to walk ten miles back to base. I'd stopped in at the bottle-o for some Jack on the way because I was so fucking annoyed. By the time I got on base, I was on my way to being toasted.

I'd grabbed my bed kit and crawled into our dorm's storeroom. I wanted to drink and to feel sorry for my sad self. And I was horny as hell. So, I wanted to pull my meat in private. But then I heard voices out in the dorm. I kept real quiet, like the nosy bastard I can be.

It was Herc and Hylas, sounding out of breath, coming back from a late-night run. I couldn't hear their words, but it wasn't a friendly fucking chat. They were arguing. Not loudly, but in that low-voiced way that's somehow worse than an out-and-out barney. I only got bits and pieces.

"This isn't right…"

"We can't fucking do this…"

"Fuck you…"

They moved into the shower stalls, and I cracked the door open an inch. They were standing in the steam, still arguing, a stand-off between two Titans.

"I don't deserve this…"

"You fucking do; I do, too…"

"You don't know me…"

"I know enough…"

There was a look between them then, an agreement.

And that's when I closed the door. I'm many things, but I'm not a fucking perv.

Later, though, I found out that someone else got a fucking eyeful that night.

❖

The following Monday when we came back to the barracks, something was different. You could see it when Herc and Hylas walked in. They'd finally released the tension. The eagle had fucking landed. There was this relaxed look around Herc's eyes. He was quicker with a smile and a kind word. He was still a mean son-of-a-bitch a lot of the time. But we all were. We had to be. We had to be better, tougher. When you're a fag in the service, you have to be ready with your armour twenty-four/seven. It's the price you pay. Sometimes, though, it's too fucking high a price.

We were all so fucking relieved that Herc and Hylas had finally done something about it. Now, it was time to wait and watch again. Was this a one-off thing? Did they just bomb the dam and it was done? Not fucking likely. There was real chemistry between these guys. Two powerful men with a lot to prove.

There was something enduring there. You felt it, but you rarely saw them act it out. They never showed it while on duty. Never. Not once. And on the job, Herc never cut Hylas any slack. Hylas never asked for it, either. We worked hard, and we didn't ask for favours. At first, we did it to prove ourselves to Herc. Then he taught us that we were actually working that hard for *ourselves,* and for the unit. *That's* how we learned to take pride in who we were.

As I said, I watched the two of them closely; we all did. How would their relationship affect the unit? Would it weaken our edge? Would it diversify our focus? We needn't have worried. If anything, it brought us closer together. Herc was the head of our team, and Hylas was the heart. We grew closer as a unit.

❖

One evening, as we were coming back from our run around the base, Herc called us together. We sensed an announcement.

"You know me…" he locked each of us in turn with his gaze. "You know what I stand for. You know my playbook. And you know I live by the rules…"

He had rehearsed and measured his words. But, uncharacteristically, he faltered.

Theo, our munitions guy, broke the pregnant pause. He produced a bottle of Black Label from his duffel bag and handed tin cups around. He raised a toast.

"To honour."

We all repeated: "To *honour.*"

"And to bending the rules," Phemus added. He winked, and we all relaxed a little.

None of us were big on words. The message was clear: it's okay, what you guys have here is okay. Because you're one of us, and we're all a part of something special now. And it's a-fucking-okay with us.

We hit the showers, hit the sack, and put the subject to bed.

❖

Slowly, other teams started to envy us, and we got a reputation. Officially, we were Team Mysia. Stupid fucking wog name. But we *were* a bunch of fucking wogs, chinks, and even a kike. They still whispered our nickname—CDT: Cock Diving Team—although no one dared say it within our earshot. We'd have fucking pummeled them.

When I say that we worked hard, it's fair to say that we also played hard. We were fags, but we were in the Navy after all. We liked to let off steam by going out partying. We didn't do drugs, but we liked a drink. It wasn't like before, though. Back before we joined the team, when so many of us hated ourselves, we drank, drugged, and drug-fucked to forget. We didn't need that anymore. We were part of something now, something bigger than ourselves. We'd worked hard to get where we were. We'd pushed our bodies and our minds to the limits, and we were the better for it. And then we partied to let off some steam.

It was early 2015, and we were preparing for deployment to [Redacted]. We had a four-day leave pass before the week of prep that led to deploying. And we were ready to party.

We hired a minibus and drove into Darlinghurst. We'd sprung for the ritzy Carlyon close to Oxford Street. We wanted to be close to the action. We'd all hired individual rooms so we could bring trade back. Except Hylas and Herc, of course, who shared a room. We spent the Friday getting ready, buying everything in bulk: party clothes, snacks, and booze. Condoms and lube were bought in industrial quantities. There would be a major dance-fest and fuck-fest that weekend.

But things didn't work out that way. Oh, it was a fuck-fest, just not in the way you're thinking. It was more like a clusterfuck.

❖

Like the song says: "Dig if you will the picture…"

Friday night, around 10 pm and we're heading down Oxford Street. We were all outfitted in various kinds of low-rider tight pants and even tighter t-shirts. It paid to advertise. We did the slow-mo *The Right Stuff* walk down the main drag. All eyes were on us. The inner-city homos thought their Christmases had all come at once: eight tall, built guys striding confidently down the street, a couple of rounds of drinks already under our belts. We owned the street. They probably thought we were strippers heading off to a gig. They were half right, because the clothes would definitely be coming off later. It was like my dad used to say: "The girls will be busy tonight 'cos the Navy is in town." Well, tonight the boys would be even fucking busier.

We'd pre-purchased our tickets to the dance party at "Pegae." It was a new venue that'd opened up, which none of us had been to before. It's a huge dance club over three levels. Once you got tired of trancing, you could head down to their subterranean sauna and spa—sex club— over two levels in the basement. Guaranteed: we'd be visiting all the levels of the venue over the next eight hours.

Just like we owned Oxford Street, we owned the club. We towered over the other guys. We weren't long in the door, and we'd already downed several drinks at the front bar. Then we were in, and up, to the main dancefloor. Shirts quickly came off. It was hot, and we were hot to trot.

Herc and Hylas moved to the middle of the room. They were soon the centre of attention. If guys weren't secretly watching them, then they were just plain gawking. Their sweaty torsos ground together. They were lost in each other's eyes and in the pounding beat. They moved and grooved, pausing only to lock lips.

The rest of us guys were pairing off with trade. The civilian guys couldn't keep their hands off us. A couple of the more game guys in our unit were even setting up their own little threesomes. We were drinking and laughing and dancing and drinking some more. Our crotches and arses were regularly getting felt up. We just laughed and encouraged it. We slid through the lasers and the hazers and the deep *doof-doof* of the music.

We thought we were so fucking good. But we were just fucking morons. We were high on ourselves, our bodies, and how impressive we thought we were. As my dad also used to say: "Pride cometh before a fall."

That is how it all fucking started; how it all went to shit.

❖

Out on the dancefloor, slick with sweat, Hylas had decided to take a break and get a drink. He and Herc engaged in a long pashing session before Herc would let him go. Every man in that room wanted to be either Heracles or Hylas, or the meat in their particular sandwich.

Hylas headed across to the bar in the opposite room. I was ahead of him, lounging on a stool against a mirrored wall. I had a drink in one hand and a twink in the other. I watched as Phemus made a beeline to intercept Hylas at the bar. But the prick made it seem to Hylas that he'd run into him by accident.

I was intrigued.

They met up and started talking. I was a bit distracted by the twink who was chatting away in my ear. He was too young and too thin—and too fucking *Kylie*—for my tastes, but he was a good kid, and I thought maybe I'd throw him a fuck downstairs to start off the evening.

I watched Phemus and Hylas at the bar. Hylas drank an entire bottle of water, then mouthed that he wanted to take a slash.

I think that must have been when Phemus spiked Hylas' drink.

Later, they found large amounts of GBH—Grievous Bodily Harm, as it's known on the streets—in Hylas' bloodstream. They found some fucking Rohypnol as well.

Phemus was such a fucking cock-juggling thundercunt.

Hylas came back and did a couple of shots—tequila, probably— with Phemus. They were laughing and carrying on like fucktards. Then Hylas downed another bottle of water in one long gulp. He and Phemus headed back to the dance floor. I took my wide-eyed twink and followed them.

They got to the door; it was a couple of steps down onto the big dancefloor. Hylas took in the view from the doorway, Phemus at his side.

There, in the centre of the room, two tall, handsome young guys were pashing Herc; one on the mouth, the other on the ear. And a third was on his knees, just releasing the base of Herc's python cock into his eager, waiting hands.

Later, I learned that—with his trademark military precision— Phemus had engineered this scene to play out just the way he'd wanted it to. I'd never known—none of us did—that we had a fucking snake in our unit.

Hylas took a step back, then went to take a step forward. He didn't seem to be sure what he was seeing. By now, the drugs must have started to kick in. Deftly, Phemus spun Hylas around and guided him out of the room. He was murmuring in Hylas's ear like a fucking devil on his shoulder.

I'd taken this all in, and the pieces slowly started coming together.

I glanced over to see Herc shoving the twinks off him—hard—and zipping up his fly. He scanned the crowd, looking for Hylas whom he'd glimpsed. By now, he'd started to sense that something was not quite right.

I ditched my drink, along with my protesting twink, and made my way to Herc. I intercepted him just as he got to the door.

"Where's Hylas?" He eyed the crowd, agitated.

"Phemus took him out. Herc..." I yelled, to get his attention. "Herc! Something is very fucking wrong here."

"I'm starting to see that..." he trailed off, not sure what to do next.

"Come on. I think they headed downstairs." I grabbed him by his arm, which was slick with sweat. We dived into the crowd. Pushing our way through the gyrating bodies, I saw one, then two of the guys from our unit. I gave them the nod and the hand signal. They knew that gesture meant business, and they made their way after us.

We came out onto the main stairs, pushing people out of the way as we headed down, down. No sign of Phemus or Hylas. It was darker in the stairwell, with its painted-black walls and red lighting. The music wasn't so loud here, though. I glanced back at Herc. I could see him processing and taking it all in. We kept heading down. I had a bad feeling in my gut by now. I knew to trust that feeling: it had saved me in the field before.

We reached the ground floor just as our medic, Theo, was about to head up. He saw it straight away in our eyes. I asked him if he'd seen Hylas or Phemus. He said he saw them going down into the basement sauna. We kept heading down, the other guys trailing behind us.

This is where we lost fucking precious time.

They made us wait at the entrance to the sauna—the sex club—because it was so packed inside. Phemus and Hylas must have made it in before the lockout. We stood in a line behind other guys. Like the stairwell, the walls were black and the minimal lighting red. It was hot, too. Some guys were pashing and groping each other. All of them were ready to get their gear and their rocks off. We waited, silently, our bodies twitching. I glanced over at Herc. His eyes were thunder.

Finally, we made it through. We were given towels and key lockers. We threw ours on a nearby bench and headed straight in.

The mood lighting down there was even worse. You could barely see in front of you. Guys were walking around in towels. Those with better bodies were just plain naked. We followed the maze further and further in.

Then Herc heard a shout of pain. It was Hylas. Herc put his ear to a black cubicle door, pulled back, then threw his weight against it. The door sprung open.

Hylas, on all fours, was on a raised padded bed. His head was lolling to the side, his face grimacing, the cry still on his lips, his eyes glazed. Phemus stood behind Hylas, mercilessly fucking him from behind. Even in the gloom, I think I saw some blood. We all knew that Phemus was hung like a rhino.

Herc was on Phemus before he knew it. He slammed him against a wall and into the corner. I heard something crack. I think it was Phemus. He cowered like a whelp, the life gone out of him. Herc rolled Hylas onto his back. Hylas saw him then. He started beating Herc about the head and shoulders and chest. Hylas pushed him back. Herc tripped back and fell onto Phemus who had the wind knocked out of him again. Then Hylas scrambled up and ran for the door. I tried to catch him as he went, but he was bigger and taller than me. And, with the drugs in his system fighting for control, he had a mind of his own. For a fleeting instant, I saw the wildness in Hylas' eyes.

Herc was tangled up with Phemus on the floor. I reached down, pulled Herc up and we were out the door. The other guys caught up with us. We headed off in search of Hylas.

Blind corridors, men in towels, the wet floor: they all conspired to slow us down. We were like rats in a literal fucking maze. Eventually, we made it to the spa pool. We stood in the doorway scanning the room.

The vast pool spread out before us, parts of it hidden by low, undulating sections of wall. Metres of black tiling on the floor, walls and roof. Towels hanging from the walls. Bodies sitting, standing, bobbing in the water. Clouds of steam. Tiny red spotlights made it hard to see anything.

Then we heard a commotion from across the pool. Still in his jeans, Herc waded out into the water.

I was about to join him when I slipped on the wet fucking tiles.

The side of my head caught one of the low walls as I fell. I was down, lying on my side, at the edge of the pool. I could hear Theo talking to me, but it was from a distance. I could feel warm blood on my face.

Across the pool, I watched as Herc made his way into the darkness. Everything slowed down then. My vision went in and out in time with my heartbeat. It seemed like an eternity was passing, kind of like when you take amyl while you're fucking.

Then I saw Herc wading back through the water: he was cradling Hylas in his arms.

Theo dragged me out of the way. He propped me up against a wall to make room for Hylas.

Herc put Hylas on his back and started CPR.

Thirty chest compresses. Two breaths. *Again.*

Thirty chest compresses. Two breaths. *Again.*

It went on. Theo checked Hylas' pulse. Herc continued trying to breathe life back into Hylas.

After a while, Theo tried to take over. But Herc pushed him back and continued with the CPR.

The lights came up. Herc continued.

Time changes when you're giving CPR. Your only focus becomes the person in front of you, the breath and the chest compresses. You shut everything out, because you are trying to give life. And Herc was trying to save the only man he'd ever truly loved.

I watched all of this through a fog. I watched him try to save Hylas.

Heracles only surrendered when the paramedics arrived. They carefully pushed him back. He went limp like a rag doll and the guys in our team caught him. The medics intubated Hylas, continued the CPR, and loaded him onto a gurney. I was lifted by two of our guys, one on each side of me, who drag-walked me out.

Hylas and I were loaded into the ambulance. I looked over at the paramedics working on him. Hylas was so beautiful. Pale as he usually was, he now looked like a ghost.

I went out of the world for a while after that.

❖

Later, I found out that the MPs [Military Police] were quick to the scene. A Saturday night in Sydney? You bet that there was at least one squad cruising the streets, keeping an eye out for soldiers in trouble or misbehaving. As they're trained to, they took over with precision efficiency. Our entire unit was interviewed by the Police, then escorted back to the hotel. They gathered everyone's gear up, and the guys were back on base before dawn.

This included fucking Phemus, of course. But he went straight into lockup. More for his own safety than anything else's, I reckon.

The paramedics told me later that they'd kept trying to revive Hylas all the way to the hospital, then in the emergency department.

But he never came around.

The drugs had fucked him up. He'd had a seizure in the spa and taken too much water into his lungs. Fucking irony for a fucking Navy diver. He just fucking slipped away from Herc, from all of us...

[Interview paused at subject's request]
[Time stamp: 19:34]

❖

[Interview resumed]
[Time stamp: 19:55]

I was released the next morning to the base hospital, then sent back to barracks that night. Nothing major, just a concussion and a couple of stitches. We'd all had much worse.

The military machine had already swung into gear by then. All of the guys had either been interviewed or were in the process. I spoke quietly with each of the guys, out of earshot of Herc. I pieced the story together. He did, too.

The next morning, a rookie cadet came by and took Phemus' gear away. We never saw him again after that. He was quickly and quietly transferred to a ship in Western Australia.

The following year, I heard that Phemus put a barrel of pure smack [heroin] in his arm and never woke up. God have mercy on his worthless fucking, good-for-nothing soul.

Preparations continued for our deployment. Two guys were drafted from another CDT to take the places of Hylas and Phemus. Like anyone could. They felt very uncomfortable. But full credit to them, they sucked it up and got down to the job. They made sure they reminded us regularly about their fucking wives, though.

The day before we shipped out they held the funeral. It went as well as could be expected, I suppose. At the service, Heracles gave a brief speech on Hylas' life and Navy career. He edited himself out of that speech, though. They gave the folded flag and medals to his mother, who wept quietly. She'd never known about her son. So, she'd never known about Herc and what they'd shared.

The Navy chaplain gave Herc just one item from Hylas' gear before it all went to his mother. It was a ring that Herc had apparently given Hylas just before we headed off on that fateful weekend in Sydney.

It was a wedding band—three thin layers of gold, white gold and rose gold—much like the Russian wedding bands that are popular with the fucking breeders nowadays. But this one had a knot fashioned out of gold connecting the three narrow bands. Herc had a matching one, although he'd never had the chance to wear it. I think it was supposed to be the knot that bound Heracles and Hylas together.

When I think of Hylas nowadays, I always think back to that line from that fucking movie, *Bladerunner*: "The light that burns twice as bright burns for half as long." I finally watched that movie from beginning to end. Twice. After that line, the guy also says: "And you have burned so very, very brightly."

And Hylas did. He really fucking did.

We shipped out to [Redacted].

Herc led us into the field, into the water, and into battle. He was a different man now, though. He'd been a hero before, but now he was reckless. It was like he wanted to die. He never put anyone else in the unit in danger—*ever*—yet he put himself in harm's way. And often.

Herc led a record twelve missions while we were in [Redacted], all of them successful. He had more scars now, but he survived. And he brought us all safely back home again. I really think he wanted to die over there in [Redacted]. He wanted a soldier's death. But I guess—and I'm very fucking glad—that wasn't to be his fate.

Our unit didn't stay together long after we got back.

Guys transferred out, new guys transferred in, most of them straight. The heart had gone out of the team with Hylas' death. And

Herc's light had dimmed. He eventually came back from the edge, though; came back into the world.

And I was there waiting for him.

I can say this all now because this will be our last tour. Herc will confirm it. We're getting out of the Navy at the end of the year.

I'd loved Heracles from a distance for so very long.

One day he saw it in my eyes. I waited. I'm a patient cunt. Amongst the many things Herc taught me was patience.

One day, Herc started talking to me. I mean, really talking, to me and with me. And the next day, and then the one after that.

Then one night, he took me into his bed.

I just held him. This man—this *soldier*—who had saved countless civilians and fellow soldiers, who had served his country with honour through so many tours; I held his scar-covered body.

Then one day he took me into his heart. We've been together ever since.

When we finish up with the Navy, we're heading up north to Cairns in Far North Queensland. We're both "twenty-year men" now. We have our savings and the pension we'll each get. We've put a deposit on a small cruiser called the "Argo." We're going to take people out diving on the reef. Fags and dykes, mostly, but the invitation will be open to whoever can cough up the money and refrain from pissing us off.

Herc says I need to stop paying out on other gay men so much. I just give him a fucking shit-eating smile. Then I tell him to stop talking like a fucking fag and to go fuck himself.

❖

I swore Heracles an oath that I would never leave him, that only an enemy would take me from his side. So far, I've been lucky. And we only have this deployment in [Redacted] to get through now.

I know he'll never be all mine, though.

There's a part of him—a part of his soul—with a very high fucking wall around it. In that compound of his heart, he keeps the shining memory of Hylas; always beautiful, always smiling, always ready with a kind word and a helping hand. Always young. I know that Hylas is Heracles' great love, and his great tragedy.

But what Herc and I have is real, it is enduring, and it will be my honour to serve by his side until the day I fucking die. He's taught me to regret nothing, to live and to love. He even tells me from time to time that I might learn to love myself one day. I usually tell him to fuck off.

My name is Nester Prusa. And this is the truth—*my* truth—the whole truth, and nothing but the fucking truth.

[Interview concluded]
[Time stamp: 21:15]

CONTRIBUTOR BIOS

MAUREEN BRADY is the author of eight books, including the novels, *Getaway*, *Folly* and *Ginger's Fire*, and the short story collection, *The Question She Put to Herself*. Her stories and essays have appeared in *Sinister Wisdom; Bellevue Literary Review; Just Like A Girl; Southern Exposure; Cabbage and Bones: An Anthology of Irish American Women's Fiction;* and *Banff Writers, among others.* Her short story, "Basketball Fever," won the 2015 Saints and Sinners short fiction contest. She has long served as President of the Money for Women Fund.

LOUIS FLINT CECI is an author, educator, and retired software engineer. His published works include poems, short stories, autobiographical essays, and a novel, as well as scholarly works on poetics, linguistics, and artificial neural networks. He is a masters swimmer, winning two silver medals and a bronze at Gay Games 10 in Paris in 2018. He won the gold medal in the Poetic Justice poetry slam at the 2002 Gay Games in Sydney, and was inducted into the Saints and Sinners Hall of Fame in 2017. He lives in Nevada City, California.

LEWIS DESIMONE is the author, most recently, of the satirical comedy *Channeling Morgan* (Beautiful Dreamer Press). His previous novels include *Chemistry* and *The Heart's History,* cited in several "Best of 2012" lists. His work has also appeared in a number of journals and anthologies, including *Christopher Street, Chelsea Station, Best Gay Love Stories: Summer Flings, Best Gay Romance 2014, My Diva: 65*

Gay Writers on the Women Who Inspire Them, and *Not Just Another Pretty Face.* He blogs at lewisdesimoneblog.wordpress.com.

JAMIESON FINDLAY is the author of two novels, *The Blue Roan Child* and *The Summer of Permanent Wants*, both published by Doubleday Canada. He is a past winner of the City of Ottawa (Canada) Book Award for fiction. A science writer by trade, he currently makes his home in Chelsea, Quebec. His enthusiasms are skiing, writing, trying different microbrewery beers and playing guitar with his musical group Buskers for Tuskers, which raises money for elephant and rhino conservation.

J. MARSHALL FREEMAN is a writer, musician, and graphic designer. His young adult adventure novel, *Teetering* was published in 2016. He is currently seeking a publisher for his queer YA fantasy novel, *The Dubious Gift of Dragon Blood*, for which he received a Toronto Arts Council grant. His story, "Curo the Filthmonger," won the Saints+Sinners 2017 Fiction Contest, and he was a finalist in 2018. Mr. Freeman proudly wears epithets thrown at him online, including Tree-hugger, and Social Justice Warrior. www.jmarshallfreeman.com

MICHAEL GRAVES is the author of the novel *Parade*. He also composed *Dirty One*, a debut collection of short stories. This book was a Lambda Literary Award Finalist and an American Library Association Honoree. Michael's fiction and poetry have been featured in numerous literary publications, including Post Road, Pank, Storgy Magazine and Chelsea Station Magazine. He is a Pushcart Prize nominee. Connect with Michael on Twitter: @MGravesAuthor. Visit his official website: www. michaelgravesauthor.com.

STEPHEN GRECO's most recent novel, *Now and Yesterday*, was featured in *Vanity Fair* and praised by Kirkus as "a book about big ideas." His stories have appeared in *Men on Men, Flesh and the Word*, and other anthologies. Greco wrote the app *Peter and the Wolf in Hollywood*, narrated by Alice Cooper, and *Peter and the Wolf in Hollywood: The Live Show*, premiered in 2017 at the Kennedy Center in Washington, D.C. His interactive show *InsideRisk: Ombres de Medellin (Shadows of Medellin)* debuted on Swiss TV in November, 2018.

J.R. GREENWELL is a playwright and author from Cox's Creek, Kentucky. His books include *In a Whirl of Delusion* (2018), and *Who the Hell is Rachel Wells?* (2013), both published by Chelsea Station Editions. His memoir, *Teased Hair and the Quest for Tiaras*, (www.jrgreenwellmga79.com) chronicles his journey to become Miss Gay America 1979. J.R. has been making the annual trek to the Saints and Sinners Festival since 2010, and attributes his literary success to networking and learning from the incredible authors and publishers who also attend.

JONATHAN HARPER is the author of the short story collection *Daydreamers* (Lethe Press), which was a Kirkus Review's Indie Book of the Year for 2015. His writing has been featured in such places as The Rumpus, The Rappahannock Review, Big Lucks, and Chelsea Station. He received his MFA from American University and lives in Northern Virginia.

W.L. HODGE is a writer from Austin, Texas. His fiction focuses on matters of religion, culture, and identity, issues he confronted growing up gender-dysphoric and Catholic in the suburbs of Fort Worth. In his spare time W.L. works 100 hours a week as the owner of an architecture firm. His short story "Stockyards Harlot" was the runner-up in the 2018 Saints and Sinners Short Fiction Contest and he recently completed his first novel, *Sister Jack*, from which this year's submission is excerpted.

AARON HUGHES is an emerging gay writer from Melbourne, Australia, who has had short stories published in several Australian literary journals, and has been the recipient of several writing prizes. He has a Bachelor of Arts in English Literature, and a Diploma of Professional Writing and Editing. He has a background in LGBTI community services, and is currently working in the university sector. Aaron writes across a variety of genres, and takes his inspiration from great storytellers, such as Dan Simmons, Anne Rice, and Clive Barker.

DANIEL M. JAFFE is an internationally published fiction writer, essayist, and literary translator. He's author of the novels *Yeled Tov*, *The Genealogy of Understanding* (Rainbow Award finalist and honorable mention), and *The Limits of Pleasure* (Foreword Magazine Book of the

Year Award finalist), as well as the collection, *Jewish Gentle and Other Stories of Gay-Jewish Living*. Daniel teaches in the UCLA Extension Writers' Program. Read more at www.DanielJaffe.com.

WILLIAM CHRISTY SMITH lives in New Orleans and has been to every Saints and Sinners Literary Festival except the first one. He is a library and museum professional and works at the Jefferson Parish Public Library. He holds an undergraduate degree in English from Westminster College, Fulton, Mo., a master's degree in Liberal Arts from the University of Chicago, and a master's degree in Arts Administration from the University of New Orleans.

KARELIA STETZ-WATERS publishes across genres and prides herself on erotic and uncompromising portrayals of lesbian sex and sexuality. She is also committed to writing happy endings. She publishes with Sapphire Books, Ooligan Press, and the Forever Yours imprint at Grand Central Publishing. She is repped by Jane Dystel of Dystel, Goderich, & Bourret. Her novels include *Worth the Wait, The Admirer*, and *Forgive Me If I've Told You This Before*. Karelia teaches college writing and lives in Oregon with her beloved wife. More at www.kareliastetzwaters.com.

MICHAEL H. WARD received a B.A. and M.A. in English Literature from the University of Nebraska at Omaha, taught at the University of Maryland's Overseas Program and Tuskegee Institute in Alabama. Later he trained in New York City to become a psychotherapist and practiced privately in Boston for nearly forty years. Upon retirement he wrote *The Sea Is Quiet Tonight*, a memoir of his relationship with Mark Halberstadt, who died of AIDS in 1984. He is currently working on a family memoir.

About the Editors

Tracy Cunningham retired after 25 years in education, having taught English, creative writing, and journalism, and entered the field of non-profit event planning and management. She holds a B.A. in English Education, a master's degree in English, and a master's degree in Educational Leadership. She has been a national speaker and writing workshop leader for the National Writing Project, and is the Co-Director of the New Orleans Writing Marathon. She is managing director of the Tennessee Williams/New Orleans Literary Festival. Her writing has appeared in *Louisiana Literature* and in various anthologies and radio shows from the New Orleans Writing Marathon.

Paul J. Willis has over 23 years of experience in non-profit management. He earned a B.S. degree in Psychology and a M.S. degree in Communication. He started his administrative work in 1992 as the co-director of the Holos Foundation in Minneapolis. The Foundation operated an alternative high school program for at-risk youth. Willis has been the executive director of the Tennessee Williams/New Orleans Literary Festival since 2004. He is the founder of the Saints and Sinners Literary Festival (established in 2003). Current fascinations include the French ice-dancing duo of Gabriella Papadakis & Guillaume Cizeron; the artwork of Timothy Cummings; getting new tattoos and Eurovision 2019.

OUR FINALIST JUDGE

JEFF MANN grew up in Covington, Virginia, and Hinton, West Virginia, receiving degrees in English and forestry from West Virginia University. He's published five books of poetry, *Bones Washed with Wine*, *On the Tongue*, *Ash: Poems from Norse Mythology*, *A Romantic Mann*, and *Rebels*; two collections of personal essays, *Edge: Travels of an Appalachian Leather Bear* and *Binding the God: Ursine Essays from the Mountain South*; a book of poetry and memoir, *Loving Mountains, Loving Men*; six novels, *Fog*, *Purgatory*, *Cub*, *Salvation*, *Country*, and *Insatiable*; and three volumes of short fiction, *Consent*, *Desire and Devour*, and *A History of Barbed Wire*. With Julia Watts, he coedited *LGBTQ Fiction and Poetry from Appalachia*. The winner of two Lambda Literary Awards and four National Leather Association International awards, he teaches creative writing at Virginia Tech in Blacksburg, Virginia. Follow him at jeffmannauthor.com.

Our Cover Artist

TIMOTHY CUMMINGS, represented by Catharine Clark Gallery in San Francisco and Nancy Hoffman Gallery in New York, journeyed to a French Quarter pied-à-terre overlooking Armstrong Park this fall (2017) provided as part of a My Good Judy Residency. The My Good Judy Foundation provides residencies for artists seeking to produce a body of work or performance in New Orleans that address culture making from an LGBTQ perspective. "Much of the inspiration for these portraits is from being in close proximity to the spirits of my favorite writers, Tennessee Williams and Truman Capote. They shaped my early adolescence. They offer a magical telling of the spirit of this place. The darkness and humor of life and the queer Southern aesthetic shows up in my work as well. Williams' "garrulous grotesque", replacing the bleak mundane of the world with a lush queer poetic eye for the shadows is part of my focus," Cummings said. You can see more of Timothy's work at timothy-cummings.com.

Saints + Sinners Literary Festival

The first Saints and Sinners Literary Festival took place in May of 2003. The event started as a new initiative designed as an innovative way to reach the community with information about HIV/AIDS. It was also formed to bring the LGBT community together to celebrate the literary arts. Literature has long nurtured hope and inspiration, and has provided an avenue of understanding. A steady stream of LGBT novels, short stories, poems, plays, and non-fiction works has served to awaken lesbians, gay men, bisexuals, and transgendered persons to the existence of others like them; to trace the outlines of a shared culture; and to bring the outside world into the emotional passages of LGBT life.

After the Stonewall Riots in New York City, gay literature finally came "out of the closet." In time, noted authors such as Dorothy Allison, Michael Cunningham, and Mark Doty (all past *Saints'* participants) were receiving mainstream award recognition for their works. But there are still few opportunities for media attention of gay-themed books, and decreasing publishing options. This Festival helps to ensure that written work from the LGBT community will continue to have an outlet, and that people will have access to books that will help dispel stereotypes, alleviate isolation, and provide resources for personal wellness.

The event has since evolved into a program of the Tennessee Williams/New Orleans Literary Festival made possible by our premier sponsor the John Burton Harter Foundation. The NO/AIDS Task Force of New Orleans provides volunteer and special event support. The

Saints and Sinners Literary Festival works to achieve the following goals:

1. to create an environment for productive networking to ensure increased knowledge and dissemination of LGBT literature;
2. to provide an atmosphere for discussion, brainstorming, and the emergence of new ideas;
3. to recognize and honor writers, editors, and publishers who broke new ground and made it possible for LGBT books to reach an audience; and
4. to provide a forum for authors, editors, and publishers to talk about their work for the benefit of emerging writers, and for the enjoyment of readers of LGBT literature.

Saints and Sinners is an annual celebration that takes place in the heart of the French Quarter of New Orleans each Spring. The Festival includes writing workshops, readings, panel discussions, literary walking tours, and a variety of special events. We also aim to inspire the written word through our short fiction contest, and our annual Saints and Sinners Emerging Writer Award sponsored by Rob Byrnes. Each year we induct individuals to our Saints and Sinners Hall of Fame. The Hall of Fame is intended to recognize people for their dedication to LGBT literature. Selected members have shown their passion for our literary community through various avenues including writing, promotion, publishing, editing, teaching, bookselling, and volunteerism.

Past year's inductees into the Saints and Sinners Literary Hall of Fame include: Dorothy Allison, Carol Anshaw, Ann Bannon, Lucy Jane Bledsoe, Maureen Brady, Jericho Brown, Rob Byrnes, Patrick Califia, Louis Flint Ceci, Bernard Cooper, Jameson Currier, Brenda Currin, Mark Doty, Mark Drake, Jim Duggins, Elana Dykewomon, Amie M. Evans, Otis Fennell, Michael Thomas Ford, Katherine V. Forrest, Nancy Garden, Jewelle Gomez, Jim Grimsley, Tara Hardy, Ellen Hart, Greg Herren, Kenneth Holditch, Andrew Holleran, Candice Huber, Fay Jacobs, G. Winston James, Raphael Kadushin, Michele Karlsberg, Judith Katz, Moises Kaufman, Joan Larkin, Susan Larson, Lee Lynch, Jeff Mann, William J. Mann, Marianne K. Martin, Stephen McCauley, Val McDermid, Mark Merlis, Tim Miller, Rip & Marsha Naquin-

Delain, Michael Nava, Achy Obejas, Felice Picano, Radclyffe, J.M. Redmann, David Rosen, Carol Rosenfeld, Steven Saylor, Carol Seajay, Martin Sherman, Kelly Smith, Jack Sullivan, Carsen Taite, Cecilia Tan, Noel Twilbeck, Jr., Patricia Nell Warren, Jess Wells, Edmund White, and Paul J. Willis.

For more information about the Saints and Sinners Literary Festival including sponsorship opportunities and our Archangel Membership Program, visit: www.sasfest.org. Be sure to sign up for our e-newsletter for updates for future programs. We hope you will join other writers and bibliophiles for a weekend of literary revelry not to be missed!

"Saints & Sinners is hands down one of the best places to go to revive a writer's spirit. Imagine a gathering in which you can lean into conversations with some of the best writers and editors and agents in the country, all of them speaking frankly and passionately about the books, stories and people they love and hate and want most to record in some indelible way. Imagine a community that tells you truthfully what is happening with writing and publishing in the world you most want to reach. Imagine the flirting, the arguing, the teasing and praising and exchanging of not just vital information, but the whole spirit of queer arts and creating. Then imagine it all taking place on the sultry streets of New Orleans' French Quarter. That's Saints & Sinners—the best wellspring of inspiration and enthusiasm you are going to find. Go there."

—Dorothy Allison, National Book Award finalist
for *Bastard Out of Carolina*, and author
of the critically acclaimed novel *Cavedweller*.